PAPER DOLLS

Lisa Bradley is a former journalist and now Director of Learning and Teaching for Journalism at the University of Sheffield. *Paper Dolls* is her first novel.

LISA BRADLEY

PAPER DOLLS

Quercus

First published in Great Britain in 2020 by

Quercus Editions Ltd
Carmelite House
50 Victoria Embankment
London EC4Y 0DZ

An Hachette UK company

A CIP catalogue record for this book is available
from the British Library

PB ISBN 978 1 52940 778 5
EB ISBN 978 1 52940 779 2

10 9 8 7 6 5 4 3 2 1

Typeset by CC Book Production
Printed and bound in Great Britain by Clays Ltd, Elcograf S.p.A.

MIX
Paper from
responsible sources
FSC® C104740

Papers used by Quercus are from well-managed forests and other responsible sources.

For all my boys

Prologue

31 July 2003

The newspapers were stacked up high – matte and musky, folds exact, edges freshly cut. The man picked up the top copy, still warm and smudgy under his fingers.

Friday commuters milled in front of the big clock, like caged tigers pacing back and forth, men in their ironed shirts, women with their dewy make-up. The muggy smell of hot metal wafted in from the automatic doors leading to Platform One, which sported professionals waiting for the city express, and friends, clumped in little twos or threes, sipping lattes from paper cups and giggling in anticipation of shopping trips and white wine before lunchtime.

The man paid for his paper at the station cafe and ordered a coffee, one elbow on the wooden counter to the left of the muffins and buttery taupe pastries. Feeling his stomach grumble, he smoothed out the pages while the machine hissed and puffed.

A young blonde girl placed her order and stood next to him, wrapping her arms around herself. She looked cold, and was shivering despite the pleasant July morning. The man looked back down and eyed a pastry again, calculating how many calories that would add up to. He'd promised his wife he would stick to the diet this time.

Sighing, he looked away, and his eyes skimmed the front of the paper. A picture of a teenager was splashed across it. Her blonde hair was pulled into a thick honey ponytail, her face scrubbed clean, no make-up like his daughter and her friends, with their bottle tans that stained the bedding and complicated hair in little butterfly clips.

Sparkling blue eyes and a plump, rosy lower lip with a handful of freckles across her cheekbones. The headline read: *Family devastated without Hope.*

He read on. A missing girl – just fifteen. Hope. The paper must have loved that one for the headline. Two days gone, model student, popular, loved horses. Some sick bastards around. He shook his head and thought of his daughter and how she'd walked home from the cinema last night on her own.

The woman called his order and he reached for his black coffee – no milk, no sugar. He sighed as he brought it to his lips. The girl next to him looked down at his paper, her hair falling over her face, and she was so motionless, so statuesque, that she was almost captivating.

The man looked away quickly, deliberately, lifting his coffee and folding the paper under his arm while he took a seat on the row of stools facing the counter. The girl carried two coffee cups over to the stand where the milk stood, with shaking hands. He tried not to watch her as she went to pick up the metal flask and caught one of the cups with her sleeve.

2

'Ow, shit, sorry.' The hot brown fluid poured out all over the counter, funnelling into a steady stream as it cascaded onto the floor. The girl grabbed a handful of napkins and dropped down, frantically soaking up the mess.

'It's all right, love,' the woman behind the counter clucked, and lifted up the flap, armed with a mop. 'I'll sort it.'

The man stood up. The girl was still down on the floor, holding her wrist and wincing. 'You OK? Did that burn you?' He leant over the table to get a better look, but she scuttled back, banging into the legs of the woman like a frightened rabbit.

'It's OK, here.' He put down the paper and went to help her up, but she was already clambering to her feet.

'I'm fine, I'm fine,' she said. 'I'm so sorry.'

'Just hang on a sec, pet, and I'll pour you another.' The woman winced as she straightened herself up.

'No, no, it's OK.' The girl looked frantically towards the platform. 'I think my train is here . . .'

'Are you sure?' The woman looked towards the doors. 'There's nothing . . .'

But the girl had already gone, pushing her way through the growing throng of suits and heels, and the people nattering into their handsets, their voices a constant drone.

The man and woman looked at each other and shrugged.

He sat back down and carried on reading – the picture still gleaming, leaping off the page. The picture of the girl with honey-blonde hair and blue eyes.

The man looked up, startled, grabbed the paper and made his way to the platform, joining the sea of people as the next arrival was

3

announced. The crowd moved and undulated, swelling and shrinking, as people tried to best position themselves to board.

Where was she? The train was pulling into the platform. The man approached a woman in a high-vis vest, gesturing frantically at his paper. She talked into her radio. The man scoured the faces, the flaring nostrils, the watchful, impatient eyes.

What had she been wearing? Something purple, maybe? Or was it pink? Purple. Purple.

The train doors opened with a swoosh and the people surged forward. The crowd was thinning but he still couldn't see her. He turned back towards the coffee and briefcase he'd just abandoned in the cafe. It was probably nothing.

And then there she was.

Her blue eyes were dim, her hair straggly and swollen with the salt of the sea air.

But it was her. She just stood there. Then she must have felt his gaze, because she lifted her eyes and stared at him. At the paper in his hand. Her shoulders were slumped, but her chin was high. She really was shivering now. Her jaw was clattering, and her fingers trembled as he took a tentative step towards her, his hand reaching into his pocket for his phone. The woman with the radio had spotted her too and moved forward, speaking again in a hushed voice into her transmitter, and the doors that should have slid shut stayed open.

The girl watched them approach her. The man had kind eyes that crinkled and a comforting pudge to his belly. His shirt strained a little against it.

'Hope?' He reached his arm out towards her, afraid she would bolt at any second.

She was cold. Deeply cold inside her bones, and the blood was pumping around her body at an alarming rate.

'It's OK. Everything is going to be OK.'

1

Now

The girl sat down on the kerb across the road and pulled out her phone from her back pocket. Every day this week. Same time, just past ten. Same cut-off denim shorts. Her hair was always different, though.

She glanced up and Leah pulled back from the kitchen window. Not so fast she looked guilty. Just casually. She wasn't staring. Not exactly. But she didn't want to look weird. Turning on the hot tap, Leah rinsed her coffee cup and watched the black water bleed out to beige as it ran over the brim. It'd been another struggle to get up this morning and she was already considering a third cup.

'Jesus Christ, Mum.' Luke appeared next to her, chewing on an overstuffed bap. It smelt of mayonnaise and something vaguely fishy. Her stomach curdled. 'Will you stop staring at kids?'

'I'm not,' Leah murmured, 'I'm washing up. It's just . . .

I feel sorry for her. She's always here. Doesn't she have a home to go to?'

Luke snorted and wiped a creamy smear from his top lip with the back of his hand. 'I told you last night, I wouldn't feel sorry for Charlie Bates. Why are you washing up, anyway? Is the dishwasher broken?'

'That's like the start of a sexist joke,' Leah said, still looking outside.

A gleaming black SUV appeared around the corner, the sun bouncing off the bodywork. Leah looked at the mud splattered on the hatchback in her driveway and puffed out her cheeks. She'd been threatening to wash it for weeks.

She watched as Hannah, her neighbour's daughter, leapt out of the passenger seat, hair swinging down her back. She threw her arms around the girl at the kerb. Sweet Hannah. So fawn-like: her wispy hair was biscuity, her legs wobbly, stance awkward and gangly. Her freckles were coming out now the sun had broken through.

'See.' Luke raised his eyebrows. 'She's not on her own now, is she?'

Bracken, Hannah's Labrador, bounded out of the back seat and jumped up at Charlie, who laughed and ruffled the top of his chocolate head, then squealed and leapt back.

'Careful, he's wet!' Hannah's dad, Sam, shouted out of his open window, and then he got out of the car, swinging the keys in a circle round his middle finger. He opened the boot and pulled out a lumpy reusable shopping bag. He was wearing shorts, classic English-summer, knee-length, combat-style shorts with too many pockets and access cords. His trainers looked new. Or at least recently washed. 'Had to jump into the bloody beck to get him. Daft bugger.' Sam slammed the boot shut.

'Who's that girl?' Leah had asked at dinner the night before. 'The one over the road, knocking about with Hannah all the time?'

Her husband Chris had shrugged without looking up, shovelling his penne into his mouth one-handed, eyes on his tablet. It kept pinging and making him scowl. Leah and Luke had been eating spaghetti with their meatballs. But Chris didn't like spaghetti. She always made him penne separately.

'Charlie Bates,' Luke said.

'Is she in Hannah's year? She looks much older than Hannah.'

'Yeah. Year Eight. Well, going into Year Nine.' He had reached over for the pepper mill and started grinding forcefully.

'Calm down. Does it owe you money or something?' Leah had nodded at the mill and raised her brows. 'You'll break it.'

'But the pepper tastes better if you do it faster.' Luke had given it one last twist.

'That's impossible. It's exactly the same.' Leah had torn off some garlic bread, then thought of her waistline and dropped it onto Chris's plate.

'Thanks.' Chris had looked up briefly and flashed her a smile. His whole face had changed. He looked stern most of the time. A bit like one of those hunters in old-fashioned paintings with a frown and a pheasant. But his blue eyes always brightened with a smile, and it seemed to make him more real somehow. 'This is lovely, by the way. New recipe?'

'No, old. Just mixed up the spices a bit.' She'd turned straight back to Luke. 'So really? This girl is only, what, thirteen? Christ . . . she looks about sixteen.'

'She vapes and gives Year Tens blow jobs.'

Leah had dropped her fork with a clatter.

'I've heard . . .' Luke hastily added.

'Who are we talking about?' Chris had looked up with sudden interest.

'Some girl that Mum's obsessed with.'

'I am *not* obsessed. It's just, you know, she's been here every day of the summer holidays. I just wondered if she was new to the area or something.'

'Nah, I think she lives up in Berry Brow Flats.'

'Oh . . .' Chris had grimaced and looked at Leah.

'Don't be a snob, Chris.' Leah had finished the last mouthful of her red wine. She had wanted another glass, but Chris hadn't even touched his. She'd waited till her bath.

'I'm not being a snob, Leah. It's you who shudders whenever we drive past.' Chris had waggled his fork at her. A bit of meatball had slithered off the prongs and landed on the table in a small pool of passata and garlic. He didn't notice as his tablet pinged again. 'God, we need to get this new receptionist in. Everyone is so stressed trying to juggle staffing the counter with appointments. No one understands the system. The booking thingy has totally gone to pot.'

'I don't shudder,' Leah said sulkily. 'It's not like that.'

'Well, what is it like?' Luke grinned. His hair was definitely darker again, Leah had noticed. When he'd been little it had been so red that he looked as if he was crowned in flames when the sun caught it. But it was burning out now, fading to conker embers to match his eyes – her eyes. 'You're the one always banging on about how you grew up on a council estate and we're not thankful enough, yada yada yada.'

Leah had looked back at the wine. 'I just wondered who she was. That's all.'

Now, Luke crammed the last of his sandwich into his mouth.

'I'm out,' he spluttered, his lips oozing with mushed-up orange crumbs and a grey sludge.

'What are you eating?' Leah turned her gaze back to Luke.

'Fish finger butty.'

'With mayo?'

Luke nodded. 'And cheese spread.'

'Is there anything more revolting than the taste buds of a fourteen-year-old boy?' Leah shuddered. 'It's ten in the morning.'

'*Human Centipede*.' Luke winked at her. 'YouTube it.'

'I'm good, thanks.'

Leah looked back at the drive. Bracken was in Sam's front garden, rolling in the borders. She could hear the girls chatting as they went into the house, not the words exactly, but the melodies in their voices overlapping, like the end of a song.

'Mum?' Luke ran his hands through his hair and ruffled it up. 'Do you think, maybe, you need a job?'

'Don't be a . . .' Leah trailed off, a slippery insult rolling like a boiled egg in her mouth. She couldn't quite bring herself to call her son a twat. At least, not to his face.

'Twat?' Luke offered.

'Just. Stop. Talking. Go down to the skate park and indulge in some light antisocial behaviour like a normal teenager.'

'Are you saying I'm not normal?'

'I tidied your room yesterday and I didn't find anything untoward. I am greatly disappointed in your general lack of civil disobedience. You need to rebel, otherwise you're going to be one of those people who goes mental in a super-market one day because they've run out of chickpeas and guns everyone down.'

'We don't have guns in this country.'

'Don't be awkward.'

'God. So moody . . . Are you on your blob?' Luke flashed his cheekiest grin. The one that used to get him an extra sweet at the hairdressers.

'Are you going through puberty yet?' Leah countered, folding her arms.

'Although . . . actually, do you still have periods? Or are you too old for that now?'

'Fuck off!' Leah went to swat her son, but he ducked and winked.

'You owe a pound to your swear jar.'

'A more cynical mother might think you were deliberately trying to wind her up to wring more cash out of her.' Leah dug in her jeans pocket and fished out some change.

'Whatever makes you think that?' Luke took the money and dropped it into the jam jar on the kitchen windowsill. 'Although, nearly full, look . . . You've been knocking about with Bunty too much.'

Leah scowled and looked back out of the window.

'Yeah, and isn't *Grand Theft Fortnite* or whatever coming out soon?'

But he'd already gone, leaving the patio door ajar behind him and the smell of the wild lavender in the back garden wafting through.

Leah drummed her fingers on the oak worktops. They needed re-oiling. Another job for the list. The coffee machine hissed and spat, and The Moog, her smelly, ageing crossbreed, waddled over, licking at some stray mayonnaise that had been dropped and abandoned by the fridge. She supposed there was a fancy name for The Moog, some ridiculous blend of breed names that commanded thousands for dogs who in reality were mongrels with designer collars. They thought he was part pug, part spaniel and part Jack Russell.

The Moog had been brought to Chris's vets' practice by an old boy who'd found him shivering behind the bins in a takeaway's car park, covered in fleas and with a severe eye infection. Chris had removed his left eye and brought him home to recover. But when they'd seen Luke's face light up, Leah had known he would never be handed on to the shelter. The Moog was about twenty – and very possibly going to outlive them all.

'If there was ever a nuclear holocaust, you do realize that

all that would be left would be The Moog and some cockroaches,' Chris had once observed, watching the dog eat leftover chicken Balti.

'Then The Moog would eat the cockroaches,' Luke had added proudly.

Still, Leah loved the dog almost as much as Luke did, and he'd been good company the past few weeks. She refreshed the Facebook notifications on her phone and watched the home screen spring back up without any little red markers of validation. She did the same with Instagram, then Twitter.

Everyone was at work, their days rotating, structured and calm. Order and lists. Goals set. Tasks achieved.

Sighing, she splashed soya milk into her coffee and scowled at the colour. It always tasted off, but in the past few months her jeans had definitely got tighter, and her stomach had started lying next to her in bed.

Last night's leftover meatball sauce winked at her, and as she went to shut the fridge she paused briefly, thinking how good it would taste heated up on bread with some extra Tabasco.

She glanced at the clock: 11 a.m. She couldn't put it off much longer.

Leah wouldn't call herself 'a runner'. She had a vision of how a runner looked: striding against the skyline, the burst of a sunset sketching out her silhouette, or slate rain pounding down on her chest, streaking her face, drenching her hair. She'd be with a dog: one like Bracken, not The

Moog with his stubby little legs and low belly, snorting and wheezing listlessly at her side. Her legs would pound a rhythm on the ground and her hips would swing. She would be one of those women who wore numbers tacked to their backs and posted maps and times on social media.

She told herself this as she strapped her phone on her upper arm, connected her Bluetooth earbuds and selected her playlist. She'd yet to hit 10k without having to walk, but she'd come a long way in a year, thanks to an app and the sudden empty hours that would once have seemed almost hedonistic to her.

She didn't stretch, because she wasn't a runner. Instead she walked up the street briskly and swung her arms to get the blood flowing where the phone straps were tight.

By the time Leah reached the park, the back of her neck was already damp and her hairline heavy. She preferred running in winter, when the streets were emptier and the park was shadowy. She loved seeing her breath in the air and feeling the tingle of her fingers in the cold. Running in summer was less romantic, and as she began to jog, she felt very aware of her tummy jiggling in the less-than-forgiving jersey shorts.

Cressheld Park was small. A war memorial, where the local teenagers would sprawl with limbs dripping, sat at the centre. Luke and his friends would sometimes skate up and down the paths that circled it, flipping their boards and speaking in tongues.

Vacant-eyed new mums would push their buggies around

the boat pond, barely holding together a conversation while their bundles screamed and writhed.

There was an ice-cream cafe in the boatshed. Not a farm-style brown-bread-and-jam artisan venue, but machine ice cream topped with sprinkles in cheap cones that disintegrated in one lick.

Leah ran on, trying to find her pace, hoping that her thighs weren't wobbling too much.

Her nineties grunge music gave her a steady rhythm and she ran upwards to the swings. The music reminded her of purple hair dye and ripped fishnet tights, Newcastle Brown Ale and wishful dreams of boys with bass guitars and German army jackets.

She focused on her breathing, always the bit she couldn't quite handle, and her feet as the field sloped upwards and away from the playground. *One in front of the other. Don't look at the top of the hill. Just concentrate on the next step.*

The trees, the spindly ones of black and silver that never seemed to leaf, were on her right, growing denser. Her breath began to stick at the back of her throat. She turned between the trees and felt the relief of the flat, if crooked, path. The track on her playlist changed to the Smashing Pumpkins and Leah adjusted her pace to match the bass line.

She thought of sticky university summers: working in bars while all her friends went home; cut-price rent in large, empty houses; rattling about and pulling double shifts to stave off the loneliness; nothing but her CDs and the conference crowd to keep her company – businessmen on work trips with white clammy faces and bloodshot eyes, pale-grey suits and damp ties. She thought of the one man in particular who'd tried to put his hand directly between her legs when she'd leant over the table for the empties, asking in a whisper, with his fat tongue and whisky eyes, when her break was.

So, at the fag end of her third year, when everyone else had been trying to eke out just one last drag, Leah had already had her boxes and suitcases piled in the hall. While her housemates had been blowing the last of their loans on the festival circuits, Leah had managed to save up a few hundred quid from those double shifts for a rusty Fiat Panda that still had a choke but no left windscreen wiper.

Her lecturer had told her there were two ways to put herself ahead of the crowd of eager graduates looking for that first break into journalism. One hundred words per minute shorthand and her own car. So she had dedicated the last semester to getting both.

There had been no way she was going to spend another summer pulling pints and being groped by townies. Her only home had been four boxes and a holdall. Not a four-bed detached on a cul-de-sac, as she had now.

She hadn't even stayed for her graduation ceremony. There would have been no one there to watch her. So what was the point?

The song came to an end and, in the pause between the tracks, Leah heard the crackle of twigs under her feet and a rustle of life in the undergrowth.

She broke into the clearing from between the velvety bark of the chestnut trees that Luke used to attack with sticks for conkers, his glossy, sappy treasures held up to her like pearls from an oyster in his chubby little hands, and she picked up her pace. Over the field, and down the left-hand side to the riverbank, across the bridge and back to the playground. She could do it. She carried on up the muddy banking and past the dilapidated caravan. No one knew how it had come to be there, but the roots of the trees had claimed it for their own now. A wax jacket still hung from a peg inside, just visible through the smeared front window, where the clutter from a rag-and-bone man's life was piled up like a barricade.

Leah often had a squint through the greasy windows as she jogged past, always trying to spot something that might indicate a new resident. Her arm buzzed violently as she was deciphering the lumps in the shadows and she shrieked.

'Shit!' Leah ripped the band off her upper arm and steadied her breath before jabbing at the answer button. Her fingers felt fat and slippery and it took her two attempts to slide the icon across.

'Dave?'

'Hi . . . Leah?'

It was always infuriating that he questioned if it was her. As if, after fourteen years, he didn't recognize her voice.

'Yeah.'

'You OK? You sound like you're in the middle of something.'

That Geordie lilt.

'Just out for a run,' she replied, with a touch of smugness. Last time Dave had picked Luke up she could definitely see the start of a double chin and a meaty upper arm.

'Oh. Good for you.'

Leah rolled her eyes. 'Everything sorted for this weekend? You're not cancelling, are you?'

'No, no, course not. Everything's fine . . .'

'OK. So, what's up?'

'Nothing, I just wanted to say . . . you know. Good luck for tonight.'

'Oh.' Leah took a deep breath and looked to the sky. The branches of the birches above her head knotted together like a tapestry. A bird broke from the top branch and set flight into the sky. On the other end she could hear rustling, a blend of voices in the background. It sounded underwater and echoey.

'So, are you staying up for it? It's midnight, isn't it?'

'Yeah. Bloody Netflix. Why can't they make it at 9 p.m. like normal channels? I feel like some *Star Wars* geek, queuing outside a cinema for the big release.'

Dave laughed, but they both knew his heart wasn't in it.

'You OK? I'm sure it will be nothing to worry about.'

'Yeah. Well. I doubt that. Fuck. Maybe I shouldn't have talked to them. I mean, I wasn't . . . feeling great at the time. I hope I don't come across a bit unhinged.'

'Don't start that . . .' He paused. 'Anyway, it's good you're out. You know. Running. How's everything generally?'

'I'm great. Listen, thanks for the call. See you next weekend.'

Leah hung up the phone without waiting for a reply, strapped it back to her arm, and began to run again.

2

She didn't run straight home. She took a left by the park and ran to St John's Church, which stood just behind the flower gardens. It wasn't a big church, there were grander ones for weddings and funerals further into town. It was the modern kind, with glass doors in the entrance foyer, blue carpets and multicoloured exhibits on the wall from local primary schools.

Inside, though, the stained-glass windows and visible beams nodded to something more traditional. It was always quiet and dimly lit, with tired flowers and loud, brightly-coloured prayer cushions, embroidered by the Women's Institute. The pews were empty.

At the front was the prayer tree: an intricate wooden and metal sculpture by a local artist, with handwritten slips of paper cut into leaves and tied onto the ends of the branches. Leah's breath was ragged and awkwardly loud as she walked up the aisle, over to the tree. Her eyes flicked to the wooden box on the table next to it. She hadn't brought any change for the donations, but she'd pop back later.

Sitting on the step, she took a smooth, ivory candle from the box. The wax was slippery under her fingers. Closing her eyes, she waited for her heartbeat to settle, and rolled the candle between her palms.

She thought of a beautiful girl, with coffee skin, wide almond eyes and thick, black, cloudy hair. She thought of a blue hooded top, embedded in the sand at the shore. She smelt the sea. Leah lit the candle and placed it in the rack under the tree. All the lights for all the souls. Then she picked up a paper leaf and again asked for forgiveness for what she'd done to Tilly Bowers.

'So, it's like a documentary?' Bunty ripped open a brown sugar sachet with her teeth.

'Yeah. Missing White Woman Syndrome. Why some kids make the papers and others don't. Not just kids. Adults too. Really, it's just a massive attack on the media. I mean, why else would they ask me on? I knew what was coming, but I was hoping maybe I'd get the chance to explain. But basically it was just a witch-hunt. Can't say I blame them.' Leah rubbed her temples. 'I'm having the horrors about it, Bunty.'

'Don't worry. Most people will look at your face, not your gut.' Bunty sat back in her chair and hooked a long leg over her knee. In her dance gear she looked like a spider, the ones with the bubble on their back. Her limbs all joints and spikes, apart from the kind of bum that could make a grown man cry, as Chris had once said.

'I don't mean about the camera adding ten pounds,

Bunty! I don't care what I look like, I just don't want to be demonized.'

'Stop tapping your foot.' Bunty smiled without showing her teeth. The gloss on her lips shone in the middle. 'Who gives a shit anyway? Wasn't it, like, decades ago?'

'Sixteen years.'

'And three days? Have you got some kind of creepy shrine to her in your spare room? Are you marking up each day that goes past? Is that why you don't let me in there?'

'I don't let you in there because it's a bomb site. And I'm not tapping my foot.' Leah crossed her legs.

'You're right. You're jiggling your knee. It's vexing me.'

'Sorry. God. I'm, well . . . I just want it to be over.'

'It will be, tomorrow.'

'It won't. It's on bastard Netflix. It will be there for bloody ever. I miss the good old days when you had to record the telly on video if you wanted to watch it again.'

'No one wants that, Leah. TV on demand is a basic human right.'

'You know, I don't think I would have agreed to do it if I had known it was going to be so . . . Netflixy. God, it was such a mistake to bring it all up again. I'm sure that's what kicked off my nerves. Christ, listen to me. *My nerves*. What do I sound like? Chris says he still thinks I should talk to someone.'

'Thought you'd already been down that road? Anyway, just, you know. Fuck 'em all. You were just doing your job. Or some cliché like that.' Bunty reached over and stole Leah's biscuit. 'Are you not eating this?'

'Knock yourself out.'

Bunty popped it into her mouth in one. Her coal-black hair was pinned up in a high, scruffy bun. She had her full face on too: bronzer, eyeshadow cream slicked across her lids, ruby lipstick that cost a fortune and took thirty-five minutes to apply. If Leah had tried the look she'd have resembled an office Christmas party on steroids. But Bunty just looked fabulous and glowing. Although that could have been shimmer body oil.

'So . . . you going to tell Luke that it's on? Give him the heads up?'

'Well. Yeah. I've told him about it. But he's fourteen, he's oblivious to everything that isn't a pair of tits or a gamer handle.'

'Not thinking he's gay any more, then?' Bunty drummed her shellacked nails on the table. 'Christ, I need a cig.'

'Why aren't you vaping like everyone else?'

'Because I'm not a fucking millennial.'

'Fair point. No, well, I don't know about the gay thing. He still has a poster of Hugh Jackman on his wall.'

'Ooh, speaking of which. I'm doing *Greatest Showman* at my summer school this year if he's keen? Won't charge.'

'You know, I think he'd love it. But no chance of dragging him away from whatever vital, all-important fuckery he does all day. He wouldn't do it, purely on the basis that I asked him.'

Bunty nodded and took a sip of coffee. 'I hear you. Immie's a right little cunt these days.'

'Jesus, Bunty!'

'Well, she is. She keeps falling out with Lottie – it's, like, constant Snapchat dramz. I've seen some of the messages. They are all vile. I mean, I know I'm salty, but you can be queen bee without being queen bitch.'

'Are you talking about being Beyoncé again?'

'Are you kidding me? She ain't got nothing on this booty.' Bunty snaked her head and slapped the side of her bum.

'Don't be such a stereotype,' Leah laughed.

'You're jealous because your skinny white bottom will never be as ripe as mine.'

'I wish it was skinny. I'm running and keeping off the carbs, but I'm still not seeing any bloody results.'

'Stop being so hung up on your weight. Especially round Immie, yeah? This self-loathing might be catching and I'm already focusing all my attention on keeping her off the pole. If she carries on in this toxic friendship group, she's gonna have zero self-esteem left.'

'Hey, actually, speaking of which, what do you know about Charlie Bates?'

'Vapes and gives Year Tens blow jobs.'

'Ah. That's exactly what Luke said.'

'To be honest, I don't think Immie knocks about with her much. Although I did see her on a group chat telling some poor girl that her eyebrows were bigger than her future. Which did make me warm to her.'

'Still going through Immie's phone, then?'

'Totes.'

'*Totes?*'

'Sorry, it's those little bastards I have to work with all day.'

'It charms and delights me how much you love your students.'

'I don't mind the little ones. A twirl, a tutu and fairy feet, and it's money for old rope. It's the older ones I hate. With their fucking jazz hands and earnest bloody faces. Why can't they go and drink cider in the park? Why do they have to come and plague me with spine-shuddering renditions of *A Million Dreams*? And that's just the boys. Hugh bastard Jackman. He's got a lot to answer for. And Zac bastard Efron. And the girls? Jesus wept. Fucking little dance-school cocksuckers.'

'Maybe that should be your school slogan?'

Bunty threw her head back and laughed her big dirty laugh. 'That'll be a hit with the parents. Mind you, they're just as bad. Wanting to volunteer backstage and demanding headsets. Why can't they just drop them off and go to the pub like *normal* parents?'

'Is there such a thing?'

'Well. You're OK.'

'Thanks. But I doubt Chris would agree.'

'Tell him to fuck off. How are you doing anyway . . . you know, with not working?'

'Well, I'm not drinking before lunchtime yet, but you know. Goals.'

'Leah, seriously . . .'

'What? You're making me sound like that man off *The Full*

Monty who starts smashing gnomes.' Leah paused. 'Or was that Michael Douglas? Anyway. I'm OK. Bit bored. But you know . . .'

'Still think you did the right thing?' Bunty eyed her closely. 'Do you think if I dip my head under the table anyone would notice if I had a quick puff?'

'Yes. To both. It wouldn't feel right, watching all those other editors go and then just . . . I don't know. Being the last woman standing. I'd get survivor's guilt.'

'You feel guilty for breathing. You must have been a shit journo.'

Leah smiled. 'I think I was a better editor than a reporter. But Jesus. All the papers, all those editors who had been there *years*. Do you know, five of those local papers don't even have offices in the town they serve now? It's a sacrilege. I think about how it used to be, having actual time to work on stories, doing decent investigations – people cared. Really *cared* about what the paper had to say. About being *in* the paper. It felt like we were really doing what we were *meant* to do. Holding power to account. Showcasing courage. Being brave. It was life. Newspapers aren't printed with ink. It's the blood that pumps round the towns, the cities. But no one cares now. Not if they can get their news on Twitter in one fucking line. And you know what gets me? It's that readers still want the news. They still want it, but for free. As if reporters should be out there 24/7, not seeing their families, like it's a public service. Which it is, I guess. But one that still needs paying for. You know, the

26

day I left, some bitch on social was slagging us off because she'd had to wait an hour to find out about a sexual assault in the park. She said it was disgusting she was being made to wait for the details. Didn't care if they were right. Just anything, everything, *now*. The heart's still there but it needs a pacemaker.'

'Well.' Bunty threw a tenner on the table. 'That was a bit fucking poetic. Let's go for a real drink.'

Leah opened the mince and dropped it into the pan, relishing the softness of the pink, squirmy ribbons between the tips of her fingers. She was drunk. Not falling-up-the-stairs drunk, but three-glasses-of-wine-in-the-afternoon drunk. She stared at the pan for a little too long, then realized the meat was beginning to catch. She poked at it with a wooden spoon and put the coffee machine on. She couldn't look pissed on a Tuesday afternoon.

Bunty had convinced her it would be cheaper to buy the bottle, failing to point out that she was on white and Leah on red. So they'd got two. It seemed like a great idea at the time, but now, standing here, making chilli for her family, it all seemed a bit embarrassing. And she'd left her car in the multi-storey car park, which would mean Chris having to take her to get it in the morning. And having to explain why. 'LUKE!' she shouted over the extractor fan. 'ARE YOU IN?'

She knew he was home. The house had been unlocked when she got in. She opened the tinned tomatoes and took

27

a big slurp of coffee, burning her tongue. She probably deserved it for being drunk and forty-one and jobless on a Tuesday afternoon.

No reply. Leah turned the heat down and wandered from their thickset, heavy island, having to duck to avoid the hanging copper pans above the butcher's block. She had thought they would look charming when they'd redesigned the kitchen with her redundancy money, but in actuality they had just been the cause of repeated yelps and 'fucks' when Leah and Chris inadvertently smacked their heads on them.

'LUKE?' she yelled again out of the double doors that led into the hall. *He must have his headphones on*, she thought, putting her foot on the bottom step. It was far too quiet upstairs.

'WHAT?' The shout startled her.

'Shit!' She held her chest. 'You nearly gave me a heart attack.'

'Why?' Luke poked his head over the banister on the second floor. 'You called me.'

'I know. I didn't expect you to reply, though.'

'Then why were you calling me?'

Luke's bedroom door opened behind him and suddenly Hannah and Charlie Bates were there. In her hallway. In her house.

'Oh. Hi, girls.' Leah took a step back self-consciously. 'Sorry, I didn't know you were here.'

'That's OK, we're just going, actually.' Hannah looked pale, her hair dangling in her face as usual, her eyes darting all over, huge behind her glasses.

'You sure? I'm making chilli, there's plenty.'

'No, it's OK. Thank you, my dad is making pizza.' Hannah was already halfway down the stairs. Charlie leant over the banister, her T-shirt almost down to her knees, The Moog in her arms.

'Ohhh, but chilli's my favourite.' She beamed at Leah. 'Can we really stay?' She looked at Hannah. 'Just text Sam. He won't mind.' She looked back at Leah. 'I'm sleeping over. Eight-day streak.'

'Erm . . .' Hannah looked as if she was trapped on the stairs, but Leah could see her eyes trying to make contact with Charlie. 'I don't want to impose.'

'It's fine.' Leah smiled, regretting even asking. 'But do call your dad first.'

'Great.' Charlie bounded down the stairs and plopped down with The Moog on the thick twist rug on the wooden floor. 'By the way, I am, like, totally stealing your dog.'

The Moog looked up at her and started padding on the rug, shifting his weight from one foot to the other.

'Well, he must like you. That's his happy dance,' Leah smiled.

'I can't believe someone would do that to him . . . Luke said Chris like, saved his life.'

'Yeah, he's a hero all right,' Leah said, somewhat dryly. But Charlie had already gone through to the den, throwing herself onto Luke's oversized floor cushion. Not a beanbag, apparently. 'Let's watch a scary film!' She beckoned Hannah over, who was on her phone, talking quietly to her dad.

'No 18s,' Leah whispered to Luke.

'Whatevs.' Luke shrugged. He didn't look entirely thrilled by the prospect of the girls staying, Leah suddenly noticed.

'How come they are here?' she mouthed as she opened the pantry for some extra rice.

'Dunno. Just are.' Luke shrugged. 'Don't wet yourself over it.'

'I'm not,' Leah said tersely. 'Just, I didn't think you liked Charlie?'

'She's all right.'

'What's an eight-day streak?'

Luke stopped and wrinkled his nose. 'Oh my God, Mum, are you pissed? You smell like a lush.'

'No.' Leah filled the kettle. 'Of course I'm not pissed. It's a Tuesday afternoon.'

'You been with Bunty?'

'Yes. But we only had one ... anyway, stop it. You're making me feel like a right cheap gutter-alkie.'

'Don't worry. I won't tell Dad.' Luke winked and grabbed a bag of Doritos from the side.

'No, it's nearly dinner.' Leah grabbed them back.

'Yeah, but you're a dodgy, unemployed, drunken mother, and you need to bribe me.'

Leah grimaced. 'Will you pack it in?'

'Love you.' Luke kissed her on the cheek. 'Nice to see you having a bit of fun again.'

Leah felt her stomach churn and she watched Luke wander back through, swinging the bag of crisps.

At dinner Charlie sat cross-legged at the table like a toddler and spooned mouthful after mouthful up at an alarming rate. Hannah was more reserved, picking out the kidney beans and pushing the rice and meat around her plate until it swirled together, oranges and browns, like mashed-up plasticine.

'You don't have to eat it, Hannah, it's fine. Sometimes I make it too spicy.'

'Mum's got an asbestos mouth.' Luke dolloped another spoonful of soured cream on his plate. Leah's mouth filled with saliva.

'Sorry, I'm just not that hungry.' Hannah smiled apologetically.

Leah smiled back and shook her head. 'No worries.'

'Well, I love it.' Charlie wiped her chin with the back of her hand and turned to Luke. 'Is it all over my face?' Her voice was lower and came with a roll from the back of her throat.

Luke glanced up and shrugged. 'Nope.'

'That T-shirt looks a bit big.' Leah raised her eyebrows. 'Or am I just hopelessly out of fashion?'

'Nah, it's Sam's.' Charlie gathered her black hair into a scruffy topknot and tied it with a band from around her wrist. 'He got me totally wet. Earlier.'

Leah felt her face flush.

'Mum's been at the pub.' Luke pushed his chair back and

31

took his plate over to the Belfast sink that Leah had begged for when the kitchen was the only thing she could focus on.

'On a Tuesday afternoon? Wow, Luke's mum! Like your style.' Charlie clapped her hands childishly then sprang up. 'Thanks for the eats.'

Hannah leant over, picked both plates up and took them to the sink.

'Just leave them, darling, I'll do the dishwasher in a bit,' Leah said.

'Thanks for having us, Leah.' Hannah smiled and looked through into the living room, where Charlie was spreading herself back out on a beanbag. 'Sorry, we'll be out of your hair soon,' she whispered.

'It's no problem,' Leah replied with a smile. 'I like the company.'

Later, after Hannah had forcibly removed Charlie from the house, Leah made two hot chocolates. She even added whipped cream for Luke. It wouldn't be long, she knew, before he'd be too cool for hot chocolate and he'd be ordering Americanos and pretending he liked them.

She handed Luke's to him with a smile and wished it was cold enough outside to light the fire.

'I kind of like you not working.' Luke put his feet up on the coffee table and rested his head back against the sofa.

'Really?' Leah curled up in the corner part of the sofa. 'How come?'

'Dunno. Just, you know. You're less agitated. And there's always tea.'

'Hey!' Leah swung out her foot and kicked him on the back of the knee. 'When have you ever not been fed?'

'I know. I'm kidding. You're less of a stress head. And you've cleaned my room twice this week.'

'Urgh.' Leah let her head fall into her hands. 'I know. I don't know what to do with myself, really.'

'It's not going to be like . . . before. Is it?'

Leah swallowed. 'No, hon. Nothing like that. I'm fine. I'm just . . . well. Bored.'

She reached over and tried to brush Luke's red tousles from his eyes, but he swatted her away.

'Maybe you should get a hobby or something.'

'What? Start Stitch and Bitch up at the community centre? I don't think so. Although, on second thoughts – you can get really good gossip up there. Did you know Sheena and Alan Peterson from number 72 are . . .' Leah mouthed the last word, 'swingers?'

'*Gross, mum.* That's . . . Jesus, I can't unsee that now.'

'I know, right.'

Luke started scrolling through Netflix, and Leah tensed. Out of the bay window the sun was beginning to droop.

'Listen, Luke. I don't want you to stay up tonight, OK? Let me just watch it myself. Then if I . . . come across badly, I can talk to you about it first.'

'Think again, you batty fish,' Luke said. 'I'm staying up.'

Leah sighed and checked her phone. She really thought Chris would have been home by now. Luke clicked on some teen supernatural drama and settled back.

'What's a batty fish?' Leah frowned.

'You.'

By the time Chris got home, Leah had cleaned the kitchen counters so thoroughly that the heels of her hands were raw from the bleach. She was too tired and anxious to be annoyed with him. Even when he put a cup of tea down wordlessly in front of Leah in a black mug. Leah hated tea in any mug that wasn't white inside. It looked strange. Of all the times, he couldn't remember that tonight?

The Moog nestled into the crook of her knees and she rubbed his head.

'You OK?' Chris sat down next to her on the sofa and put his hand on her shoulder.

'I will be when it's over.' Leah gave him a tight-lipped smile.

'You know, you'll probably only be on for about two minutes.'

'I know. I know.'

Luke wandered in, a slice of toast in one hand.

'Is it on yet?'

'In a minute,' Leah said, refreshing the home page.

'Have you disabled your Twitter?' Chris asked quietly.

'Yeah, I did it last week,' Leah said.

'Facebook?'

'Just put my privacy up to max. *It's here.*'

Leah selected the title under Netflix Originals. *Missing White Woman.*

Luke dragged the beanbag across to be beside the sofa and plonked himself down.

She knew the narrator. A dark-haired man called Carl, who Leah had met a couple of times during her crime reporter stint and never quite warmed to. He did mainly voice-over work now. His tone had that velvet richness to it. Accentless. Reassuring.

The script was dripping in clichés, of missing teenagers and the mystery surrounding them. Dark secret lives. And the cruel, unrelenting, unforgiving media. Leah cringed as her headlines flashed up on the screen.

'Sixteen years ago, Tilly Bowers went missing from the North Yorkshire seaside town of Whitby after she failed to return home from a friend's house. Now, on the anniversary of her disappearance, her parents are campaigning for the media to give equal attention to all missing children cases, and not to adhere to what is commonly referred to as Missing White Woman Syndrome.'

And there she was. In full colour on the screen. Tilly Bowers, her face filling the entire frame, her golden-brown skin gleaming over her cheekbones, her hair in waves around her face. Her eyes, almost black, were shaded by a blue hooded jumper. The one they'd found. She had a split-ting smile, displaying her big white teeth. Her skin, slightly puckered in places on her temples and forehead, was blos-soming with teenage acne. There was a tiny mole on her chin and freckles on the bridge of her nose. Leah knew every detail of this picture. Not the picture the police had used, but the one circulated after.

'Jesus Christ.' Luke's jaw fell open. 'She looks *just* like Charlie Bates.'

'I know,' Leah whispered.

3

30 July 2003

Leah's palms were sweating, and she looked down the list again. Leads, down pages, fillers. She had half an hour to the morning meeting.

Mark placed her Buffy the Vampire Slayer mug next to her.

'You've got this.'

'Jesus, Mark. I'm bricking it.'

'You're in the chair.' Mark raised his eyebrows in amusement. 'I can't actually get my head round the fact that you're my boss now.'

Leah closed her eyes to soak in the drone of the newsroom and the clatter of keyboards, the banging of phones on desks. Five things you can hear. Five things you can smell. Five things you can see. Don't panic. Think about your counselling.

'Christ.' Mark bobbed down beside her desk. 'Is this because of Paul?'

'Mark, it was awful. He thinks I'm crap.'

'If he thought that would he have given you the job?'

'Well, it wasn't entirely up to him, was it? There were other people on the panel. He told me after I got it, he thought they should have advertised externally. That was like taking a bullet.'

'It's all mind games.'

'He hates me,' she said.

'He's not even here. So lead it. Own it. Prove you can do this job. You can. You're a great news editor, Leah. No offence, but you're an even better news editor than you were a reporter. You treat the team well. You give them time back. You see the big picture. Look . . .' He motioned to the team. 'You're half the age of some of these people, and has anyone given you any shit?'

Leah opened her mouth.

'Apart from Paul?'

'Not to my face. But the Bitches of Eastwick probably think I shagged someone to get this seat. I know I wasn't exactly the first choice.'

'OK. So we all thought Ben was getting it. I'll give you that. But that's exactly why you've got this, Leah. Walk into that conference room like you did at your interview and fucking smash it. You've nothing to prove to anyone but yourself. Be that news bitch you know you are.'

'Oh, fuck off. Can I run these front-page options past you and see what you think?'

'No. Trust yourself. Although, something to add to your list. Missing girl. Fifteen. Police just put it out. Not much detail, though, and a generic appeal for her to get in touch. Looks like a runaway.'

'OK. Pics?' Leah started scribbling on the bottom of her pad.

'Yep. Police ones. Nothing more at the moment. I'm going to call Dave, though, and see if it's worth more.'

'OK, thanks.'

Her phone said 8 a.m. She took a deep breath, picked up her list and her coffee and headed to the editor's office. She was the first there. She hesitated for a second, then went round the desk and slid into the big black leather chair. Paul's chair. The editor's chair. Her chair, today.

The back of Leah's neck felt damp and she could feel her hair beginning to swell at the roots already. She'd hacked a good few inches off before her interview in a bid to be taken more seriously. The News Bob. The nose ring had gone. She'd even invested in a fancy pair of straighteners. Ceramic and everything. They'd cost approximately a third of her monthly income, but they made her feel grown-up. The shoulder-length hair, though, as thick as it was, was prone to kinking and bulging in humid conditions. Or whenever she felt nervous.

Graham, the chief subeditor, and Samantha, the picture editor, filed in. Graham looked at where she was sitting and raised an eyebrow but didn't say anything. His smirk said it all. Leah scowled internally and picked up her pen.

'OK. So, here are the main leads for today. I think we have three options. I know none of them are ideal, but . . .' Her voice trailed off as she caught Graham wince and give her a sharp, almost imperceptible shake of his head.

'. . . but with a bit of fairy dust, I'm sure they can be great.' Leah sat up straighter. Mark was right. She had to own this.

'Fairy dust?' Samantha asked, deadpan.

Leah laughed at herself. It sounded tinny. 'Polish. OK, so, first of all, we have the new artist's impressions of the super hospital. I know hospital stories always sell well, and the pics are pretty good, but then

39

we did something similar with the new shopping centre last week – and I thought people might be getting artist's impression fatigue. So maybe a page-three lead instead?'

Graham and Sam nodded and held their pens poised. Neither argued with her, which was a good sign. Meant she'd called it.

'The second option is a three-year-old boy, needs life-saving treatment, community rallying round to raise the money so he can be treated in America. Pics and interviews.'

'That sounds OK but familiar,' Graham said. 'We done it before?'

'No.'

'What's his name?'

'Oliver Higgins.'

'What area?'

'Oakwood.'

'Bit fringy for us, isn't it?'

Leah took a deep breath. 'I know it's edging out of our patch, but Scott has done an incredible job with the pics. They are gorgeous. Great quotes. It's all done and ready to go.'

'Hmmm, not sure Paul would like that. We're not big sellers in Oakwood. Maybe for page five or seven.'

'Paul's not here.' Leah bristled but looked back down at her list. 'Last option is gunshots in the Lupton estate last night. Might just be air rifles but loads of old folk scared. Dan is out knocking now.'

'Sounds the best of a bad bunch.' Graham sat back. 'Is that all you've got?'

'No. We'll get some stronger lines, "prisoners in our own homes" kind of thing. Can hopefully get some decent pics.'

Leah knew she was clutching at straws, but Graham, with his

snivelling nose and bald spot, was in Paul's pocket. She knew he'd be scuttling back to him at the main office, whispering in his ear about what a shit job Leah was doing now he was based at the regional office, juggling eight titles. But she wouldn't lose face.

'So, we'll meet back in an hour, see where we are, and I'll make a call.' Leah started scanning down the list. 'There's the care home closures up for discussion, but that item isn't up until the end of the meeting, so we'll miss the presses. I've earmarked it for tomorrow but running a pre-piece. Other than that . . .' Leah paused and looked Graham directly in the eye, while feeling sick to her stomach. 'Let's get cracking.'

She stood up. The others stayed put and she felt a stab of paranoia. Would they all be talking about her the minute she walked out? Holding her head up, she marched to the desk and started making calls.

'Bad news, Leah, no one's being named. Just called the police press office and it doesn't even look like any shots were reported. Could be a car backfiring for all I know.'

'Shit.'

'Sorry. I'll keep trying.'

'Thanks, Dan.'

She hung up and closed her eyes. She had nothing. Maybe there was something else she could do to jazz up the hospital story? She was just on her way to speak to the health reporter when Mark started flagging her down from across the room, phone wedged under his chin.

She jogged over, eyes wide. 'What? Missing girl better than we thought?' she whispered. He shook his head and carried on knocking out his shorthand, pausing only to spin the screen round.

41

It was an email from Dave, one of the friendlier police press officers.

Heads up, press call this afternoon. Another missing girl, but a good one. Totally out of character, possible abduction.

Thank fuck. Leah started trying to decipher Mark's notes as he wrote, but he batted her away.

'What time, what time?' Leah whispered.

'3 p.m.,' Mark mouthed back.

'Can we get the release early?'

'I'm on it.' He motioned her away.

Leah checked her watch. Two hours until absolute deadline. She looked round the room. She could pull Katie and call Dan back. Get them to the girl's house. Knock the neighbours.

Mark hung up the phone.

'Her name is Hope Hooper-Smith. Fifteen. Sandbrigg. Last seen yesterday leaving school. No reason to run away, perfect student, loads of friends.'

'OK. Great. So, school, street address? Pic?'

Mark shook his head. 'All at the police press call this afternoon. At the station. I'll call it in from there.'

'That's too late. Please push Dave for the release earlier. And the pic. Tell him we'll splash for tonight's paper. They'll want that, surely? Parents at the conference?'

'No, too upset to speak, apparently.'

'That's bollocks. OK, you lean on Dave and get to the conference. KATIE!' Leah called across the room. 'Can you go through the electoral roll, Hooper-Smith in Sandbrigg. Missing girl.'

Katie nodded and started typing.

'Mark, can you hit the schools? It'll be grammar, won't it, if she's from Sandbrigg. Unless private?'

'I'll call Dave, get as much as I can.'

'Found them!' Katie shouted over.

'Great, can you go out? Mark will brief you.'

Leah's heart was pumping. 'Really need a picture, guys.'

Katie was already on her way over, zipping up her coat. 'Chav or posh?'

'Middlish. Hope Hooper-Smith. Fifteen . . . ah, yes! Dave is giving us the pic.'

'Oh, thank fuck. Katie, go go go.' Leah's knees were almost weak with relief. Mark grinned at her and she smiled back. 'You've saved my life.'

'Don't be daft.'

'Seriously, thanks, Mark. Oh, by the way, what's the deal with the other missing girl?'

'Oh yep, here. Headshot and some details. Dave said she's run away about a billion times before. Nothing suspicious.'

Leah looked down at the pic. The girl was heavily made-up in the picture, hair scraped back in a scrunchie, sports top zipped up to the neck. Her hand had been blurred out, making Leah think she was very likely giving the finger.

'Worth putting them together? In one tale?'

Mark wrinkled his nose. 'Not sure. They sound very different.'

'OK. Check with police, though, yeah? Make sure they are not connecting the disappearances or anything.'

'Will do. I reckon Dave would've said, though. I'll ask at the presser.'

'No, don't, everyone else will link them then. Ring first.'

43

'Right you are.'

By 10.30 a.m. Leah had it all. Katie had managed to get the parents at their home, holding a picture of Hope; the police press office were unusually helpful; even the headteacher of Hope's school had given a comment. There was some extra CCTV footage of her leaving the school premises, and a beautiful school picture, her blonde hair tied up in a ponytail, blue eyes sparkling. It would make the page pop. Subs were already working on the headline by the time she called everyone back together.

'Right,' Graham said when she'd finished. 'Sounds in the bag. Good work.'

'OK.' Leah turned to leave and then paused. 'Just one other thing, there's another missing girl. Tilly Bowers. Same age, but different school, other side of town. Police think she's a runaway. I was thinking we should maybe put them together . . .'

'Two girls better than one. Are police linking them?'

'No. Well, I don't think so. I've asked Mark to check. But it sounds like two very different sets of circumstances.'

'Where's she from?'

'Berry Brow Flats.'

'Prozzer?'

Leah bit her tongue. 'I don't think she's a sex worker, no. But even if she was, she's still a child.'

'But nothing to link them other than they're both missing? Nothing suggesting the same person might have taken them?'

'No,' Leah admitted. 'Police think she's just run away again. But they think Hope might have been abducted. Or hurt. It's totally out of character.'

'We might be in for a whole world of pain with this Hope's family if we lump the two together, then.' Graham sat back in his chair. 'What's your gut feel?'

Leah felt the blood rush to her fingertips. Behind her eyes. She didn't feel qualified to make this call.

'Well, two missing girls is obviously bigger news,' Leah started tentatively. 'Maybe we could spin it? Maybe this Tilly's parents will be pissed off they are not getting a press call. Could it be . . . you know, a race issue?'

'Jesus, Leah.' Graham raised his eyebrows. 'You can't do that unless it's water fucking tight. You'll have to call our lawyers.'

Leah gulped. 'Well. OK. Hope's case seems to be a bigger deal. Police are seriously concerned. Maybe it would be a bit out of context to combine the two,' she conceded. 'Just, you know, looking for the best angle.' She nodded briskly. 'But I think we've got enough. I'm happy just going with Hope. Simpler.'

Graham nodded: 'Yeah. We don't want our P45s on our desks tomorrow. Good call.'

Back at her computer, Leah looked at the picture of Tilly Bowers. A pirate smile and a go-to-hell look in her eyes that Leah had seen before in her own reflection.

'What we going with, then?' Mark bent over her desk and nodded at the screen. 'Police reckon she's with mates, trying to piss off her mum.'

Leah looked at the image on the screen and sighed. 'OK, keep it tight.'

When the time came to lay out the pages, Hope Hooper-Smith's face beamed out of the front page. Four hundred words and a turn to page two.

45

Leah scrawled 'missing kid 2' on the flat plan of page eighteen and handed it to a down-table subeditor to lay out.

Tilly Bowers was seventy-five words and a headshot at the bottom of the page. Underneath a lead story about a boy who had saved a hedgehog from a lawnmower.

'Well. It could have been worse,' Chris said as Leah opened the fridge.

'Could have been better.'

'You looked hot, at least.'

'Fuck's sake,' Leah hissed. 'Do you actually think that's what I care about? Anyway,' she added, 'I had at least three chins.'

'Night, Mum.' Luke poked his head round the door.

'Night, buddy,' Chris said. Leah smiled.

'I'll come up in a second.'

'I don't need tucking in.' Luke rolled his eyes. But Leah knew he'd be waiting with his lamp on low until she came up the stairs. She poured herself a white wine and Chris furrowed his brow.

'Now? Isn't it a bit late? It's gone 1 a.m.'

'Well. What have I got to get up for?' Leah knew she was being antagonistic, but she didn't care. *Former editor.* That's what her caption had said. *Former editor.*

She was itching to check Twitter. See if she was being slated. She cringed at how cheesy she'd sounded. How earnest. 'If I could turn back time, I would do it differently. Hindsight is a wonderful thing.'

Ugh. She wanted to slap herself.

She gulped down her wine and locked up. Chris had already gone up by the time she had finished emptying the dishwasher.

Then she went back to the living room and replayed the programme from the start.

'Leah Wallace, who until last year was editor of the *Eastern Post* in North Yorkshire, came under fire shortly after the disappearance of a fourteen-year-old girl who came from the Berry Brow council-owned estate. On the day of Tilly Bowers's disappearance, Ms Wallace chose to run a front-page story covering the disappearance of another teenager, Hope Hooper-Smith, a Caucasian girl from a middle-class area. As a result, Tilly's parents reported the paper to the Press Complaints Commission. Ms Wallace maintains her decision to give more exposure to Hope's case was neither a race nor a class issue. But, regardless of why the *Post* decided not to feature Tilly on the front page, Ms Bowers's parents believe that the lack of press coverage was a major factor in the police's inability to find Tilly. Hope was found only two days after her disappearance, recognized by a member of the public who had seen the news coverage. The discrepancy in how the two cases were handled by Ms Wallace was branded at the time as symptomatic of the press's institutional racism and general tendency to prioritize the Missing White Woman, which is maintained to this day.'

The camera panned on Leah walking down the pier. Her legs looked awkward and stiff and her arms hung at odd, poky angles. She would never have survived in broadcast journalism.

The pier was sparse and grey; they'd shot out of season, of course, and the wind ruffled her hair and they did the typical moody profile shot of her leaning over the railings, looking mournfully out at the east-coast sea.

'I made the best call I could at the time, with the facts I had in front of me . . .'

Leah mouthed along. And then rewound. And played it again.

4

Leah had cleaned the house from top to bottom, reordered all the drawers the Kondo way, and rolled up all the towels into fat sausages. Over the past week she had even cleaned out the garage and taken her cuttings, all her boxes of old newspapers, up to the attic. She was sick of seeing them every time she went into the garage to go on the cross trainer. She never actually used the machine, she just sat in her gym gear eating pork pies and watching *Glee*.

She'd done her emails, skyped her dad in Singapore, changed their gas supplier and was now considering making an appearance at the community coffee morning. It was 11 a.m.

The street was dead. Luke was at his dad's for the day. No squeals or squeaks from Hannah and Charlie on the trampoline. No cat calls or even birds in the sky. No cars in the drives. The air was grey and cottonish, not warm or cold. Flowers drooped and the tarmac was dull.

This life had seemed blissful for the first few months after leaving the paper. She'd done the school run, baked for the church; she'd even thought about doing costume for the amateur dramatic group at the community centre before realizing that she was taking it a step too far.

The novelty had worn off after a couple of months. All this relaxing didn't seem relaxing when there was nothing to actually relax from.

'You're winding down from being a busy, working single mother and high-profile newspaper editor,' Chris had kept reminding her. 'You need the break. *We* need you to have a break. It's been tough on us all.'

So she'd tried. She'd filled her days with coffees with Bunty and some of the other mums from school who didn't work. They'd talked about the horrors of mothering teenage boys, which Leah thought wasn't even that unnerving any more since they seemed to all be so bloody anxious these days. There was no underage sex or contaminated ecstasy; middle-class Gen Z teenagers were all clean-eating and mindfulness courses now. The most popular kid in Year Nine identified as non-binary and, instead of a prom, the Year Elevens had asked to volunteer en masse at the food bank. Who *were* these kids? She longed for Luke to beg her to buy him a couple of cans of cider to take down the park. Or for her house to be crammed full of his friends – boys taller than her who would eat the contents of her fridge. But as Luke explained, they all played online together now. It was easier to do it from their own homes so they could all play at once and grunt at each other over headsets.

So she'd hosted Temple Spa parties, got 'giggly' over a few Proseccos and tried not to swear too much in front of the other mums. She cooked with ingredients from fishmongers and farm shops, and she'd even attempted to bash out that book she was convinced she had inside her, but had quickly become bored and agitated.

She'd researched PhDs and business loans for sandwich shops, courses for counselling. She'd volunteered at the local primary school to be a reading buddy then never actually got around to completing the DBS checks. Her days had become tedious and lacklustre. She'd started projects she'd never finished. Vegetable gardens. Dumb-bells gathering dust. Blogs unwritten. Pictures unprinted.

She'd heard other mums saying, 'I don't know how I had time to go to work,' and had absolutely no idea what they were talking about. As if drinking lattes and spending two hours a day at the gym was a productive use of time. As if these women were not, like her, on the edge of howling at a moon they couldn't see because the sky was too blue. There was so much daylight in her life now. Constant brightness, when all she wanted was the familiar warmth of dusk. Like the way the shards of sun highlighted the particles of dust, it just seemed to shine on the flakes of nothingness she had to fill her days.

Leah had been practically housebound for a month, since Netflixgate. She hadn't even popped out for milk, just drank her tea black and asked Chris to get some for her on the way home.

She'd spent her days scrolling through Twitter on Chris's log-in, looking out for vile comments and horrendous judgy attacks.

She'd was a racist bitch. Journalist scum. How would she like it if her kids went missing? One user had even threatened to bundle Luke into a van to see how that felt.

She'd stopped sleeping after that.

There were others. Warmer ones. Sympathetic. Loads of journalists and editors backing her. More attacks on the police, to be fair, than her. But for every hundred supportive remarks, there was one that hurt so much it was like someone was scraping the meat from her bones.

She made Luke text her every hour.

She could feel it.

It was coming back.

That evening she made Luke his dinner and pushed hers around her plate, feeding chips to The Moog when her son wasn't looking.

'Mum. You've not been on Twitter again, have you?' Luke asked as Leah stared out of the bi-fold doors. They'd run out of money before they could get blinds fitted, but Leah had liked the view and the feeling of the garden being an extension, another room. But now she felt exposed. On stage.

'No, honey,' she lied smoothly. 'I'm just tired.'

'Promise me you'll go out tomorrow?' Luke said and put down his fork. 'You look like shit. Can't you, and I can't believe I'm about to say this, meet Bunty for a drink?'

'Ugh. I don't have the energy,' Leah said, but she felt her heart twitch. She did need to call Bunty back.

'Well. A run? A walk? No one is going to recognize you, Mum. No offence, but it hasn't exactly made you an A-list celebrity. Even C-list. Or D. *Love Island* isn't going to come knocking.'

'Don't I know it.' Leah forced a smile.

'Mum.' Luke reached out and grabbed her hand. She looked down and saw he still had little dimples where his knuckles should be, and for some reason it made her want to cry. 'Please. For me?'

'If I go for a run tomorrow will you stop nagging me?'

'Deal.' Luke grinned. 'And call Bunty. She's snapchatting me now and it's embarrassing.'

Luke disappeared upstairs after tea and Leah took a bottle of wine to the sofa. Chris had texted to say he was going to be late again because he'd sat in on the new receptionist interviews all afternoon and was way behind.

She couldn't exactly be mad.

Instead she surfed Sky, not Netflix – never Netflix – for any old trash, and settled on an episode of *Friends* she could recite word for word. She let it wash over her, as she looked out onto the street. Car doors slammed. Dogs barked. More *Friends* came on. It all seemed to roll into one.

The sounds of the last raspy breaths of the day made her eyes grow heavy and her limbs thick. By the time dusk had fully settled in, she was fast asleep.

When she awoke with a jolt, she assumed it was because of

the front door going and Chris coming home. But it was dark in the living room. The TV had turned itself onto standby and the lamp was off. There was no light creeping in from the hallway either, but she was covered in the throw from the back of the sofa so Luke, presumably, had tucked her in.

Leah reached over and tapped the base of the table lamp, but the bulb flashed and cracked, blowing the fuse. Her heart jumped and she swore under her breath. Her phone said it was just past 11 p.m. But there had been no word from Chris. She stood up and shivered, inexplicably. The air still felt thick and soupy from the heat of the day, but the tops of her arms were dimpled and rough.

Wrapping the furry throw back around herself, she walked over to the main lights and switched them on. There was a strange static crackle.

Perhaps there is a storm on the way, she thought. It was early for Luke to be asleep but there was no movement from upstairs, no blare of the games console, or tinny sound of late FaceTime conversations.

She walked down the hallway and into the kitchen. The entire back wall looked out at a copse of skinny woods climbing up the banking beyond her secret garden. The huge patio doors ran from one side of the room to the other, framed in a dark-grey composite. During the day it was like living in a tiny private forest, until the ramblers and dog walkers wandered through the trees on the purpose-built path.

But at night, it was just blackness. No lights. Just the

stoic silence of the trees. Leah always came back inside when night fully fell, and locked the doors, the snaps and crackles of foxes or rabbits making her feel nervous and a little exposed. At dusk the trees became spindly and creaked like scarecrows.

It was even colder in the kitchen, and as soon as Leah walked in she realized something wasn't right. It took a couple of seconds to work out what. The back wall was all black, but a section was even darker. The doors were half pulled back.

'Shit,' Leah whispered.

Dropping the blanket, she went quickly to the door and pulled it shut, not daring to look outside, locking it and checking it twice. Standing back she could see her reflection in the glass pane, lit by the spotlights underneath the cream drop-down hood over the range. She looked like a child holding a torch under her chin. Trying to scare someone.

Her heart was pounding and she walked backwards slowly. There would of course be a rational explanation. She must have left it open earlier when she was cooking. Or maybe Luke hadn't shut it. That was probably it.

'Luke?' she called up the stairs, hating how loud, how vulnerable her voice seemed. 'Luke? Are you asleep?'

It was unlike him not to come and say goodnight. Even at fourteen, he liked the end of his day to be bookmarked by her. Up to the age of six, she'd lain with him to get him to sleep every night, feeling his little pudgy hands on her face. Even as a baby, when he'd refused to be cuddled and arched his back every time she'd tried to snuggle, at night-time he'd lain there, blinking at her, with those huge, beautiful, conker-brown eyes, like she was his own personal lullaby.

When Chris had moved in, or rather when they'd moved in with him, he'd come and woken her. Told her she was making a rod for her own back. That Luke would never learn to sleep without her. She'd just shaken her head and laughed and said he wouldn't still be getting into bed with her at fifteen.

But night-time Luke, there was still something magical about kissing him goodnight. Kissing away his bad days. His bad thoughts.

There was no reply from upstairs, so she went up, hand on the banister. It was dark in the hallway. Even the bathroom light was off, which Luke always left on.

She knocked softly, something she'd been doing for the past year after hearing horror stories from other mums about the possible sights beyond a teenage boy's closed door, then pushed it open when there was no reply. Luke was asleep, fully dressed, on his stomach, his Xbox blaring quietly through his headphones like the sea through a shell. The Moog's head lifted from the end of his bed, then dropped back down again between his paws.

'What kind of watchdog are you?' Leah murmured, and went to draw the curtains against those unfriendly trees. She peered down into the garden and froze. There wasn't just blackness now.

A light, just one. Flickering. Like a firefly. She stopped dead and held onto the windowsill. It was a candle. A white church candle placed in her orange and red stained-glass hurricane lamp in the centre of the table.

It flickered and undulated as she stared. She hadn't been outside for the last few days. She had lit a candle on Saturday evening. But there was no way that could still be burning. And how would she have missed it when she was in the kitchen just now? She watched to see if it was just the moon-light catching the colours. But it wasn't. The candle was definitely there. Burning strong.

Someone had been in the garden. Someone must have been in the garden when she'd put her arm out to pull in the patio door.

There was a sudden bang downstairs, and Leah screamed. Luke bolted up from his bed and The Moog growled.

'What the fuck?'

Leah put her hand on his chest and a finger to her lips. 'Ssshhh.'

'Why are you in my room?'

'Shut up. I think . . . I think someone's in the back garden.'

'Wait . . . what?' Luke's eyes widened in panic and he scuttled to the head of his bed, wrapping his arms around his drawn-up knees.

'Be quiet,' Leah mouthed and positioned herself in front of him, her arm reaching around behind her to hold him.

'Mum . . . what's going on?'

There were footsteps in the kitchen. They looked at each other and Luke grabbed his phone off the bed.

'Is that Chris?'

'I don't know.'

'Well . . . *check*?'

The footsteps came closer. To the stairs. Leah heard the bottom one creak. She closed her eyes to listen harder.

'LEAH? LUKE?'

'See!' Luke jumped up and flung open his bedroom door. Leah realized her hands were shaking.

'What's going on?' Chris padded up the stairs, looking exhausted.

Leah sank down onto Luke's bed. 'Oh my God.'

'Mum thought you were some psycho coming to kill us.' Luke sounded scornful but there was a wobble in his voice.

'What . . . why?'

'The back door was open. And . . . someone lit a candle.' It sounded stupid with Chris there, in his vet's scrubs still, a shadow on his jaw, his hairy arms folded and his expression amused.

'What's going on in here?'

'Jesus.' Leah shook her head. 'Chris, sorry. I just got really spooked.' She looked at Luke and laughed. 'Sorry, sweetheart. It's me. I'm going mad.'

'Christ alive. You *really* need a hobby.' Luke put his head-phones back over his ears and glared at her.

'No.' She went to remove them, but he ducked.

'I need to recover from the shock. I can't go to sleep with all that adrenaline.'

'Fair enough. But only ten minutes.'

Leah kissed his cheek.

'Night, buddy.' Chris followed Leah out of Luke's room and began to head towards their own. 'I need a shower.'

'Wait.' Leah grabbed his arm. 'I really think someone was here, in the garden. They lit a candle.'

'Leah, why would someone do that?' Chris looked weary.

'I don't know, but please will you go outside and check? I'm seriously freaked out.'

'Leah, I'm knackered. I've been doing those bloody interviews and I've just had to put down a horse and her foal after a road traffic accident. It's been a long night. I just want . . .'

'*Please*, Chris. At least see if it's still lit.'

'Fuck's sake.' He stormed down the stairs and Leah heard him opening and banging the patio doors.

'Be careful,' she called, following slowly.

There was a silence. She could feel the night air blowing through the kitchen and up the stairs. It smelt of dead barbecues.

A rustle, and then more footsteps. She crept further down the stairs, her fingers on the oak-cladded rail.

'Chris?'

The patio door banged shut and she heard the lock click. She turned the corner on the stairs and saw Chris walking towards the kitchen table with her hurricane lamp. The candle was still lit.

'Is this what you mean?' He set it down, his tone a little less aggravated.

'Yes.' Leah came over, her eyes on the blackness outside. 'That's it. Was there anyone out there?'

'No. Not in the garden. And you have to cross that beck to get over our wall. Are you *sure* you didn't just light it and forget?'

'I'm sure. I swear.'

'Leah . . . have you been drinking?' Chris looked down at her. There were new lines around his green eyes. He wasn't what you'd call handsome. His nose was bigger than average and his incisors were pointy. But he had a lovely dimple in his chin that Leah used to put her pinky in when they first got together.

He wasn't smiling now.

'I had a couple this afternoon,' she admitted. 'But I wasn't *drunk*. I cooked tea for Luke. I'd remember lighting a candle.'

'Well, what have you been doing all evening? Didn't you hear anything?'

'I was asleep. On the sofa,' Leah said.

Chris looked around the kitchen and his eyes rested on her empty wine glass.

'Could you have been sleepwalking again?'

'I haven't done that for ages.'

'I know. But you have been . . . on edge, the last few weeks.'

Leah paused. Then she shook her head. 'Chris, I'm sure I wasn't sleepwalking.' She thought of all the lights that had been turned off. Had they been on earlier? Or had it still been light outside when she fell asleep? She put her hands up to her face and screwed her eyes shut.

'Leah.' Chris put his hands on her shoulders. 'How many glasses did you have? Be honest.'

Leah sighed. 'The best part of a bottle this afternoon. Then one, maybe two, after tea.'

'OK,' Chris said. 'I think it's best if you get some sleep now. I'll stay up for a bit, so you don't have to worry. You're safe.'

Leah leant forward and rested her head under his chin and breathed in the smell of his scrubs, of rubbing alcohol and sweat. His arms tightened around her and for a second she felt trapped. Her chest crushed against his. Then just as she was about to gasp for air, he let go so quickly she almost stumbled, and went to get a beer from the fridge.

Leah looked at the candle in the lamp, making the shadows dance on the wall. But there was something else. Something stuck to the base of it. Leah turned it towards her. On the bottom, there was something cut from newspaper. A figure. No, two. Holding hands. Two paper dolls. Damp had stuck them to the glass jar when Chris had picked it up. *How weird*, Leah thought, peeling off the paper and dropping it into the bin. The candle flickered again and Leah peered closer. The hairs on her arms prickled and stood high and for a second she could swear an icy breeze whipped past the back of her neck as she closed her eyes and blew the candle out.

5

'Something totally weird happened last night.' Leah nestled the phone under her chin while she crouched in the cupboard under the stairs, rooting for her running trainers.

'Did Chris give you an orgasm?' Bunty replied. 'Is that what you *finally* rang me to report? Because I've got a class full of fat toddlers in tutus and mothers with resting bitch faces in the studio waiting for me. And I think I've got thrush.'

'Go and get a pessary. I keep telling you those tablets do nothing. You need something that works, you know, *directly*.' Leah dislodged an Ugg and watched her favourite brown crocodile heels tumble from the shelf.

'God. OK, I will on my lunch break. Quickly tell me, then.'

'OK, last night I fell asleep on the sofa.'

'Standard.'

'And when I woke up it was all dark.'

'What time?'

'11 p.m.?'

'Again. Standard.'

'It was freezing in the house. I mean, absolutely freezing. And the patio door at the back was open.'

'Well . . . that explains why it was freezing.'

'And there was a candle in the back garden. Like, a lit one, one of those white church ones. Not mine.'

'Oh, that's weird. How can you tell it's not yours, though? You've got loads of those. Oh shit, I've got to go, that cow with the horsehair extensions owes me money and she's about to dump and run.'

'But no, wait . . .'

'Got to go, I'll call you later, but pick up, you elusive bitch. I know you've gone underground but it's time to be fabulous now, sweetie. Stop moping about and get those tits up. Love you, byeeeee.'

Leah shook her head and shoved her phone in her back pocket. This morning the garden was friendly again. The pinks, yellows and whites of the clematis and honeysuckle clambered up the side of her wall, making the bricks look like packets of Refreshers. Sprawling pots of azaleas, rosemary, lavender for luck, hyacinths.

Leah was the only one who ever sat in the back garden, really. It was tiny and compact, like most new-build gardens. The square footage had gone on bricks and mortar. But she still loved the smooth green turf she'd laid herself, shaven and shorn like a grade one, and her mosaic table with the wrought-iron chairs. She'd fought against Luke and Chris who wanted those beige wicker sofas and a trendy fire pit. They lacked romance and imagination. Not to mention the faff of having to cover them up when the weather turned. There was only one thing more romantic than sitting in her garden, drinking tea from a mismatched cup and saucer she'd sourced from the charity shop, with the hurricane lamps and her chimenea blazing, and that was watching the wind howl and rattle the china, the rain like machine guns on the mosaic and the dragonflies on the jars painted brighter by the grey rain.

Luke thundered down the stairs while Leah was tying her shoelaces, her mood ambivalent at best.

'Hey. I'm out.'

'Wait, where are you going?' Leah called after him.

'Skate park. Remember you promised to go out today.'

'I will. I actually have to. Chris left my car in for its MOT on Tuesday and it's miraculously passed. I'm supposed to pick it up today before noon . . . Chris was going to give me a lift.'

'Looks like you missed your ride.' Luke paused as he grabbed his board from the coat cupboard.

Chris had headed off early without waking her. But he'd left her a tea on the bedside table, uncharacteristically. It was tepid by the time she'd come to. She'd only slept in fits and starts, her legs restless and her dreams shallow. It had been around 5 a.m. when she'd finally drifted off.

'Sucks to be you. You'll have to run and get it,' Luke grinned.

'*Noooo*.' Leah let her head fall between her legs. He was right, though. She could just run. It was only a couple of miles, but it was embarrassing to run on the road and turn up a sweaty mess at the MOT centre. Her belly would jiggle and there was no chance she could stop and walk and keep her pride.

She checked on her taxi app, but it said no drivers were available.

'Dammit.' She zipped her car key into her top. 'How are you getting to the skate park?'

'Sam's giving me a lift.'

'Sam? How come?' Leah asked.

'Hannah and Charlie are coming,' Luke said, and patted his back pocket to check his phone was lodged safely.

'Hannah's going to the *skate park*?'

'Yeah.'

'With *you*?' Leah scraped her hair back into a ponytail.

'Why is that such a big deal?' Luke said.

'It's not. I suppose. I just didn't know you guys were hanging out.'

'You say that like we're engaging in group masturbation, smoking crack and hacking into the Dark Web.'

'Yeah, yeah, very funny . . . anyway, do you think I could jump in? The garage is only around the corner from the skate park.' Leah pulled her hair loose of her scrunchie.

'Dunno,' Luke shrugged. 'Ask.'

Leah stared at her phone. It totally solved the car problem, but was it weird to ask? She could wait for a taxi, but if Sam was going in that direction anyway . . . Leah was never sure about the etiquette with things like this. But a minute's awkwardness was worth not having to run. And she had his number from when he'd brought Bracken in to see Chris.

'Hey. It's Leah, I hear you're dropping the kids at the skate park. Any chance I could hop in? I need to collect my car near there. No worries if not!' Emoji or not to emoji? No, definitely no emoji.

The three little dots appeared.

'Sure.' Smile emoji.

Five minutes later she was in the front of his fresh-smelling car with spotless leather seats, Luke looking mortified in the back and making desperate eyes at her not to turn around and talk.

'So, you girls like skating?' Leah turned her head. Luke would hate her, but she couldn't cope with the silence. Charlie was quieter than the last time Leah had seen her. Her hair was down and loose, and judging by how crumpled her outfit looked, she was wearing yesterday's clothes. Hannah looked fresher, in a pair of leggings and pink sports top, her hair down, and, if Leah was not mistaken, slightly crimped. Did they even have crimpers these days?

'No, just hanging out.' Hannah blushed a little and looked at Charlie, who was transfixed by her screen.

Sam raised his eyebrows and whispered, 'I think they go for the view.'

'Really?' Leah mouthed back. She looked in the wing mirror to try and catch a glimpse of Luke. Had his hair been a bit more artfully tousled than usual this morning?

66

'So, are you going to the gym or something?' Sam turned right and headed down towards the park.

'No. I hate gyms. I was going to run for my car, but it's a little further than my usual route so you have saved me the effort,' Leah admitted, wishing she'd told him to hang on for a few minutes so she could have got changed.

Sam pulled over in the car park and Luke opened the door quickly. 'Thanks, mate.' He dropped his board and headed towards the bowl, not waiting for Hannah and Charlie, who were climbing out of the car and looking a little less confident now they were surrounded by older teenagers and the stink of burning rubber.

'Gentlemanly,' Leah muttered, but Sam just laughed, telling the girls to text when they wanted picking up.

'So, fancy a coffee before we swing by the MOT centre?' Sam popped his arm over the back of Leah's seat and reversed one-handed.

'Oh.' Leah was surprised. She tried to think of an excuse but came up blank. 'Sure. Well. Oh God, to be honest I'm trying to keep a low profile.'

'What? Why?' Sam held the car on the biting point.

'Oh, just that Netflix thing.' Leah looked down.

'What Netflix thing?' Sam pulled out of the way to let a Land Rover pass, his forehead crinkled in confusion.

'What do you mean, "what Netflix thing?"'

'I mean, I have no idea what you're talking about.' Sam laughed, and put the car in neutral.

'Oh. Did Hannah not . . . ? Well . . . I was interviewed as

67

part of a crime documentary. About a decision I made a long time ago. A bad one.'

'You were on Netflix? Well, I need to hear this. Where do you want to go?'

'To be honest, Sam, I'm not really feeling like being out in public.'

'I'll protect you. Promise. We can go somewhere small and out of the way if it helps?' He smiled, flashing his straight white teeth.

'Well,' Leah started, 'I'd love to tell you I'm a big fan of some hipster artisan coffee place in some poky alley that looks like an ironmongers and I'd rather die than give my money to corporate takeovers who don't pay tax properly. But actually, I really like Costa lattes.'

'Can't get more anonymous than Costa.' Sam spun the car around. 'And I don't want a gluten-free vegan muffin. I want a cake made of lard.'

'You're a man after my own heart,' Leah said, then immediately felt weird. There was something intimate about being in the front seat of a car that wasn't being driven by her husband and had no kids in the back.

Sam seemed relaxed, though. He chatted easily about the stress of summer holidays, the pitfalls of being a freelance project manager and it being tough to keep the kids out of the house so he could do a Skype conference call.

By the time they'd settled down for their coffee, she was used to the gentle rhythm of his Scottish twang and the way you could see the gold tooth at the back of his mouth when he smiled. His face was tanned, and his skin was weathered, but not lined as such. More rippled than ridged. His arms were hairy, with blond fuzz that caught the sun, and with those shorts he looked like a climbing instructor at some kind of outdoor pursuits centre in France. He had footballer's calves. She bet he could mix a decent Bloody Mary and do the grouting at the same time.

'So, you seem to have adopted an extra kid this summer?' Leah said as they sipped their coffee, overlooking the harbour. They'd even managed to grab one of the outdoor metal tables. The sun was fresh and the dirty pavements warm.

'Yeah.' Sam scratched the back of his neck. 'She's a good kid, though. So it's nice, really. Keeps Hannah from getting bored.'

'I can imagine.'

Sam smiled at a harassed-looking mum negotiating a double buggy past them, packed with a screaming baby and a toddler eating a jam doughnut who was wiping the sticky contents down her white top.

'Glad those days are over,' Sam whispered to her.

Leah nodded. 'Yeah. I couldn't wait at the time. But it seems so far away now.'

'You and Chris not planning a second, then?'

'Not now. And it would be Chris and mine's first. Luke's got a different dad.'

'Shit, and I knew that.' Sam visibly cringed. 'Sorry.'

'Nothing to be sorry about. But no. It never happened,

really. I did want another. My friend Bunty, she says you know when there's another baby out there for you. I always thought I knew. But I guess it wasn't to be.'

'Did you think about IVF?'

'Yeah, we thought about it. But we were way down the list, given I already had one. So it would mean going private. And I don't know. I think I wanted it more than Chris. It seemed selfish to spend all that money.'

Sam looked at her. 'Really? I wouldn't say it's selfish.'

'Anyway,' Leah said quickly, 'it's good having just one, right? No arguments over Xbox turns. Only one set of school trips to fork out for. Although, like I said, you seem to have gained another mouth to feed.'

'Yeah, I know. They're an odd mix, really. But you know, opposites attract and all that. Hannah could do with coming out of her shell.'

'That's good, then. And I bet Hannah's a calming influence on Charlie.'

Sam shook his head. 'Well, I hope they are good for each other. I know she can be a bit full-on, but Charlie's got a really good heart, you know. I don't think she has it easy at home.'

'Luke said something similar.'

'Yeah. I think, well, maybe she gets taken . . . advantage of sometimes. I'm not sure she's got much of a – what do they call it now? Support network?'

'Well. Good she's got you guys.' Leah smiled and wished she'd bothered with mascara. Her hair was bulging in an unsightly off-centre ponytail and her fringe had started to curl.

'Yeah, we like the company.'

'How long has it just been . . . the two of you?'

'Julie died when Hannah was seven.' Sam tore open a sugar packet with his teeth.

'I'm so sorry, Sam. It must have been very difficult.'

'Being a widower dad?'

'Being a widower parent.'

'Or widower step-parent. Sometimes I forget she's not even mine, you know, biologically.' Sam let the brown sugar crystals trickle into his coffee then gave it a stir. 'I adopted her, around the same time we found out Julie wasn't well.'

'Actually, I didn't, did I know that?' Leah leant forward. 'Not that it matters. Being a dad has nothing to do with the sperm that wriggled its way in.'

'No. We went out for a special dinner to celebrate. But, you know, it was under difficult circumstances, so it never really felt like a happy occasion, so we didn't shout about it. She looks so much like her.'

Sam stared straight ahead, and Leah shifted in her seat.

'Does she see her biological dad at all? Or is he not on the scene?'

'Never was. And I'd kill him if he ever turned up now.' Sam's jaw tightened. 'Is it like that with Luke's biological dad? What happened there?'

'Oh, Dave's OK.' Leah stifled a yawn. 'He's harmless, to

71

be honest. We were never actually together, so, you know, he didn't have time to turn out to be a total twat. I've never had to threaten him with the CSA or anything. He's always been there for Luke. That's more than I can say for my mate Bunty's ex. He's not seen Immie since she was a baby. Never paid a penny. Worst thing is, his other kids go to the posh music school opposite Bunty's place. So she has to see Immie's half-sisters all the time, getting dropped off. And they don't even know about Immie. It's so messed up.'

'Sounds like a dick to me.'

'Bunty uses much more colourful expressions.'

'What about Chris? Are he and Luke close?'

'Kind of. I mean, yeah, they're comfortable with each other. It's easy. Luke's pretty independent and Chris, well, Chris loves his job. He's set up a second practice, more like a shelter, he got this funding grant from a charity. So he's been up to his ears lately running his surgery and getting the new project off the ground. They could do with some quality time.' Leah sipped her latte and cringed inwardly. She hated those women who slagged off their partners constantly and nailed themselves to the cross.

'God. People like Chris make me feel really shit about myself.'

Leah laughed. 'We can't all be frontline. But I know what you mean. I used to come home from work, and we'd talk about our days and I'd tell Chris about all the stories I'd run, or how much I'd pissed off the council or the police or whatever, and then he'd tell me he'd saved twenty-seven kittens from some smackhead drug farm or something.'

'What a guy. Although you had a proper sexy job. Newspaper editor.'

Leah shifted in her seat.

'Not as sexy as it sounds. Especially towards the end. I became a bit disillusioned.'

'Please tell me you did a big Jerry Maguire and flipped out in the middle of the newsroom holding a fish.'

'I wish I could. I actually took voluntary redundancy.'

'Wow. Big decision.'

'Yeah. But, well, long story. I didn't want to stay and watch the paper get butchered. I couldn't run it the way they wanted and feel like I was actually doing my job properly.'

'Frustrating . . .'

The word hung in the air and Leah looked down into the swirls of foam sinking into the dregs of her coffee.

'So you took the moral high ground?'

'Or I was a rat deserting a sinking ship.'

'Don't be so hard on yourself.'

To her horror Leah felt her eyes prick with tears. She looked down and Sam had the good grace not to notice.

'Anyway, you're not too old to start again.' Sam busied himself with his phone until the danger had passed. 'You're what, mid-thirties?'

'I'm forty-one.'

'You don't look it.' Sam leant forward. 'I'm not just saying that to be smooth. You really don't.'

'I feel it.' Leah looked away, feeling her cheeks burn. 'I actually think I'm going senile.'

Leah told Sam about the previous night, albeit with a lilt in her voice and smile on her face. She didn't want to seem like a crazy person. But Sam leant forward, concerned.

'Leah, that's really weird. Call me if anything like that happens again, OK? I am literally over the road.'

'OK.' Leah felt her stomach drop. 'Why? Do you think there was someone, you know . . . prowling?'

'Well, who knows? But it's not nice to be scared, Leah, is it?'

Her name sounded different coming from his mouth. She finished her coffee and enjoyed the burn down the back of her throat.

By the time she got to the garage, she realized she hadn't even mentioned the documentary. And what's more, she hadn't thought about it. So, by the time she was home, she actually felt like going for a run.

Changing into her cropped running trousers and an old grey top, she took her usual route, feeling the burn in her lungs through the park and into the woods. Her legs felt heavy and her blood sluggish. She couldn't seem to find her rhythm and for the first twenty minutes it was like wading through waist-high water. The ground was mossy and the bark damp. She carried on, Nick Drake whispering in her ears, so the brook was silent and the twigs uncracked. Her ankles were mud-splattered and she was too hot, but she couldn't strip down any further. She knew her hair would be curling, her skin flushed. She carried on, feeling the vibrations of the earth under her feet. She managed the slight incline into the deeper thicket and tried to keep to the path, but the brambles were overgrowing and the bushes throbbing midsummer. She slowed down and twisted her body, turning to the side, raising her arms to avoid the spiteful nettles and thistles, when a flicker of light to her left caught her eye.

The caravan, ever more nestled in foliage, stood clinging onto the slope. But through the filth on the window, an amber light was burning. Leah stopped still.

The light was moving. It was too isolated, too soft, to be electric. She ripped her earbuds out and stared, the tinny echoes of her music distorted.

She looked around and listened for the drumming of small feet, or the smell of cigarettes. Kids in the woods? She guessed the caravan could make a good den, although Luke was always convinced some lunatic lived in there, sewing together a new skin made of dog walkers and teenagers. She used to laugh, but it had terrified him. Still did, she suspected. He used to hold his breath every time they walked past in case the devil inside tried to claim his soul.

She took a step forward. There was no noise and the rest of the caravan was still. The filth on the window made it too hard to make out. The light seemed to flicker.

'Hello?' Her voice bounced from the branches and a bird broke from the ash tree ahead and took flight.

She tried not to think of a ghoulish face grinning at her from the window. Unstrapping her armband, she held her phone tight and unlocked it, just in case. She took a step closer.

The wax coat was hanging there, just like always. She could make out the outline of it, along with the stacks of paper. And the light. It was a naked flame. Surely that would be a fire hazard? The entire caravan was stuffed with kindling.

'Shit,' she whispered. Should she call the fire brigade? No, they'd think she was crazy. For a candle. Just blow it out. She held up her phone and took a picture. There must be someone in the park she could call. A warden or something? She didn't want to try and rattle the door. Even with her sensible head on, there could be anyone in there. Someone who didn't want to be disturbed. Sleeping rough. On something?

She took one last brave step. She was about a foot away from the window now. She craned her neck and saw something hanging in the window, something draped like bunting. But oddly shaped.

She took another step, heart beating in time to the bass line still pounding from her earbuds. She looked down and swiped the screen, so all was silent.

And now she was face to face with the window, there it was. A thick white church candle. Burning. With a string of paper dolls tied across the window. Cut from newspaper.

Leah felt as if the ground was tilting and her lungs seemed to be getting smaller and smaller until there was no air. It was as if the trees had eyes in their knots and the birds were circling too fast. She took a step back, and if the woods had not been so deathly silent she might have even screamed.

Instead she turned and ran as fast as she could towards the clearing. By the time she got home there was a thudding in her ears and her lungs were on fire. Her neck was stiff and her shoulders sore; she'd kept looking over her shoulder as she ran. Sinking down onto her front step, Leah ran her hands through her hair and tore off the tie-dyed band she was using to keep it off her face.

'Wow. Tough run?'

Leah looked up to see Sam's car slow down as he crawled past the house, window down.

She couldn't even answer, just nodded and leant the back of her head against the front door.

'Hang fire, I signed for a parcel for you earlier. I'll just grab it.'

She watched as Sam parked up then jogged to the house. Here, back on the street, she felt a bit ridiculous. It could have just been kids, in fact it probably was kids. Building a den or something. But no. The dolls. Exactly the same as the pair in her garden. It couldn't be a coincidence.

Sam came back out of the house and walked up towards her. Still in those cargo shorts even though it was cooler today. He was wearing some kind of expensive Japanese label hoody, all logoed and surfy. It was the brand Luke always insisted on, but she made him pay for it himself. Actually, Sam looked like an overgrown teenager in general. Only with a less complicated haircut. And thicker-set arms and calves.

He looked like he'd free-climbed and played a lot of football in his younger days. He smiled, blondish stubble across his chin, and handed her a packet, a Jiffy bag with a recorded delivery sticker on it.

'Thanks.' She took it and turned it over for the return address. She couldn't think what she'd ordered, but she seemed to be doing that more and more recently. Green smoothie recipe books. Web cams for The Moog, iPad magnetic stands, 1,000 brown paper bags. The curse of Amazon Prime.

'You OK?' Sam said. 'You look a bit . . . freaked out.'

'Yeah. I am, a bit.' Leah took his extended hand and pulled herself up. 'Remember that candle thing I told you about?' Sam nodded. 'Well, I've just been running, and I could swear I just saw another one, a candle, I mean, lit in the caravan in the woods. You know the one? In the pines behind the park?'

'Yeah, yeah, of course, I've walked Bracken up there. A candle? Sounds a bit like a fire hazard.'

'I thought so too. There was a light coming from inside. And when I got closer, there were . . . well, they looked like paper dolls. Hung like bunting in the window. Just like the ones on the Hurricane Lamp that someone left in my back garden.'

'Yeah, that's weird. We should probably call the fire brigade. You can't have naked flames in the woods.'

'Yeah . . . Maybe they could check it out. I wonder if someone is living in there?'

Leah shuddered at the thought.

Sam shrugged. 'Is there a Friends of the Park or something?'

They looked blankly at each other.

'I'm not even sure if the woods count as the park?'

'I'll google it.' Sam sat on the step next to her. 'Here, it's council-owned. Want me to call?'

She did. 'No, I'm a big girl,' Leah smiled. 'I'll do it. Just need to catch my breath.'

'OK,' Sam said. 'Do you want me to come in or anything? I don't like leaving you like this.'

Leah shook her head but she really didn't want to go into the house alone. Sam raised his eyebrows as if he could see the scenes running through her head.

'Actually, yes. Sorry. I feel so pathetic. Will you just make sure there's no mentalist wearing a patchwork skin suit lurking about?'

Sam looked at her for a second too long. Then he stood up and held his hand out. 'Copy that.'

6

2 August 2003

Paul tapped his biro against the desk in two beats. A pause. Two beats.

'So. I thought it worth bobbing in. See how you're all doing.'

Leah nodded her head. The office was stifling. Her top was damp under the arms. It's not sweat – just melting deodorant, she felt like calling out. She wanted to ask Paul to open the window, but neither of the men looked at all uncomfortable. Samantha, she noticed, was wafting the news list in front of her face.

'I liked your splash last week. Nice work. Good timing that she didn't get found overnight, though. That's the risk with missing kids. They get found before we've hit the stands and it's too late to recall. It can make you look very outdated. Risky.'

'We had a fairly strong steer from the police . . .' Leah tried to explain, but Paul cut her off.

'You got lucky there.'

'Well. I went with my instincts.' She regretted the words as soon as they came out of her mouth.

Paul let out a dry laugh and shook his head. 'Like last time?'

'No,' Leah said quietly. 'Not like last time.'

'You planning on following up?' Paul pushed his chair back and stood up.

'We did try. They're not talking. Which is understandable, but annoying really since it was our front page that meant she was found.'

'What have they said?'

'The usual. I've got a fairly weak statement, needing family time, so relieved, pressure on young people. Respect their privacy. Enough for a reasonable lead but I don't think it's enough to make a decent splash. It's been everywhere now, anyway.'

Paul nodded, sniffed and turned his back to her. Hands deep in his pockets, he looked out of the window.

'God, I do miss it here. Miss that sea.'

Leah decided not to point out that he was looking at the staff car park, which backed onto a Wilkinsons.

'Anyway, so I was thinking page-three lead. Although this Tilly Bowers is still missing. Another runaway. I was going to send Mark down to the flats this morning and see what more we can get. Might be stronger on the back of Hope being found. Could make a page one? Get some heads saying something about exam pressures?'

'Not exam season, though, is it?' Paul sat back down. 'You don't want another missing kid lead. And she looks like a smackhead anyway.'

'Leah wanted to put them together last week. We talked her out of it.' Graham coughed into his fist.

'Ah. This famous instinct of Leah's.' Paul smirked. 'Well, two missing girls are better than one. But I can't imagine the other family being best impressed at their gymkhana princess being lumped in with . . .'

Leah felt bile bubble and burn the back of her throat.

There was a knock at the glass door and Mark poked his head round. 'Sorry to interrupt. Just been on with Dave at the press office. I know you wanted me to go knocking, Leah, but social services are involved now. It's all a bit . . . dodgy family stuff. I'm not sure we want to go there.'

'What are they thinking? Still that she ran off?' Leah leant back in her chair and twisted her neck so she could see him properly.

'Yeah.'

'Still has legs, then?' Leah turned back to Paul.

'Bit involved now, don't you think?' Paul wrinkled his nose. 'Go with council tax hikes. That's if you want my advice, of course. Or go with your gut . . . see where that gets you.'

7

'How are you feeling now?' Chris came up behind Leah and wrapped his arms around her waist.

'Weird.' Leah sipped her wine and stared out of the patio doors. It was dusk in the woods and the sun was falling behind the trees, the colours of the day becoming watery and thin.

'Come away from the window, Leah. It's making you . . .'

'See things? They were there, Chris. The dolls. In the caravan window.' Leah let herself be cuddled, but her back felt stiff.

'They've probably always been there. I'm proud of you for going out today, though. I know you haven't wanted to leave the house much since they aired the documentary. Are you still glad you did it?' Chris swiftly pushed the caravan conversation to one side.

'I think it would have been worse if I hadn't.' Leah shrugged. 'I wish I had stayed at the paper a bit longer, though. Their media team and lawyers would have sorted it all. I feel a bit . . . vulnerable on my own. Do you think people around here have watched it? I mean, will people in the Co-op start accusing me of . . .' Leah shook her head and groaned into her palms. 'Do people think I'm racist?'

'Leah.' Chris kissed the top of her head. 'You didn't make those decisions because she was black. Or from Berry Brow. No matter what people say. And anyway. It wasn't you. It was the police who tipped you off.'

'Yeah, but I've ignored steers given by the police loads of times. They always told us not to go knocking. To respect the family's privacy. We never did. We always tried to get them. And half the time, the family wanted us there. Wanted to talk. It's just something the police always say. I could have made someone go and track down the family. I did with Hope . . . I shouldn't have been governed by what the police thought was newsworthy. What kind of journalist am I?'

'Leah—'

'Was. I should have said . . . was.'

'Was what?'

'I *was* a journalist.'

'Come on. You're still a journalist.'

'Am I?' Leah took another sip of her wine.

'Well. If you're not, what are you?' Chris gave her a squeeze. 'Come on. Stop staring at the woods like a sailor's widow. There's nothing there. No one there.' Chris sighed. 'Do you think, maybe, it might be a good idea to make a doctor's appointment?'

'Why?' Leah gulped down the rest of her wine. 'You think there's something wrong with me?'

'I think you're very stressed. And I think you've struggled with this redundancy.' Chris took the glass out of her hand. 'Look, it's natural. You've worked so hard, all your life. The paper. Luke. No wonder you feel . . .'

'Redundant?'

'Lost.'

Leah looked up at him.

'Remember that day? When I came down to the shelter?'

Chris smiled. 'Of course. You still look exactly the same.'

'You're a massive liar. But that's what you said to me. You look lost.'

Chris kissed her on her nose. 'How do you remember that?'

'Because I was having a bad day. Like, one of my really, really bad days. Luke had been screaming when I dropped him off at breakfast club. They'd had to prise his little fingers off me one by one. Then I got into work late and we'd had a call from the Press Complaints Commission and one of my reporters was crying after being called a leech by some paramedics. I'd totally forgotten about our meeting for your campaign. I pulled up in your car park, and for a minute I just felt like putting my foot down. Ramming the accelerator to the floor, unbuckling my seat belt and driving as fast as I could into that garage wall. I could hear the metal crunch. I already knew what it would feel like. The snap of my neck.'

'Leah . . .'

'You look lost. That's what you said when I wandered in. I must have looked a bit dazed. But I thought you meant . . . well, the way you looked at me. That smile. It's like you understood.'

'Actually, I just thought you'd walked into the wrong building. With your heels and your jacket. All shiny hair and perfect lips.'

'Just shows, I guess . . .'

'It's almost our anniversary. We should do something.'

'Like what?' Leah rested the back of her head against his chest.

'Weekend away? When Luke's with Dave? Just us.'

'Actually, I was thinking we could do with some family time.' Leah remembered her conversation with Sam. There had been truth in what she was saying. It wasn't just bullshit to fill a guilty silence.

'That sounds less intimate. But OK. If that's what you want. Come on. Let's get you upstairs. A bath and an early night will work wonders.'

Leah felt a surge of annoyance and moved away.

'I'm fine,' she said and held her hand out for her glass. 'I'm not six.'

'Really?' Chris handed it back. 'Don't you just want to get some sleep?'

'I'm hoping it'll make me sleep better,' Leah said and filled her glass halfway. 'Do you want some?'

'No. Better not.' Chris looked at the clock. 'Well. I'm going to go up and watch TV in bed or something. Early start and I'm knackered.'

Leah leant against the counter. 'I'll be up soon.'

Chris gave her a reproachful look, but she couldn't bring herself to follow him. Instead, with their conversation weighing on her mind, she went back into the living room and selected the documentary again on Netflix. Maybe it wasn't as bad as it had seemed a month ago. Maybe she wouldn't be shunned as a racist bitch after all. The programme began with a reconstruction. Tilly leaving her friend's flat, the CCTV footage. No bags. Nothing with her. It hadn't been that warm a day. She was in cut-off denim shorts, baseball boots and a blue zip-up hoody, carrying one of those mini backpacks that couldn't hold much more than a phone and a purse. It was 2003. Tilly didn't have a phone. She'd said she was going home.

She'd never arrived.

Leah remembered the almost-interview with the friend. Dakota. She'd rocked up in reception at the paper with some other friends. Grief vampires. Red Converse and cornrows. She'd said she was Tilly's best friend. Leah hadn't been able to talk to her, though, without her parents' permission. She'd had to call them there and then, but they'd demanded cash. Said the *Sun* wanted to sign them up and could we beat their price?

They couldn't.

She watched now. *Adele and Darren Bowers*, read the caption on the screen. Adele was smaller. Not the warrior queen she remembered. Or was that imagined?

'If her photo had been put on the front of that paper, then maybe somebody would have seen her. We might have got her back. But they didn't. They weren't interested.' Adele sat in her tiny, cramped kitchen. Cutaway shot of the tower block. Back to Darren's hands on his coffee mug. All the shots by numbers. 'You know. She was just a kid. She'd run away before, like. But this time it was different. But no one would listen. There was no conference. No reporters came knocking on our doors, you know? They didn't even ask. Didn't care.'

The scene cut to another headline. Another girl. The voice-over continued.

'Missing White Woman Syndrome is a suggestion by some social scientists and media commentators that, out of the thousands of people who go missing in the UK every year, if the person is white, middle-class and female then they are likely to get much more media attention than peers of a different ethnicity. In 1999, when a five-year-old Asian girl, Saya Ahmed, was reported missing . . .'

Leah closed her eyes and rubbed at the bridge of her nose.

'Mum?'

She opened her eyes and Luke's silhouette was in the doorway.

'Why are you sat in the dark?'

'I'm just watching . . .' She looked up. But the TV was on standby. 'Oh. That's odd. It must have turned itself off.'

'Why don't you go to bed?'

'God. Not you too.' Leah got to her feet. 'Are you coming up?'

'Yeah.' Luke waited until Leah was in front of him. 'Mum. What was Tilly's full name?'

'Tilly Bowers.'

'No, I mean, what is Tilly short for?'

'Matilda. Why?'

Luke paused. 'No reason . . . Mum?' Luke put his hand over hers on the banister. 'Could you, maybe, come and chill in my room for a bit?'

'What?' Leah turned around and noticed that Luke seemed very pale. 'What's wrong?'

'I don't feel great,' Luke said quietly.

'Me neither,' Leah said and stroked her son's head.

She followed Luke upstairs and got changed in the dark into the crumpled pyjamas she'd left on the bed. Chris was snoring lightly, like a puppy. She breathed in the slightly sour smell of his sleep and, pausing just for a second, she picked up her pillows. She crept down the hall. Luke's bed-side lamp was on and he was curled in a ball on one side of his bed, the covers up tight beneath his chin.

'Aren't you a little old for a night light?' she said jokingly and flipped off the hallway light. He turned over and gave her a rueful smile.

'Sorry. I'm just a bit freaked out.'

'Is that my fault?' She fluffed the pillows on his bed and sat herself down, leaning against them. 'If it's the candle thing last night, I was just being stupid. There's nothing to be scared of.'

Luke didn't say anything and looked up at the ceiling.

'Luke. Seriously. I lit the candle and forgot. That's all.' She hadn't mentioned the caravan and decided not to. Luke tended to fixate on things. She couldn't imagine where he got that from.

He nodded. Then opened his mouth and shut it again, like a goldfish.

'What? What's the matter?'

'Nothing.' He let his head roll towards her and she wanted to put her hand on his cheek, no longer chubby, but sculptured and angled. He wasn't handsome, her son. He was beautiful.

'Want me to stay for a bit?'

'Just until I go to sleep.'

'OK.' Leah pulled his navy fleece rug up over her legs and scrolled through her phone.

She knew the exact second when he drifted off. The change in his breath. The heaviness in his limbs. But she stayed for a few minutes anyway. To be sure.

When she woke, the pale sun was filtering through the curtains and Chris's alarm was bleeping in their room.

'Do you think it's cold in here?' Leah pressed a pod down into the coffee machine and waited for her toast to pop. She couldn't face another morning of plain scrambled eggs.

'Not really. You're probably just cold from sleeping under that little blanket.' Chris dug his spoon into his porridge. 'I can't believe you slept there all night.'

'I know. But he seemed really unsettled.' Leah pulled her

dressing-gown cord tighter. 'You're right, though. My bones are cold. I can't warm up.'

'Well. Maybe he's picking it up from you.'

'Don't.' Leah hit the button on the toaster impatiently. The bread was barely brown. But it would have to do.

'How are you feeling today? Any better?' Chris asked.

'I'm still a bit freaked out by the caravan. Those dolls. But . . . I guess it's just one of those things that never gets explained.'

'Like where my North Face jacket went?'

'Yeah. Or like that time I locked myself out of the house and found the keys *inside* the house.'

'I still don't get why that one is weird.'

'Because how could I have left the house and locked the door without having them with me?'

'I still think Luke locked the door.'

'When does Luke *ever* lock the door?'

'You're imagining things.'

'Chris.' Leah looked up sharply. 'Do you actually think I'm delusional?'

'I didn't mean it like that.' Chris scraped the last of his porridge out of the bowl. 'But I do think it's worth seeing someone – maybe they can tweak your anxiety meds? Did you call the doctors?'

Leah grimaced. 'I will.'

'What are you going to do today?'

'I don't know. Clean up. Might see if Bunty is free.'

Chris smiled. 'Good. Although don't get pissed up again in the middle of the day.'

Luke walked into the kitchen, hair messed up at the back.

'The Kraken wakes.' Leah smiled. 'This is early for you.'

Luke grunted and opened the fridge, still in the shorts and the stained T-shirt he'd slept in.

'OK, see you tonight.' Chris kissed Leah on the top of her head. 'See you, buddy.' He raised a hand at Luke and grabbed his keys. 'Leah. Make that appointment.'

'What time are you home?' Leah asked.

'Late. I've got to spend some time with the new girl, Alice. She needs more training on the system. Yesterday she organized all my appointments as Facebook events rather than in the diary.'

'Is that really your job?'

'What kind of place would the world be if we all had that attitude?' Chris pulled on his coat. 'I'll be home as soon as I get done.'

Luke brought a bowl of sugary cereal to the table, milk dribbling down his chin.

'You eat like an eight-year-old,' Leah said.

'Stop buying me kiddie cereal, then.'

'Fair enough.' Leah went to push her chair back, but Luke signalled to her to wait, his mouth full of Honey Loops.

'What's up?' she asked. He waited for a second until the front door clicked shut.

'What were you talking to Chris about?'

'When?'

'Just then. About imagining things.'

'Oh God.' Leah laughed. 'Nothing. Just Chris thinking I'm nuts. Nothing new.'

'But what about? I mean specifically. Have you . . . seen something else?'

'No.' Leah lied smoothly. 'OK. Come on, kid. Talk to me. I know something's up.'

'Well . . . you know the other day. When I was hanging out with Charlie and Hannah?'

'Sure.'

'We were just messing about. And Charlie was telling us about one of her brothers doing a Ouija board.'

'Okaaaay.' Leah tried to keep her face straight.

'And, like, obviously I said it was bollocks.'

'Obviously.'

'But she was saying her brother is like *nails*, and he didn't believe in them either. But then he did one. Up at the flats, with some mates. And they got in contact with some guy who said he was called Frank and started telling them shit. Like shit *no one* would know. Like, about Charlie's brother wetting the bed until he was six.'

'That's not a very nice thing to share.'

'Or, like, his mate having a teddy called Blue that used to be his dead sister's.'

'OK, but—'

'And it turned out some methhead called Frank killed himself by jumping out of that tower a few years ago.'

'Right.'

93

'Anyway . . . so . . . we did one.'

'Did what?'

'A Ouija board.'

'Oh, Luke, you didn't?' Leah's mouth dropped open.

'I thought you said they were bullshit!' Luke's eyes opened wide.

'I do. But that doesn't mean to say I think you should mess about with stuff like that. Just in case. It's . . . bad energy.'

'I know. I know. I wish we hadn't. But you know, she was teasing me. When I said I didn't want to do it, she said I was a pussy.'

'And . . . hang on, who? Charlie? Did Hannah go along with this? Where was Sam?'

'Well, at home. But we didn't do it there.'

'Where did you do it?' Leah asked slowly.

'In my room.' Luke looked down. 'You weren't in.'

'*In this house?*' Leah squealed.

'You always said they were bollocks,' Luke said defensively.

'So did you,' Leah replied stonily.

'Well, I'm not sure now.'

'Where the hell did you get a Ouija board from?' Leah stood up and immediately felt light-headed. She steadied herself on the worktop.

'We just made one. You use a coin, and then write the letters and numbers on a big bit of paper.'

'Where is it? Now?'

'I binned it.'

'It had better be out of this house. I mean, I don't believe in them, but I've seen *The Exorcist* . . .'

'It is. I put it in the outside bin.' Luke stood up. 'I'm sorry. It was weird. It really freaked me out. It's been freaking me out ever since. I keep thinking . . . thinking someone's watching me. And it's always cold in my room. And . . . and . . . yesterday . . .'

'What?'

'The weirdest thing happened. I woke up and someone had left a cup of tea next to my bed.'

'What?' Leah laughed, but she wasn't quite sure if it was hysteria. 'Well, that sounds quite nice. What are you complaining for? Anyway, it was probably me.'

'You were out. I heard you go out. Then I went back to sleep and when I woke up there was a tea there. And it was red hot.'

'Well, I don't know. Maybe you made it and forgot.'

'You get mental when Chris says something like that to you.'

'You're right. I'm sorry. But OK. Tell me what happened, then. With the Ouija board. Did it work?'

'Yeah. I mean, the coin really did move and we weren't pushing it. The person . . . the girl we spoke to . . . she said she was murdered.'

'Oh, for God's sake. It will have been Charlie. It can't move of its own accord. You don't really think a spirit was pushing it?' Leah knew she was being snappy now, but there was a sick feeling bubbling in her stomach.

95

'No one was pushing it, Mum. Honestly. You could tell. And Charlie, like, flipped. We stopped it ... as soon as the spirit said she was murdered. The Moog was, like, whimpering at the door and everything.'

'Well, what else did it say?'

'It said ...'

'What?'

'Mum ...'

'*What*?'

'It said her name was Matilda.'

8

It had been a strange week.

After Luke's revelation, Leah had cleaned out his room and scrubbed the house from top to bottom. She'd read up on crystals, feng shui, put her bed northwards and bought plants. Chris had watched her quietly.

The sinks shone and the house smelt of lavender, bay and rosemary. She constantly moved, ducked and weaved in and out of rooms.

Luke wasn't sleeping well. She heard the tinny sound of the Xbox through his headphones late at night, the lamp on the lowest setting. They had laughed off the cup of tea eventually, but every day there was something else. His game cases were stacked vertically and not horizontally. She never touched his Xbox stuff. Strictly a no-go area. And they both knew it. But neither of them mentioned it. She'd seen him trace his fingers along them, confused. But when he'd looked up, she'd just smiled and carried on folding his laundry.

Then all the shoes in the cupboard – the ones both she and Luke just tossed in and quickly slammed the door on so they didn't tumble out – were all lined up neatly. Leah told Luke Chris must have done it. After all, it used to drive him mad. But he'd barely been there all week. And she didn't dare ask him.

She hadn't slept well either, jumping at every noise, every snuffle from The Moog. She'd jostled Chris awake twice last night, once thinking someone was breaking a window, which turned out to be the ice-maker in the fridge refilling, and again at about 5 a.m., convinced there was someone in the back garden. Of course, there was no one there.

She and Sam had called the Friends of the Park committee, who said they'd send a volunteer down to have a look at the caravan. Make sure someone wasn't living in it and check for fire hazards. Probably kids building a den, they said. Sam had suggested they go back together, but Chris had got a little agitated and started muttering about enabling.

To keep herself busy she'd pruned and potted and clipped and weaved in the back garden and strung globe lights across the fence. She'd power-washed the patio and drank her coffee at the mosaic table. She'd lit the candles in the hurricane lamps, even though it wasn't dark, and left them to burn.

She'd spent her days wiping down the kitchen and looking out of the window at the girls in Sam's garden, Luke skating and mounting the kerbs in front of their drive in a series of clicks and whooshes.

But the house still didn't *feel* right. So Leah had kept cleaning. Moving.

Then she'd found the package. The one Sam had handed her when she'd been trembling on the step after the caravan incident. She'd shoved it on top of the big American shiny steel fridge-freezer that she'd blown the last of her redundancy on. Then yesterday, while she had been wiggling the ice compartment aggressively to dislodge the build-up, it had tumbled down.

At first it had seemed empty. She hadn't been able to see anything inside, so she'd pinched the sides to widen the mouth and seen, there at the bottom, bits of newspaper. Plunging her hand in, she had hooked her finger around the shapes and pulled them out. Paper dolls. Two triangles for dresses and circles for heads, holding hands.

The newspaper had been crinkled. Not silky and fresh. She'd smoothed them out. They'd been cut carefully, with no ragged edges. Peering back into the envelope, she'd looked for something, anything, to explain – a slip, a note.

But nothing. Just two paper dolls staring at her with their inky featureless faces.

'You've got a stalker, babe,' Bunty had told her.

She'd come straight round. Chris hadn't answered his phone, as per usual.

'Well. At least I know I'm not a crazy person. Although there is someone sending me newspaper dolls and lighting candles in my garden. Quite frankly, I don't know which is worse.' Leah squeezed a lime around the edge of two glasses.

'Yeah. I agree. It's weird. But, look, it's just been on TV. It's probably her parents, isn't it? Or some nutjob campaigner.'

'That's what Dave said.'

'You spoke to Dave?' Bunty puffed on her vape.

'Don't do that in here.' The crushed ice crackled as Leah added the gin.

'Why? It's just, like, incense.' Bunty glowered but she put the vape down. Her hair was the messy side of cool, tied up with a Seventies scarf, black tendrils escaping like tentacles. A look Leah often tried to achieve, but it always seemed like she'd been dragged through a hedge backwards.

Leah gave her a glass. 'It's slimline.'

'I'm not on a diet, thanks.'

'No, but I am.'

'You're not fat, Leah.'

'That's because I'm on a diet.'

Bunty rolled her eyes.

'So, what's the score with the fit dad over the road? Any more coffees?'

Leah blushed. 'No. And he's not that fit. I just meant. You know. He's a bit fit. For a dad.'

'Well. Someone to put your lipstick on for, I suppose. He clearly thinks your curves are just fine.'

'It's not like that.'

'If you were a munter, he wouldn't have invited you for coffee.'

'Maybe he thinks I'm nice? Or funny.'

'Nope. I'm the funny one. You're the unhinged one. Stick to your part, please.'

Leah sipped her gin. 'Anyway, I called Dave after you. I didn't know if I should report it to the police. You know, officially. Dave said he'd have a word with a few people and call me back.'

'Does Luke know?' Bunty took a deep sip.

'No. I don't want to worry him. He's still freaking out about the Ouija board incident.'

'So, seriously. Do you think there is anything in it?'

'The paper dolls?'

'Yeah. Well, the dolls and this Ouija board. I mean, would the kids have known that name? Tilly Bowers?'

'Well, yeah, Luke watched the programme. That's how he recognized her name.'

'What about one of the girls? Playing some kind of prank?'

'They'd have to have watched the show. And are kids really bothered about documentaries? At their age?'

'Yeah . . . Well. There's only one way to find out.' Bunty downed the rest of her drink.

'What?' Leah caught up and reached for the bottle.

'We'll have to do one ourselves.'

Leah nearly choked on her slimline tonic.

Half an hour later and there they were. At the kitchen table, Leah feeling like the biggest hypocrite there ever was.

'Look. It'll just prove it's all bullshit. Then you can put it out of your head and move on.' Bunty was writing numbers and letters on a piece of printer paper. Leah was sure it was meant to be more sinister than this.

'Are you sure this is all it is?'

'It's what YouTube says.' Bunty shrugged and held up her iPhone.

'God. And people get in a moral panic about social media challenges, when all you need is a bit of paper and a crayon to get possessed,' Leah said.

'You don't get possessed by a Ouija board!'

'That girl in *The Exorcist* did.'

'Yeah but . . . that was a proper one.'

'What's the difference?'

'I don't know. Shut up,' Bunty said and fished in her giant vintage brown leather handbag for a coin. 'I don't think I have any cash. Who even has coins these days?'

'Here.' Leah got up and went to the swear jar. 'What do we need?'

'Dunno. Two pence?'

'Cheap date. We don't have two pence swears in this house. You'll have to have a pound.'

'That'll do.' Bunty took the coin off Leah and sat cross-legged on the bench side of the table, her back to the woods. No fear.

'Speaking of cheap dates . . . how is your love life?' Leah asked.

'Shite. I'm too old to be sending Belfies.'

'Your boobs are great!'

'I *know* that, but I'm not sending them to geography

teachers called Craig in return for a dick pic. Which are never attractive. Why do they send them? They're all aggressive-looking and unsightly. Like veiny bicycle pumps. I don't want to see it. I'd rather get sent a screenshot of his bank statement and a clean STI test.'

'No one with potential at all?'

'No . . . I don't want someone to shag. I can sort myself out quicker and better. And I don't really want a relationship, either. I've got enough on trying to keep Immie's legs together. I don't have time for anyone else's shit.'

'Where is Immie tonight?'

'She claims she's studying at her mate's house. Clearly she's performing group fellatio in some dogging area.'

'Bunty!'

'Just being realistic. Where's Chris?'

'Same.'

'Nice.'

'He's still at work with this Alice chick.'

'Definitely group fellatio, then.'

'Maybe come off Tinder. It's warping your brain.'

'No. I like the Super Likes.'

'I give up.'

'Right. Come on. Shall we light some candles and shit?'

Leah looked around. 'I had a bit of a candle purge, I've only got a Glade air freshener candle.'

'That'll do. Dim the lights.'

'What if Luke comes in?'

'Where is he?'

103

'Over at Hannah's.'

'Well, he's probably going at it.'

'Performing group fellatio as well? Seems everyone is doing it.'

Bunty did her big dirty laugh and even Leah managed to smile.

'Come on. Right. What do we say?' Leah leant forward, her nerves beginning to chatter.

'Hang on. The guy says there's fourteen rules when using a Ouija board.' Bunty screwed her face up. 'Shall we not bother with that?'

'Wait, isn't this like the time we painted your raw plaster and ignored all the warnings that we had to treat the wall first? Look what a disaster that was, and this involves tormented spirits in my house,' Leah said.

'OK. But we'll just skim through. OK. So burn a white candle.' Bunty looked at the Glade candle and its fake flicker. 'Good enough. Don't ask about God or Death yada yada, oooh, if it does a figure of eight or goes to all four corners it's an evil spirit trying to get out, and you have to say goodbye.'

'Fucking hell,' Leah spat her gin back into her glass.

'Ohhh, hang on, OK, always close the portal.'

'How do we do that?'

'Dunno. Say "This house is clean," maybe?' Bunty said in a high-pitched squeaky voice.

'Stop quoting *Poltergeist*. I'm properly shitting it,' Leah said.

'Oh my God. Listen to this.' Bunty read off her screen:

'"Never burn a Ouija board. If you do and hear a scream, you have thirty-six hours to live."'

'Nope. Fuck this for a game of soldiers. I'm not doing it.' Leah pushed her chair back.

'Oh, come on, you massive pussy. You said you didn't believe in it! It's all bollocks.'

'Right, fine then. Let's do it at your house.'

'Not a chance.' Bunty looked down at the board and grimaced. 'Ah, let's have another gin instead. It'll have been that bellend Charlie pushing the coin. Honestly. Do you know what she did to a girl in Year Seven? Told her if she saw that bloody Momo character it would pin her chest down in her sleep and make her feel like she was dying. Poor kid drank coffee for three days straight to stay awake.'

'Are we doing this or not?'

'I thought you didn't want to?'

'Now who's chicken?'

'Index and middle fingers on the coin, bitch.'

Leah did as she was told and let out a shaky breath.

'Is anybody there?' Leah asked, and suddenly both of them started to giggle.

'No, you've got to respect the board.' Bunty tried to keep a straight face.

'OK. Sorry, I'm just nervous.' Leah wriggled and tried to sit up straighter, ignoring the darkness outside the window and the reflection of the candle in the glass.

'Is anybody there?'

Leah was quiet. She could hear Bunty's breath and the murmur of the dishwasher.

'Is anybody there?'

The coin moved. Just a millimetre. Leah's eyes widened and Bunty's breath caught.

'Is anybody there?' Bunty said, more confidently.

The coin seemed to wriggle under their fingers then began to inch slowly forwards.

'Shit,' Leah whispered. 'Is that you?'

Bunty shook her head, her eyes fixed on the board.

It felt to Leah as if there was a magnet under the table dragging the coin.

It came to rest on the word *hello* that Bunty had scrawled on the paper.

'Hello,' Leah whispered. She locked eyes with Bunty.

'Can you tell us your name?' Bunty asked, not breaking eye contact with Leah.

The coin began to move straight away.

Leah felt as if her chest was about to burst as the coin headed towards the *T*. She knew it would.

'Oh my God.' Her voice was a squeak.

T. Then *I*.

Her hand began to shake as she waited for it to move towards *L*.

But it jerked suddenly and flew towards *T* again. Then, as Bunty burst out laughing, *S*.

'TITS? Oh my God. I knew it. Oh, this is such bollocks.' Bunty lifted her fingers off the coin, but Leah yelped.

'No. NO. Put them back. We have to close the portal. Or whatever.'

'Oh, for crying out loud.' Bunty was still laughing as she put her fingers back. 'Goodbye, spirit. We hereby close this portal.'

The coin didn't move.

'You bitch.' Leah stood up. 'Was that you? That was you, wasn't it?'

'No, honestly, I swear. Well. Not to start with. It did feel weird. But then, I don't know. I just started thinking of the word "tits" and I couldn't help it. God, that is proper bizarre about the "hello", though. And the "T". I didn't do that bit.'

'Well . . . that's what they say, isn't it? That it's telekinesis. Or, like, you're sub-consciously pushing it.'

'Whatever, babes, I think we can safely say you are not being haunted by a malevolent spirit.'

Leah sighed. 'I need another drink.'

Bunty started laughing again. 'Oh my God, that was so funny. Your face.'

'What do we do with this?' Leah picked up the bit of paper.

'Burn it?' Bunty suggested.

'Fuck off, I don't want to be dead in thirty-six hours.'

'Well, lob it in the recycling, then. You can't get less macabre and more middle-class than that.'

Leah had done as she was told. But she'd not been able to warm up all night. Like there was a coldness, almost a cloud, around her. Bunty hadn't seemed to feel it, howling and shrieking at the Tinder guys and swiping right, no goosebumps on her bare arms, her feet swinging merrily from the bar stool by the kitchen counter. She had been a welcome distraction. But when Chris had driven her home later, and Luke had settled down upstairs, Leah had sat back at the kitchen table and risked a look out into the woods.

She had only really been able to see herself backlit by the spotlights, so she'd turned out the lights, just for a minute, and gazed out into the fresh navy darkness. The longer she'd looked, the more she had been able to see shapes in the trees, the branches. It had been like cloud-watching. Tall figures with long dripping fingers. Squatted, hunched ones with thick legs. And a silhouette carved out of the dusk, of a young girl with thick black hair and a soaking wet blue hoody standing in the middle of the path.

Leah had snapped on the lights quickly. The window had been fogged with the condensation of her breath. She'd swiped at it but it had just smeared her view. She'd stood to the side of the patch, but all she could see was herself, staring back.

9

The beach was quiet. It was Leah's favourite time to walk across the tightly packed sand, just as the tide was going back out and before the day trippers turned up. The Moog waddled next to her, grunting with the effort, his squashed face turned up to her, the sea lapping between his pads.

Leah breathed in the salt air and listened to the waves break until she found a rhythm. She'd heard people say that they couldn't live anywhere but the sea, that they were called to it. But when Leah had first moved here she hadn't heard the Sirens. Instead she had followed the smell of the printing press and the musky ink. She'd sent off fifty letters to editors in her final year. Begging for a chance. Her clippings from the university paper backed on black card. References from news editors at papers where she'd toiled for free and let herself get treated like shit for the sake of a joint byline. More than half of those papers didn't exist any more.

She'd been headhunted when Luke was almost two. Offered a news editor's job on the *Manchester Evening News*.

God, she'd wanted it. She still wasn't sure why she'd turned it down. Why she'd turned them all down. Joni Mitchell said it was the bright red devil keeping her in a seaside town. Leah knew different.

The gulls were gathered ahead at the crags like a pack of thugs, with their black eyes and round heads. Leah stopped and looked out to the view, the dark waters scraping the granite sky. She let her breath fall in and out of time to the beat of the waves.

They bobbed and swelled and made her feel dizzy after a while, so she turned and began to walk, trying to feel the overwhelming sense of insignificance she normally felt at the shore.

But it didn't work.

She had started thinking about the paper and now she couldn't stop thinking about Tilly Bowers.

Tilly was dead. She'd always known it. And even if it wasn't her fault exactly, had she reduced the girl's chances? She thought again of that moment, that fast reflex, scribbling the words: missing girl, page eighteen. Dropping it in the tray. And she'd known. She'd known she should have put them together.

Crouching down, she scratched between The Moog's ears. He gave her a googly-eyed dribble and the waves broke around her toes.

But she hadn't trusted her instincts back then. Not after *it* happened. She'd been twenty-two. It hadn't been her first death knock. There had been plenty. In the days before vicarious trauma was a buzz word and the mere mention of how upsetting you found a situation was met with derision. Grief tourists.

Paul had sent her. A house fire. The dad had done it. Dragged his two little boys into the attic and waited for the flames to take them. The younger one, Liam, had been found half way down the stairs. So close to escape. His ten-year-old brother, Sam, curled up against his father's chest. Faithful to the end.

Funny how easy it is to love a monster.

Leah had driven down the road. The curtains had been drawn in the cul-de-sac. The grass had been scorched, the windows blown. Teddy bears and candles lay like a blanket across what had once been their garden. Footballs. A signed Middlesbrough shirt. Leah had pulled the car over and taken a deep breath, before fishing in her bag for her notebook. The house hadn't been habitable, of course. But she'd thought the neighbours might give good comments. Or know where she could track down the mother. No journo had got close to finding her.

Just as she'd been scribbling with her biro to make sure her pen hadn't dried out, Leah had seen someone, two people actually, walk around the corner. Both women. One wearing tracksuit bottoms and a hoody, hair pulled back haphazardly. Her body had been crumpled like a Coke can, all unnatural angles and jagged points. The older woman, her mother perhaps, had been in a wool coat and gloves. She had practically been holding her upright. Leah's hand had flown to the car door handle.

They'd stopped for a second, and as they'd approached the

house the younger woman had buckled. She'd fallen so hard to the floor the cracks of her knees sounded like gunshots.

Leah had watched, motionless, as she'd bent double, her hand reaching out for the teddies, clawing them towards her. She hadn't cried so much as barked. Guttural, raspy sounds that Leah had heard in her sleep every night for a week after that.

The street had stayed still.

Leah had gulped, and with shaking hands turned the key in the ignition, reversed into the road behind her and driven back to the office in silence.

She'd thought about lying. Telling Paul there had been no one there. But the look on her face said otherwise.

'I'm sorry,' she'd said. 'I couldn't. There was just no way I felt right doing it. I . . . I just couldn't. It felt too intrusive.'

'You couldn't even ask? Asking isn't intrusive . . . not leaving and harassing her would be. You didn't even ask?' Paul had looked at her. It would have been easier if he had looked angry. Or disappointed even. But his craggy face had been like stone.

'She wouldn't have talked, no way,' Leah had said. 'Seriously. I just know.'

The next day the Yorkshire Post had run a full-length interview with her on the front page and Paul hadn't looked at her for two weeks. Mark had even drawn up a pretend P45 and left it on her desk. As a joke, apparently.

Ahead, a figure was running along the wet sand. Faster than a jog. A real run. She watched as it got closer. A man.

With sandy hair. A tribal tattoo on his calf. Jogging shorts and a faded old Creedence Clearwater Revival T-shirt. She could almost taste the salt on his skin.

Exactly on time.

'Sam?' Leah called and held a hand up.

Sam squinted and slowed down, a slow smile of recognition appearing on his face. He pulled his earbuds out and wiped his forehead with the back of his arm.

'Oh, hi!' His hands massaged his waist, catching his breath.

'I forgot you said you ran here.' Leah smiled and hoped she looked convincing. 'Don't break your stride for me.'

'Nah, it's a great excuse.' Sam put his hand to his chest. He looked ruffled. He laughed nervously and took a step back into the white horses of the shallows. 'Oh, shit.' He jumped forward again.

Leah laughed. 'Mine are soaked too.'

'What are you doing here so early?' Sam ran his hands through his hair, leaving it sticking up in little tufts and peaks. Leah could smell his deodorant.

'Couldn't sleep.' At least that part was honest.

'Still got the heebie-jeebies?'

'Something like that. Hey, did you hear Luke and the girls have been messing about with Ouija boards?' Leah folded her arms.

'Jesus Christ. *Where?*'

'My house.' Leah shrugged.

'Shhiiiitttt.' Sam looked out at the sea. 'Mind you, we all mucked about with stuff like that when we were kids, right?'

113

'Not me.' Leah shook her head. 'I'm, well, let's just say I get anxious.'

'Really?' Sam motioned for them to continue up the beach and Leah nodded. 'I wouldn't have had you pegged for the anxious type. Recent events excluded, of course.'

They began to walk, slow and measured. The Moog shuffled along in the shallows.

'I'm a good blagger. I hide it well.'

'You do. I get a bit like that sometimes too, you know.'

'Really?'

'Yeah. A couple of years ago, I even had counselling for it.'

'What happened?'

The gulls squawked and circled like vultures. Leah wished she'd brought a bigger coat.

'It sounds so stupid. I convinced myself I was going to die.'

'Really, what brought that on?'

'I had a bump. You wouldn't even call it a car accident. Someone went into the back of me on an exit road off the M1. Nudged the bumper. Not even worth going through the insurance. But I started thinking about what would happen to Hannah if I died too. After that, every time I got in a car I started to panic. It's not you on the roads you have to worry about. It's everyone else. I wouldn't let her get lifts off other people. I worried every time I was in the car alone. Somehow it would be OK, if she was with me. If we went together.

'Anyway, one day, it was snowing. In fact, do you remember? The schools all closed. Although it was probably just after we moved here. I went to pick Hannah up from school and I was going really, really slow. Trying to get up that hill, you know, by the sports hall?'

Leah nodded.

'Well, another car was coming down and lost control. I saw it coming straight towards me. It was almost as if it was in slow motion. I froze. I just waited for the impact. I was convinced this was going to be it. That everything I had been frightened of was coming true. Then I had this image of Hannah. She was there, by the gates, screaming, and I knew I had to try. So I wrenched the wheel at the last minute. The car missed me, literally by an inch. When I opened my eyes, she was there. Hannah. Just like I'd pictured her in my mind.

'I actually cried. I blubbed like a baby. I felt like I'd been given a second chance at life. I was euphoric. I quit my job, went freelance. I wanted to do everything, see everything. I started climbing. I took a sky-diving course. I thought I was Patrick fucking Swayze in *Point Break*! I even . . .' He slowed his pace. 'I even thought it would be OK to meet someone else. You know. But I had so much guilt every time I noticed another woman. As if I was cheating on Julie. Which is ironic, really. Given that she was cheating on me.'

'What? Sam, oh my God. When? What happened?'

'It was, well, just as she got sick. You've got to swear you won't mention any of this to Hannah, though, or even Luke. I don't want it getting back to her. She idolized her mum. I don't want her to know the truth.'

'Who was it, that she was with?'

'Someone at work. The ultimate cliché. I think she had just found out. Just found the lump. Remember that special dinner I told you about? When I adopted Hannah? She'd been late to it. Said she'd been held up at work. She lied.'

'How did you find out?'

'Good old-fashioned emails. All in the cloud. She was shit with technology. She obviously thought she'd deleted them. But I was going through everything, after she died, looking for an insurance reference. The messages were all there.'

'Oh, Sam. I'm so, so sorry. That must have been so hard to deal with. Especially because you couldn't even confront her.' Leah slowed to an almost-halt. The sea breeze was beginning to pick up and toss her hair into her eyes. She grabbed it with one hand and held in back in a bunch.

'Well. That's the thing. Would I have? She was so sick.'

'I am sure it was just some kind of moment of madness. I can't imagine what goes through your mind when you get news like that . . .' Leah bit the inside of her cheek and a trickle of blood pooled around her back teeth. She tried not to wince.

'Well. Funny that. You'd think it would be your family, wouldn't you? Pretty hard to swallow that she wasn't thinking about us at all. Yet she still wanted me to adopt Hannah. Pretty screwed up, in my opinion. In fact . . . Nah, forget it.'

'What?' Leah tucked her hair behind her ears as the sea breeze whipped it across her face again. 'You can tell me.'

Sam kicked a stray piece of petrol-coloured driftwood into the breaking waves. 'Well. I dunno. Maybe she wanted to leave me, but didn't want Hannah to be alone. I couldn't help . . . feeling tricked. I know how awful that sounds.'

'But you love Hannah?' Leah said.

'I do. I mean, of course I do. But . . .' Sam's jaw clenched. 'It's complicated.'

'Sam.' Leah laid a hand on his arm and they stopped walking. 'I'm glad you told me all this. I'm always here if you need to talk.'

'Thanks. Sorry. I didn't mean to unburden on you. I don't know why I did.'

'Trick of the trade.'

They were close. Leah looked up into his face, glad she'd put her make-up on. Not too much. Just enough to cover her tiredness and frame her eyes. Just in case. There was a line, a thick one, between the edge of his nose and the corner of his lip. She was scared she wouldn't be able to resist reaching out and touching it. A sudden gust whipped Leah's hair forward again and she had to use both hands to scrape it back.

'I understand, you know. About anxiety. A few years ago I got a little bit . . . fixated,' Leah said.

'On what?'

'Sounds so embarrassing now, but on Luke. About him being safe. I wouldn't let Dave, that's his dad, take him to the beach in case there was a tsunami. I did a story at the paper about a dad who left his handbrake off and his car, with his kids inside, went into the canal. They were banging on the windows but he couldn't get them open. They all drowned. The minute I filed that story, I went out and bought a claw hammer. It's in my glovebox now. In case I ever need to smash a window to get Luke out of the car.

'If we did a story about a house fire, I started imagining him burning alive. Reaching out to me, the agony he would be in, and how I would have no choice but to set myself on fire just to be with him through it.'

Leah paused and took a deep breath. 'Shit, sorry. I know it's dark.'

'Hey. We're on the same page here.' Sam briefly threw his arm around her shoulders and gave her a squeeze.

'Anyway. I think, if I'm honest, that's one of the reasons I took the redundancy. I mean, I had some therapy. I have coping strategies now, and it comes in waves. But. It became harder. Every crash. Every kid with cancer. I could just see Luke's face.'

'So it's not true what they say. About becoming desensitized?' Sam nodded in the direction of the pier and they began to walk again.

'Well. No. You get used to it. And there's always a gallows sense of humour.'

Leah looked ahead. The pier was still and the shutters on the kiosks down. The noise from the harbour on the other side was catching the wind.

'Do you think you'll go back?' Sam asked.

'Nothing to go back to. I know that sounds dramatic, but it's not the same industry I left.'

They climbed the stone steps and the shouts and laughs from the boats began to get louder.

'So, if you don't go back . . . won't you get bored? Or will you find something else to fixate on?' Sam smiled as Leah scooped The Moog up in her arms, his short stumpy legs struggling with the steps.

'I'll have to do something,' Leah said. 'Or I'll go out of my mind. Chris thinks I have already.'

'And what do you think?' Sam stopped and shoved his hands down in his pockets. He looked like a schoolboy, shifting his feet about.

The Moog's wet, sandy paws were making a mess of Leah's top, but she didn't care. She was used to it.

'I don't know . . .' Leah said. 'It's been a crazy week.'

'Doesn't mean you're crazy, though.' Sam smiled.

'Not yet,' Leah replied quietly.

The two of them looked out to the harbour.

'So. What next?' Sam asked.

Leah looked at him. 'Want a lift home?'

He paused, gave a rueful smile and nodded.

10

24 August 2003

'Right. Before we start, I just need to tell you, and only you three – no need for this to go out to all and sundry – that Tilly Bowers's family are taking legal action. I got a solicitors' letter yesterday.' Paul shut the conference room door a little too hard and moved behind his old desk automatically.

'Oh God.' Leah ran her hands through her hair. 'What are they saying?' Her stomach was a lead ball and her ribs felt ready to buckle.

'I'm not going into the nitty-gritty, but basically they are accusing us of racism because we buried Tilly's story at the back.'

'So you mean me. They are accusing *me* of racism?' Leah felt as if the office was spinning.

'Leah. We would have all made the same call,' Graham said. Then added, 'Probably.'

'There's nothing they can sue us over. We are not a public service, there's no accountability for editorial decisions. It's not a crime to be racist. It's only criminal if you've committed a hate crime.'

'But I'm not racist!' Leah raised her voice.

Paul looked at her and leant forward slightly, hands together, with that calm down, dear expression that made Leah even more on edge. 'Our lawyers say they've got nothing. They can take us to the Press Complaints Commission, but there's no code of conduct you've broken. It was your editorial judgement.'

'Right.' Leah nodded. Keep it together, don't cry.

'So, any notes that Mark has in his notebook from that conversation with the police press officer? Anything on email? Giving you a steer that she was a runaway, no suspicious circs? Anything we've got, can you gather it together? Soon as?'

'Of course,' Leah said.

'Right. So. Today's leads. What have we got?'

Leah took a deep breath. 'Well. Police have appealed again. There's a new photo of Tilly. And a picture of the locket that they found under the pier.'

'And what . . . reading between the lines . . . are they thinking suicide?'

'Yes, or accidental death maybe. They're not ruling out murder, though.'

'Is it an official murder enquiry?'

'No, not yet.'

'Definitely Tilly's necklace, though?'

'Yes. Her family say it's hers.'

Paul sighed. 'Shit.'

Leah knew what he was thinking. She'd made the wrong call. And a girl could be in the gutter somewhere because of it.

'Right, I'm going to run it past the lawyers, but you will have to go with that on the front. Say that police are refusing to rule out murder, yes?'

Mark was out on a job by the time the meeting was over, so she circled the newsroom, gave out the deadlines, got updates and sat down to copy-edit. Her foot was jumpy as she went through passive intros and weak second paragraphs without changing much.

The snappers had left an updated contact sheet of the pictures. Tilly's photo, a much more media-friendly one this time, with a wide smile and soft hair, was at the front.

She felt sick but carried on reading through the pieces. Library break-in. Pensioner left on trolley for twenty-four hours in A & E. Angry residents demanding traffic-calming measures after kid breaks his leg dodging a speeding car on the school run. Same stories. Different faces.

The phone rang and Leah picked it up. 'Hello, newsdesk?'

'Leah? It's Dave from the police press office.'

'Oh hi.' Leah sat up straighter. 'How are you?'

'Yeah, good, thanks. You?'

'I've had better days,' Leah said flatly. 'I needed to give you a ring, actually. About Tilly Bowers.'

'Ah, well. That's what I'm ringing about.'

'Any updates?' Leah reached for a pen.

'No. Not yet. I'll let you know when we have. But listen, what are you planning on doing with it for today?'

'Giving it some space,' Leah said cautiously. 'I take it the family still don't want to talk to us.'

'Sorry,' Dave said. 'I'm doing my best. But listen, we need to get this out there as much as we can. I might be able to get you something else from the DI. Would that help?'

'Sure. Anything that hasn't been anywhere else will push it up higher.'

'OK. Leave it with me.'

'Great. Listen, while you're on. I need to . . . um . . . you know when you told Mark that the Tilly story was a bit complicated and social services were involved?'

'That was off the record,' Dave jumped in. 'That's not to be reported.'

'No, I know. But . . . I need to put a statement together. Saying why we ran with Hope on the front and not Tilly. I need to explain, really, why I didn't put them together.'

'Well, why didn't you?' Dave's voice turned cold. 'We gave you both releases.'

'But Mark said you told him that the police weren't taking the Tilly case as seriously . . .'

'Whoa, whoa, whoa.' Dave's voice got louder. 'That's not what I said.'

'But . . .'

'Leah. Is that what Mark said I said?'

'He's not here right now, but that was the general impression we got,' Leah said carefully, trying to keep the panic down. 'Is that not . . . what you recall?'

'Get Mark to call me,' Dave said tersely. 'I'll try and get this DI for you. But don't hold your breath.'

11

The tower block loomed on the skyline, the jaunty attempts at brightly coloured shutters and balconies almost embarrassing. Like a girl in a tattered prom dress. It was still early, not even 8 a.m., despite feeling much later. They'd walked for almost two hours. The beach always seemed to gulp down time.

Leah slowed the car down and indicated right into the car park. There weren't many others there. She felt very conscious of her white-woman, middle-class car and was glad for the mud splatters and The Moog, who was pressing his snout up against the back window.

'What are we doing here?' Sam looked straight ahead, confused. A balding man in a green anorak with an Alsatian walked past and stooped for a second to look in the passenger window.

'Leah? You OK?' Sam nudged her. 'Do you need me to drive?'

'Sorry.' Leah started and rubbed her face. 'God, sorry. It's . . .

a bad habit. I sometimes come here. Normally after I've been walking. I forgot I had you with me for a second.' She gave him a sideways glance. 'Must have been on autopilot.'

Sam peered up out of the windscreen.

'This is where Charlie lives. I've dropped her off a couple of times. Why do you come here? I can think of more attractive thinking spots.'

'It's where Tilly lived,' Leah said quietly.

'Tilly?'

'She was a teenager who went missing about sixteen years ago, she's why I was on that Netflix documentary. My paper decided not to give her disappearance much in the way of column inches when she first vanished. Well, I say my paper. It was my call, really. Another girl had gone missing and it seemed like a bigger story at the time, and the police were swaying us that way too. Tilly's parents accused us of being racist for sticking the white girl on the front page and burying Tilly in the back. They said that the lack of media exposure is why she was never found. They blamed us, or me, rather.'

'And she lived here?' Sam unbuckled his belt and turned towards her, his knee pressing against the gear stick.

'Yeah. I come here sometimes. It makes me feel closer to her, somehow.'

'I don't think we should be here,' Sam said nervously and started fishing for his seat belt. 'Do her family still live here?'

'I don't actually know. I think so. God. You're right. The residents might recognize me now. After that bloody show.'

Leah started the car.

'How often do you come here?' Sam looked relieved as she began to reverse.

'When I was little, I had a baby sister. She died when she was just a few weeks old. Meningitis. My mum, before she left us, used to go to the hospital for months afterwards. At night. Just to walk the corridors. Dad said it made her feel closer to her.'

'I'm sorry, Leah. Wow, you've really been through it.'

Leah stared ahead at the green, rusting metal bins.

'She didn't cope well. It's why she left. I don't think she could handle being a mother. It was almost as if it was too much of a reminder.'

'How old were you?'

'Seven.'

'Same age as Hannah when her mum died.'

Sam reached out and put his hand on her leg. Halfway between her knee and hip. Leah looked down at it.

'Leah, you're incredible. You're one of the strongest women I know.'

Leah shook her head and furiously blinked her eyes as she put the car into gear. 'You don't really know me, Sam.'

'That's what you think.' His voice was low and heavy.

'What do you mean?' Leah sniffed and looked over at him. To her anger she could feel her eyes becoming damp.

'Hey, I'm here, you know. Any time you want to talk.'

Leah forced a thin smile. 'I can't believe I'm offloading on you like this. I'm so sorry. I don't know what's come over me.'

'I'm a good listener,' Sam said. 'Besides, didn't I just do the exact same thing on the beach? You've earned a turn. But I like that you feel you can talk to me.'

'Fair enough.'

Leah turned onto the main road. There were more cars on the road now, runners on the pavement. Little clusters at the bus stop. It made Leah feel oddly unsettled. As if all eyes were on her.

'My friend Bunty thinks I'm a nutjob.'

'Is that the Rihanna lookalike? The one with the . . .'

'Big tits?'

'Actually, I was going to say Audi.'

'Oh.'

'I'm more of a bum man, anyway.'

Leah smiled and checked in her rear-view mirror. There was a car behind her. A black one. Not quite a 4 x 4, but a bigger car. She was sure she'd seen it earlier. Parked by the beach. She recognized the bumper sticker because it was grammatically incorrect.

'Or a killer smile will do it.'

There was a loud silence.

'Leah? You OK?'

'Sorry.' Leah looked back in the mirror. It was too far behind to see who was driving. 'Look behind you, do you recognize that car?'

Sam swivelled his neck. 'No, which car?'

'That big black car. It was parked by the beach.'

'And?'

127

'Well. Just a bit weird that we were on the beach and now it's behind us.' Leah braked slowly and the car fell back in rhythm.

'This is the main road to the beach.' Sam leant forward and switched the radio on. 'It's just a coincidence.'

Leah felt herself relax a little. Sam was right.

The twang of Placebo started and Sam started drumming the dashboard with his fingertips and blasting out the chorus. His voice was fantastic, alto and rich. He hit every note and got louder as they went along.

'Oh my God, this song makes me feel like I'm eighteen again.' Leah almost had to shout over his voice.

'I *know!*' Sam beamed. 'Let's drink Newcastle Brown and smoke Regals!'

'No way, man. Marlboro Reds all the way.'

The car was still there. A blue Vauxhall Insignia had nestled between them now.

'Moshers' Marlboro. I can proper imagine you in DMs.'

'I was indeed a grunge queen. I used to dye my hair purple with that cheap stuff that turns it a bit weird and grey when you wash it out.'

'I was a grunge wannabe.' Sam leant forward and turned the volume down. 'I even had the cardigans. And the Nag Champa. And I could stand at the front of gigs and do that wavy head thing.'

'Like a toddler at fireworks?'

'*Yes.*'

Leah checked and the black car was indicating. It turned

left up the road towards the church and Leah let out a sigh of relief.

'No man apart from Kurt can pull off the cardigan look,' she quipped, suddenly feeling lighter.

'I know. I realized that too late.'

'I can see you at festivals, though. Woven tops, acoustic guitars and roll-ups? Did you draw CND signs on your shoes?'

'Yes, but only with Tipp-Ex.'

'Is Tipp-Ex still a thing?'

'I don't actually know. Is CND?'

By the time they had got back to the cul-de-sac they were both laughing, and the day was ripe with the promise of hot showers and fresh coffee.

'Thanks for the chat.' Leah smiled as she turned off the engine. 'I promise next time I won't be so weird.'

'Next time?' Sam looked at her. But he didn't smile this time.

'I mean. You know.'

'Any time.' Sam leant forward and kissed her cheek. His breath was salty. 'I mean that.' He whispered it so close to her ear she could feel the moisture of his lips.

Leah drew back, half in surprise. But he just grinned and his eyes crinkled like weathered paper. 'Right, see you later. Got to go and pretend to do some work.'

He reached over and ruffled her hair, before opening the car door. Leah felt suddenly very childlike.

Inside, the house still smelt of sleep and stillness. But she could feel the warmth of Sam's hand on her thigh and the graze of his stubble on her skin. She was very, very awake.

By the time Chris was up and eating the porridge Leah had made him without complaint, even though she knew it was too runny, Leah was feeling calmer and the early morning on the beach suddenly felt like days ago, not hours. She felt a bit silly now. Like when she was fifteen and used to walk the long way home from school every night just so she could go past Ben Duggleby's house and accidentally bump into him as he was on his way back from rugby. Not that she'd even speak to him. But she liked to think about him seeing her. About him being aware of her existence.

'So. How's your new girl working out? Good hire?' Leah picked up a banana.

'Yeah.' Chris nodded and looked up from his phone. 'She's been working hard. She's clearly not daft. And she's amazing with the customers. And the animals. Some people just have that connection, don't they? Anyway, I'm going to see if I can up her hours, write a bigger role for her into the funding bid for the shelter. She said she wants to train up.'

'Great.' Leah looked back out of the window.

'What are you up to today?' Chris brought his bowl to the sink. It was still half full.

'Not sure. Washing. Big food shop. Living the dream?'

He smiled and startled her by putting his arms round her.

'We should go away for that weekend. Get you some fresh air.'

'We live by the sea. Isn't that fresh air?'

'A break from this . . .' Chris tapped her forehead with his finger and Leah had to stop herself from slapping it away. She heard her phone vibrate.

'I need to stay until closing tonight to show Alice how to do all the alarms and stuff. If there's someone else who can man the out-of-hours, I can be home early more often.'

Chris's hands squeezed her waist, then travelled up her ribcage. He moved them round towards her breasts.

She stiffened.

Chris tentatively touched her, massaging her breasts, and he started to breathe deeply. He grabbed her hand and moved it towards his crotch, but she broke free and turned her back to him quickly.

'Pack it in.' She tried to inject a playful tone into her voice. 'Or you'll ruin it for later.'

They both knew she was lying. It had been months. But every time he tried to touch her, she felt stale, somehow. It was normal, she told herself. All relationships went through a dry patch. They were both exhausted. It was the drudgery of routine, being in their forties. They weren't teenagers.

But when she thought of the way Sam kissed her cheek, she felt sixteen again.

'Hi. Mark?' She hadn't expected him to pick up his phone, really, and she was midway through repotting her lavender plants in the back garden. With the patio doors wide open and the smell of the damp earth, she felt almost normal.

'Leah?'

'Yeah. Sorry, are you at work? Well, of course you're at work, everyone is.'

'I am, yeah, but it's fine. Hang on, I'll shut this door . . . It's good to hear from you, I keep meaning to call. I heard about the redundancy. You OK?'

'Yeah, oddly. Well. You know.'

His voice was the same. Melodic, almost. She thought of all the times he'd calmed her down on the metal steps outside their office.

'I never thought I'd see the day when you'd walk away. Must have been a good package.'

'Yeah. I got about a year's salary. Just taking a bit of time out, to hang out with Luke, reassess. You know.'

'Sure. How is Luke? How old is he now?' Mark asked.

'Fifteen.'

'You're fucking *kidding* me?'

'I know, right?' Leah gently prised up the roots from the pot, her neck beginning to ache from holding the phone between her shoulder and her ear.

'Oh my God. I remember the day he was born.'

'How are your two?'

'Great. Josh's off to university in September.'

'Jesus, now that does make me feel old.' Leah popped the lavender in the larger terracotta planter and took the phone in her hand, rolling her neck around slowly.

'You should come round for dinner. You and Chris?'

'Absolutely,' Leah said enthusiastically. *That'll never happen,* she thought. There was a crack in the right side of her neck and she almost moaned with relief.

'Anyway, what can I do for you? It's nice to hear from you, but I'm guessing there's a reason for your call?'

'Yeah. Sorry. Have you seen it?'

'Christ, yeah, I did. That's another reason I meant to call. Sorry, I'm a shit friend.'

'Don't be daft.' Leah started to pack down the compost with one hand.

'It could have been worse. I got accused of identifying a sexual assault victim last month and she tried to top herself because of it.'

'Jesus, Mark, what happened?'

'Nothing, really. I didn't identify her, but you know the drill. Someone on Twitter did based on the fact she'd been at this club . . . oh, listen, that's by the by. Just saying. Shit happens. I hope you're not still carrying it around.'

'You sound like . . . never mind. I'm not, but listen, I want to go and see her parents. Just to say sorry.'

'Do you think that's a good idea?'

'Well, Paul would never let me, remember? He said it implied we'd done something wrong.' Leah's nails were thick with dirt, all around the beds and under the tips. That was £30 wasted, she thought, looking at the rose-coloured gel manicure that she'd got with Bunty just a couple of days before.

'Well, they weren't the easiest of customers, Leah.'

'What did you call them again? Fucking vile?'

'Yep. The dad chased me out of that block and hurled a few choice insults my way. I still think there was something else going on there.'

'What do you mean?'

'Weird family. Especially the mum. She was angrier at us than at the fact her daughter was missing. All very strange.'

'Yeah, I remember that. Dave said they were a total nightmare to deal with. Weren't the police sniffing around the dad for a while?' Leah stood up and felt her knees click.

'Maybe. It was all so long ago. He was just dodgy in general, though. Sad, really. Poor kid never had a chance.'

'Do you think she's dead?'

'Who knows? Probably. She was probably pissed up and fell off the pier. Or jumped. I know it's awful, Leah, but you'll never know, so try to stop torturing yourself.'

Luke's face. Bloated and purple. His hair fanned out in the water. The panic as his lungs filled with black water. Flailing. Thinking of Leah. Where was she? Why wasn't his mum there?

'Listen, I know they used to live in the Berry Brow Flats, but have you still got their address? I'm guessing a number would be out of date by now and I don't have access to the electoral roll any more. Thought I'd save myself some time and legwork if you had it to hand.'

'God, I doubt it. Well, I don't know, actually. I'd have to dig about in my contacts books, but they're all buried in the garage somewhere.'

'Oh, OK. No worries. I just thought I'd try.'

'Well, Dave will have the details, won't he?'

'I'm not asking Dave.' Leah looked back out into the woods. She was sure she'd seen someone weaving between the branches out of the corner of her eye. One of the girls, maybe?

'Why not?'

'First off, he'd go all Dave on me, and second, he wouldn't tell me anyway. He won't be allowed.' The trees stood sentry, alone.

'OK, listen, leave it with me. I've been threatening to clean out the garage anyway. If I find the book I'll give you a buzz.'

'Thanks, Mark.'

'Don't go knocking.'

'I won't,' Leah promised. 'I'm too long in the tooth for that carry-on.'

They spoke for a few more minutes, trying to stretch out the conversation, but it became thin and transparent fast.

She spent the rest of the afternoon repotting and pruning. She tied the clematis to the trellis and weeded the border wall. The hyacinths were out, and their heady perfume made her think of red wine and Wonderbras. She couldn't remember the last time she'd worn a dress and heels.

She dug out the dandelions and thistles and power-washed the drive, then set about scrubbing weedkiller deep into the cracks. Mid-afternoon she tied up her hair with a scarf like Bunty and let her knees and hands get muddy. She plucked out stones, cut back the hedge, and scraped the inside of her arms gathering the weeds into a black bin bag. Chris always said she was at her most attractive when she was scruffy. He'd called her 'attractive in a farmer's wife sort of way', though, which she thought deserved a swift kick to the bollocks.

'What?' he'd said. 'You're all Nigella Lawson. It's hot.'

'Nigella bakes, not gardens.'

'Nigella can do whatever she wants!'

At 4 p.m. Sam reversed his car out of his drive and drove past her with a wave.

She waved back and watched the back of his car disappear out of the cul-de-sac and onto the main road, running her hand over the back of her hair to check for lumpy knots.

Then she went inside and showered until her skin was steaming. Her arms prickled with red, itchy, slightly sore bumps. Typical that the things she enjoyed the most were the things that disagreed with her. Luke had inherited her sensitive skin. Baths with Oilatum and bumper tubs of E45 cream throughout his primary years. He always smelt slightly medical, even now. She flicked the switch on her hairdryer, which was kicking out a rather alarming singed odour that she'd been ignoring for too long, and for a moment she closed her eyes while the air blew around her face and made her feel like she was driving fast through a desert. Her hair streaming back, and only the long, long road and the brown dirt ahead. Violet skies and tiger's eye rocks.

She couldn't tell how long she'd sat, how far she'd driven, but her cheek began to burn and her eyes were starting to sting. She turned off the dryer and the sudden silence was almost sinister.

The free-standing oval mirror on her dressing table was wonky and smeared. But she was too tired to try tightening the screws. Her arms ached from the stubborn weeds. Instead she cocked her head to the side like a spaniel and rubbed a thick layer of age-defying cream onto her face, its glossiness reviving her complexion, if only for a few minutes. She pulled at the thirsty skin around her temples, while it still slid under her fingertips from the grease, and let it bounce back. Back in her twenties, when she'd thought she was fat and tired and looked old, that was when she'd had been beautiful. That was the best she would ever look, when her thick hair shone, her stomach didn't crêpe and her arms were taut. Even in the midst of her Luke exhaustion, her clothes would drape and hang, instead of catching on lumps and humps. Her smile had still reached her eyes.

It all felt a little too late to be trying to turn back the clock with the eye creams she was suckered into buying at beauty parties, and serums that made her feel like she was injecting some kind of elixir back into her skin. But she carried on relentlessly. Until there was a sound. For a minute she thought it was a tricycle. A creak. A long, slow squeal.

'Luke?' Leah paused, the lid of her moisturizer still in her hand.

The house was quiet, but it felt to Leah like it was holding its breath. She sat listening, head cocked.

'Luke?' Leah shouted a little louder.

There was no reply. Her heart began to quicken and she suddenly felt very exposed, sitting with only her towel wrapped round her. She turned and grabbed the jeans on the floor by the wash basket and yanked them on, not even bothering with underwear, and pulled the old Fleetwood Mac T-shirt she'd slept in last night over her head.

There was something not right. About the house. It felt full. Like the way the walls and ceilings seem to swell during a party, stretching to accommodate visitors. Leah opened the bedroom door. And stopped dead in her tracks.

The ladder to the loft was down and the hatch was swinging softly with a creak.

'Fuck,' she whispered. The word came out fast and sharp, like the spitting of a lemon pip. She took a deep breath and heard her heart in her chest.

She stood frozen for a few seconds, then took a step forward and peered up into the darkness of the entrance, with visions of Luke's skin-man tormentor from the caravan. She was almost afraid it would appear, like a Polaroid picture, developing out of the darkness, wraith-like hands reaching down. She stepped back fast.

'Hello? Luke? Chris?' Her own voice was weak and she knew it, but it still rose and rolled around the high attic space, like the pennies she used to drop into spiral charity boxes when she was little. Round and round through the cold, dank air.

'I'll fucking kill you, kid,' she muttered. 'It'd better not be you.'

She quickly retracted that thought, then took a deep breath and went to the bottom of the ladder.

'Hello?' she called again. Her voice ricocheted from the roof.

She put her foot on the first rung of the ladder and told herself to stop being so daft. This was a cul-de-sac, for crying out loud.

She checked her back pocket for her phone, slid it to unlocked, and started to climb. One rung at a time. But by the time she was almost at the top, her legs were shaking and she was gripping onto the ladder so hard her fingers were red. Just as her head was about to come up into the darkness, she flipped the torch on her phone and, before she could think about it, yanked herself up so she was sitting on the edge. And there it was. In the middle of the floor. A thick, white church candle, burning brightly, shadows licking the walls like darting tongues.

Her fingers fumbled on the flooring for the light switch and she snapped it on. The room flickered, once, twice, then the fluorescent bar caught and buzzed as the harsh white light flooded the eaves.

Leah's head swivelled so fast around the attic she felt the tendons in her neck give way and ping. Her eyes searched the gloomy corners for crouched figures, women in white, Japanese ghost girls with long black hair. Every terrifying image flashing into her mind like a flick book. She felt the room spin once, twice. Before it came to the slow standstill of the last spin of the carousel.

And there was no sound but the fizz and crack of the wick. Not even her own breath.

She pulled her legs up, scared someone could grab them and yank them from below, and held up her phone. There was no way anyone was telling her she'd made this one up. She snapped a pic. And then another. And another.

The candle was surrounded by boxes and files, and Luke's old Moses basket, which she couldn't bear to throw away. It was basically all kindling. She needed to put the candle out.

She crawled forward. The candle was only a couple of metres away from her. As soon as she got to it, she blew it out. A thin plume of black smoke whispered into the air, and a small pool of clear wax was puddled in the centre of the cylinder. It hadn't been long lit. Leah sat back on her haunches and cast another look around. It wasn't the kind of attic filled with old chests and mirrors. The hatch was too small to get anything up. They mainly used the garage for storage.

But anything she was worried about getting damp, that came up here. Contacts books, cuttings. Christmas lights. When she first started reporting, she'd saved everything. Every short. Every picture story. Then she'd stopped and just saved the page leads. Then the splashes. And, when she'd stopped reporting, she'd kept a copy of every paper she'd edited. Until they'd all begun to blend into one. Same stories. Different faces.

She was asked sometimes, once she became editor, if she missed the reporting. The thrill of the byline. Knowing it was her that had gone out and got it, done it, achieved it.

She'd smile and say she wasn't after the glory. That ink

was in her blood. That holding the entire paper in her hands was better than any byline.

And it wasn't a total lie. She would always go down to the press hall on Thursday nights, when the newspaper was still printed in the building, run her fingers over the silkiness you only ever felt when the paper was fresh and the ink warm. She would inhale the smell of the machines and feel the drop-drop-drop of each paper, like a metronome. A heartbeat she'd created.

All her papers. They were all here. Stacked up. From the side they looked like some kind of abstract art. A jagged unformed picture made up by the colours on the folds.

Then she realized. One paper was not on the stacks. It was under the candle. Leah didn't need to move it. She recognized it. Would always recognize it. The face of Hope Hooper-Smith under that headline. *Family desperate without Hope*. But something wasn't right. With a sick, writhing stomach, Leah leant over it. The shape of two paper dolls, carefully cut out from where the girl's eyes once were.

12

'I want the locks changed.' Leah crossed her arms and leant back against the kitchen counter, turning her head away from her reflection in the glass of the doors. She felt as if she was in front of a two-way mirror. Only she had no idea who, or what, was on the other side.

'Leah.' Chris bowed his head. He was still in his vet scrubs. Leah wondered if he was actually planning to go back to work. She'd been grateful he'd come straight home, but perhaps she'd been wrong to assume he was here for the rest of the day.

'What? If you won't let me call the police, we can at least do this. Someone. Was. In. The. House.'

'I'm just saying let's not rush into anything. We don't know what happened. Let's talk to Luke when he comes home.'

'No. There is *no way* I want him to know about this.'

'Leah.' Chris pinched the bridge of his nose. 'It was probably those bloody girls across the road. You've already said

142

they were dicking about and pretending to talk to ghosts. They were probably trying to scare Luke. I think I'll go and talk to Sam. He seems like a good guy.'

'NO,' Leah barked. 'No. I'll talk to him. I don't want you telling him . . . I don't want him thinking . . .'

'Thinking what?' Chris stared at Leah and she let their eyes lock.

'That I'm mad. You're going to tell him I'm going crazy. Aren't you?' Leah took a step closer to Chris. Her fingers were curled like claws.

'Leah.' Chris put his hands on her shoulders. 'I love you. You're not mad. But I do think it's time you booked an appointment and got your medication reviewed.'

'You're not seriously telling me that I made this up? I . . . Look.' Leah scrunched up the paper that was still lying on the counter and held it up in a ball to his face. 'It's right here. In front of you.'

'No. I don't think you made it up. But, and I'm just saying *but*, do you think there is a small possibility that you've started sleepwalking again? Just a chance?'

'Sleepwalking?' Leah's jaw dropped incredulously.

'It makes sense. The documentary. The guilt. It wouldn't be the first time you've reacted this way to stress.'

'I can't believe you think I'm doing this,' Leah whispered. 'Just how crazy do you think I am?'

'I don't think . . .'

'Fuck you,' Leah spat. She felt her eyes shining with tears of anger. She wouldn't cry. She would not cry.

'I'm not talking about this while you're being unreasonable.'

'Unreasonable?' Leah ran her hands through her hair. 'You're treating me like the madwoman in the attic. Please. We need to change the locks. Please, Chris.' Her voice cracked. 'Please.'

Chris sighed. 'OK. If that's what we need to do to make you feel safe. But on one condition. You get a GP appointment.'

Leah gave a slight, sharp nod. There was no fight left in her.

'I will. Can we get someone out to do the locks tonight?'

'I'll make some calls.'

The locksmith came about an hour later. Once the locks were changed and Chris had shown the man out, he came back into the kitchen where Leah was waiting anxiously.

Chris leant over and went to kiss the top of her head. The front door slammed, making Leah jump, and her head hit Chris's jaw, which clamped shut.

'Shit. Ow.' Chris backed away from her. 'Jesus. Owwwww. Fuck. My tongue.'

'I'm home!' Luke called out as he pounded up the stairs.

'Don't say anything to him. Promise me. I'll tell him my key broke in the lock.' Leah glanced over at Chris, who was spitting blood out into the sink. 'You OK?' she added as an afterthought.

'Fine.' Chris glared back and wiped his mouth with the chicken-printed tea towel.

Leah opened her mouth to apologize, then closed it again.

'I'm going to bed,' she said. 'Now Luke is back, can you lock the front door? And make sure every single door is locked and . . .'

'Yes. And I'll check the attic.'

'And . . .'

'And put the padlock on.'

Leah headed for the stairs.

'Night, then,' he called after her. 'I'll be up soon.'

'Night.' Leah didn't turn round, but she paused, one hand on the stair rail. 'Actually. Can you stay down here for a bit? Wait until I've gone to sleep?'

'Sure.'

She could hear a slight sigh in his voice. But she carried on up the stairs and went to kiss Luke goodnight.

'Who are you texting?' Bunty peered over Leah's shoulder.

'No one.' Leah ducked out of the way.

'Oh, is it the hot dad?' Bunty raised a perfect brow.

'No. I mean, yes, it's him. But I don't fancy him.'

'You are *so* full of shit.' Bunty licked her ice cream and shooed away a scavenging seagull from her feet. 'Beady-eyed fucker.'

'Sam?'

'*No*. The seagull. Why are you texting him?'

'Just checking in. Luke's over there. Again.'

Bunty laughed and licked her ice cream provocatively. 'You'd better give him the talk. Charlie Bates will breed like a rabbit.'

'If she's as . . . sexually mature . . . as you claim, she'll be on the pill.' Leah blew on her freshly fried doughnut. 'Do you think these are less calorific than ice cream?'

'Whatever gets you through the night.'

'Ow. Fuck, this is hot.' Leah dropped half her doughnut back into its striped paper bag and did a less than attractive open-mouth chew of the other half. 'Jesus.'

'You're out of practice.' Bunty leant over and nicked one of the golden sugary rings. 'These are amazeballs with ice cream.'

'Hoooow are you so thin?' Leah wailed.

'Because I spent all afternoon rehearsing "Thriller" with my summer camp kids. And they're shit. So we had to do it fifty zillion times. And they still look like they're having seizures.'

'Thanks for meeting me. I hate being in the house.' Leah picked up her double-shotted coffee and blew on it through the drinking hole.

'Just call the police already. Fuck what Chris says.'

'I called Dave.'

'He's not the police. He's the police's spin doctor.'

'Well . . . anyway. It sounds utter bullshit, though, when you explain it out of context. But I feel like I'm being watched. All the time.' Leah sipped her coffee and looked out at the busy beach. The sun was only just poking through the clouds, but there were still families with rainbow windbreakers and blue-tinged toddlers being coaxed into the sea.

'Or maybe you *are* sleepwalking?'

'Bunty, if I am capable of going to sleep while drying my hair, going into the attic, lighting a candle, cutting out paper dolls and sending them to myself . . . I need more than the police. I could have burned down the house.'

'Charlie Bates. I'm telling you.'

'But why? What have I done to her?'

'Maybe she's jealous. Maybe she fancies Sam.'

'Eww. No, anyway . . . Nothing to be jealous of.'

'Babe, since we've been talking your phone has buzzed six times. You're only ignoring it because you know I'll snatch it out of your hand. What is he sending you? Dick pics?'

'*No.* Don't drag us down to your level!'

'Oh, now there's an *us*?' Bunty grinned.

'We're friends.' Leah pulled her knees up on the bench. 'He's funny. He's easy-going. It's sort of good to know there's someone around. There's nothing in it. I mean, seriously. Are we that backwards that men and women can't be friends without one of them being accused of being a homewrecker?'

'Hey. Dude. I'm not judging. Knock yourself out. He can roll you round the bedroom for all I care. Lord knows you need it. Just know what you're getting into, that's all. Don't shit on your own doorstep.'

'That is such a charming phrase.'

'Babe. Just . . .' Bunty looked like she was about to put her arm round Leah but thought better of it at the last minute. When Leah had first met her, when Luke and Immie were in pre-school, they'd gone on a hideous 'mums' night out', which basically meant loads of squealing women dancing provocatively with much younger men and then weeing in the bus station because no one had a pelvic floor. Leah had sat with Bunty. Bunty had Afro hair then and was managing not only to pull off wet-look snakeskin leggings, but to make them look as if they had been designed for her alone. Leah had felt very mumsy next to her in skinny jeans and a tunic top.

'Well. This is fucking ghastly,' Bunty had murmured to her at the bar, refusing to join in the Prosecco rounds and ordering herself a whisky. 'Are you normal or do I have to spend the next hour talking about nap routines and catchment areas with you?'

'Normal,' Leah said hurriedly. 'I've just been trapped by that woman over there who wanted ideas about what to do with Weekend Bear.'

'What the fuck is Weekend Bear?'

'Has yours not had it yet? You get it sent home and you have to do activities with it and take pictures of it with your kid. And then fill in the diary.'

'Just what every single working mother needs. What kind of activities?'

'Don't ask me,' Leah had shrugged. 'I forgot and had to take a picture of me and it at the off-licence on Sunday night.'

'I like you,' Bunty had said. 'Sit down.'

Leah had tried to hug her at the end of the night during the flurry of air kisses and screeches.

'I don't do hugs,' Bunty had said, stepping away. 'Nothing personal. I don't like being touched.'

Leah looked at her friend now, her beautiful glowing

chestnut skin and the devil in her eye. She'd idolized her to start with. Become nervous when Bunty hadn't texted her back. Replayed conversations in her head, over and over. That was before, though. When she hadn't been well. She didn't idolize Bunty now. It was hard to once you'd seen someone have diarrhoea and be sick into a bucket at the same time, after a vicious weekend in Dublin. They'd reached a nice, balanced groove. As Chris had pointed out once, you couldn't have an equal relationship when one person thinks they are eclipsed by the other.

Now the two of them looked out over the sand and listened to the crash of the waves and the humming of the beach.

'Tide's coming in,' Leah said after a while.

'Yep.' Bunty nodded.

'Better get a move on or we'll be caught up in the traffic.'

'You know you can stay at mine. Any time,' Bunty offered as she zipped up her pink cropped sweatshirt.

'Bunty.' Leah stopped outside one of the rock shops on the promenade, where offensive T-shirts hung garishly on the racks outside next to the sugar dummies and candyfloss. 'Do you think it's Charlie? Really?'

'Honestly? Probably not. I mean, why would she? Although kids are in general little fuckers. Especially tweenagers.'

'So you think it's all in my head?' Leah looked straight into Bunty's big lash-extensioned eyes.

'I didn't say that either. I do think you need to let go of this, though. Go back to that tower block. Find Tilly's parents. Say sorry. The universe will be realigned. And you can move the fuck on.'

Leah drove home without the radio on. Background noises were starting to irritate her. She needed it to be quiet when the inside of her head was so loud.

But when she got home, she couldn't bring herself to get out of the car. Parked on the sloping drive, she looked up at the house. The windows with the sage-green frames. It was as if the house was raising its eyebrows at her. Leah stared through the windscreen. It looked as if something was moving in the living room. Like someone was crouched under the windowsill – a bobbing brown head.

She unbuckled her belt and sat up straighter. It was definitely a head. A shiny round head. 'Shit!' Leah reached down into the coffee holder for her phone.

Then suddenly the head started to rise up. Leah braced herself, ready to look into whoever's face it might be. But instead of two eyes, there was a stumpy, waggy tail, as The Moog turned himself around in a circle and settled on the back of the armchair.

'Jesus Christ.' Leah's head fell back against the car headrest in relief. But only for a second as a loud hammering jolted her forward again.

Sam. Knocking cheerfully on the driver's window.

Leah let out an involuntary gasp and, heart still pounding, opened her car door.

'Hey. You scared me.'

He had different shorts on today. Same length. A dark-grey,

trendy hoody with some kind of American sports team logo on the front. He was holding a paper bag.

'Why are you sat in your car?'

'Honest? I'm a bit freaked out about going in.' Leah opened the car door. 'Is my son making a nuisance of himself?'

'Nah, they've gone to the pictures. With some of his mates.' Sam frowned. 'He told me he'd texted you. Didn't he?'

Leah pulled her phone out of her back pocket. 'He did.' She furrowed her brow. 'I must have missed that. Sorry. Are you playing taxi again?'

'No worries. It gave me a chance to pick this up.' He held out the bag.

'For me?' Leah blushed. She never knew the right way to act when she got a present.

'Open it.'

Leah peered inside and started to laugh. 'Oh my God. I love it,' she said, pulling out a little pot of bright-violet hair dye.

'Did I get the right one?'

'You did. Where on Earth did you find this?' Leah said, turning it over in her hands. 'I thought they'd stopped making it.'

'One of those awful hippy shops by the pier.' Sam grinned and followed Leah as she unlocked the front door. 'Here, let me go first if you're freaked.' He waved her aside.

'I can't believe you remembered. Do I actually have to dye my hair now?'

Sam wandered into the hallway and automatically headed for the kitchen. 'Why not? I'll help.'

For a minute Leah had an image of herself bent over the sink in just her bra and Sam's fingers massaging her wet hair.

'Maybe later,' she said quickly, feeling herself going red, as if he could read her mind. 'Thanks, though. Love it.'

'Good,' Sam said. Without smiling this time, he turned around. 'Hey. Love your windows. Oh, I mean doors. What a great view. Are they new? I don't remember it being like this when you moved in.'

'Yeah. Thanks. Although it's been creeping me out recently.'

'Well. That's another reason I'm here.' Sam vaulted himself onto the worktop, which seemed somewhat over-familiar to Leah. He'd only been inside the house once or twice. She liked how comfortable he was, though. 'I thought we might take Bracken and The Moog down to the woods. Exorcise some ghosts?'

'You mean, by the caravan?'

'Yep. Let's check it out. Hopefully, nothing will be there and then it's another thing to cross off your list of worries, isn't it?'

'Sam . . . that's really kind. But you don't need to do that. You don't need to get caught up in this crap.'

'Hey. What can I say? It's keeping me out of mischief. And I need to walk Bracken anyway. I'd like the company.' He raised his eyebrows. 'Come on. I'm doing it for you. Don't tell me I have to force you.'

Leah looked down at The Moog in his basket.

'Moogie? Walk?' The Moog looked up at her and thumped his tail twice. But he didn't move.

'God, that's a first.' Leah went over and patted his head. 'What's up, buddy? Aren't you feeling good?'

The Moog gave her hand a wet lick.

'Come on. Walkies!' Leah patted her knees.

But he didn't move, even when she dangled his lead from the utility room in front of him.

'Poor baby.' Leah squatted back down. 'Are you tired?'

She rubbed between his ears and on his belly and he obligingly rolled over for her.

'OK, tiger,' she said. 'Just stay put.'

'Must be handy having a vet in the house,' Sam said as they left the house and walked across the street to pick up Bracken.

'Yes. Although, touch wood, The Moog's healthy. I know he looks like a walking tumour, but he's pretty sprightly.'

'I've got to ask. Why is he called The Moog?' Sam opened his front door and whistled. Bracken came tearing out and galloped three loops around the bottom of the drive before Sam managed to fasten the lead to his brown leather collar.

'*Willo the Wisp*? Don't you remember the dog?'

'Vaguely.'

'Weird-looking thing. We thought it fitted.'

'But why The Moog? When you call him, do you shout "Come here, The Moog"?'

'Ha ha, no. I call him Moogie. But I kind of like the title. Gives him grandeur.'

'And why would we begrudge that?'

The walk towards the park seemed longer than usual. It was as busy as ever, the paddling pool was full, and the water sprinklers were being harassed by children in nothing but T-shirts. Leah shivered just looking at them. The gulls were coming further in to the mainland, swooping and rooting around the edges of the playground, undeterred by the dogs tied to the green fencing around the woodchipped play areas. The dogs barked, the birds squawked and the children laughed and screamed and cried, and the noises bundled together like an ever-growing ball of wool inside Leah's head.

Sam was talking but she couldn't quite focus on what he was saying – the way the top of his arm brushed hers was making her stomach twitch. Sam was tall. Taller than Chris. And broader. It made Leah feel dainty.

'So. What do you think?' Sam glanced at her. 'You're not listening to me, are you?'

'I am. Sorry, I'm just nervous.'

They began to head up the hill.

'Am I making you nervous?' Sam asked after a pause. There was something lower about his tone.

'Yes,' Leah replied after a while. Then she added, 'Do I make you nervous?'

It was a gamble and she knew it. Sam paused. Then looked at her.

'A little.' He smiled and it reached his eyes, before he looked down at the ground sheepishly, hands stuffed low in his pockets.

Leah tried to pretend she wasn't getting out of breath as they climbed the hill. She hadn't dared go out for a run since her last visit to the caravan and she could feel it.

'Can I ask you something?' Sam said as the trees beckoned them closer.

'Sure.' Leah's stomach leapt, but she didn't quite know why.

'Are you religious?'

'Wow. That's a bit out of nowhere.'

'Sorry. It's too personal, isn't it?'

'It's . . . no. I don't mind. I do believe in something. I don't know exactly what, but the thought that this life is it scares me stupid.'

'Same.'

'Why do you ask?'

'Charlie said she saw you going into the church, a couple of weeks ago. St Peter's? I just wondered. She said she's seen you there a couple of times. I hadn't pegged you for the church type.'

'Charlie? What, is she spying on me?' It came out harsher than Leah had intended.

'No. She just mentioned it in passing. I think she likes you, actually. Looks up to you. Not sure how many decent female role models she has in her life.'

'I think she likes *you*.' It came out of her mouth before

she had time to stop it. She cringed and waited. But Sam breezed past it.

'I think she likes the family set-up. I get the feeling hers isn't around that much.'

A thought struck her. 'Did Charlie come into the church? After me?'

Sam shrugged. 'I don't know. Why?'

'No reason.' Leah thought of the prayer leaf and the candle for Tilly.

All the candles for Tilly. Was that what the candles in her house were about?

They turned into the woods and Bracken dashed ahead into the undergrowth, heading for the stream. Suddenly Leah wondered if Bunty could have been right about Charlie and a feeling of relief rushed through her.

'So. How long have you and Chris been together?'

'Eight years. Married for five.'

'How did you meet?'

'Through a story. Well, a campaign, actually,' Leah said. 'It was Christmas and the paper needed a splash. A front page, that is. We decided to do a "dogs on death row" story. The same one we always churned out. But we made it more of a campaign through the paper and we needed a shelter to join up with. We had just done a story from court, an animal cruelty case. Chris had saved the life of three labs who had pretty much been left to rot in cages in this man's garage. I thought as a vet he would probably know of a decent shelter that deserved the publicity. So I went to see him, and it turned out he was trying to raise funding for one, as there wasn't actually a big enough shelter on the east coast to cope with the demand. So that became the story, really.'

'So . . . love at first sight?' Sam stamped down a patch of nettles and stood to the side to let Leah through.

'How chivalrous.' She smiled. 'Thank you. No, though. I don't believe in love in first sight. But any man who is kind to animals is halfway there. Or waiters. Or taxi drivers.'

They walked along. 'Can I ask you something else?' Sam said, glancing at Leah.

'Right. New rule. You can just ask me, you don't have to ask my permission to ask me a question.'

'I'm not as forthright as you.'

'You think I'm forthright?'

'I think you're . . . direct.'

'Occupational hazard. But ask away, I can always give a no comment.'

'Why isn't Chris here with you?'

Leah frowned.

'Um, well, he's at work.'

Sam stopped. 'You know what I mean.'

'Hey.' Leah started walking again. 'It was your idea to come.'

'Wait.' Sam grabbed her arm. 'It was an excuse. Not an idea.'

It was going to happen. Leah felt her body fill with adrenaline.

'What do you mean?' She knew exactly what he meant. But, all of a sudden, she didn't want him to say it. Because if he said it, it would be over. She wasn't ready. Either way.

'Look, I really appreciate you taking me seriously. Chris just thinks I'm nuts,' she said. 'He says he doesn't, but he does. Thanks for being such a good friend. You've been a proper mate.'

Sam let go of her arm sadly. 'That's OK.'

'Chris isn't trying to be cruel or anything.' Leah's voice started to quicken. 'He's just very pragmatic. He always has been. He thinks it's all me. Sleepwalking. Or just forgetting. When I got a bit poorly, last time, he once found me wandering through the woods. It was the middle of the night and I was wearing just a T-shirt. Not even any shoes. The soles of my feet were bleeding. I'd climbed over the back wall and gone through the stream and everything.'

'Jesus, Leah. Really?'

'I hate thinking about it. I barely remember it. It's like, you know when you're drunk, and you go to sleep and have those really lucid dreams? The kind that blend reality and something else? It was like that. Like a drunken memory. It really scared me. Chris thought it was my work. That it had all got on top of me. Having to watch all the redundancies. Watching my paper get ripped to shreds. And then that's when I started projecting all that fear, all that loss of control, onto Luke. Maybe it was a good thing me and Chris couldn't get pregnant. Maybe I would have fucked that one up as well.'

Leah felt her eyes well up.

'Leah.' Sam put his arms around her, and she didn't step back. 'I don't think you're crazy. And Luke? He's incredible. You're incredible.'

He pulled her towards him, just gently, and Leah rested her forehead on his chest. Not the nook of the shoulder like Chris. It was a whole new jigsaw. His stomach felt solid and his arms strong and she thought about what it would be like if he pushed her against the gnarled oak behind them. His wide hands under her top and his lips, his stubble on her neck. Warm, damp words. The burn of her jeans against his thigh, the movement of her ribs under his chest. Her hands crept to his waist and he stroked her hair. She could dig her fingers into his sides, just softly. Just to let him know. His breathing was slightly deeper. She could move her hands. To his chest. In seconds they could be kissing. She knew it. She could feel every twitch of resistance.

She wanted the emerald moss to stain her clothes. And to feel the bark against the back of her head. She wanted to feel awake. Wanted. Alive. Her fingers pressed into his waist and his arm tightened around her lower back.

They were so close, her breath became shallow and she could feel him ready to move.

The air cracked as Bracken bounded over a fallen tree and came skidding to a stop beside them. They both pulled away, but Leah could still feel static in the air.

'Sorry, boy. We're coming.' Leah reached down and ruffled his shiny head.

'You OK?' Sam asked, holding out his hand to help her over the trunk. She took it, even though she was perfectly capable.

'I'm fine,' she smiled. And let go of Sam's hand.

13

The caravan was there. Leah had almost expected it to have disappeared, like a strange twist in the tale, as if it was also just in her head. When she was younger, she'd sometimes thought, what if the dream world was real and that was the true reality?

She'd stopped sleeping well after that, frightened of where her thoughts would take her.

But the caravan was there, of course. Like the centrepiece of a dark fairy tale, with the branches bursting through the roof and the thorns and brambles crawling underneath. There was no glow in the window this time. No flicker. No life.

Sam looked at her. 'OK. All good?'

'Yes,' Leah said. 'Let's do it.'

They walked to the window and Sam cupped his hands against the glass and peered in. 'OK, tell me what you saw. Christ, this glass is filthy.'

'I definitely saw a candle. And bunting? It looked like

bunting. Something hung up in there. I could swear they were paper dolls.' Leah looked furtively around her. 'Do you think someone is living in there or something?'

Bracken sat on his haunches and let out a low growl. Sam reached down and clipped his lead on.

'No. It's not steady enough. Look.' Sam reached out and pushed the caravan. It rocked visibly in the dirt. 'It's half sliding down this bank.'

'Careful!' Leah stepped back. They waited but there was no movement from inside. Or the outside. The woods were still quiet, apart from the pound in the earth of Bracken's solid paws as he ran around them in circles.

'I can't see anything. Look, I'm going to try inside.' Sam jiggled the handle of the caravan door. It rattled but jammed, and the whole frame shook.

Leah took a step closer. 'Is it locked?'

'No,' said Sam. 'Just rusty. Hold this.' He handed over Bracken's lead and grasped the handle with two hands and gave it an almighty yank.

The smell hit Leah before anything else. Mould. Rotten leaves, wormy compost. The kind of smell only the dark can create.

'Jesus.' She held her sleeve over her nose.

'Leah, no one has been here in a really long time.' Sam stepped gingerly into the caravan. 'Ooh, it's creepy as fuck though. Look.' He turned around. 'Come on. It's safe.' He stepped further into the caravan and Leah climbed up the steps.

162

Inside was no better than the outside. There was life in here, just not human. Like when her old cat Biscuit would bring in a shrew and hide it somewhere for days. It was only when they were all retching from the smell that they would find its maggot-infested corpse.

There were colourful china plates piled near the sink. Probably even worth something. Bold red roses and once-gold trim. Saucers filled with pools of brown water. A teacup with a broken handle.

'Someone must have lived here once,' Leah said, looking at the broken shelves, old road atlases spilling on the floor. An A–Z of Norwich. Damp blankets were piled in the corner, washed-out colours and bleeding grey water.

'Or used it for holidays. It's a touring caravan. I reckon someone just dumped it here. There's no number plate.' Sam opened one of the cupboards under the sink, and Leah hid her eyes, fearful of dead animals. Or face masks made of skin.

'How old is it, do you reckon?'

'Fifties, maybe?' Sam bobbed down to get a better look.

'It's a bit sinister how the woods have just claimed it. Almost.'

'Hang on.' Sam pulled out a Tesco carrier bag. 'This is newer.'

Leah crouched next to him. 'What's in it?'

Sam opened the bag and they both looked in. 'Some kind of jumper. It's a bit gross, though.' He went to put it back but Leah stopped him.

'Wait. Can you just empty it out?'

Sam looked at her. 'Why?'

'I . . . please. Just please do it.'

Sam shrugged. 'OK, but I'm not touching it.' He turned the carrier upside down and the jumper, dirty and cold, fell with a thud onto the floor. It had been blue once. Not as bright any more. Salty and stiff.

Leah would have known it anywhere.

She took a deep breath and gingerly picked it up, looking for a name tag in the back. But nothing.

'This is the same jumper Tilly was wearing.' She looked at Sam. 'This is the exact one.'

'Why do you think that?' Sam stood up so fast his knees clicked. 'I'm sure it just looks the same.'

'It's not.' Leah turned it over in her hands. 'Look. *Look*. There it is.' A tiny sewn-on rainbow on the pocket. She fished out her phone and brought up Tilly's picture. 'Here. Look.' She shoved it in his face.

'Was she wearing it? When she disappeared?' Sam took her phone and stared at the picture.

'Well. No,' Leah admitted. 'But look, it's exactly the same.'

'Hold on.' Sam crouched back down and checked the label. 'It's New Look. There were, like, millions of these.'

'*Sam!*' Leah stood up. 'Don't shut me down. Please. Not you too. Someone is trying to tell me something. Someone wanted me to find this. The dolls, the bunting, the candles. Someone *is* watching me.'

He paused. Then put the hoody back into the carrier bag.

'OK,' he said softly. 'Maybe it's time to go to the police.'

14

23 August 2003

'Look. I'm not saying that I didn't give you a steer,' Dave said, lighting a cigarette. 'But I did not say, and will not be quoted as saying, that we weren't taking it as seriously.'

Mark stayed silent. He was stressed. The sleeves of his shirt were rolled up, but his tie was still straight.

Leah took a sip of her pint. The beer garden, albeit more of a beer yard, was gorgeous after the stifling day in the newsroom. Paul was paranoid and they weren't allowed to keep the windows open. Security risk, apparently. The sea breeze and the clatter of glasses were a welcome relief. But it made the conversation all the worse.

'OK. But look, I'm in a lot of trouble here,' Leah explained. 'I just need us to agree on something, something you said that made us think the Hope case was more urgent.'

'Listen, mate, it's not as if we're after a favour.' Mark sat forward. 'We've had a billion of these chats. It's just this is the first one that's come back to bite us.'

'I said it was off the record.' Dave smoked very quickly, his wrist a blur of sharp flicks. 'We're not being dragged into a race row over this.'

'How come, though?' Mark put his glass down. 'I mean, it was obviously serious in the end. How come you didn't want to run a conference?'

'I'm not talking about it. I can't discuss police procedure and details of investigations. You know that. At that time, we had reason to believe she was with a family member.'

'Right. And we can say that, then, too? Police thought she was with family?' Leah asked.

'No. Like I said. I'm not commenting officially on the investigation.' Mark sighed. 'This is a right fucking mess.'

'I don't see how,' Dave shrugged. 'We send out four, five releases a week. A day, sometimes. They don't all make the front, do they?'

'I know. But most of them aren't directly comparable. I don't know what I was thinking, not putting them together.' Leah took a gulp. And then another. Before she realized it, most of her drink was gone.

'If Tilly had turned out to be with her sister, or holed up in some smack house somewhere, you wouldn't think anything of it. You're not psychic. How were you to know? There's a billion missing-person stories that come to nothing and a handful that go the wrong way. You used your instincts. That's all you can do.'

Mark gulped back the last of his drink. 'Are we having another?'

'Not having to get back for the baby?' Dave asked.

'That's why I'm not going back yet,' Mark said.

Leah nodded at Mark when he looked at her empty glass with a raised eyebrow.

166

Dave nudged her foot with his under the wooden table.

'Don't beat yourself up. You couldn't predict this.'

'Hard not to. What do you think happened to her?' Leah asked quietly. She looked around the beer garden, packed with the after-work crew rather than with tourists, who wouldn't know the little suntrap round the back of the Blue Anchor even existed. The pub was dark and gloomy. Worn red carpets, ornaments on the walls, the mahogany-coloured bar scratched and sticky. The kind of pub that the mums with buggies, or the groups of teens who had come here on the train, or the stags and the hens, wouldn't even look twice at. They would walk past it, tucked away behind Gypsy Rose Lee's great-grand-daughter's fortune-telling caravan, and head for the smarter bars on the harbour, all chrome and fairy lights.

It was only the ones who lived here who knew of its cheap craft ales and cut-price wine – those on entry-level salaries, those who lived here rather than tore through the place.

'Who knows?'

'Do you think it's going to turn into a murder enquiry?'

'If it does, you'll be the first to know.'

'Thanks, Dave,' Mark said, returning from the bar. But Dave's eyes were on Leah.

After they'd finished their next drink, and Mark's phone had been flashing consistently for a solid half-hour, they left the Blue Anchor and headed out onto the street.

The early evening smelt of vinegar and batter mix. Sleepy children were being bundled into cars and wrapped in damp towels, sand between their toes. The funhouse and the ladybug ride had switched on their lights at the end of the pier, and the tide was rolling.

'Night, then, you crazy kids without parental responsibilities.' Mark waved before he headed towards the bus station.

Dave jiggled his hands in his cheap grey suit trousers and looked at Leah. His eyes were dark and wide, and his hair the kind of golden brown that Eighties movie stars traded off. He barely looked old enough to be in a suit, even though Leah knew he was a couple of years older than she was. She'd asked Mark his age the first time she'd seen him at a press call.

'One more? Or are you rushing off?'

Leah thought of her grimy terrace with her squealy housemates, who no doubt would be at home, jostling for the mirror and rooting through IKEA wardrobes for a dress, deciding between low-cut and knee-length, or high-top and legs out.

They were sweet enough. They humoured her love for DIY SOS and always left her a plate when they'd cooked a lasagne. The day she'd got her first splash, they'd bought her a bottle of cava and took her 'round town'. She'd never felt more alone.

'Sure. Another would be great, thanks.'

Dave looked up towards the pier. 'Shall we head up that end?' he said.

Leah knew what that meant. Wooden floors. Imported lager. A mojito menu. A far cry from the Blue Anchor.

'Why not.' She smiled at Dave. 'Can I scab a cigarette?'

He lit it for her, and they walked toward the noise, stepping over pools of melting ice cream on the pavement. He scooted his chair closer to her in the Owl and the Pussycat wine bar, and they discussed the other press officers, the other reporters. Journalism training. Dave's old reporting job before he moved to the 'dark side'.

'The money's better and I feel like I'm making a proper difference. It's not like I'm a press officer for a bank or anything. It's worthwhile.'

'You don't need to justify it to me,' Leah laughed. But she knew he did.

When she went to the toilets, she reapplied her blusher and added some gloss to her lips. Her hair was big from the sea air, and she tried to pat it down. She wriggled and tried to adjust her work clothes, which had become attached to her skin after a long day. Her brown tartan skirt was firmly sitting at her waist rather than her hips and her cream fitted shirt with the ribbon round the waist looked limp, like a leftover birthday present that someone had forgotten to open. It was no longer the Sex and the City look she'd been going for. More Working Girl, secretary pool.

She sighed and went back to her seat, her feet beginning to throb in the faux-crocodile Mary Janes she hadn't been able to resist in the sale.

Dave was lighting up a cigarette for both of them.

'I owe you a pack,' Leah said apologetically. 'There's nothing more annoying than someone crashing off you all night.'

'I don't mind, seeing as it's you.' Dave smiled. His eyes were a little unfocused. 'So. Is there a Mr Leah?'

'No,' Leah said. 'Why, is there a Mrs Dave?'

He looked foggy. 'Not any more.'

'I sense there's a story there.'

'Always the journo.'

'Always the press officer, avoiding the question.'

'Louise and I split up a couple of months ago.'

'I'm sorry. What happened?' Leah saw the rebound warning above his head like a red flashing beacon.

169

'Ah, just wasn't working. She lives in Leeds. Works there. Long distance not really happening.'

'Could you not move closer together?'

'Both got jobs we love. I guess if we actually loved each other as much as we should, that wouldn't have come first.'

'I actually get that.' Leah picked up her fifth pint and knew that by the time she was at the end of it her speech would be slurred, and she would no longer be tipsy. She would be drunk. The conversations around her had become thick and blurry.

'When was the last Mr Leah?' Dave was closer to her now. She could smell his stale aftershave. It wasn't unpleasant, though. If he didn't have such a baby face he could look almost cop-like. The way he sat with his knees apart. His tie was off and his shirt untucked. He wasn't as scrawny as she had first thought, either. Leaner. Solid. She pictured them together sober. At the cinema, maybe. His arm around her. Curled up on a sofa somewhere. Eating toast. He wasn't tall. Perhaps an inch or two taller than her. She'd have to wear flats. She could handle that.

'Not for a while,' Leah admitted. 'I was seeing someone, this guy, for a while.' Try two months. 'But it didn't really work out either.'

He'd slept with her a handful of times. The barman. He'd liked that her name was on the music column in the paper. They'd gone to a few gigs, he'd introduced her as his girlfriend. Then one evening she couldn't make a barbecue at his friend's house. A court case had overrun and she'd had to prepare two backgrounders for the morning, ready for the trial verdict going either way.

He'd been pissed off. She'd only seen him once after that. He'd made up excuses about the bar being busy. The texts had dropped off. She'd found out later through one of her housemates that he had a new girlfriend. A friend of a friend of hers, who'd met him at a barbecue, apparently.

Leah hadn't really been that fussed about him until then.

The new girl was a singer-songwriter, waitressing in her spare time. Her hair was long, her tongue was pierced. She had a record company keen, apparently. Why would he want the girl who writes about the music when he could have the girl doing the music? A girl who could perform.

Leah had gone to his bar a few times afterwards. He had the heady title of assistant manager. She'd sat in the corner with the housemates, trying to make eye contact. Trying to be noticed. Remembered. He'd always been friendly. Slipped her the odd free shot. But he'd never looked over. He'd never looked back.

She'd stumbled out of the bar one night and he'd been there, smoking a cigarette on his break, looking pissed off. It was the height of pop punk and his bleached hair matched. Black at the roots, a shock of spikes. Gangly and loose.

'Hey.' His eyes had lit up when he saw her. 'Long time no see.'

She'd been served by him the night before.

'You going home? Want to share a taxi?'

To her shame, she had.

She hadn't asked about the singer-songwriter. Leah had already known she had a gig in London. The next morning, she had cried in the shower. She hadn't been back to that bar since.

'I'm surprised,' Dave said. 'I can't believe you're single.'

'Why not?' Leah's tongue felt heavy. She still had half a pint to go.

'Because. Look at you. You're talented. You're driven. You're gorgeous.' The words were like nectar. 'I fancied you from the first time I saw you. At that press conference. I asked Mark about you.'

'Really?'

'I would have asked you out. But, you know, I was with Louise.'

'Oh.' Leah's words were drying out. She needed fresh air.

'Really.' His breath was close.

'I'm pretty drunk,' Leah said, the room beginning to tilt. 'I should have eaten.'

'Let's go back to mine and get a pizza.' Dave stood up unsteadily.

It's already written in the stars, Leah thought. She let Dave order at the counter of Bits and Pizzas. She hated herself for her lack of assertiveness when he'd asked what she wanted. She was too drunk to care and had just waved her last fiver at him, saying Bits and Pizzas over and over again in a Liverpudlian accent for no reason. He'd taken the fiver and ignored the rest. She'd had to wait outside because the strip lights were playing havoc with her depth perception, and when he brought it out, she ripped off a piping hot slice of Meat Feast from the grease-soaked box and blistered the roof of her mouth.

They had devoured it by the time the taxi came, wiping cheese strings from their chins. She didn't care what she looked like any more, she just wanted to sit down. She put her head on his shoulder in the back of the cab and watched the blackening sea as the last of the sunset hit the water.

His flat was exactly how Leah had pictured it. A framed Tarantino poster. Huge TV and speakers and cheap flat-packed furniture. An interest-free-credit beige sofa and a damp-towel-scented white bathroom that could do with a reseal.

The sex was awkward. By the time they were both de-clothed and

172

in bed, Leah could have happily gone to sleep. It took Dave a couple of attempts with the condom, before he threw it down the side of the bed.

'Fuck it, I'll just pull out, yeah?'

It seemed like a good idea at the time. They had been crazy kids with no responsibilities.

15

Chris hadn't wanted the police coming to the house. He was still looking at her as if she was a sinner about to go into a confession box. The police hadn't said much. They'd agreed it could be anyone's – the hoody. The dolls – a prank. The attic was still going unexplained, but there were looks exchanged between the officers.

She curled up that night on the grey fabric corner-sofa in the kitchen, the one Chris liked, all smooth lines. A little modern for her taste. The Moog slumped on her lap – he still wasn't eating. They stared together out of the doors into the woods until the shadows became as tall as the trees.

'You know the attic?' Luke said, sitting down beside her and scratching The Moog's ears. The dog's tail thumped.

'Yeah?' Leah sipped at her herbal tea. No wine tonight.

'Well, I was reading about a maniac who, like, *lived* in people's attics. You know, like the whole row up and down the street. They are all connected. So I was thinking, maybe it was a neighbour. Or something? Someone who'd seen the show? All they had to do was go into their attic and then . . . hop along.'

'Luke,' said Leah. 'We live in a detached house.'

There was a pause. 'Oh yeah.'

'Sorry, baby, this is why I didn't want to tell you. I knew you'd worry. Look, it probably has a really rational explanation.' Leah paused. 'Maybe it was me sleepwalking again.'

'Do you really think that?'

'Well, we've just had the locks changed. So we are 100 per cent safe now.' Leah reached out and ruffled the dark-red mop on his head before he could keep prodding. 'Your hair needs a wash.'

'But do the police think it's got anything to do with the jumper? The one you found in the woods? And it doesn't. I washed my hair, like, yesterday.'

'No, honey. I was just handing it in. That's all. In case anyone was looking for it. Just being safe. And no, you didn't, because I know you didn't shower yesterday due to the lack of sopping wet towels all over the floor left for *someone* to pick up.'

'Oh.'

'So. What's going on with you and Charlie, then?' Leah changed the subject. 'Or is it Hannah you like?' *Please be Hannah. Please be Hannah.*

'Neither,' Luke practically shouted. 'They just like hanging around me, that's all. They're like flies round shit.'

'You realize you've just called yourself shit in that scenario.'

'Shut up.' Luke left the kitchen and stomped up the stairs.

Charlie and Hannah had been out in the street when Sam and Leah had arrived home, watching Luke flip and ollie on his board. She'd wanted the police to come to the caravan. Leah had been worried about disturbing anything by taking it away. But a random dirty hoody didn't warrant any crime-scene action. No yellow tape. Nothing, really.

Charlie had jumped up when she saw them, and bounded over to Sam.

'Sam, Sam, pleeeeaaaase can I sleep over?' she begged. 'Me and Hannah want to make it another seven-day streak. Pleeaase? I'll cook!'

Leah looked at Hannah. She wasn't begging. But there was something in her eyes. Something almost beseeching. She glanced at Leah and Leah tried to smile, but it must have come out crooked, as Hannah put her face down and her hair hung over her cheekbones.

'I'll leave you to it,' Leah said and went towards her front door, clutching the Tesco bag. Luke just carried on clicking and whooshing on his board, like the ebb and flow of the sea.

'Wait. You want me to come in? While you call?' Sam had said, while Charlie bounced up and down on the spot. She needed a better bra, Leah noticed.

'No. It's OK.' Leah looked pointedly towards Luke. 'I'll give them your number though. Is that all right?'

'Of course. Call me. OK?'

176

Leah nodded, feeling stiff and disjointed. As she turned to shut her front door, she heard Sam laugh.

'Yes, OK. But only if you make me your killer cheese on toast.'

'*Yes!*'

Leah watched Charlie throw her arms around him. Sam hugged her back. Stiffly. Then Sam caught Leah's eye and drew gently back. Leah shut the door.

She did as she promised and texted him after the police called round. Chris even came home from work on time, raving about his new girl.

'She's so amazing. The animals just, I don't know, it's like they all just roll over for her. Like she has some kind of magic power. She's smart, too. She helped me with the funding bid wording. And she's reordered my entire diary so I get alerts and everything. She's set up an office iPad. She's great. Absolutely great but . . .'

'I would have helped you with the wording. Why didn't you ask?' Leah felt herself prickle.

'Well. We were just at work and she knew I was struggling, so she pulled a chair over and we had it done in two hours.' Chris reached out to stroke her hair. 'You've had so much on your mind, I didn't want to bother you with it.'

Chris pulled Leah's feet into his lap. She crunched her toes up and flexed them, making them crack. Chris winced.

'I hate it when you do that.'

'Sorry.' Leah rubbed The Moog's tummy and he did a

grumbling fart. 'Oh Christ.' She retched and held her hand up to her mouth. 'That stinks. Is he sick?'

Chris leant over him and felt his stomach. 'It's a bit tender. Hang on.' He got up and went to the cupboard over the top of the big fridge and pulled out a black leather washbag.

'He didn't want to come out today,' Leah said. 'Not like him.'

'Maybe he's psychic.' Chris pulled out his thermometer. 'Sounds like it was a shit day.'

'Yeah,' Leah nodded. 'It's not been great, although I feel almost . . . justified now.'

Sam. Sam. Sam. Sam. He hadn't texted her back.

'Justified how?'

'Now I know it's not all in my head.'

'Leah . . . we don't know that jumper had anything to do with Tilly. Or the dolls.'

Leah lifted the The Moog off her lap onto the cushion and stood up. 'Don't be such a *twat.*'

'Mature,' Chris muttered under his breath and pulled out a bottle of Sauvignon Blanc that Leah had been saving, although she wasn't quite sure for what.

'So, it's OK for you to drink, but every time I do, you act like my fucking *dad*?'

'Your *dad* isn't around, Leah. Since when did he *ever* look after you?' Chris slammed the fridge door shut and the bottles and half-empty jars on the shelves rattled.

'Erm . . . he gave me a deposit for a house? Flew halfway

round the world when Luke was born?' Leah made for the stairs.

'When are you going to admit it?' Chris called after her.

'Admit what?' Leah turned around.

'That you're in a bad place again. You ... need ... a ... fucking ... GP ... appointment.'

Leah walked back into the kitchen. 'You know what you are? You're like one of those Victorian men who couldn't cope with their wives having emotions, or liking sex, or just not being a fucking robot, so had them locked up in a lunatic asylum or locked them in the goddam attic.'

'You're saying I want to lock you in the attic?'

'I wouldn't put it past you.'

'You're insane.' And the way Chris looked at her, for that second, gave Leah chills down the back of her neck. She could feel it all the way down her spine. Her calves. He really thought that. He thought she was going insane.

Leah grabbed her phone off the counter and took the stairs two at a time, slamming the bedroom door. She was shaking and her heart was about to burst from her chest.

'Bastard.' She kicked the door then slumped down next to it, head in her hands.

It was coming back. The fear. The sense of doom. Of everything closing in. It had first started after Luke was born. She'd heard people say that maternity leave could be lonely. Especially for a young single mother. The health visitors, the midwives. They'd all warned her, given her checklists to fill in, to rate her feelings. She hadn't minded the loneliness.

She was used to it. It was the horror she couldn't bear. The feeling she might accidentally kill her newborn baby boy: fall asleep and smother him or drop him on his head and see it split open in front of her.

She had pushed Luke in his pram for hours and hours around the park to stop his constant screaming, while seeing other mums in pairs drinking coffee and pushing their kids on the swings. The baby group gang had looked down on her. Not that they weren't perfectly pleasant, cooing over Luke's ginger hair, *Oooh, where does he get that hair from? Is your partner red?* Then she'd have to explain she didn't actually have a partner. The faux compliments over her figure. Her youth. How much energy she must have at her age. She'd had no interest in Buggyfit. Or baby yoga. Or Rhyme Time, or any of the banal sit-cross-legged activities designed solely to stop the parents climbing the walls, since the babies would just lie there like potatoes while everyone sang 'Wind the Bobbin Up' and tried not to gouge out their own eyes with a bottle teat.

She'd just wanted to lock the door and keep the world away. But then the house would become oppressive and silent. God, the silence. The only thing worse had been the screams.

Breastfeeding had been agony. She couldn't get the latch right and Luke would pound on her breasts with little fists of fury, his face purple, his cries becoming a husky bark. She'd given up after a couple of weeks. The health visitors had watched her give him a bottle of formula and looked at her as if she'd introduced him to crack.

The nights had been cold and long in her armchair, feeding in the dark. Too exhausted even to go back to bed, she'd let her head loll to the side and sleep with Luke, all swollen with milk, in her arms. Another sin.

She'd used a dummy, she'd fed him jar food. She'd seen grandmas cooing over the other babies' chubby little legs, bouncing them on their knees, and she'd wanted to howl. Her mother hadn't even known Luke existed. Her dad had flown back from Singapore for the first two weeks. He'd been brilliant, of course. When he'd been there. He'd come armed with lambswool pram liners and onesies and baby powder. He'd let her sleep, blissfully sleep, and refused to answer the door when Dave called. He'd doted on Luke and given Leah wads of cash in a Morrisons carrier bag. She'd held her breath the first time she'd used one of the fifties in the newsagent.

And then he was gone. He'd called, they'd skyped. He adored his grandson. But his life, over there, was complete. He'd be back soon, he'd told her. Soon as he could.

Six weeks later Leah had found herself curled in a ball in the kitchen, biting her lip so hard she could taste blood while Luke screamed in his cot. Controlled crying. Routines. Baby-led feeding. Nothing had worked. He'd screamed and whinged and fussed. He hadn't liked to be held – he'd hated cuddles. She had become convinced he could smell the fear on her.

She'd stunk of milk vomit and her skin had become rough like sandpaper, her eyes dark and hollow. She had become puffy and her hair had thinned. Every night she'd tucked Luke up after his feed and watched his eyes grow heavy and blue as he'd drifted asleep to the sound of her breathing, his fingers around her thumb. Tears had run down her cheeks, but she'd kept her thumb steady.

She had been losing herself. Days had been unfriendly and purplish-green – bruised and sore to touch. Even so, when Dave had taken him, she hadn't been able to bear it when they walked away, seeing his little face over Dave's shoulder.

In her new house the kitchen had smelt slightly damp even though it had been proofed. She'd been able to hear next door rowing and the bark of their Staffie when he wanted to be let in. But it had been all hers. Her name on the mortgage that took up half of her salary. She could have continued to rent. But it hadn't felt right for her and the little apple pip inside her tummy. She'd wanted something permanent for Luke. Something for him, for them. So she'd borrowed her deposit, guilt money from her dad, and while five months pregnant had bought a house on the edge of the city; a white-painted terrace with a shocking-pink front door and an electric-blue ceanothus bush in the tiny front garden. She'd had to pay full price. In 2004 the market had been booming. £80,000 for a two-up two-down, with a freezing bathroom containing a rather bizarre yellow bidet she'd eventually potted plants in and an old bath with cracked enamel that always looked filthy no matter how hard she scrubbed.

The house had been a little crooked, the cellar had had mushrooms growing in it and you couldn't get hot water and heating at the same time. But it had been warm and bright and filled with blankets and cushions, and mismatched furniture she'd bid on at house clearance auctions. She'd had a Victorian writing desk as a dressing table and a creepy old wardrobe she'd regretted buying once the delivery men had put it in her room. Unnervingly, the latch hadn't worked and the door had had a habit of swinging open in the middle of the night.

Luke's room had been tiny. Just an armchair donated by Gloria, a sales rep from work, and the cot. But it had been a soft blue, with glow-in-the-dark stars on the ceiling, and a gorgeous rotating wooden mobile that work had sent just after the birth. She'd hung windchimes in the window.

It had been perfect. It had been theirs. It had been all theirs.

The day after she'd sobbed herself raw, she'd booked tours around nurseries. Two weeks later she'd gone back to work. And slowly she'd come back to life.

It wasn't until ten years later that the black dog of depression had come back and howled her name.

Leah banged the back of her head on the bedroom door and pulled her knees up to her chest. She checked her phone, still no messages. Hurling it at the bed so hard it bounced, she shoved her fists into her mouth, trying to choke down a scream.

'Mum?' There was a rap on the door. 'You OK?'

She took a deep, shuddering breath. 'I'm fine, babe. Just going to have a bath.'

She listened for his footsteps, but all was quiet. Sighing, she slid back up the door and opened it slowly. Luke was standing there, pale and smaller, somehow.

'Come here.' Leah wrapped her arms round him. 'Sorry. I'm just due on or something.'

That would normally make Luke laugh. Instead he put his arms around her and they stood, locked for a minute, before Leah began to gently sway, her hand on the back of his head.

And suddenly he was three again and it was just him and her, him and her against the world. Two peas in a pod, two eggs in a pan. Sometimes she thought it would all be so much easier if it was just them. Leah and Luke. Mummy and Luke.

'You are the love of my life,' she whispered to him.

'All right, don't get weird,' Luke said and pulled away.

'Not long until Devon now, hon.' Leah faked enthusiasm. 'Be good for you to get away. Your dad and Louise are looking forward to it.'

'Yeah. You'll be OK, right? Without me?'

Leah's cheeks began to ache with the effort of smiling.

'Of course! I'll miss you though. But we can FaceTime.' She took a deep breath. 'Actually, me and Chris are thinking about going away as well. For a couple of days. To get a break.'

'That sounds good.' Luke nodded happily.

'OK, kid. No more worrying. I'm going to have a bath, all right?'

'OK.'

Leah watched him trot back to his room, then went into the en suite and turned on the hot tap. Chris could never understand the way she drew baths, he always mixed the cold and hot water through the single tap, so it was at a perfect temperature all the way.

Leah liked the long way round. She watched the scalding-hot water run and hiss and spit against the white tub, the steam rising and the windows fogging. She liked to smell the lavender and the bergamot oils as they hit the water and puffed up in clouds. It felt purer, as the ribbons of steam curled around the room like ghosts. She could breathe in the steam and feel the heat in her lungs.

Text me back.

She sat, chin on the edge of the bath, watching it fill. Listening until the swell drowned out the noise in her head.

Bunty pushed her way through the throng at the bar and leant over, her card in hand.

'What do you want?' she shouted back to Leah.

'Gin and slimline tonic, please.'

'Can we have two ultimate margaritas? Cheers.' Bunty winked at the young bartender, who grinned back cockily.

'I don't even know why you ask.' Leah squeezed her way through the crowd to stand next to Bunty at the bar.

'Salt rim?' the barman asked, flashing his dimples at Bunty.

'Absolutely,' Bunty said slowly and Leah rolled her eyes.

'You're old enough to be his mother.'

'Ha, I'd prefer hot aunt.'

'Well, I'm sure I read somewhere that younger men work harder, thinking they've got something to prove. Maybe it's not such a bad idea?'

'Babe, in my experience they just want anal and a bloody

motivational speech in the middle of it because they're so insecure.'

The barman handed over their drinks and raised his eyebrows at Bunty.

'Think I came in at the wrong point of that conversation.'

'Or the right one,' Leah said.

Bunty laughed and held out her card. 'See, I told you it would be good for you to get out.'

Leah found herself agreeing. Neither Chris nor she had apologized yet and they had reached a stalemate. She hadn't heard anything back from the police and it had been two days since she'd handed in the hoody. Surely they'd know something, anything, by now? She hadn't heard from Sam either. To be fair, she hadn't asked a question, she told herself. Just told him what they'd said. It didn't technically require a response. But still. Two days was a long time to wait.

There'd been no more candles. No more paper dolls. But she still couldn't shake the feeling that there was something in the air. Something suffocating and wrong, like two magnets being forced together and pushing back.

'God, I'd love it,' Bunty had said when Leah had rung the day before. 'But you know me, anything for attention or a bit of dramz. Shall we go out tomorrow? Immie's at a sleepover, and I can't face another night of watching *Naked Attraction* on my own and feeling like a deviant.'

Leah did feel better in the crowded bar. They'd made maximum effort and gone into York for the evening. They were surrounded by students and creatives, tourists and townies.

It made her feel comfortingly anonymous among all the colours and the shopping bags.

Bunty spotted some twenty-something girls with tattoo sleeves, prom dresses and trainers gathering up their satchels and anoraks at a high table with two stools near the door. 'Grab it, grab it, grab it.' She nudged Leah forward. 'I've got the drinks.'

Leah headed to the table and smiled apologetically at the girls. 'Sorry, I feel like I'm jumping into your graves.'

'No worries.' The one with the purple hair grinned. 'Watch out for the sharks, though.' She nodded at a group of men closer to Leah's age standing around the next table, all polo shirts and tanned biceps. The modern middle age.

'Far too old for me, darling.' Bunty swept in behind Leah and put down the drinks. 'Love your dresses, ladies.'

'Oh, thanks! It's an iconoclastic statement.' The purple-haired girl's slightly chunkier friend smiled winningly.

'Of course it is,' Bunty beamed. 'Off you fuck now. Have a *great* night.' Her voice was so warm the girls left, looking bewildered as to whether they'd just been insulted or complimented.

'What a state. Art school Barbies.'

'You're in a good mood.'

'I know, right! I've got my period so I'm not pregnant, but I'm not menopausal either. These are obviously the golden days. Plus, my summer singing camp has sold out, which means I can keep up with my eyelash extensions, pay the car lease and feed Immie for another month.'

'Are things tight, hon?' Leah sipped her cocktail and decided it was a definite upgrade on the gin and tonic she'd requested.

'When are they not? What about you? How's one-salary life?'

Leah shrugged.

'Well, I've still got a bit left from the redundancy. So that's keeping the wolf from the door.'

'Sounds delicious, I wouldn't mind a wolf at my door.'

'When was the last time you had sex? You're more hyped-up than usual,' Leah noted.

'Oh, I don't know. A month? Maybe more. I *am* itchy,' she admitted.

'Still got thrush?'

'*No*. Shut up. I meant. . . .'

'I know.' Leah laughed. 'Is that why you're making eyes at the teenager behind the bar?'

'Nope. I mean, you know, I would. But I can't be bothered with the ego boosts required by that generation. Anyway, look at him. He's like a little foal or something.'

They glanced over at the bartender, who clocked them looking at him, puffed up his chest and began to try and banter with his harassed-looking co-worker.

'Oh, God love him. You'd eat him for breakfast.'

'And I'd still be starving.'

'Barmen are all mouth and no trousers anyway.' Leah took another sip. 'This is really nice. From now on you're doing all my ordering for me.'

'You're looking hot,' Bunty said. 'Have you lost weight?'

'I don't feel like I have. I can still count the change in my pockets after I've taken off my jeans. Which is sexy.'

Bunty laughed. 'Well. Just don't take your jeans off in front of other men, then.'

'I wouldn't dare,' Leah said. 'Saying that, my sex life has totally dried up.'

'Well. You're married. That's normal. Is it him or you? Or both?'

'Both. But mainly me,' Leah admitted.

'Close your eyes and pretend he's someone else.'

'That's just another thing to do. I'm too tired to have to add something else to the to-do list. I've no imagination at the moment.'

'Hmmm. Do you fancy other people, or are you clamped shut in general?'

'Clamped shut,' Leah lied smoothly. 'And please don't tell me to spice it up. The idea of wearing some horrendous highly flammable cheerleader's costume makes me cringe.'

'Could you . . .'

'I am not sending pictures of my tits to him at work.'

'Fair enough.'

'Bunty, what was it like towards the end with you and Pete?'

'Well, Pete was a dickhead and Chris may be boring as fuck, but he's a good guy. It's not the same kind of thing. I woke up one morning and the thought of spending one more hour with that arsehole was more than I could bear. I made all the money. Did all the childcare. Left fucking

London for him. For what? To be woken up by seagulls and teach talentless kids who will never ever end up on the stage because they just, quite frankly, don't have either the fight or the talent for it.'

'Was it easy? You know, the logistics? Of leaving.'

'Yeah. We weren't married, though, were we? House was rented. I literally just packed his bags.'

'God. You were so brave.'

'Not really. He did make me laugh, though.' Bunty looked rueful. 'There's a lot of fit men out there, but not all of them will make you laugh so hard your tea comes out of your nose. Most of them just shag your mates when you're not looking, once you're that age.'

'Ain't that the truth. Mind you, I don't think women are always much better.'

'Hmm, maybe. Why the break-up digging, anyway? Are things really that bad?'

'No. Not bad. I just . . . I don't know, Bunty, there's got to be more than this. Sometimes, when he looks at me, it's like he's seeing straight through me. Like I'm not even there.'

'Have you talked to him?'

'About what? I don't even know what to say. I'm not unhappy. I'm just . . . going through the motions. Doesn't seem enough to pack and go. Sometimes I wish we'd have a big, massive fuck-off row. I know sometimes I even try to provoke one. But he's just so calm and passive and patronizing. I feel like some kind of demanding toddler in a tiara around him.'

Leah closed her eyes for a second. The first time she'd met Chris she'd not exactly fancied him. But she had been drawn to him. It was perhaps the dark hair, the wide, almost flat nose. Those big, gentle hands. He wasn't exactly a talker. In the end she'd made up his quotes for the article entirely, as she'd barely been able to get a sentence out of him that made sense.

He'd told her later it was because she'd made him nervous. It had been the first time Leah had ever really felt like she'd had the upper hand in the attraction stakes. She'd been thinner back then. Her blonde hair less bleached, her forehead smooth, the skin around her eyes taut.

His forearms were sturdy. She'd noticed, as he'd handed her a kitten that had been brought in after being found with his tabby brothers and sisters in a taped-up box under a viaduct.

The dogs had wagged their tails at him as he'd taken her round the shelter. He'd let his fingers trail down at his right side by the cages so they could lick or sniff him. The first time they'd slept together he'd undressed fast and with confidence, whereas she'd panicked about her stretch marks. There had been no lazy Sunday mornings, no montage of brunches, her wearing nothing but his shirt, all lazy-limbed and doe-eyed. No picnics in the park with her head on his chest or long dinners and frantic sex up against the fridge. Not with an eight-year-old around. Instead, it had been snatched coffees on lunch breaks. When Dave had had Luke for the weekend, she'd been so exhausted she'd fallen asleep on Chris's sofa. And he'd let her. She'd never let him stay at hers, so worried Luke would smell the intrusion like a dog.

After six months Chris had met Luke at an ice-cream parlour. Chris hadn't said much and Leah had been cross, until she'd realized he was just nervous.

But Luke had loved everyone. He'd let Chris buy him a chocolate brownie ice cream with extra sprinkles and then finished off Chris's vanilla cone too. He'd talked incessantly about the varying powers of the villains in superhero movies, not noticing that Chris had grown paler by the second. He'd told Leah later it was like being naked in the most gruelling interview of his life.

Then there had been trips to wildlife parks. Cinemas, where Luke would spill popcorn all over the floor, and Leah would get a blinding migraine. Chris had cleaned up. He had taught Luke front crawl and how to hit a six at cricket. Luke would beg him to practise batting in the back garden every morning and every time Chris had promised he would, when he got back from work. And unlike other dads, he'd kept his word.

And then came the treehouse.

Luke's eyes had been like saucers when Chris had strung fairy lights in the branches. It had been like something from Enid Blyton, which Luke would never have read, but the magic had still been there.

Bunty nudged her. 'Well, you've got to remember, life isn't normal for you right now. You're, like, in that weird bit between Christmas and New Year when you're eating

192

selection boxes for breakfast and you don't know what day it is. You *are* like a toddler. You need a bit of routine. Don't be making any hasty decisions when you're a bit fuddled.'

'*Or* you could say I finally have some clarity now my life isn't all work, racking up speeding fines trying to get to Luke on time, and doing the food shopping on my mobile while I'm having a wee because there's quite literally no other second in the day.'

'Same again?' Bunty circled her finger round their drinks.

'It's my round.' Leah grabbed her purse.

'No, give me your card and I'll go. I want to torture the child.'

'You're like a bloody cat with a mouse. Just put him out of his misery.'

'Where's the fun in that?' Bunty hoisted her huge breasts up inside her bra. She looked incredible in her skinny jeans and Bardot black top. Her hair was swingy and poker-straight and she smelt of honey and orange groves. Leah watched roving eyes fix on her and follow her as she squeezed back to the bar. She wasn't long for this town, Leah thought, not for the first time. She'd go back to London. Leah knew it and a bubble of panic began to rise up. She wriggled in her seat and caught her reflection in the mirror over the bar.

Bunty had been right. Her clothes were looser. For some reason she hadn't had much of an appetite recently. And her hair was behaving, sculpted accidentally into the loose waves that she kept, unsuccessfully, trying to achieve with products. She'd even dared to go strapless tonight, with a handkerchief-type knotted top that fell just below the forgiving high-waisted jeans. It was more Stevie Nicks than Bunty's Rihanna approach, but she felt good.

She pulled out her phone and checked Facebook. Sam's page was still up on the tab from the last time she'd looked. His status about going out tonight still unchanged. She tapped her toe against the bar stool and considered for a second that she might, outrageously, post a selfie, before coming to her senses.

She'd wait for Bunty to do it.

The bar was becoming darker and the floor syrupy with splashes of stray drinks and drying saliva. Voices were raised against the music and the babble, bodies touching, eyes catching. The laughter of the sharks behind them was beginning to get drowned out by the bulge at the bar.

Bunty put down their drinks right on cue. 'Shall we have a pic before we start looking sloppy?' she said, almost as if she'd read Leah's mind, and whipped out her phone. 'Ready?'

'Hang on.' Leah brushed her hair forward and pulled up her top. 'OK.'

Bunty snapped and there was a shout followed by a surge of laughter from behind them. They turned round to see a sniggering man behind them, one of the polo shirt crew.

'Oh, thanks for that!' Bunty waved her phone screen at them.

'What?' Leah looked back at Bunty.

'Facebombed us.' Bunty showed Leah the picture, the two of them all highlighted and cheekboned, with a pouting goon in the middle pushing together his pecs.

'Nice moobs,' she called out to him.

'Sorry, ladies, I was just mucking about.' The man, in a pink shirt, was not unattractive. Mousy-haired and sparkly eyed, big-eyebrowed and broad.

'Paul, you wanker,' one of his friends brayed.

Paul, the wanker, stepped towards them. 'Do you want me to take a pic for you?'

'No thanks, Paul.' Bunty raised one eyebrow. 'We can manage ourselves.'

Another one of them, skinnier, looped his arm round Paul the wanker's neck, like a monkey. 'Sorry, girls, is he bothering you?'

'No, he was just offering to buy us a drink, actually,' Bunty said and Leah felt her stomach drop, realizing this would mean at least half an hour of polite conversation with Paul's friend before the inevitable awkward brush-off from Bunty, and Leah feeling a bit like she should really pay them back for time wasted.

'Not my round,' Paul said, then turned around and tapped his friend on the shoulder. The friend was standing with his back to them, deep in conversation with someone else. 'Sam, Sam, it's your round, you twat. We've got another two here.'

Then Leah's stomach really did drop.

'Shit!' Sam's eyes widened. 'Leah!'

'And that's why you wanted to come into York,' Bunty hissed quietly in her ear. 'You sly fucker. I'd better get shit-loads of free drinks for this.'

'I didn't know,' Leah said through gritted teeth.

'Hey.' Sam pushed his way through Paul and his friends, who were looking deflated now the women were known, which Leah took to mean that they were disappointed they could no longer harass them or attempt to stick a tongue into any orifices without wives finding out. 'What are you doing here?'

'Girls' night,' Leah said, then cringed at her own term. 'This is Bunty.'

'Hi. Nice to meet you.'

'I've seen you before, you're Leah's neighbour, yeah?' Bunty shook his hand and then leant forward to kiss him on the cheek.

'Yes. I've seen you coming and going too. I heard about the seance.'

'Ha, what a load of bollocks. I hear you've been caught up in the middle of all this carry-on.' Bunty nodded towards Leah and she bristled. 'Thanks for looking after her for me. I appreciate it.'

She truly was in full-on dazzle mode. And Leah felt like a troublesome teenager.

'I haven't done anything really,' he said. 'Any word from the police?' He looked at Leah.

'Nothing yet.'

'But we're not talking about it tonight,' Bunty said. 'She needs a break.'

'Agreed,' Sam smiled. 'So, I hear it's my round?'

*

Leah knew she was drunk because her head was spinning when she sat down on the toilet. It was always the first sign. When there was no incessant chatter and loud music, it always hit her. She just sat, on her own, jeans around her ankles, reading the graffiti on the back of the door.

She shouldn't feel this pissed, she told herself, as she pulled herself back up and realized the balance was all wrong in her feet. She needed some fresh air.

She opened the cubicle door too harshly and it slammed against the one next to it.

'*Jesus!*' the girl next door shouted in alarm.

'Sorry. Sorry.' Leah steadied herself on the door frame. *Bunty?* Bunty was holding court downstairs. *Was Bunty mad at her?* She kept kicking Leah under the table. Sam smelt like liquorice.

She stumbled over to the sink. She definitely wasn't tipsy. She was pissed. Running the tap, she washed her hands and considered splashing water on her face before coming to the conclusion that drenching herself and causing her make-up to run would not do much for her attempts to look normal. She hoisted her handbag onto the sink and unzipped it, glancing up to check her reflection.

Her face was white, with black shadows under her eyes – a mix of tiredness and smudged mascara. But it wasn't her reflection that made her head spin and her stomach churn. They were stuck to the mirror. Just like the others. Two paper dolls. Leah felt her legs wobble and she clutched the side of the basin.

There was a flush and a cubicle door opened. Leah saw a tall blonde in a crisp white top from the corner of her eye. She was the wrong way up.

'Are you OK?' she heard a voice ask.

Then everything went black.

16

Leah moved her head and felt her tongue push against the roof of her mouth. Her feet and ankles felt heavy and her stomach acidic.

There was a panicky sensation in her chest and her eyes flew open to check why. She was in her room, the weight of Chris next to her. It was still dark in the bedroom, but the grey curtains strained against a muted light from outside.

Her hair smelt of smoke and her mouth tasted sour. The pillow was too soft under her heavy head.

Her mind raced back through the night.

How had she got home? She remembered the back seat of a car, Sam's hands on her leg. Her hands on his waist in the bar. Before she'd ... had she fainted? Then Bunty holding back her hair outside the bar.

Oh God, no.

She struggled to sit up and looked around the room.

Her clothes were on the floor, splayed like the chalk outline of a murder victim. She leant down and, for a moment, thought she was going to pass out from the rush of blood to her head. Her fingers rooted until they found her bag and she pulled it up onto her lap. Purse and cards still there, thank God. Her lipstick. Phone.

She hit the home screen and checked her messages and missed calls.

Four from Chris, the last at 2.45 a.m. Shit.

One from Bunty at 1.25 a.m. Why had Bunty called her? Why hadn't she been with her?

No, no, no, no, no, no, no. Leah swiped to delete and felt a gurgle in her throat. Throwing back the covers she bolted to the en suite, the pain in her head blinding, and all of last night's tequila and shame wrenched up through her guts and into the white toilet bowl.

It was horribly early. Just past 5 a.m. But there was no way Leah could go back to sleep. Half of her wanted to violently shake Chris awake and confess everything, at least everything she could remember. The other half wanted to run so far away that none of this would ever matter.

She wrapped the furry throw around herself and quietly headed downstairs. The morning sun was delicate and sweet, and, body shaking, she curled up on the sofa in the kitchen and listened to the vacuum of the silent house.

The satisfying, empty feeling in her stomach that vomiting always brought was beginning to give way to nausea again, becoming thicker by the second. Leah's mouth was filling with saliva and her heart was beating like that of a hunted fox.

She went back to her phone, wanting to call Bunty, but the world was not yet awake.

The dolls.

Sam's lips on hers; even if just for a second, they were there. She knew they'd been there. They'd laughed, taken the piss out of each other, which was when Bunty had started to look more worried. She, of course, had her pick of the men. But she'd stuck very closely to Leah's side. She'd kicked her under the table when Sam's fingers had laced over hers.

She'd been sick in the toilets and obediently let Bunty mop her up, like a toddler with a scraped knee. Oh God, she'd passed out.

The dolls.

Leah rubbed her face and thought of Chris sleeping upstairs, and for a minute she wanted to claw her fingers into her eyes. She was too dehydrated to cry, but her body still convulsed with sadness. What had she become? Some kind of desperado, flirting with the school dads. Sponging off her husband. Getting so pissed she was sick in the gutters of alleys, the red lights from the bar sign reflecting in the puddles. Hugging her knees to her chest she let her hangover engulf her, feeling it was only what she deserved.

At some point she must have fallen asleep again, because when she opened her eyes it was brighter and there was a glass of water on the table in front of her, along with two paracetamol.

Which just made it all worse.

Her phone was buzzing and her head was pounding, but the sickness seemed to have passed, which she was grateful for. Her lips felt too fat and clumsy as she tried to answer.

'And how are we feeling, princess?' Bunty said, not even waiting for Leah to say hello.

'Fucking horrific. I have serious horrors.' Leah sat up slowly and popped two of the painkillers out of the foil packaging. It seemed disproportionately difficult.

'So you should, you gutter slut.'

'Oh God, Bunty, seriously.'

'What did Chris say when you got in?'

'I have no idea. I don't remember getting in. He's left me out water, though, so he can't be that mad. I have loads of missed calls from him.'

Leah checked her phone. It was just after 9 a.m. 'I don't actually know where he's gone. I thought he wasn't working today.'

'And . . . anything you need to confess?'

'What do you mean?'

'Well. I got out of the taxi at about 1 a.m. and you promised you'd call me when you got back to yours . . .'

'Sorry, I think I just passed out.'

Leah looked back at the missed calls on her phone. 2.17 a.m. 2.25 a.m. Where had she been? Her house was only ten minutes away from Bunty's.

'And Chris called me at about 2.30 a.m. looking for you, which leads me to believe you did not, in fact, go straight home . . . ?'

'Fucking hell, Bunty. Really? What did you say? What did he say?'

'I didn't answer as I didn't want to drop you in it. But you've gotta fess up now.'

'I can't remember.' Sam's hands on her waist, his face in her neck, whispers. 'I don't think I did anything. But . . . maybe. I . . . Fuck. *Fuck*.' Leah's eyes started to well up and her chest tightened. 'Oh my God, oh my God, I can't breathe.'

'Pull yourself together. I am assuming you weren't doing it doggy style over the bonnet of his Volvo or anything? What *can* you remember?'

'Nothing, really, after being sick in that loo. Bunty, did I say anything about paper dolls in the bathroom?'

'You were babbling all sorts of shite. I did have a look, but I couldn't see anything. Some stranger had to come and find me because you just went down like a tonne of bricks.' Bunty paused. 'You were really hammered, hon . . . had you been drinking before we went out?'

'*No*. Not at all. I don't understand why I was so pissed. Bunty . . . there were dolls, though. Stuck to the mirror.'

'Well, I didn't see any. Are you sure you're remembering right? Might have been one of those weird, drunky dreams. But listen, that Sam. He's trying to get into your knickers and don't be a dick and pretend he isn't.'

'I think I might have been just as bad.'

'Well. Pack that in now. Chuck it in the fuck-it bucket and move on. Unless you want to go down that road, which is totally your choice, but just look at the state you're in now.

Can you *imagine* how crippled you'd be if you *did* actually have sex with him?'

'Do you think that's all he's after? Just sex?' Leah said quietly.

'Oh babes, please don't think this is the start of a romantic, star-crossed-lovers kind of thing. It is always, *always*, just sex.'

'But . . .'

'Leah. He's just a man. He's not the answer to anything. At the end of the day, ask yourself, will he actually make you happier than Chris?'

Leah thought about it for a second. 'He makes me laugh. I feel like, I don't know . . .'

'If you say "like a teenager" then we can no longer be friends.'

'I feel myself again with him,' Leah said.

'And if you left Chris for him, in two years it would be exactly the same. The same dull sex life. The same boring relationship. The same waiting and wishing for something, anything, to happen. Only you'll have a moody teenage girl to add to the mix, and her jail-bait mate, who will probably end up stalking you, stealing your bras, getting herself pregnant by basting herself with cold semen from a chucked-out condom she found in the bin, and then claiming it's Sam's.'

'Bunty . . .'

'And just remember that if you're ever tempted. Cold semen in the bin. Psycho-girl watching you sleep. And if you ever just think, oh fuck it, I'm just going to shag him and get it out of my system, can I just paint you a little picture?'

'Do I have a choice?'

'So, let's pretend you're over at Sam's. The kids are out and you're having an innocent coffee. But the kitchen is ramped up with sexual tension.' Bunty adopted a breathy, high-pitched voice. 'Then he picks the coffee cup out of your hands. And pushes you up against the counter and starts kissing you. And it's so hot and you're so into it you forget everything else. And it's all just incredible and you're on fire and you've never felt like this, so you open his belt and you're soaking wet and pull down his jeans and he reaches under your skirt and rips your knickers to the side. Then he has you, your legs wrapped around him and his cock is massive, and then he bends you over the counter and makes you come so hard you almost see spots.'

'Bunty, this is not helping me . . .'

'*Wait.* So, he's come on your back because you didn't have a condom, and now he has to wipe you up. And you're there, seeing him having to shuffle to the bathroom with his jeans round his ankles, his legs all white and like a schoolboy. You have dried semen on your back because he's not bothered to wipe it up properly. And all of a sudden you wonder where Luke is, and what he's doing, and what he'd think if he knew his mother was being screwed by some passing sailor like a cheap whore.'

'Jesus.'

'And then it's all so awkward you can't even finish your coffee. And you are terrified that when you see Chris it's just going to all get blurted out. So you leave his house and you walk home and all you feel in each step is dread and you have entered the Cold Moment.'

'You have talked far too much about semen for 9 a.m. on a Saturday morning.'

'The Cold Moment, Leah. Just keep thinking of the Cold Moment. You'd shrivel up like a barren old hag from the guilt.'

'I know. I know you're right. I don't ... eurgh, it's not even him. I don't really fancy him. I don't think. Ah *fuck*. What did I do?'

'My guess is you probably snogged him and had some weepy conversation about what-ifs yada yada. Nothing to destroy your marriage over. If you can't remember, it didn't happen. Now look, I've got to go and choregraph eighteen little knobheads to 'Revolting Children'. Oh, the irony.'

'OK. Thanks, Bunty. And thanks for last night. Sorry I was such a mess.'

'No worries. But seriously, it wouldn't surprise me if that bastard put something in your drink. I've seen you drink double that and still be standing. Now go and shower and do something useful.'

Leah padded upstairs and stuck her head round the door of Luke's room. He was awake and scrolling down his phone.

'Morning, babe.'

'Hi. How's your hangover?'

'God, did you hear me come in?' Leah asked.

'No, but you were out with Bunty and that only means one thing.'

'Fair enough. I was a bit rough when I woke up, but I'm OK now,' Leah lied smoothly. 'Going to have a shower. What are you up to today?'

'Dunno,' Luke shrugged. 'Graffiti something, maybe? Do the Momo challenge. Might steal a car if we get bored.'

'OK. Just remember to burn it out so they've not got fingerprints.'

'Good call.'

Leah shut the door and headed to her room, stopping short in surprise to see a Chris-shaped lump under the duvet. It groaned and rolled over.

'Hey. I thought you'd gone out.' Leah sat down gingerly on the side of the bed.

'Why would you think that?' Chris opened one eye. His breath smelt warm, stale and cheesy, but Leah knew she couldn't complain, given how much she must smell.

'The water and the tablets. Downstairs. Thank you.' She cranked out a smile.

'I don't know what you're talking about it. I just woke up. I'm surprised you're up.'

'Sorry.' Leah took a deep breath. 'I was pretty worse for wear last night.'

'I gathered. I called you, like, ten times. Why didn't you answer?'

'I'm so sorry. I was hammered.'

'I called Bunty too.'

'Did you? Sorry. I . . .' The guilt was lurking inside her like a parasite. She took a huge gulp and swallowed it down.

'I'm sorry. Bunty and I shared a taxi back with Sam. I was pretty much passed out.'

'Sam? What was he doing there?'

'Oh, we bumped into him. He was on some godawful work do. They were all twats.' Leah attempted a rueful laugh.

'I thought he was freelance?'

'Well, ex-work or something. Anyway.'

Chris was quiet.

'I'm sorry,' Leah said again.

'I was really worried.'

'I know.' Leah bent down to kiss him on his lips. He let her, but it felt like she was kissing a cold, wet fish. She wanted to shudder.

But mostly, she wanted to feel clean.

The shower helped. By the time she was out, washed and conditioned, having gargled away the stale nicotine, scrubbed although hardly glowing, Leah felt more human. There were no messages from Sam. Part of her wanted to run over there with a giant bottle of Tipp-Ex that would erase his memory, or better still, make it never have happened at all.

But there was no undo button in life.

Leah dried her hair and pulled on a loose, soft grey T-shirt and skinny jeans. With her pink trainers she'd look more demure than she felt. She kept her make-up simple. Rosy shimmer powder, nude gloss, mascara. She was so pale today – any more make-up and she'd look like a clown.

Chris was reading the paper on his iPad when she got

downstairs, for which she felt an irrational sense of rage at him, as if he had single-handedly brought about her redundancy.

Her stomach growled, taking her by surprise, and she knew the only way to get through the day was to stuff it with carbs. While waiting for the toast to pop she felt her phone buzz in her back pocket and her heart lurched. But it was only Mark.

Sorry Leah, looked for that contacts book. No joy.

Half relieved, half disappointed, Leah texted back not to worry and spread a thick layer of salted butter on her toast, watching it sink in and ooze a golden syrup onto her fingers as she raised it to her mouth.

Chris looked up. 'Luke wants a lift to the skate park,' he said. 'I'll take him. You're probably not fit to drive.'

'Fair enough,' Leah said. 'Thanks.' Her toast suddenly tasted like brown envelopes. 'Is Hannah going?' she asked.

'I dunno,' Chris shrugged. 'He just came down when you were in the shower and asked for a lift.'

'OK,' Leah said.

'Do you have plans today?' Chris asked, as he rinsed out his mug before putting it in the dishwasher.

'No. Why do you do that?'

'Do what?'

'Rinse stuff before you put it in the dishwasher?'

'Because I'm not an animal.'

'You're a psychopath.'

'Says you.'

Leah laughed and Chris's eyes crinkled and she felt a surge of love.

'Chris. I'm sorry. I really am. About last night.'

He sighed and came over to her. 'Do you need to talk to me about anything?'

Leah went cold, to her feet.

'No. Like what?'

'I miss you,' Chris said.

'I'm right here.'

'No,' he said sadly. 'You're not.'

'Mum!' Luke called from the hallway. 'Can we give Hannah and Charlie a lift too?'

'Sure. Is Charlie at Hannah's?' Leah called back, breaking eye contact with Chris.

'No. She's at hers. Can we pick her up on the way?'

'OK.' Leah called back. She looked back at Chris. 'I feel fine,' she said. 'I'll take them.' It was clearly a sign.

Leah swung into the same visitor parking space she'd used last time.

The air smelt pickled and tart through the window Leah had insisted on having open, despite Luke whining in the front.

'I'll go.' Hannah climbed out of the back seat and walked slowly, almost gingerly, on coltish legs to Block B, her hair hanging down her back in a point. Leah looked at her and remembered the way her own thick, coarse chestnut hair had looked in plaits and all the times she'd sat and imagined what it would be like to have a mum brush her hair.

Fucking horrific, according to Bunty, who claimed it was akin to an exorcism and that Leah didn't know how lucky she was, just ruffling Luke's head with water and occasionally wax, before he started to slap her hand away and refuse her fashion interventions.

Leah often wanted to encourage him to ask for something a bit cooler at the barbers: a bit more height, side-swept, quiffs in the ironic way. But she was so paralysed with fear of invoking later life issues caused by a controlling mother that she kept her gob shut and let him continue walking the halls looking like the ginger dickhead from *Happy Days*.

There was every chance, however, this was now back in vogue, the newest hipster style. At least he wasn't cultivating a bumfluff beard and wearing waistcoats like some of her friends' kids. She'd even seen a cravat on Instagram.

There was a fat crossbreed sniffing around the recycling bins without a lead and a man in a green parka smoking nearby. He was so thin, his cheeks were hollow and his arms long and wavy, like reeds. His hair was floppy and his coat stained. He was the epitome of Nineties indie, and if she and the man had both been fifteen, she would have found him wildly attractive. But they were not.

A group of kids, not much older than Luke, were skating at the other end of the car park, with clicks of boards biting tarmac and whooshes of wheels. Luke, she noticed, had sunk down in his seat.

The tower blocks rose like lighthouses.

'Have you been to Charlie's before?' Leah asked Luke.

'Nah.' Luke shook his head, then sneaked a peek up at Leah. 'It's a bit grim, innit?'

'Mmm,' Leah agreed. They watched as a couple of residents punched in a code to the doors of Block C. The woman was ageless. Black hair snaking down her back, all tangled in the way that was desired now. Coarse, not glossy, and twisted. Her fake sheepskin boots were off-centre, the sole slipped to the side, and her black wet-look jeggings made Leah feel sticky just looking at them. Her eye make-up was heavy but her lips bare. The man seemed younger. Gauche somehow, and sickly. His hair was shorn unevenly, making his head patchy like the light-up globe Luke had as a child. He kissed the woman and she put her arms around him, pressed up against the intercom.

'Get a room, you slags,' someone hollered from a flat above.

'Fuck off, Benty, and let us in, you knob.' The man looked up and flipped the Vs. The woman lifted her chin and grinned and looked like the world was there in front of her.

Hannah was watching too. Leah saw her flinch and start swaying from foot to foot at the next block along. She'd been quiet all the way here. It wasn't as if she was usually a chatterbox, but she'd barely muttered two words. Her hair might have looked lovely, but her skin was patchy and raw, as if all the moisture had been sucked out of it. Her top was too big for her, swamping her skinny little ribs and draping back at her slender wrists. It was the height of summer and she was wearing a giant hoody. Was that the fashion? Who knew? It made her look wraith-like.

Leah's headache was back and the smell from the bins was making her stomach vault. She closed her eyes and listened to the tick-tock of the skateboards, the gush of the doors being opened and closed and the brash melodies of the banter between the open windows.

It was like coming home.

Her first memory of her mother was of her in a tower block like this. She'd been holding her hand in a long corridor. Leah had been eating a bread roll with margarine on it. Her mother wearing a dress with birds on it.

'Sorry, had a total wardrobe crisis.' Charlie was shuffling across the back seat and beaming, smelling of knock-off perfume and mischief. Hannah slid in after her.

'You look lovely.' Leah smiled at Charlie in the rear-view mirror. She was sporting a Seventies vibe with little velour rainbow shorts and an American baseball T-shirt. It was so innocently provocative.

'Thanks, Leah,' Charlie beamed as she clipped in her seat belt, her hair wound up in two messy French plaits, one on each side of her head. Funny how dressing like a toddler seemed to make her look older.

'So, Charlie,' Leah asked as she turned the car round, 'do you have brothers and sisters?'

'Yeah. Two sisters and a little brother,' Charlie said. 'He's cute.'

'What's his name?' Leah asked.

'Bailey. He's three.'

'Oh. Big age gap.'

'We've got different dads,' Charlie explained.

'I see. What about your sisters?'

'Yeah. Well, Frankie is my full sister and Chanelle is my half-sister.'

'Must be nice, having a big family,' Leah said.

'Not really. Channy's moved out now. But it's cool cos it means Bailey doesn't have to share with us any more.'

'How old is Chanelle?'

'Sixteen.'

For fuck's sake, thought Leah.

'Yeah, she's just in Block D, though. With her boyfriend, Paul.'

'How old is Paul?'

'He's, like twenty-nine. Old.'

I bet he's been twenty-nine for some while, thought Leah, then felt bad for being such a judgemental bitch.

'Actually, I used to know some people who lived near you,' Leah said.

'Oh yeah?'

'Yeah.' Leah took a deep breath. 'The Bowers.'

'Shit, really? I think Paul's mates with one of them. You mean the *Bowers*, Bowers?'

'What do you mean?' Leah's heart began to thud.

'Everyone knows the Bowers round here.'

Leah could have sworn she saw Charlie's eyes narrow for a second.

'How do you know them?'

'Just . . . from my old job,' Leah said, willing Luke to keep quiet.

'Your old job?'

'Yeah. Where do they live again?' Leah felt her voice become too high, ringing with winging it.

'Block A, I think. Why?'

'No reason. Block A. Is that nice? Same as yours?'

'Same shithole, but at least we've got a better view.'

'Here we are,' Luke said loudly as Leah pulled the car over. The skate park was already getting busy, the bowl lined with younger teenagers sitting on the edge, dangling their legs over and perfecting their resting bored faces, surrounded by a cloud of nonchalance. It would have taken weeks to rehearse, Leah thought wryly.

'Don't you girls get fed up just watching?' she asked, as they scooted out the back.

'No.' Charlie looked out the window. 'It's just good have somewhere to, like, get away.'

Fair enough, Leah thought, thinking of her days drinking 20/20 in the park and waiting for something to happen.

The doors all slammed and the kids dispersed into the clumps and cliques. Leah watched Charlie's rainbow shorts bob as she weaved and pushed to the prime spot of the bowl, past the older girls with their facial piercings and the alternative girls with unicorn hair. She strutted as if that bowl belonged to her. Which Leah had to admire. It wasn't a sexual thing, she realized after waiting a little too long to watch them settle. It was power. She oozed confidence, charm and a little bit of go-fuck-yourself, like a churchyard cat who is fussed over by everyone but belongs to no one.

The outfit, Leah noted, was not turning the heads of the fifteen-year-old boys. After all, the way she was dressed was the fantasy of much older men. Hannah pulled her hood up and shoved her hands deep into her pockets.

Leah screwed up her eyes, checked her phone, and then headed back towards Berry Brow Flats.

The car park was empty again. Leah checked her appearance in the mirror and was glad to see she looked pretty rough. The last thing she wanted was to knock on the door of Paul Bowers and look all coiffed and middle-class.

Block A was over to the right. Four blocks in all, two at the front and two slightly set back. Its glass entrance door was splintered, like a cobweb. It was almost beautiful, Leah thought as she approached it.

She hadn't rehearsed this. She hadn't door-knocked anyone for years.

There was an intercom that appeared to be there just for show, as the door opened smoothly when Leah tried it. The bank of lifts was there right in front of her, gunmetal grey and covered in the usual lazy graffiti.

She pressed the button and watched it light up, which was a good sign. When she was little, she feared lifts like these. Dark and smelly, trapping her with those aggressive slamming doors and buttons that wouldn't light. She would cling onto her dad's hand, even when she was too old.

She'd been eight when her dad had had to give up his job on the rigs. After her mother had left them, he had done his best to make their flat cheerful. The corridors, the stairs, the room on the sixteenth floor. Pink walls in her room. Fairy lights. A dressing table he had found in a skip and sanded down for her.

She would look out of her window, watching the twinkling lights of Manchester at night, and listening to the gush of the traffic, just as soothing as the sea.

They'd given up the flat when Leah got her university place, all fully funded as it was back in the day, and her dad had taken up a job offer in Singapore with one of his old mates from the rigs. She hadn't blamed him at all. A new adventure for both of us, he'd said, when they'd packed up his Ford Escort with cheap bedding and a basic saucepan set and driven up the M62, the castle in the rear-view mirror.

'You'll never have to come back here again,' he'd said, as if it was a promise.

But it had been her home. She'd loved the block, the community. She'd loved Smelly John and his French Bulldog, Strongbow, and the way everyone looked out for each other. When her dad had worked lates at the warehouse, her neighbours had dropped in with leftover spaghetti bolognese or packets of Hobnobs. The kids, the little ones, had run in and out of the flats, doing circuits, riding tricycles up and down the hall.

The noise, the constant noise. She had loved it.

She didn't remember much about her mother. Not really. She'd sent cards at first. Birthday ones with money rather than gifts. Called for a couple of Christmases. She'd even turned up once. One autumn. In a furry coat and darker hair. She'd taken Leah out for pizza, then admonished her for eating it with her hands. She'd asked too much about her dad and not enough about Leah. She hadn't wanted to hear about the ballet lessons Leah wanted so much, or the fact that Emily in Year Four had a boyfriend and was going to have a birthday party at the local Italian and that Leah MIGHT be invited.

Her mother's eyes had been glassy and her skin yellow.

She'd dropped Leah home with a cold wet kiss and said they'd do it again soon.

Leah had never heard from her again.

For a while she'd pretended her mother was dead. It seemed easier that way, easier than explaining to the other kids that her mum just didn't love her. Then a teacher had called her dad. After that, she'd stopped explaining anything. Stopped asking friends round for tea. Her dad hadn't questioned it.

The lift pinged and the doors opened onto the top floor, where Charlie said the Bowers lived. Leah had no idea which door it was, or whether they'd be in.

Taking a deep breath, she turned to the first door, and remembered the day she had done her first knock.

She'd had a right to be there. She had been there to tell a story. To get a voice heard. To make a difference. Could she say the same now? Perhaps she could.

Her knock echoed down the long, empty passage. She listened for signs of movement inside, but the fire doors were thick, she remembered from experience.

After a few moments she moved onto the next one, where she had more luck. A young-looking elderly woman, the sort with matching outfits and neatly bobbed hair, answered the door, keeping it on the chain.

'Can I help you?'

'Sorry to bother you.' Leah gave her most winning smile. 'I'm actually looking for the Bowers but I can't remember which flat it is. Don't suppose you know?'

The lady looked suspicious. 'Are you a social worker, love?'

'Good God, no. I used to know the Bowers, a long time ago. Do you know if they still live here?'

'I don't know.'

The door slammed in Leah's face.

'Right,' she said to herself and moved along. The next two doors she knocked on simply ignored her. She could hear shouting inside one, and quickly moved on, and music inside the other. She knocked for half an hour without much joy. One clean-shaven man in a grey suit answered and told her they lived on the seventh floor. Someone on the seventh lied smoothly and said they'd moved out last week. Most of the flats were empty. Eventually she paused for a break and looked out of the window at the end of the corridor to the flat grey strip of sea beyond.

And wondered, just for a moment, if her mum ever looked out at the other coast of the same, sad sea.

17

28 September 2003

'Can I speak to the news editor?'

The voice was gruff and already accusing. Leah felt her hackles rise and her teeth clash. Her body flooded with adrenaline. Fight or flight.

'Yes, speaking.' Leah wedged the phone between her neck and shoulder and reached for a pen.

'What's your name?' the voice said.

'Leah Wallace.'

'And you're the editor?'

'That's right.'

'You're the one who put that rich girl on the front of your paper and shoved my daughter at the back.'

Leah's heart sank. She knew she recognized the voice.

'Who am I speaking to, please?'

'You know damn well who you are speaking to.'

'Hello, Mrs Bowers. It's a little difficult for me to talk to you at the moment as I believe legal teams are involved. But can I please just take the opportunity to say we're doing everything we can to assist the police . . .'

'But you didn't, did you? You didn't do everything you could. If you had done, then Tilly would have been on the front of that paper too, and maybe we would have found her. Someone might have seen something. She might have read it. Now my daughter is dead. That white girl is at home and my Tilly's lying in a ditch somewhere, raped or, or . . . or . . . mutilated. I don't know. I DON'T KNOW WHERE MY DAUGHTER IS.'

'Mrs Bowers—'

'How do you sleep at night? Why wasn't our girl good enough for you, for your paper? Because she's black? Because we don't live in the fancy part of town? Does that make her life worth less?'

'Please, Mrs Bowers, if we—'

'I bet you don't have children. If you did, you'd know.'

The phone went dead.

'Another one?' She felt Mark's hand on her shoulder.

'Yeah. Her mum this time.' Leah rubbed her eyes and realized she'd smeared mascara all over her face.

'You OK?'

'Been better.'

'Fag?' He held up his packet.

'I've quit.' Leah smiled thinly.

'Jesus, of all the times to pack it in.'

'I know. But I've started now.'

'Come out for some fresh air, then, and you can passively smoke mine.'

'Sure.'

Leah followed Mark out onto the steps and sat down, resting her head against the brick.

'I bet you don't have children.'

'What?' Mark lit up his cigarette and respectfully exhaled in the other direction.

'That's what she said to me. "I bet you don't have children."'

'Leah. She's distraught. Of course she's lashing out. She needs someone to blame.'

'Did it change for you?' Leah asked.

'Did what change?'

'The death knocks. The RTAs. Is it different when you have kids?'

Mark hitched up his trousers and sat down next to her. 'Yeah,' he admitted. 'You do think about it more. Remember that accident? The one with the toddler stuck in the car.'

Leah nodded. It had been a harrowing front page to edit.

'I never told anyone, but when we went up, I went with Scott. To get the pics of the car. The body . . . it was still there.'

'Oh fuck.' Leah's hands flew to her mouth.

'I mean, we couldn't get near, and obviously, you know, we weren't trying to see that. We just didn't know. And the dad. God. He was being put in the back of an ambulance. Those noises coming out of him.'

Leah thought back to the mother on her knees outside the burned-down house.

'The car was a total wreck, just all burned out. I could smell it, Leah. And all I could think of for weeks was that little girl. Her skin, blistering and cracking. Fat melting out. Screaming for her dad.'

'Stop. Please, Mark.'

'We're human, Leah. People think we're not. But we are. Sometimes I think we should have specialist counselling services, like the emergency services, to deal with what we report on. But we don't make those things happen, and no one would know about them if we weren't there to see it all first.'

'He called me a vulture. Tilly's dad. Last week. Said I was a vulture, feeding off other people's misery.'

Leah felt the tears begin to burn the back of her eyes and her throat begin to close.

'Hey . . . come on.' Mark put an arm clumsily around her shoulder. 'You didn't do anything every other news editor wouldn't have done. You made the best call you could with all the information you had in front of you.'

'That girl is dead and somehow, in some way, when I scribbled her name on that page eighteen, I could have been writing her death sentence. I should have gone with my gut.'

'Leah, you are a great news editor. The whole team respects you. They work hard for you. They do night jobs, weekend jobs, you push them, and they accept it. They are better because of you. This paper is better because of you. It has a fucking heart now.'

Leah just cried harder.

'Ah, come on now.'

'I just want to say I'm sorry.'

'Well, tell them, then.'

'I can't. Legal said I wasn't allowed to. Paul says we can't say sorry as it admits liability. He hates me.'

'He doesn't hate you.'

'He does,' Leah spluttered. 'Last week he called up and chewed me out for every literal in the paper, from misplaced commas to spelling mistakes. He was all, "So, Leah, I'm assuming you're happy with this level of attention to detail from your reporters. That this is the baseline." It was so embarrassing. But he's right. I've totally taken my eye off the ball. I'm not sleeping. I feel sick.'

'Leah, maybe you need to see a doctor. There's no shame in it.'

'I already have,' Leah said, taking a few deeper breaths.

'And what did they say?' Mark asked.

'She said . . .' Leah calmed down very suddenly. She felt her body go limp, as if all the fight had been knocked out of her. 'She said . . . I'm pregnant.'

18

Leah didn't dare give herself the luxury of hesitating. If she bottled it now, she would never come back. This was the door. Two neighbours had happily confirmed it. Mrs Bowers owed number 118 a tenner.

Leah raised her hand and knocked sharply. It was darker here, the light blocked by the adjacent tower, and the square floor felt more closed in. It smelt of reheated chip fat and aftershave.

There was a rustle inside. Leah waited for the steps in the corridor. But there was a scrape, a pushing and shutting of drawers. She waited for a couple of minutes and knocked again.

'Just a minute,' a voice hollered, and Leah took a deep breath. She felt on the edge of something, only she couldn't put her finger on what.

The door opened. It was her. So much smaller than she remembered. Less make-up, brighter clothes. She was in a red velour zip-up track top and loose blue sweatpants. There was a sweet, musky smell wafting from behind her, almost chocolatey. And Leah could see plants everywhere. The hall was like a jungle. Big thick ferns, indoor trees, spider plants. Scary black, twisted lumps with only dribbles of light oozing through the leaves. Her face was almost shrouded.

'Mrs Bowers?' Leah cleared her throat.

'Yes?' The woman stepped outside the door and half closed it behind her, her eyes squinting, searching Leah's face. 'I know you. Don't I?'

'My name is Leah Wallace. I . . . I used to be the editor of the *Eastern Press*. We've spoken before . . . but, well, well of course you'll know me. I was on the documentary too.' She was gabbling and she knew it, but the light flicked on, then fizzled out, in the older woman's eyes.

'What do you want? What are you doing here?'

Leah's breath came out ragged. She knew Mrs Bowers could hear it and she felt, for a second, like a mouse under a cat's paw.

'I'm here to say I'm sorry.'

And in that one second, Leah felt as if the ground was shaking and the walls around her were her cracking. Then everything became very, very still.

Mrs Bowers looked her up and down.

She pushed open the door behind her. 'You'd better come in.'

Leah could feel her hands trembling as she followed Mrs Bowers into the corridor. The door slammed shut with a whoosh behind her and made her jump.

'Should I take my shoes off?' she asked.

'No. Unless they're muddy.'

'I don't think so.' Leah looked down at her Nikes.

'No, I don't suppose they would be,' Mrs Bowers said and walked straight up the hallway. Leah assumed she was meant to follow her.

The living room was much the same as the hall, the walls and corners crawling with foliage and even a trellis nailed up one side. It felt like being in a greenhouse. The window in the living room opened onto a balcony, with an uninspiring view of the block next door. Leah wondered how the plants were thriving with so little light but thought better of asking.

Mrs Bowers sat on the armchair and nodded to the sofa where a fat ginger cat was snoozing in a nest of its own hair. Leah sat down gingerly next to it. She was always a little nervous around cats, anxious they would flatten their ears until they looked like owls, hiss at her, then pounce, all sharp claws and needle teeth.

But it opened one yellow eye lazily, appraised the situation, then went back to sleep. Leah looked around the room for something to compliment her on. A huge television. More plants. An old-looking gas fire, the kind with heating strips like they used to have in her dad's flat. A wall of framed photographs. And there, right in the middle, was the one of Tilly, the one they'd used in the paper. The second time, of course.

'Such a beautiful picture,' she said quietly.

'So.' Mrs Bowers lit a cigarette. 'Are you here for a story?

Because we've signed up to an agency. Anniversary and all that. The *Mirror* are doing a special and I'm not allowed to talk to the *local* press.' She said it with a sneer. Leah didn't blame her.

'No. Mrs Bowers, I'm here because when Tilly went missing, I made the wrong decision. And I'm really sorry about it.' Leah raced on without looking for her reaction. 'My reasons for doing so were, well . . .' She halted. There was no point in passing blame; she needed to confront her own culpability. 'Well, they probably wouldn't make much sense to you. But I can assure you, it was nothing to do Tilly, what colour she is, where she comes from.

'I should have pushed harder. I should have pushed the police into letting us talk to you, into finding out more. I was young. And inexperienced. And I'm sorry.'

Mrs Bowers looked at Leah for a long time without saying anything. A trick Leah used to use herself when she was trying to get an interviewee to talk.

'I'm not asking for your forgiveness.'

'Then why are you here?'

'To tell you I'm sorry. Not over a screen. Face to face. I owe you and Tilly that.'

Mrs Bowers held her cigarette and stared at the wall. Her cigarette was burning down and turning into a pure cylinder of grey ash. Leah watched it crumble on the arm of the chair and didn't say anything.

'Mrs Bowers . . .' Leah said. The woman's eyes were glassy,

peering up, and her chin was down, almost rested on her chest.

'She was always my clever one. Could've gone on, you know. A levels and that. First in the family.'

'Mrs Bowers . . .' Leah moved off the sofa and knelt on one knee by her armchair. 'What do you think happened to Tilly?'

'A mother knows. I knew. I knew two days later. I couldn't *feel* her any more. Do you have kids?'

'Yes. A son. He . . . he's almost fifteen now.'

'Oh, that's why you're here now?'

Leah opened her mouth but Mrs Bowers carried on.

'My grandma. She knew. She said she knew the minute her son Ralph was killed. When the bullet was fired. In France. In a field. She didn't have to wait for a telegram. She couldn't *feel* him. The way you feel when you hold them for the first time, and you sense their little soul. She said it was like a candle had been snuffed out inside her.'

'Is that how it felt for you?'

'My daughter was murdered. I know they reckoned she ran away. But why would she run away? She had the brightest future of the lot of us. She was loved.'

'The police told me she'd run away a lot before. Is that not true?' Leah's knees were beginning to creak, but she couldn't move.

'She'd go off for a bit. See her sister. Sleep at her friends' houses. Her dad would go mad. Call the police. You didn't have mobiles then. Well, kids didn't, anyway. We didn't know all her friends. You can't keep track of them all when you've got four. You just . . . I thought she was off again. She was a spirited little thing. When things didn't go her way. She'd be off.'

'Things like . . . ?'

'Rows with her brothers. Not wanting fish fingers. Because the sky was blue, but she said it was black. You name it. Defiance. But that's what I loved in her.'

'What about her sister?'

'What about her?'

'You said Tilly liked to go and see her.'

'She hitch-hiked coupla times. Got as far as Birmingham once. Twelve bloody years old. Got picked up by the police at a services. Some truck driver called her in. Couldn't keep her caged, that one.'

'Do you think,' Leah drew a deep breath, 'that it could have been . . . an accident?'

'I know the police think she jumped from the pier. They haven't said it like that, but that's what they think.'

'But you don't.'

'She wouldn't do that. Like I said, she was defiant.'

'And you don't think she fell?'

'She hated that pier. Hated this town. She even hated that beach. She was never the kind of kid who wanted the sand between her toes. She wouldn't be there. Someone put that necklace there. Someone killed her. It was like a snuff. I felt it. Something unnatural. It was like an eclipse.'

Leah shifted her weight and felt the hairs go up on the back her of neck.

'She's haunting you, isn't she?' said Tilly's mum.

Leah lost her balance and toppled to the side, putting her arm out quickly to stop herself going over, jarring her wrist.

'What do you mean?'

'You're not just here out of guilt. Are you?'

'What do you mean?' Leah whispered again.

'Buildings like this. Blocks like this. You all look down on us. In your shiny cars and five veg a day. We're a family here. We have each other's backs. You wrong one, you wrong us all.'

'Mrs Bowers, please listen to me. I am sorry. Please, whatever is happening, whatever anyone is doing. Please make it stop.'

The woman paused, then stubbed out her cigarette.

'I don't know what you mean.'

'Someone is watching me. Following me. Lighting . . . candles. Sending paper dolls.'

'Paper dolls?'

'Cut from the newspaper. The one we printed when Tilly first went missing. I know, I know you hate me—'

'Don't flatter yourself. I barely think about you any more.'

'But the TV appeal . . .'

'I still want justice for Tilly. But you? You and your earnest eyes and your silly mistakes. What's that to me now? It doesn't change anything. Whatever you say is happening to you, it's nothing to do with me. Now have you actually come here to say sorry? Or to clear your conscience? Because you've said sorry now. I can't help you with the second one.'

Leah stood up. 'I understand.'

Mrs Bowers stood up too.

'Can I ask you one more thing?' Leah said.

'Go on.'

'If you think Tilly is dead . . . why are you still looking?'

'You think death is the worst thing that can happen?' Mrs Bowers let out a scornful laugh, more like a bark. 'It's not knowing that's worse. It's not knowing what happened. Where she is. Whether her body is at the bottom of the sea or chopped up in a bin liner.'

Leah flinched.

'I don't know. And that's what's worse. I have no idea what happened to her. She left that girl's house. That bloody girl with the gob. And that's it. That's all we know. And if I had anything, *anything* – someone spotting her at the bus stop, or at the train station, outside a pub – it would be a start. But I don't. Because no one knew to look for her. It's like she stepped out into an empty void. And that's where she'll always be.'

'Mrs Bowers. I want to help. I want to help you find out what happened.' Leah stepped towards her.

'And what do you think you can do that the police didn't?'

'I don't know,' Leah said. 'But I'm going to try.'

'Go home, you stupid woman.' Mrs Bowers shook her

head. 'And don't come back here again. I know you're sorry. But sorry, how does that help me? Live with it. Just live with it. Don't come running to me for forgiveness. It's not mine you need.'

Leah nodded. Then she took a deep breath and walked stiffly to the door. Mrs Bowers didn't follow.

'Mrs Bowers. Thank you,' Leah called from the door. 'Thank you for letting me in.'

There was no reply.

She drove home too fast and ran straight up the stairs without even shouting hello to Chris. His car was in the drive and the door to his study was shut. She unhooked the attic trapdoor and yanked down the metal stepladder with a clatter.

The study door opened and she heard Chris call up the stairs. 'Leah? Where've you been?'

She ignored him and climbed up the ladder, hand feeling for the light switch, less fear this time. The light flickered while she pulled herself through the hatch and by the time it was fully on she was already emptying boxes, turning them over, shaking them, spreading the contents across the floor.

'Jesus Christ.' Chris stuck his head up through the hatch. 'What on earth are you doing?'

Leah knelt down and ripped masking tape off the seams of a large box and pushed it onto to its side so papers spilled like sand all over the floor.

'It's here somewhere. They all are.' She kicked out in the

papers. 'Where the *fuck* are they?' She grabbed another box. A plastic container this time, and barely noticing the burn in her palms she wrenched the airtight lid off.

'What are you doing?' Chris vaulted up into the attic.

'*They're here*' Leah plucked out spiral-bound notebooks, old address books, notepads.

'What? What are you looking for?'

'My old contacts books.' She sat down with an inelegant thump and crossed her legs, grabbing a book and starting to flip through it. Chris winced as a cloud of plaster smoke puffed up.

'Not this one,' Leah muttered, throwing the book over her shoulder with a clatter and reaching for another one.

'Leah. *Stop it.*' Chris grabbed her wrist. 'Tell me what you're doing.'

Leah ignored him and pulled her hand back, carried on flicking through the books, muttering quietly.

'*Leah!*' Chris bent down and grabbed both of her shoulders and Leah looked up, as if surprised to see him there.

'*What* are you looking for?'

'I'm looking for someone,' Leah said and tried to pull herself free.

'Who?'

'A girl. A girl. She was friends with Tilly. Tilly was last seen at her house. We couldn't do the interview because she wanted paying.'

Chris stood up. 'Leah, we need to get you to the doctors. You are becoming obsessive.'

234

'What do you expect? Someone has been *coming into our house*. Someone is watching me.'

'The police called when you were out,' Chris said flatly. 'That jumper wasn't Tilly's. It was only made four years ago.'

'What?' Leah dropped the book. 'No. No. It was hers. I swear.'

'It doesn't even look that similar on the picture, Leah.'

'But . . .'

'Leah. Come downstairs,' Chris said calmly.

'*No.*' Leah picked up the book. 'I need to find this girl.'

'Why? What are you trying to do?'

'Mrs Bowers just told me she didn't know who her friends were. Maybe . . . *Oh my god. It's here. This is it!*' Leah leapt up. 'Dakota Lockwood. It's *here*.'

'What do you mean, Mrs Bowers *just* told you?'

'I went to see her,' Leah said. She knew how she sounded. Defiant.

'When? Just *now*? Is that where you've been?'

'Yes.'

'Fucking hell, Leah. Please wait.' Chris leant forward and grabbed her arm. 'Just please stop a second. It's happening again. You have to see that. I love you. We all love you. But you're going back to that dark place.'

'It's not the same.' Leah pulled her arm back, but Chris held on and Leah felt her shoulder jar.

'Leah. I know it's not always clear. The memories, I mean. But this is how it started. You were obsessed with Luke. I'd find you in the night, just stood over his bed. Staring. You'd follow him to the park, hide behind trees.'

'I WANTED HIM TO BE SAFE,' Leah yelled.

'He *was* safe, Leah. You were fixated. Fixated on the insane idea that someone, or something, was going to take him away. It wasn't rational. Remember what the doctors said? It's, what was it, "warped thinking". It's the same now. I know it feels real to you . . .'

'It *is* real.'

'It's not, Leah, please, please listen to me. You didn't remember the stuff you were doing back then, either. The sleepwalking. Hiding all the sharp objects, sellotaping over plug sockets. You couldn't remember doing it. You were sick . . .'

'I wasn't *sick*. I don't have a disease! And yes, I had problems before, but that doesn't make any of this, what's happening, any less real. Chris, listen to me.' Leah's voice dropped and she steadied her eyes on his.

'There is someone in the house. Someone is watching me. Us. Luke. You might not believe me. Dave might not believe me. But I believe in myself. And I'm *not* in that place any more.'

Leah yanked her arm away, feeling the blood rush back to her wrist, and pushed past him, a ragged old spiral-bound notebook in her hand.

'Jesus, Leah, be careful.' Chris wobbled by the entrance to the hatch and grabbed onto a beam to steady himself.

Leah climbed down the ladder, missing the last two steps in her haste and crying out as the metal scraped her shin.

'Leah, wait!' Chris shouted, but Leah was already making for the stairs. *The glass of water and tablets*, she thought. *Chris didn't leave them out. Luke didn't leave them out.* Someone had been in the house. Someone who knew she'd been drunk the night before. She felt for her phone in her back pocket and headed for the front door. She didn't know where she was going until she was out in the street.

She jogged over to Sam's drive and hammered on the door. He answered, looking sleepy in those shorts again and a crumpled grey T-shirt. He hadn't shaved but his blue eyes flashed with something when he saw her.

'Leah . . .'

'Can I come in?' she said, pushing her way into the hallway without waiting for an answer. 'Listen, I'm so sorry, I'm hiding from Chris. He . . . he thinks I've gone crazy. That jumper, it wasn't Tilly's, but I woke up this morning on the sofa and there was a glass of water next to me, and paracetamol. But I didn't put it there and no one else was awake. I'm not going mad, Sam, I'm not. There is someone coming into the house.'

'You slept on the sofa?' Sam asked.

'I went to see Tilly's mum today.'

'Shit, really?' Sam rubbed his eyes. 'Sorry, I've, like, literally just got up.' Sam filled the kettle. 'I need coffee. Christ. Are you not hanging?'

'I was, but I'm over it.'

'I'm not.' Sam turned to look at her. 'Over it.'

Leah felt butterflies but couldn't pinpoint what was going on in her head or her stomach.

'Can I just make a call? Here? Chris won't let me at home.'

'He won't *let* you?'

'I told you. He thinks I'm nuts.'

'Knock yourself out.'

Sam turned and started making coffee for them both. Leah took a deep breath and went into the hall. She'd never been inside the house before. It was plain. Wooden hallway. Wooden banisters. Beige curtains. Black-and-white framed arty photographs on the walls. Someone in silhouette on a snowboard. Sam? Through open double bi-fold doors she could see the living room. Oatmeal carpet. A gas stove that pretended to be the real thing on a sandstone hearth. A taupe corner sofa. She felt as if it was all closing in on her. She kicked off her shoes and padded through to the living room without being invited and gently closed the doors.

The book, a battered black-and-red spiral-bound one, with contacts painted on its once glossy front in Tipp-Ex, was still open at the right page.

Leah took out her phone and dialled.

It only rang twice.

'Hello?' A man answered, the kind of mid-octave voice that could have said he was anything from 28 to 65.

'Hello. I wonder if you can help me,' Leah said, trying to keep her voice normal. 'I'm looking for a Dakota Lockwood.

This was her number, or her parents' number, a while back . . .'

'Sorry, wrong number.'

'Well, it's the right number. Just wrong person, I guess. Sorry to bother you. You don't have a forwarding address or anything, do you? This was her family's number in 2003.'

'There's probably been about three or four people through this flat in that time, sweetheart. Sorry.'

'OK. Thanks. It was worth a try.'

Leah hung up the phone, then was startled when it began to ring again immediately. It was Chris. She sent it straight to voicemail.

'Coffee?' Sam poked his head round the living-room door, which he'd pushed open with his foot, brandishing two steaming cups.

'Thanks.' Leah took hers gratefully and sank down into the sofa. As bland as the room was, it was starting to feel very soothing. 'I'm so sorry to burst in like this.'

'It's OK.' Sam sat down next to her, his thigh pressing against hers. 'I was going to call you anyway.'

'You were?'

'Yeah. I guess to apologize. If I was a bit full-on last night.'

'It's OK.' Leah tried to smile. 'I don't really remember that much, if I'm honest.'

'No? You don't?'

'Do you?' Leah blew at her coffee, not sure what she wanted the answer to be.

'Yeah.' The silence hung there for a while.

'Dare I ask?' Leah attempted to laugh but it sounded so fake, she cringed.

'I know you remember some of it . . . or you wouldn't be asking.' Sam's thigh was radiating heat through her jeans. She would only have to turn her head. She could hear both their breathing, could see his chest rising and falling. Her leg twitched.

'I think . . . something might have almost happened,' Leah whispered.

His arm was touching hers. He smelt of rumpled bed sheets and wax. Leah shifted her weight and Sam turned his face to hers.

'Yeah. Pretty damn close,' he said, his mouth near her ear.

'I'm sorry,' Leah said. 'I shouldn't . . .'

'You've nothing to be sorry about,' Sam said. His finger traced the join between their thighs.

'I'm a married woman.'

'I wish you weren't.'

'Sometimes I wish I weren't too,' Leah said. Then she shook her head. 'I really shouldn't have said that. I didn't mean it.'

'Are you sure?'

'I don't know. I don't know what I mean any more.'

'I lied. I'm not sorry about last night.' He leant forward so his forehead was grazing hers. 'It's like, this whole crazy thing. It's awful, but it's brought us together. I want to protect you. I believe you. I believe you.'

He lifted her chin and kissed her. She let her lips touch

his. *If I don't open my mouth, it's not cheating*, she told herself. His arms snaked around her waist and she pressed her lips harder on his. He pushed back and his lips parted. She pulled back.

'Sam. I can't.'

'Of course you can. You might be married but you don't belong to him.' He kissed her again and she let him part her lips. His breathing became deeper and then she felt his tongue in her mouth, his hands gripping her tighter. 'I want you so fucking much,' he whispered. 'I can't stop thinking about you.'

His lips moved down her neck, over her collarbone, and his hands up to her breasts. She wanted to cry. She wanted to kiss him back hungrily, she wanted him to push her onto the floor and unbutton her jeans and to feel his fingers inside her. She wanted not to be married, just for an hour.

'Sam . . .'

'Leah, come on. It's OK. I just . . . I just want you so much. It's OK . . .' He carried on kissing her. She felt cruel and brutal but it squeezed her heart until she thought she might burst.

Leah stood up and pulled Sam to his feet, kissing him again. His hands grabbed her waist and he bent his knees and picked her up, pushing her against the wall. She couldn't breathe and, mercifully, couldn't think.

She kissed him until her lips were swollen and her chin felt scraped.

'Let's go upstairs,' he groaned into her neck, and he

gently set her down on the floor. Leah had a fleeting stab of insecurity that it was because she was too heavy to hold any longer.

At the top of the stairs she closed her eyes and felt his hands start to move up to her breasts. Her body was pressed up against the wall, facing away from him. The hardness under his shorts was pressed into her lower back and he began to grind himself against her. One hand started to reach lower, towards the waistband of her jeans.

'Wait, I just need a second.' Leah pushed herself back. This was it. She was either doing this or she wasn't.

'It's OK, what's wrong? Don't think about it, Leah, just let it happen.' Sam tried to push her back, but she wriggled away. The door to the bathroom was propped open and Leah ducked into it and leant against the door. There was a strange and unfamiliar sweetness – girls' body spray and hair products. She breathed in, her body shaking. He wanted her. That must mean something. It must all fit together. It all happened for a reason. It was happening. She could do this. She should do this. It was her choice. She was the one in control.

She unlocked the door and walked back onto the landing. Sam stood leaning against the door frame of his bedroom. His shirt was off. His torso was tight and firm, with just a smattering of golden hair. There was another tribal tattoo on his chest, the kind the girls at university had inked across their lower back.

'Come here,' he smiled. And she did. She needed to feel his

arms around her, the smoothness of his skin. The breadth of his chest. He pulled her T-shirt off over her head and Leah automatically sucked in her stomach. 'Just relax, baby,' he whispered. 'Let me take care of you. It's OK now.'

He drew her to the bed. Freshly made. Grey sheets. She lay down and he moved over her. His arms were strong and the weight of him between her legs made her arch her back as his mouth moved down her chest and his hands moved underneath her.

Sam was kissing her again, gently this time, his fingertips swirling on her inner thighs. But she couldn't feel it any more. She couldn't feel anything. Her eyes were on the pillow beside her. Underneath the grey-and-white-checked pillowcase she could see a bobble, a pink, fluffy bobble poking out. It made Leah think of Hannah, and of Luke. What would this do to the kids if anyone found out? Luke loved Chris.

Her hands gripped Sam's and stopped them.

'I can't.'

He stopped but there was a dim, cloudy look in his eyes. Leah felt her throat tighten and she turned her head.

A chipped mug was on the bedside table. An upturned Lee Child book.

'Leah. Why do you let him control you?'

'What?' Leah tried to sit up, but Sam's body pressed down on her harder.

'I can see it. In your demeanour. The way you talk about him. Sometimes, you're like a scared rabbit. Leah . . . you know I'd always protect you. You never have to be afraid of me.'

His hands went to the buttons of her jeans.

'No, Sam. Please.' Leah turned her hips, and for a second a flash of fear went through her body like an electric shock. Was it too late to walk away? Could she walk away now? Had she come too far?

'No. I need to go . . . Sam, I'm sorry . . .' Leah used all her strength to sit up, not caring about the muffin top that was rippling over her waistband. 'I can't do it.'

Sam sat on the edge of the bed, his legs out in a manspread. 'I don't understand, Leah. You've been giving me "fuck me" eyes all week.'

'Sam . . . I'm sorry. I didn't mean to. Well, I did. I mean, I'm sorry. I didn't think it would go this far.'

Leah pulled her T-shirt back over her head. 'It's not that I don't want to. I do, but—'

'You're scared of him. Aren't you?' Sam stood up but he didn't make an attempt to put his shirt back on.

'No. I'm not. I'm scared of myself.' Leah turned and went downstairs, then had the indignity of lacing up her trainers and searching the living room for her phone. She found it wedged between the sofa cushions.

'I do like you, Sam. A lot. You're the only person who has been here for me. But I have so much guilt right now. I can't handle any more.' She turned to go.

'Leah,' Sam said as she headed towards the door. 'Whatever is happening, just let me be here.'

Leah turned around and nodded at him, trying not to clock the hurt in his eyes. His T-shirt was back on and his hands were in his pockets.

Her phone started to ring and Leah looked down to see Chris's number flash up again. She felt sick. She felt sad. She felt shame. But most of all, she felt very, very alone.

19

It had been a week. She avoided even looking across the road. Chris would barely talk to her. And yet here she was. The doctors' office was packed. Full of coughing pensioners and scabby-looking toddlers. It smelt of germs. She remembered the way she used to be able to tell if Luke had a bug by the way he smelt. Chris used to call her some kind of witch doctor.

She'd left Sam's house that Saturday and driven round and round, out along the A roads, away from the pier, the sands, the park, the beach. Her phone had vibrated: first Chris, then Bunty, then Sam, on a tortuous loop, until she'd switched it off – and then had to pull over into a lay-by to turn it back on again. She was a mother. She didn't have the luxury of being able to block it all out. She texted Luke to ask him to call Chris for a lift home, then pulled back out onto the ring road. It was soothing and grey and curved, and she followed it round and round until the diesel light had flashed and she was too exhausted at the thought of dealing with a petrol station.

When she came back to the house, she heard Luke's voice in Sam's garden and felt sick to her stomach at the thought of her son in that house, getting a Coke from the kitchen where his mother had been pressed up against the wall just hours before.

There was another car in the drive. Dave's.

'What is this, a fucking intervention?' she muttered as she got out, refusing to look up at Chris's face in the living-room window.

'What are you doing here, Dave?' she called as she came in, hanging her car keys on the hook in the coat cupboard. 'Have I forgotten something? Are you having Luke?'

'No. Not exactly.' Dave and Chris shuffled out into the hall from the living room, holding half-full beer bottles.

'Well. Isn't this cosy?' Leah said. 'What is it? If you're here to tell me I'm being a terrible mother you can—'

'Leah,' Dave interrupted. 'You know whatever happened, I'd never think that.'

He looked tired, Leah thought. She wondered if Louise was feeding him properly. Dave had bought a lot of takeaways when Luke was little, interspersed with the odd serving of beans on toast. His hair was receding now, but he still tried to keep it in style with a messy, waxed, spiky effect. *It would be better if he just went for a grade two all over*, Leah thought, then admonished herself. This really wasn't the time, and it wasn't as if she was looking her best right now either.

'Leah, come and sit down,' Chris said.

'Don't treat me like a child.'

'Sorry, I really don't mean to.' Suddenly she realized that, if Dave looked tired, Chris looked exhausted. Beyond exhausted. As if he hadn't slept in months. His skin was grey, and his hands were shaking. 'Please, will you just come through.'

Sam's tongue in her mouth. His hands on her breasts. She'd told herself all week that didn't count as cheating because she was wearing her padded bra, so it wasn't like he was feeling anything. Her head whirred.

'I'm coming.' Leah considered asking for a beer too, then thought better of it. She hadn't eaten anything since the morning, and to her shame, she realized she was ravenous.

The living room was tidy, as it always seemed to be these days, since Luke had become surgically attached to the Xbox upstairs, and Leah spent most of her time out. Walking on the beach. Even at Bunty's dance school. Anything to avoid the house.

The Moog looked up as Leah came in, and he thumped his stumpy tail.

'Has he been out?' Leah bobbed down and patted his head.

'No. He's been a bit out of it today,' Chris said, as he and Dave sat down together on the sofa.

Leah looked up. 'He's been like that a few times this week. Can you check him over later?'

'Of course,' Chris said.

Leah sat down on the armchair opposite the sofa. 'I feel like I'm at a job interview,' she said, then promptly burst out into giggles. Dave and Chris just looked at her, which made her laugh even more. It wasn't helping her case and she knew it. But she couldn't help it. She laughed and laughed until her ribs ached and her throat burned from the gasps of air. It was only when Dave said he was here to see if she would agree to Luke coming to stay with him for the rest of the summer, that the laughter stopped.

'No way.'

'Leah, just try and think clearly for a second,' Chris said leaning forward. 'You're not in a good place. Luke is worried.'

'What, why? Wait. Did he say something?' Leah's face dropped.

'He doesn't have to,' Chris said. 'He's out of the house all the time with those girls. He's sullen. He's grumpy.'

'No, he's not,' Leah said.

'He is with me. He's worried,' Chris said. 'I know you don't want that. Dave and I, well, we thought since he's going to Devon in a week—'

'Ten days,' she butted in.

'Ten days . . . anyway, maybe Dave could take him a bit early. To give you a rest,' Chris said.

'Nope.'

'Leah,' Dave said.

'I know what my name is.'

'Please stop being so defensive.' Dave looked concerned.

'OK. I'm sorry.' Leah tried to sound genuine. 'But you can't take my son away from me. If you think I'm on edge now, can you imagine what that would do to me? You *know* what I

249

get like. I'm already terrified about you getting into a pile-up on the way to Devon. Or him eating a dodgy prawn and being sick without me there. Or a fucking tsunami on the beach. Basking sharks. Terrorists. They're all there, Dave, in my head, jumping about like cartoons I have to grab hold of and try and scrub out. Please. I'm dreading Devon enough. I can't lose him for longer.'

'I'm just thinking of Luke,' Dave said.

'So you're the parent? And I'm being selfish?'

'No.' He looked at Chris and her blood boiled. They'd been sat there. Talking about her. Being the ones in control. Poor mad Leah.

'You know what you're doing, don't you?'

'Just trying to work out what's best for you both,' Chris said.

'You know this is gaslighting, right?'

'Neither of us are trying to make you think you are mad,' Dave said. 'But from what Chris has said, you sound very stressed. And all the calls . . .'

'What do you mean? What calls?'

'Leah, I know you've been calling the station.'

Leah looked down.

'Sometimes three or four times a day.'

'Only because no one was telling me anything.'

'Because there is nothing to tell.' Dave's tone was gentle. 'Some idiot sent you those paper dolls. Someone who probably watched the show. But there haven't been any more, have there?'

'There *have*. Inside the attic . . .' Leah started.

'Sweetheart. I think what we need to do is have a chat with someone. I just wonder if all this guilt . . . do you think there's a chance, a chance you made those dolls yourself?' Chris said.

'W-what?' Leah could barely form the word.

'It just makes so much more sense. This appeal. The stress. It's brought it all back. All that guilt. You being at home. It's starting to feel like last time.'

'Last time? What do you mean? When I got upset at work and got a bit overprotective of Luke? It's hardly the same as being stalked by some nutter with a pile of newspapers and some craft scissors, is it?'

'You don't react well to stress. Extreme stress, I mean. The woods. The wanderings. The sleepwalking. But let's maybe go private. It can't hurt, can it? And then, if we're wrong, we can just rule it out.'

'That's why they're not taking me seriously,' Leah said to Dave. 'You've told them it's me, haven't you?'

'No,' Dave said. But Leah didn't believe him. He couldn't look her in the eye.

'And even if I had, there's protocol to follow. But the only fingerprints on those dolls are yours.'

Leah let it sink in. 'They must have been wearing gloves.'

'Leah. Let the police do their job. There have been calls since that programme. The case isn't cold. No case is, really. I didn't quite understand the impact all of this had on you.

I think you need to talk to someone. There are . . . special centres.'

'What? What do you mean, a special centre? Are you trying to send me away too, Dave? What *is* this?'

'No. No one's trying to send you away. We just want to make sure it doesn't get that far.' Chris leant forward. 'You and Luke need each other. Do it for him, if not for us.'

'So, what seems to be the problem?' Dr Elmwood tapped on his keyboard, then looked at Leah with an encouraging smile.

He was an attractive older man. Twinkling greyish-blue eyes, lean and tall. His shirt was crumpled but his face clean shaven.

'Well. I guess I'm here because, well, my husband thinks I'm a bit more on edge than usual,' Leah said, hating how the words sounded. How submissive she must seem. How Chris could so easily be a Victorian anti-hero and she the madwoman in the attic.

'And what do *you* think?' Dr Elmwood sat back in his chair and started to click his ballpoint pen, as if he was itching to write something with a flourish.

'I *am* on edge. But I've reason to be. Things are . . . a little chaotic at home,' Leah said carefully. 'I'm not sleeping. I, I feel, well, felt, as if someone is . . . watching me.'

'And why do you feel that way, do you think?'

'Because someone *was* watching me. Sorry, look, I know

how insane it must sound, but I got sent some paper dolls in the post. It's a long story, but it was a threat. Or a warning, maybe. I don't know. And there were candles . . .' Leah trailed off. 'But now I feel confused. My husband thinks I've been sleepwalking.'

'I see you're taking Citalopram. Are you happy with the dose?'

'Yes. I don't feel depressed. Just, I don't know, anxious isn't the right word.'

'And these . . . concerns. Is it something you need to contact the police about?'

'I have contacted the police.'

'So they're taking it seriously?'

'I'm not sure,' Leah said honestly.

'OK. So, can you talk me through some more of this, what you feel has been happening?'

Leah explained it all. Without passion. Without emotions, just the facts. The way she was trained. Dr Elmwood's face was poker-straight.

'Right,' he said when she'd finished. 'I'm going to give you a number to call. I do think we need to get you to talk to someone sooner rather than later. But there's a triage assessment first. They'll address the urgency. I don't think the wait is too long, but . . . well. See what they say.

'In the meantime, I'd like to up your dose, say to 40mg. Just a little bit. How does that sound?'

'Fine,' Leah said unenthusiastically.

'I see you've been up to 40mg before. So you shouldn't have much in the way of side-effects, really. You mentioned sleepwalking?'

'Apparently.'

'High levels of stress, Leah. They present in very different ways. Sleepwalking is one of them. Is your husband supportive?'

'Of me being here? Very.'

'Well. I meant more at home.'

Leah shrugged. 'He wants me to get better, to talk to someone.'

'OK. I'd like to see you again in a few days, Leah. And you'll call this number as soon as you get home?' He handed over a card and a prescription.

'Will do.' Leah stood. 'Thanks very much, Dr Elmwood.'

'You take care of yourself.'

'I will,' Leah said. Then she walked back to her car, tossing both bits of paper in the bin along the way.

The image on the screen was chalky and jumpy. But she could see it. A flashing bulb, almost. A tiny kidney bean.

'Oh my God,' she whispered. Dave squeezed her hand and she looked up at him and smiled.

'I can't believe it,' Dave said. 'I just, I can't believe it.'

'It's too early to tell the sex,' the sonographer said. 'But look, everything is in order. Here's the arms, and the legs.' She pointed to white blurry things on the screen. It mystified Leah, but she didn't care.

'Everything's OK? It's really OK?' Leah asked, a huge smile on her face.

'Absolutely fine.'

Dave ruffled her hair and she leant her head against his shoulder.

'You can print off pictures in reception. They are £2 each. I'll just give you a reference.' The woman in the green scrubs scribbled something on a piece of card. 'And that's all done. I'll leave you to get dressed. Congratulations.'

Once she left, Leah awkwardly manoeuvred herself to a sitting position, trying not to flash Dave in her open-backed gown.

Dave looked away as she wriggled into her jeans, then perched on the bed next to her. 'I'll give you some privacy in a sec. I just want to check, you're sure we're doing the right thing?'

'Are you kidding me? How can you say that when we've just seen our baby's heartbeat?' Leah's eyes widened.

'No. I mean you and me. I still think this could work.'

'I know. But I just can't take the risk.' Leah leant forward and rested her head on his shoulder. 'You've been incredible, Dave. But I can't focus on a new relationship when I'm growing a baby. And I'm scared I'll end up hating you. I don't need that right now.'

'I could have really loved you, Leah,' Dave said.

'I could really have loved you too.' Leah's mouth was dry and tacky. She never was a good liar. 'Friendships have started with worse.'

'OK,' he whispered. 'We'll do it your way.'

Leah looked at the tiny bean and waited for that huge rush of love, the one she'd read about in Pregnancy and Birth magazine. The one all the advertising reps had told her about after she'd been caught being sick in the staff toilets.

Her baby. She was twenty-six years old and a single mother. Her choice.

She stared at the bean. It just looked like that. A very tiny little bean. She waited for it. The rush.

But she just felt like her bladder was going to burst.

20

Leah headed home. She'd taken to looking in the rear-view mirror. Checking the back seat of her car. She was convinced she was going to see Tilly's reflection one of these days. A grotesque, blue, puffed-up face, one eyeball trickling down her cheek, her skin like scales.

Bunty had of course told her to get a grip. Especially now she could connect the dots between Charlie and the Bowers so easily.

'Of course it was her, pushing the glass. Plus, didn't you say she's seen you? At church? You write that name on the prayer leaf or whatever the fuck you do. It's her. She's messing with Luke. Trying to mess with your head. Watch it there, Leah. She's like a little Lolita. Thank fuck you don't have any rabbits.'

'But why?' Leah had folded herself up on the love seat in Bunty's apartment, which overlooked the harbour. She was torn between trying to keep out of the house as much as possible and wanting to spend every waking second with

Luke before he left for Devon that weekend. It would be half relief, half horror for her to know he was so many miles away.

'Because she fancies Sam, and Sam fancies you.'

She didn't even bother to deny it.

'I find it hard to believe a thirteen-year-old girl would be doing this. And I think . . . I think she's pretty vulnerable. I mean, her age, she's impressionable. I think she just wants some security.'

'Hmm. Well, that may be, but it doesn't mean to say she's not going to take you out with a crossbow while you sleep.'

'Where will she get a crossbow?' Leah asked.

'Crossbow shop?'

'You've watched too much *Witcher*.' Leah sipped her red wine and felt it in her toes and her jaw. 'So what should I do? Talk to her?'

'No. Just, fuck it. Stalk her back. Send her creepy dolls. Pop up everywhere, when she's least expecting it. Like, you know, her wardrobe.'

'Because that won't put me in prison.'

'And how's the Sam infatuation?'

'Fun,' Leah said flatly. 'I keep thinking I'm going to burst out with it. Tell Chris everything. I hate being around him, in case I accidentally say it.'

'That's not what I asked, actually, but a good sign, I feel. So, still have the major horn or have you finally had the cold moment?'

'Swings and roundabouts. Some days, or *hours* I guess

would be more like it, I want to go straight round and rip all my clothes off, and then others the thought of him touching me makes me want to get into the bath with a plugged-in toaster.'

'Standard. But, listen, you do right to keep schtum. Make sure you keep that massive gob of yours shut. You are a loss to the Catholic Church. You and your precious guilt. You're like Gollum.'

'What a lovely thing to be described as by my best friend.'

'Dude? I'm your best friend? Now I just feel sorry for you.'

'Am I not yours?'

'Well. You're the only person I can stand to be around without wanting to rip my own arm off just to have something to throw at them.'

'I'm going to take that as a yes. But I still think I should be honest.'

'But why? It's selfish. He'll be devastated. I mean, I know I'm a bit mean about him, but I wouldn't want to see him hurt, and if I think that – when I'm ambivalent towards him at best – then you should be taking fucking heed.'

'Heed? Hark at you ... Well, you say that. But I've been on Mumsnet.'

'Jesus Christ, don't listen to those self-righteous, jam-making fannies. They'll have you in the stocks for even thinking about Ed Balls when you masturbate and *don't pretend you haven't.*'

'There's a lot of threads saying he deserves to know the

kind of person he's married to. The kind of person. I mean, God. Is that what I am now? *That* kind of person.'

'Your mistakes do not define you, Leah.'

'Have you been on Insta again?'

'I know, right? I'm like an old fishwife. But it's true. It's your actions afterwards that count.'

'But . . .' Leah was confused. 'My actions were to almost shag my neighbour. So isn't that the same thing? Besides, if it was the other way round, everyone would be telling me to leave. If he did it once, he'll do it again. So how come it's different for me?'

'Because you *didn't* shag him. End of. Do you think every little office Christmas party kiss has been disclosed to the wronged spouse? Every dick pic from a fit dad at school? No. People are, in general, full of fucking secrets. If you tell him, you'll hurt him. Simple as. Even if you *did* shag him. It's your body. *Your* choice. Unless . . . you *want* him to leave? Then there is an argument that this self-sabotage is all for a reason.'

Leah swilled the wine in her glass. The traces of the red were there still, sliding down. What did that mean about the wine? When it had legs? Good? Bad? She had no idea.

'OK. So, I see you're going to artfully avoid that one. I'm bored of your cheap-airport-thriller dramz now.' Bunty smiled and reached out one long waxed and fake-baked leg and nudged Leah's shin. 'Come on. Let's get pissed and judge people on Tinder.'

'OK.' Leah smiled in spite of herself. Her phone had been flashing in her bag. She'd even taken the vibrate off now. 'But I can't get hammered. I've got another GP's appointment first thing.'

'Dr Elmwood again? Do you want me to come with?' Bunty's eyes twinkled.

'No, you gutter slut.'

'Top-up, then?' She stood and held out her hand for Leah's glass.

'It would have taken me days to get out of that beanbag,' Leah said. 'You're just one perfect lean machine.'

'Floor cushion. And I told you. Hot yoga.'

'The last time I went to hot yoga my hairband snapped and I ended up with Chaka Khan hair.'

'Chaka Khan's hair is awesome.'

'On you, maybe. Not on a forty-one-year-old white woman.'

'Well. Aren't we full of first-world problems? Shall I order a pizza?' Bunty called over her shoulder as she waltzed into the glossy kitchen section of the open-plan room.

'Sure,' Leah said distractedly, as she tried to read her screen while her phone was still in her bag. Didn't Bunty ever go to the toilet?

I can't stop thinking about you. I want to fuck your brains out.

Her heart fluttered, then sank again as soon as it had taken flight. She was an aeroplane disaster at take-off.

Come over tomorrow?

No. No. No. No. No.

Leah could almost see the words being typed in front of her on an old-fashioned Underwood typewriter. A crisp white sheet of paper.

She sipped her wine and let Bunty curl up next to her, pretending she wouldn't reply.

She went home in a taxi before midnight. Chris had offered to pick her up, but Leah hadn't wanted Luke left alone in the house.

While she was in the car she messaged Sam back.

We need to talk.

That sounded good. She could go and see him. Draw a line under everything. Get some closure. Like with Tilly. Tell him again, once and for all, it wasn't going to happen. But this time, actually mean it. And the promise of seeing him the next day lit up that tiny spark inside her. It was as if the pilot light had been fixed. And then, as the taxi pulled up outside her house, it was blown out just as fast.

You're right. We do. Soon.

Leah turned her phone off and went into the house.

Chris was up. Of course. In his checked pyjama bottoms and greying T-shirt that had once been white. He smelt damp, like it had been left in the washing machine too long. It probably had.

'How was your night?' Chris put down his iPad and paused the TV. It irritated her massively that he couldn't just pick one entertainment device but had to multitask them all at once.

'Good. You were right, good to get out.' Leah kept her face

turned. Every time she saw Chris she felt like she was going to accidentally blurt everything out.

'What are you doing tomorrow?'

'You know what I'm doing,' Leah said pointedly.

'I meant after the doctors.'

'I don't know. Taking The Moog out, I guess.' Leah bent down and was treated to a warm lick. 'How is he?'

'He's fine. Observations all normal.'

'Must have just eaten something, then.'

'Because I thought maybe we could go out for lunch? Or brunch? After your appointment?'

'No. I need to get the washing on for Luke. Get him packed. I should probably be around, really, shouldn't I? If it's affecting him as much as you say it is.'

It was a cheap shot. She knew it. Chris looked at her with sad eyes.

'OK. Doesn't matter. It was just a thought.'

'Maybe, you know, when Luke's away,' Leah offered. She looked at him and waited for a surge of something. Either way. Love. Repulsion. But there was nothing.

Which was worse.

'Night.' Leah turned and climbed the stairs.

Leah let her head fall against the headrest in the driver's seat, indicated right and drove past the pier. It was the long way around, but she needed to feel the wind in her hair. It was not particularly warm, but she wound down the windows as the white sun split through the clouds and tickled the sea. She'd really intended to go to the doctors. But when she'd pulled up, she hadn't been able to face going in. No amounts of medication or cognitive behaviour therapy would make the paper dolls disappear. Or this noise in her head.

She would see Sam. She would stop whatever this was. She would get everything straight. She had lain awake all night and when she'd finally drifted off at the thick and stagnant time of 3 a.m., the hour of ripe breath and damp pillows, she'd dreamt she was on the pier shouting at a girl on the beach. She had been screaming, trying to warn her. The tide had been coming in, and the girl had just sat there. Cross-legged, holding something shiny between her fingers. The waves had folded in, the layers becoming stronger, taller, the waters untold. Leah had been holding the edge of the pier wall, but her voice hadn't been there. It had been lost on the wind and her throat only croaked out bleats and mews.

Leah carried on driving. She didn't want to go home. So she drove past the pier, alongside the seafront and up to the abbey. It was quieter than usual and she managed to get a car parking space. There were still tourists in their multi-coloured Pac-a-macs struggling up the infamous 199 steps to the ruins, despite the grey skies and the fact that it was a midweek morning. She tucked her phone in her back pocket and walked to the side of the building where there was the best view of the sea. She breathed in and out with the tide and had started preparing herself for her conversation with Sam when her phone buzzed.

'Mark?' Leah answered with a smile. 'It's OK, I found . . .'

'Leah, thank God.' Mark let out his breath in one long sigh.

'Hey. What's the matter?' Leah frowned.

'Leah. Erm. OK. Something weird has happened.'

21

'What's this?' Chris looked up from his laptop as Leah slammed the newspaper on his desk at the veterinary surgery.

'It's my fucking obituary,' Leah spat.

'What are you talking about?' Chris frowned and pulled the paper towards him as Leah jabbed at the right-hand column with her finger.

'My obituary. Someone placed it in the births, deaths and marriages.'

'Couldn't it just be another Leah Wallace?' Chris's voice trailed off as he started to read. 'Oh. I see.'

'Luke. You. My job. Oh my God, Chris, this is a threat.'

'Leah . . .'

'It says I died suddenly.' Leah was shaking. 'You can't tell me I'm making this one up.'

'OK. OK. But calm down a minute. Couldn't it just be a joke?'

'What kind of SICK joke is that?'

'OK, don't shout. I'll call the police.'

'I already have. And the paper. I mean, I don't know whether to be offended or not that nobody spotted it when the proofs came in.'

'Well, what did they say? Who placed the ad? Surely they can trace the payment?'

'Someone came to front desk. Paid cash. Left a fake number.'

'Right. And what did the police say?'

'Nobody will speak to me.' Leah sat down with a thud. 'No one will call me back. Dave said he's going to try and see what he can find out.'

'You told Dave before you told me?'

'Oh come on, please don't make this some kind of pissing contest.'

Chris rubbed his eyes. 'OK. What time is Dave picking Luke up?'

'Teatime. They're staying in a Travelodge or something halfway there.' Leah shook her head. 'I'm almost relieved. I don't want Luke knowing anything about this, Chris.'

'I agree,' Chris nodded. 'OK. I'll talk to Dave then, make sure he says nothing to Luke. And maybe I'll, I don't know, look at our security systems. You know what they say, though, if anyone was really wanting to hurt you, they'd just do it. They wouldn't give you a warning.'

'That's comforting.' Leah scratched at her thigh.

'It was meant to be. Don't give them the satisfaction of letting it get to you, Leah.'

Leah nodded.

'Should we change your number?' Chris picked up a pen.

'I'm not sure what good that will do. They know where I live.'

'Leah, please don't, that sounds very unstable.'

'What does? '

'They know where I live.' Chris smiled gently. 'It sounds a little paranoid.'

'Well, why the fuck do you think I'm paranoid?' Leah kicked the desk leg and Chris pulled back in his chair.

'You need to calm down. I'll ask Alice to drive you home.'

'I don't need someone to drive me home!'

Chris sat forward. 'You shouldn't be alone when you're feeling like this. Want me to call Bunty? Look, I've got reconstructive surgery to do this afternoon. Some bastard knifed open a stray cat's face. He's already prepped. I'll come straight back after that, then maybe I'll call the police. See if we can get someone over.'

'OK.' Leah shook her head. 'OK. But nothing to Luke. Promise me.'

'Of course.'

There was a knock at the door, and Leah looked up briefly to see a tall, pretty blonde holding a mug.

'Oh sorry, Chris, I didn't realize you were with someone. I made you a coffee.' The woman, Alice, Leah presumed, smiled.

'Oh, thanks, Alice. How's that prep going?'

'Ready when you are.' Alice smiled back. She glanced at Leah. 'Oh, wait, are you *Leah*?'

Alice held out her hand with a beautiful smile. Her nails were unpolished but immaculate. She smelt of mid-range celebrity perfume. 'I've heard so much about you.'

Leah shook it quickly without quite meeting her eyes. This wasn't really how she wanted to appear. 'You too. Chris says you've saved his life.'

Alice glanced at Chris and her smile widened. 'Oh, I don't know about that. He just needed a bit of organizing. Why am I telling *you* that? You know what he's like.'

Chris looked down, trying to hide his own smile and shook his head.

'Don't start ganging up on me, you two.'

'Hey.' Leah looked at him in surprise. *Don't be painting me in that light.*

Alice gave a slight grimace. 'Anyway, lovely to meet you.' She smiled then left, shutting the door gently.

Leah stared at Chris for a second too long. 'I'll let you get on, then, shall I?'

Chris watched her silently as she leant forward, took back the paper and folded it up into her bag.

'Right. I love you. FaceTime me.' Leah pulled her son towards her. They were the same height now. She hated not being able to wrap him up, hold him to her chest. She could feel Luke's ribs through his Hype T-shirt.

'I'll let you know we've got there OK,' Dave said, kissing her on the cheek and shaking Chris's hand. 'Just call me, mate, if you need anything.'

'OK. Thanks.' Chris winked. Leah felt sick. She bent down and waved at Louise though the passenger window. 'Have a great time.'

Louise smiled. She looked good. Thin, Leah noticed. Perky tits. In the words of the late, great Carrie Fisher, your basic nightmare.

'Thanks, Leah. Hope you get some rest. Long lie-ins, no teenage boys to cook and wash for!'

Oh, fuck off, she wanted to say, but instead Leah smiled thinly. 'Bliss.'

Luke got in the back of the car and put his AirPods in straight away, Leah was pleased to note.

'I'll miss you,' she said brightly. 'Have an amazing time.'

Luke nodded. 'I will. I'll call.' He put his arm out of window and his hand found Leah's. He squeezed it. 'Love you, Mum.'

Her smile was so stretched her jaw ached, and the skin on her lips felt paper-thin.

Wrong. It was all wrong. The pavement tilted slightly.

It was almost a relief when the car disappeared at the end of the cul-de-sac. A great relief and a huge, all-encompassing horror. Leah sat down on the kerb and put her head between her knees. *Five things you can hear. Five things you can see.*

'Leah.' Chris's hand was on her shoulder. 'Come inside.'

'In a minute,' Leah replied. 'I just need to sit here for a while. Catch my breath.'

Chris bobbed down until he was at her height. 'I'm sorry, baby, but I've got to nip into work. Alice called. There's a couple of papers I haven't signed, and we can't get some drugs ordered without them. I'll be back as soon as possible. OK? And then we'll talk. Make sure all the doors are locked.'

'OK.' Leah didn't look up, even as she heard the engine roar and smelt the rubber of the tyres backing down the drive. She counted to twenty, then opened her eyes. There was a pair of trainers in front of her, and a muddy pair of black paws. The thunder in her ears rolled back a little and she looked up, squinting in the early morning sun. Bracken nestled his head into her lap and started sniffing her crotch.

'Oi.' Leah leant back and tried to swing her knees to the side. 'Stop it.'

'Bracken.' Sam's silhouette said. 'Come away.' He gave the dog's collar a sharp tug and held out his hand to Leah. Leah allowed herself to be pulled up.

'What are you doing lolling about in the gutter, you tramp?' Sam said with a smile.

'Just waved Luke off.' Leah looked into his eyes. They were mischievous, like a child caught with his hand in the sweetie jar. Sorry, not sorry.

'Where's Chris gone? Just saw his car,' Sam asked pointedly.

'Work,' Leah said, breaking his gaze.

'Want me to come in?' he said softly, stepping towards her. She could smell him. Yesterday's aftershave. Mixed with something slightly salty. 'I know you don't like being alone.'

'No.' Leah shook her head, and her eyes filled up. 'I'm OK.'

'Why are you crying?' he almost whispered. He put his hand on the top of her arm. 'Jesus, Leah, what has he done to you?'

'Nothing. I'm just, I don't feel right when Luke is away from me.'

'Baby, look at me.'

I'm not your baby, Leah wanted to scream.

'Leah, come on. I think about you all the time. I can't get you get out of my head.'

'Why?' It was provocative and she knew it. But she needed it. *Tell me you love me.* Leah's heart started to race. She felt her tears spill. *Tell me you need me.*

'Why? You know why. I want you so much.'

Leah felt her stomach drop in disappointment.

She shook her head. 'I'm sorry, Sam. I can't. It was a mistake.'

'Leah . . . I just want to help. Come here.' Sam wrapped his arms round her and she let her head rest on his chest.

It would be so easy to invite him inside. To curl up in his wide lap, let him take care of her, stroke her hair and whisper the world away. She gulped and it hurt.

She pulled back gently. 'I'm sorry,' she said, then went inside and closed the door.

For a minute she wanted to run back outside. But it wasn't the answer. Sam wasn't the answer.

She went upstairs, flopped on Luke's bed and smelt the sheets. Hair wax and grime. Her mind drifted to Luke as a toddler. Chubby little legs, a squeal. The excitement of running away. Knowing you were being chased, the thrill of those arms around your waist. Being tossed in the air.

The front door slammed, and Leah sat up.

'Leah?' Chris called from downstairs.

'Up here.' Leah walked to the top of the stairs.

'Can you come down?' Chris said. There was something in his voice she hadn't heard before. Something that made her obey. Her feet felt like lead on the stairs. *He knows*, she thought.

He was in the kitchen. Leaning on the island, arms folded, his face turned, looking out into the woods. *He knows.*

'What's the matter?' Leah said. She had a sudden compulsion to burst out laughing.

He didn't move for a few seconds, then swivelled his head towards her. His eyes were red. That was the worst. She could have handled anger, disappointment, even disgust.

She realized, at that moment, she had never seen him cry.

'What's wrong?' she said again, moving towards him.

He didn't say anything. He just looked at her loosely. Like his eyes could barely fix on her. They were wet and cold and dark.

'What?' Leah couldn't help it and a nervous laugh rose up and bubbled out. 'What?'

Still he didn't say anything. Leah's nerves turned to fear and her chest tightened.

'Chris, stop it, you're scaring me. What's wrong? Is it Luke?'

'You know what's wrong,' he said limply, then looked away again, back into the trees. 'How long?'

'How long what?' Leah's voice was shaking.

'How long have you been fucking him?'

Leah closed her eyes.

'Chris. I swear I haven't.'

'Don't you fucking lie to me!' The coffee mug that was on the counter was suddenly airborne and smashed into the one of the cupboards. Leah screamed and ducked.

'I'm not lying. I swear. I didn't have sex with him.'

'Oh, OK. What then?' Chris shouted. 'Go on, give me all the gory details.'

'It wasn't like that.' Leah's tears were flowing fast. 'You have to believe me.'

'I don't have to believe you at all.' Chris slammed his fist into the butcher's block and winced with the pain.

'Ask him. Please, Chris. It was just a kiss. I was going to tell you.'

'Just a kiss. *I want to fuck your brains out? I can't stop thinking about you?*' Your fucking account is linked up to the iPad. I went into work and charged it up, and it was there. Just on the fucking home screen. All your notifications.'

'What . . . what do you mean?'

'Your notifications. They all come through to the home screen when you turn it on.'

'I'm so sorry.' Leah shook her head. 'Please . . .'

'*Come over tomorrow?* Is that what you've been doing? Every day?'

Chris pushed past her and stormed up the stairs. Leah ran after him, taking the stairs two at a time. He yanked a suitcase out of the wardrobe and unzipped it roughly.

'No, Chris, please. Please don't go.' Leah tried to close the case, but he pushed her off and started pulling his clean clothes out of the drawer.

'Chris. It was a kiss. A stupid kiss. And I am so, so sorry.'

Chris grabbed the side of the suitcase as if he was holding onto the bars of a rollercoaster. His knuckles were white and his entire body tense. Then all the fight seemed just to fall out of him, and his shoulders slumped.

'Why, Leah?'

'I don't know.' Leah hiccupped through her tears. 'I was mad and confused and . . . and . . .' Everything just sounded like a horrible cliché.

'No.' Chris looked up at her, still holding onto the case. His biceps were bulging with the effort, his face grey. 'Why do you want me to stay?'

'Because I love you,' Leah said.

'No. You don't,' Chris said sadly. 'You haven't for a long time.'

And there it was.

'I do love you,' Leah said. 'But . . .'

Chris stood straight and flexed his fingers. 'You love me . . . *but*? This is marriage, Leah, not a contract with a fucking loophole.'

Leah remembered. The tiny service at Gretna Green in the old Blacksmiths Shop. Her beautiful vintage pleated cream dress and Luke's fat little fingers inside hers. They'd held hands and said their vows, but Leah hadn't felt it. Not until Luke had come to them and put his head through the circle their arms had made and wrapped his arms around her waist.

Nick Drake had been playing and Luke's eyes had been so wide and full of love. And Chris had stroked his head. And she'd felt it then. She'd felt this man would let no harm come to her son.

'Chris,' she pleaded.

A minute passed before either of them spoke.

'I'm going to get a hotel for a couple of days. We need a bit of space,' Chris said.

'So you're not leaving for good? It's not over?'

'I don't know. Is it? It feels like you left me a long time ago.'

'But I didn't.'

'I never wanted you to stay out of obligation.'

'I do love you, Chris.' Leah's voice cracked.

'I don't think you love me the way I love you.' Chris's eyes were dry now. Leah felt like she needed to shove her fist in her mouth to stop herself from screaming.

She watched as he threw his jeans in his case. Some pants. Part of her wanted to help, to sort his washbag out for him. He'd forget to take deodorant, like always. Every time they were on holiday he ended up having to borrow hers. But she didn't want to have any part in him leaving.

He came into the living room, the one they barely used now. He put his bag on the floor. 'I spoke to Dave.'

Leah nodded mutely.

'I told him that you'll be in the house on your own. So he's spoken to the police. They've logged it all and will call in later.'

'OK,' Leah said quietly.

276

'Dave said something else, Leah.'

Leah looked up.

'He said the word "suddenly", the word used to describe how you died . . .'

'Yes?' Leah knew what was coming.

'That's what they use when it's suicide . . .'

Leah looked down. 'I know.'

'They spoke to the receptionist, Leah. She couldn't remember exactly, but she thought the person who placed the ad . . . well. The description she gave . . .'

'Yes?' Leah urged.

'Sounded a lot like you. Just think of Luke and don't do anything stupid.'

The front door closed. The engine revved, and it was the most heartbreaking sound she had ever heard, since she'd watched her mother do the same thing when she was seven. It was raining outside that day, and she had run after the car in just her socks. Even as it sped up, she'd run and run, her legs trembling and her vision blurred. She'd watched the tail lights disappear up the hill but she'd still run until her dad caught up. His hands had circled around her waist and he'd lifted her up onto his hip.

This time, there was no one in the road.

She didn't call anyone. She left the shattered mug in pieces on the floor and only ventured into the kitchen to make sure the doors were locked. Her heart hammered and she didn't look up as she twisted the key and checked the handle. Once. Twice.

Then she scooped up The Moog and went upstairs and climbed, fully dressed, into her bed. The Moog curled up in the crook of her knees and she cried herself to sleep with all the lights blazing.

It was just past 8 a.m. when her eyes flew open. It took her a minute to process where she was, and that it hadn't all just been a horrendous dream.

Rolling over, she checked her phone. No calls from Chris. No FaceTime from Luke. There was a text from Dave, though, saying they'd got there safely and were going to some celebrity chef's seafood place for dinner.

Leah's throat was dry and her skin was stinging. She felt her swollen face. Falling asleep crying had left her with two eyes so puffed up she imagined she looked as if she'd gone five rounds in the ring.

'Moogie?' she called out, waiting to hear his shuffle. The Moog wasn't there any more; there was just a warm patch where he'd been curled up.

There was an odd glow. She couldn't quite work out what it was. At first, she thought it was the light bleeding in through the blackout curtains. But then she smelt the wax. Heart in her mouth, she crawled forward to the edge of the bed, already knowing what she would find. Candles. Lit and flickering like a coven's circle all around her bed.

And a paper doll. Stuck to the middle of her dressing-table mirror. In the three-way glass it seemed to go on forever, a never-ending tunnel.

Leah opened her mouth and screamed.

Her legs flew out of the bed and she ran for the stairs, her body hot and cold all at once. Her skin felt like a hive, swarming, itching, smothered. She missed the last two steps, and her feet flew out from under her. She grabbed the banister to stop herself falling but wrenched the small of her back, crying out in pain.

And then she saw him.

The Moog was lying on the floor in the kitchen doorway. There was something not right. His chest was moving rapidly and he was panting. Leah bent down and cupped his head. 'Moogie?' He opened his eye drowsily, then closed it again. A small puddle of brown vomit was just to the side of his head.

'Oh my God,' Leah whispered. 'Baby? Are you OK?'

He closed his eye and his breathing became even faster.

She dropped to her knees and stroked his head. 'We'll fix you. It's going to be all right.'

She reached toward her back pocket for her phone, when there was a noise. A creak. Her head flew up and she froze. It was a heavy kind of quiet. Just the rasp of The Moog's breath. Then she heard it again. A scrape and another creak. Like someone walking on loose floorboards.

Leah jumped up and pulled a carving knife from the butcher's block. They were still here. Whoever it was. They were here.

The only sounds she could hear were her own rattled breath and the dog's deep, laboured breathing. She ventured into the hallway, lit with the gossamer strands of early sun like fireflies, with its familiar smell of pine and wax.

'Hello?' Leah called. She listened to her voice bouncing off the walls. She tiptoed carefully into the den. Skate magazines and empty crisp packets were abandoned across the floor. The living room: picture frames unmoved, books in haphazard stacks on the shelves as usual. Leah's grip on the knife was becoming sweaty.

She put her ear to the cupboard door in the hall and held her breath until her chest was about to burst. She couldn't hear anything. Feeling for the handle, she grabbed it and closed her eyes. Then, counting to three, she yanked open the door as fast as she could.

Just coats and wellies, and The Moog's lead.

She turned back towards the kitchen, and saw that the bi-fold doors had been opened. And a figure stood bent over her dog.

Leah let out a blood-curdling scream, and the intruder jumped back and hit their head on the copper pans, the clang and clatter vibrating round the room like a gong.

'Jesus Christ! You mad bitch,' Bunty squealed. 'I nearly just weed my pants. Put down that knife before someone calls the police.'

'And you're sure Chris didn't do it? I mean, it looks like a bit of message, doesn't it?' Bunty stood with her hands on her hips in Leah's bedroom, staring at the doll and the candles.

'This isn't Chris. I mean, Christ, how cruel would that be?'

'Yeah. He also knows you've had your tongue down someone else's throat.'

'Don't, Bunty. Anyway, why are you here at this time of the morning? And how did you get in?'

'Couldn't sleep. The door was open. I didn't think you'd be up. Actually, I was going to come and make you breakfast.' Bunty bent down. 'Let's get this cleared up.'

'No. We need to leave it for the police. They need to see it.' Leah rolled her head around slowly and Bunty flinched as her neck cracked.

'Eww. Stop it. Come on, I'll make you something to eat. There's eggs on the counter.'

They headed downstairs, but not before Leah had closed the bedroom door tightly, with a shudder. She'd half expected to come upstairs and find it all completely vanished.

'And I was right,' Bunty said once they got back to the kitchen. 'I told you this would happen. I can't believe you didn't think about the iPad.'

'What can I say? I'm not used to the complexities of adultery.'

'Clearly.' Bunty put her arm around Leah and gave her a very quick squeeze. 'Come on. It's going to be OK. He'll come back. It was only a kiss.'

Leah stared down at The Moog. 'I need to take him in to see Chris. He's sick. Hang on.' She looked back up. 'How can the doors have been open? I checked them. I checked everything. No one has the keys apart from me and Chris.'

'Dunno, babe, you didn't answer the front door so I went

around the back to see if you were in the kitchen and it was open. Look, he's just mad. I bet he did this. I really do. It's a dick move but, you know, I'd probably do it. If I was him. I've done worse. Why don't you just text him and ask?'

'I can't . . . Not after . . . I just can't. He thinks I'm insane anyway.'

'Well, it's a slippery slope. Walk about the house and howl for a while, wringing your hands. Oooh, whack some Kate Bush on Spotify. You could come and stay at mine for a few days?'

'The Moog isn't well, Bunty. I can't leave him here. I've got to get him to a vet, anyway.'

'Well, I suppose you could bring him.' Bunty wrinkled up her nose. 'I mean, I'll try not to gag.'

'Are you sure?'

'Course. Get some stuff together. When did the police say they were coming round? We can go straight after.'

'They didn't give me a time. God, it's driving me mad. I feel like I'm just sat waiting for something to happen. I can't go on like this. No one seems to think that I'm in danger. Dave and Chris think I'm doing it all. Do you really think it's possible? That I did all this myself? That makes me a whole different kind of crazy. I know I can go a bit wobbly sometimes, I know I sleepwalk. But I wouldn't wander round lighting candles and sending dolls to myself. I mean, why would I torture myself like that?'

'You tell me, love,' Bunty replied. 'You seem to do it on a daily basis. But no. As on the edge as you are, I doubt very much even you would place your own death notice without remembering. Unless you're stringing me along and I'm going to end up in a bathtub without a kidney.'

The Moog let out a soft moan.

'Oh God. He needs to go the vets.' Leah bent down. 'I'll have to take him now. Do you think Chris will be mad if I turn up at the practice?'

'Oh my God. I can't believe I am going to say this. I'll take him.'

'What?'

'I'll take him. Just. Don't. Carry him to the boot of my car before I change my mind. You get packed and wait for the police.'

'Oh Bunty, thank you. So much.'

'It's OK. Can we line the boot with towels or something though? I don't want his stink all over the upholstery.'

'You can take my car.'

'No thanks. It might explode.' And with a Chanel kiss on the cheek, Bunty hopped into her car.

22

Leah opened her bag and started to pack, trying not to move any of the candles. The view of the tall trees from her bedroom window was the same as from the kitchen but there was something about being high up – she felt as if she could monitor everything. Like a cat or an owl. The roof of the treehouse had caved in slightly, a branch poking out of the corner. Luke had spent hours in there with his comics and his Nintendo and peanut butter sandwiches. Leah had never been able to relax, even though Chris had assured her it was fine. He'd power-drilled the boards into the tree trunk and swung off them himself to check. But she'd sat up in the bedroom, watching, just in case.

She opened the window and listened for the sound of children playing, the thundering paws of dogs, the babble of the stream. It was a different place when the sun filtered through the fingers of the trees, as if they were playing peek-a-boo.

Leah breathed in and out. The honeysuckle beneath was ripe and the smell of the damp earth was rising. On another day she would be outside, her hands burrowed into the pots. Lavender for luck. The heady, thick smell of the rosemary.

She threw some more clothes into the suitcase, along with her make-up bag, and moisturiser. She didn't want to stay in her room any longer and headed back downstairs. She felt too vulnerable in the kitchen, exposed to the woods, so she took a glass of water into the den and curled up on the beanbag – sorry, floor cushion, surrounded by Luke's things.

Luke. She wondered if he had posted any pictures yet. She flipped open the laptop she shared with Chris and clicked on her Facebook tab. But it was Chris's profile that popped up. Her eyes wandered around the screen, coming to rest on the messages, which had a red alert icon. She couldn't help it. She clicked on it.

And there it was. Just one message. From Alice Smyth.

No conversation. Just a picture.

God. NO. NO.

Leah's hand flew to her mouth.

Alice's hair hung in loose curls, not fastened in a bun like the last time Leah had seen her. Her back was bare. She was standing side view on in a full-length mirror. White lace knickers – nothing else. Her flat stomach rippled with youth and her plump, apple-like breasts were covered by her arm.

For a second Leah felt nothing but relief. All the guilt she'd been wearing, her crown of thorns – she could cast them off. But the feeling lasted a split second.

Then she stood up and hurled her glass of water at the floor.

The glass shattered and Leah screamed and pounded the wall with her fist until her hand was bright red. She kicked the door and was furious when her foot wouldn't go through it. Then she stormed back to the machine and started scrolling up and down. No messages. No conversation. Just that fucking picture.

Leah's foot was tapping, and her heart was shaking. Is that where he'd gone? To hers? The room began to spin, and the family photograph on the wall blurred before her eyes. Her stomach squirmed and she had to hold onto the edge of the dresser to steady herself.

It was just so clichéd. *And why the fuck did he leave his Facebook logged in? Did he want me to see it?* She felt sourness rise in her throat and ran to the bathroom. She vomited until all she could taste was the rank yellow bile from her stomach.

She had no real idea how long she crouched there, her forehead resting on the rim of the seat. But her knees began to ache, and her stomach eventually stopped churning, so she went down to the kitchen and took three big gulps of red wine, straight from the bottle. It hit her empty insides and burned. She took another gulp and another. Unsteadily, she reached for her phone and sank down to the floor, back against the fridge.

The phone buzzed and she looked down. Just Bunty telling her The Moog was fine and had been seen by the nurse. No sign of Chris. *Was she there? Was he with her?*

Leah looked at the time and was surprised to see it was almost past noon. She had another gulp of wine and tapped the Google app on her phone.

The front door slammed and Bunty shouted from the hall. 'Honey, we're home. Have you been raped and killed, or shall we have a glass of wine now it's socially acceptable?'

'I'm alive,' Leah shouted from the floor. She heard the pad, pad and click, click of The Moog's paws coming towards her.

'Open a bottle, then . . . oh, I see you already have.' Bunty raised an eyebrow. 'This will not do you any favours. You've not started slicing your fingerprints off, have you?'

'Hey, Moogie.' Leah stroked his head as he clambered into her lap. 'What did Chris say? Did you see Alice, by the way?'

'Chris wasn't there, so we just saw a nurse. Who the fuck is Alice?' Bunty sat down on the floor next to Leah and took her glass. 'Actually, wasn't that a song?'

Leah stroked the folds in The Moog's face and inhaled his slightly stinky, musty scent. He always smelt a bit like a damp cardboard box that had been left to dry in the garage. She opened her mouth to tell Bunty about the pictures but couldn't bring herself to say it aloud.

'Never mind,' she whispered. 'What did the nurse say?'

'She said he was dehydrated. Gave him some kind of shot. OK. So I was thinking on the drive back – we should make a list.' Bunty pulled out her phone. 'Let's think logically. Assuming you aren't a total loony who has been doing this to herself, who else do you know that had anything at all to do with this case?'

'Mark. Called him. Dave. Tilly's mum. Tilly's friends . . . though I only ever met one of them, Dakota, and I didn't even get to interview her. I wanted to. *We* wanted to, but her parents would only speak to the papers with the chequebooks.'

'What did she say to them?'

'She said Tilly left her house at 3 p.m. Tilly told her she was going home but she never turned up. And then just, you know, the usual. What an amazing person Tilly was, but she reckoned her friend had secrets. What they all say. They'll say anything to get an interview, really. It's so ghoulish. Everyone wants their fifteen minutes. Or money. Even Tilly's so-called best friend.'

'What about looking for her on Facebook? Have you tried there?'

'Yeah. I tried to find her, but no luck. Besides, what am I going to say?' Leah ran her hands through her hair. 'I mean, what does she have to do with anything? Except she knew Tilly way back when.'

'What's her full name?'

'It was Dakota Channing. But she might be married by now . . .'

'Found her.' Bunty held up her phone. 'She works at that dodgy nail salon just off the pier. She might have only known her once upon a time, but she's probably the closest you're going to get to working out who might still have some kind of grudge. Since Tilly's mum was a no-go.'

Leah looked over Bunty's shoulder at the headshot. Dakota

looked a lot different now. Much older. She hadn't aged well. Her hair was in braids and her forehead had deep lines. Far too deep for a thirty-year-old.

'*Shit!* Bollocks, I forgot I've got to pick up Immie from football. Are you ready to go?'

Leah paused. She wanted to tell Bunty about the picture, Alice, everything. But she could see her friend's foot tapping. She'd been enough of a burden.

'Actually, I'm going to stay here.'

'What? Are you *nuts*?'

'No, honestly. I think I'd rather stay here and wait for the police to show up. I need to show them everything. You go. Get Immie.'

'Well. OK. I'm going to have to. But call me as soon as they've been, and I'll come back and pick you up, OK? We'll go see this Dakota tomorrow.'

After Bunty left, Leah put on the coffee maker, popped some toast in the machine and opened the laptop again. She only needed to type in the 'T' for Tilly Bowers, and a purple list of search entries appeared, all the ones she'd already clicked on. Again and again.

But this time she tapped on images. There it was. The stock pic, the police release pic. The beautiful headshot. Not the first one, the one she'd shoved at the back. It had probably never been used since.

Leah opened the kitchen dresser and pulled out her book. She'd never kept this one in the attic. The hardback, glossy presentation book, filled with every story they'd done on

Tilly. She'd started it on the lawyers' advice, once the complaints began to come in. After that first story, every lead, every splash, every news-in-brief. She'd saved it all in the A3 portfolio. It was her body of evidence.

Leah mouthed the words, although she already knew them by heart.

Police have appealed for information about a teenage girl, last seen on Saturday afternoon leaving a friend's house.

The parents of Tilly Bowers, 15, said their daughter, a pupil at East Riding High School, had been in good spirits and would not have run away, despite previous attempts.

Tilly, of Berry Brow, was last seen walking down Carver Street wearing a blue hoody and jeans.

Police and Tilly's family are asking anyone with any information to come forward.

Call police on 0800 555111.

The picture was used across two columns. The angry one with the pixelated finger gesture. Leah stroked it. The girl in this picture, with her scraped-back hair and dark eyes, was smiling. No. Grinning. But she wasn't happy. It wasn't a free smile.

Leah took a picture of the clipping with her phone and then entered it into Google reverse image search. It was a trick she'd used at the paper many times when trying to verify an image on social media or one sent in by a reader.

She'd been amazed how many people tried to reuse old

pictures, from old stories, claiming they were brand new. After all, a riot is a riot. A fire is a fire.

She tapped on the image and searched. She'd done it before. With the other picture. Nothing had come up, despite it being a perfect profile pic. But she'd never tried it with this one.

The results flooded the screen. Leah scrolled down looking for a listing where that picture had been published online before. Her old paper's website. And the *Yorkshire Post* site. The police website.

Myspace.

Bingo. Leah sat up and wiped at her face.

She clicked on the link and there she was. Tilly Bowers had a Myspace page. As discoveries went, this was hardly a massive breakthrough. She assumed the police already knew and had rooted through it for dodgy conversations. Old men pretending to be teenage boys. She clicked through the gallery of pictures but there weren't many. One of her and Dakota. What looked like a family birthday in a pub. That was definitely her mum. Smoke was coming out of her nostrils like a dragon. Back in the days when you could still smoke in pubs.

Not much in the way of connections. A handful of people her age. They looked like school friends. A few bands Leah had never heard of. A couple of clubs.

A picture of Tilly at a gig. Some band called Annalise's Day Off that Leah vaguely remembered. It had been at the Memorial Park, an all-day bank holiday event that had tried to pretend it was a festival but died out after a few years. The band had done OK for a local gig. A couple of pop punk singles in the charts. The town had traded off their name for a couple of years, then, when they'd faded into obscurity, pretended they'd never known them, and those who had done claimed it was always tongue-in-cheek.

The picture of Tilly wasn't great. In fact she was ducking behind her hand, hiding from the camera, gripping a beer. It was a sunny day and her eyes were hidden by sunglasses. But that big toothy smile was there. An honest smile with rosy cheeks and velvet skin.

Leah drummed her fingers on the counter and looked at the picture again. She wondered who had taken it. It had been taken in the days before selfies, before the fear of missing out was so rife that if it wasn't on social media, it didn't really happen. Tilly had lived her teenage years without all that documentation.

The park behind Tilly was packed. People lounging on the hill in little clusters. Cider and camping chairs. The odd grubby kid in a baseball cap and a Spiderman mask. Daisy chains. Crisp packets.

She couldn't see any of Tilly's squad sitting with her or near her, none from the other pictures on Myspace. Just Tilly: pink long-sleeved top, hair in two topknots either side of her head.

Leah put her portfolio back in the drawer and jumped as her toast popped. She chewed at it miserably. Even with butter it was dry and unyielding. She let it slide directly from her plate onto the floor by The Moog's feet and carried her coffee through to the living room. It was gone four o'clock and the police still hadn't stopped by.

She hadn't managed to drink even a third of it before her head lolled back and she was fast asleep.

Her dreams were lucid and brutal. She was at the pier again, shouting at a girl down on the beach, hood pulled up over her hair, crouched in the breaking crests of the grey waves. Leah was screaming Tilly's name, trying hard to make her look up, but the wind whipped her voice from her throat and carried it far away, down the empty pier to the dead carousel and its horses with the empty eyes. Leah turned and ran down the steps to the beach, past crisp packets and spilt slushies in pools on the concrete. A seagull picked over a tray of chips, so covered in grease that they lay solidified. The gull looked up at her with black eyes as she tried to get down onto the beach. Tilly was still crouched in the waves, which were bulging higher by the second, now swirling around her waist.

Leah tried to call her name again, but this time her mouth was caked with sand and her tongue couldn't form the words. Her feet became too heavy to lift and she was using all her strength to pull one foot up off the floor.

She tried to scream, and the girl turned her head. She was wearing sunglasses even though the day was dull. The sunglasses in the picture. She looked at Leah and began to smile, the white-toothed shark smile. Leah stopped trying to move. Something was wrong. The smile was wrong. Tilly reached up to her neck and unclipped the necklace around it. Then she slowly tipped her head back like a snake. Her jaws opened, and she fed the chain slowly into her mouth, letting it pool on her tongue, the way a child would suck up a strand of spaghetti. Finally she dropped the locket in. And swallowed it in one gulp.

Leah's legs began to move again and she ran towards the girl at the edge at the sea. But by the time she got there, Tilly's body had turned to sand and was melting into the salty waters. Leah reached out and tried to grab the last bit of her, but was left with just the necklace in her hand.

It was the smell that woke her.

At first she was confused, thinking it was morning. But the light was too syrupy for dawn. Too heavy and tired. She inhaled and gagged, holding her hand over her mouth, thinking for one sickening moment that the smell was her.

It was putrid and cold, acidic. Wrong. But a with tinge of familiarity. She sat up on the sofa and looked down at the heavy, dead weight on her foot.

The Moog was cold and meat-like, his head lolled to one side and his soft brown eye glassy. He was surrounded by light-brown pools of runny faeces and a biley, greenish-grey vomit.

'Moog?' Leah whispered. She leant down but knew that he was dead even before she touched his little body. 'MOOG!' Falling to her knees, she felt the fluids seep through her jeans and the stench worsen. His nose was still wet. She grabbed her phone from the coffee table and hit the speed dial for Chris. It went straight to voicemail.

'Oh, baby.' Leah started to cry as she pulled her dog into her lap. She kissed the top of his head and rocked him, the way she used to rock Luke. 'I told them,' she cried. 'I told them you weren't well. I'm so sorry. I should have taken you myself. I should have known.'

Outside the sun was beginning to set, and the oranges and reds gave a strange, almost otherworldly, glow to the room.

Leah felt the warmth on her cheek as she kissed his head and muzzle, then went to Luke's room and brought down one of his baby blankets. The blue one her Dad had brought to the hospital, still soft and furry like a peach. She ran the bath and washed The Moog's slippery fur, feeling his muscles, his fat. He was even heavier wet, and when she lifted him out of the bath he slid out of her arms and hit the side panel, falling with a thud. She cried then until her throat was raw.

After he was dried and swaddled in the blanket, she tucked him up in a cardboard box from the garage and placed another blanket on top of him.

Chris's practice would be closed now. She tried calling again, but it only rang twice before her screen flashed and died. She couldn't remember the last time she'd charged it.

Leah taped up the box and kissed the top of it. The Moog was very, very dead. And she wanted an explanation. She wanted the nurse, and Chris, to look at his stiffening body and tell her there had been nothing wrong.

Leah sat down next to the box and remembered all the times she had cried, or panicked, or had a bad day, and The Moog had climbed into her lap. He'd always taken care of her. And she hadn't taken care of him. She had known he was sick. She knew it. And she didn't do enough about it. She'd let Chris tell her it was OK.

Suddenly, all the lights in the house went out and she was plunged into blackness.

Leah stood up fast. 'Hello?' she called out, but she wasn't sure if she actually wanted an answer. Feeling along the wall for the switch, she flicked it. Nothing. She tried again, off and on, but nothing was working.

'Just a fuse,' she murmured to herself. Her mouth was dry and her ribcage tight. Her shins hit the box The Moog was nestled in.

She waited for her eyes to adjust to the dark and fumbled with her phone to turn the torch on before remembering the battery was dead. The thought of running to Sam's house crossed her mind fleetingly but she cut it off, refusing to play the role of the damsel in distress.

She felt her way along the cement walls and found the door handle into the hallway. There was a touch of light here from the street lamp outside. *So it's not a power cut then*, Leah thought and her heart quickened. The fuse box was back in the garage, but the torch was in the kitchen drawer.

As she stepped into the room, she felt like she was in the middle of a black glass dome. With no inside lights on, the woods outside were so clear that it felt as if she was in the middle of them, with nothing around her but the spindly trees, their crooked fingers and wrinkled, knotted eyes. She took a deep breath and stepped towards the window, forcing herself to look. Just woods in the night. Nothing to be afraid of. The same trees she knew were beautiful in the day, that grew and blossomed like her beloved potted plants. Just shrouded in the night. They breathed. They had life. There was no death here.

In between the two nearest trees, a light appeared.

Leah sucked in her breath and felt her blood begin to pump. A flickering candle in a hurricane lamp. Her hurricane lamp. She took a deep breath and opened the patio door.

'Hello?' Her voice was shaky, but still rang out into the darkness. 'Who's there?'

The woods rustled in reply and the leaves swayed in the light breeze.

'WHO ARE YOU?' Leah yelled as she stepped out into the garden. There was a shape. Something dark, in the trees. 'JUST SHOW YOURSELF! I'M NOT SCARED OF YOU!'

It was higher than the candle. It looked like a figure. She squinted. The candlelight wasn't enough. She wanted to run, but she was scared of turning her back, scared when she turned around again that it – whatever or whoever it was – might have crept closer.

Leah stepped back and lost her footing, tripping over the patio sill. She landed painfully on the bottom of her spine and felt nausea run through her. Scrambling to her feet, she ran to the counter and felt around for her phone, but she couldn't find it. She yanked open the drawers and felt for the old torch she knew was there somewhere.

Paper, photos and old birthday cards spilled onto the floor until her fingers closed around the thin metal. She flicked it and the batteries were still miraculously alive. A yellow beam shot out of the end and she stumbled back to the open door, slipping on the papers on the tiled floor. Grabbing to the door frame to steady herself, she was about to shine the torch into the woods when she saw the candles. More candles, lined across her back wall. Some in the glass lamps. Others standing in jars. All plastered on the inside with newspaper, cut into the shape of a paper doll. Leah watched with horror. All the faces. All cut from pictures of Tilly. Tilly. Tilly. Tilly. They caught fire and began to burn, crinkling and melting one by one. Leah looked up, into the dead centre of the trees, and raised her torch. There, hanging above the lamps, was a figure wearing a soaking, dripping blue hoody, her body swinging from a noose.

23

'OK. Sounds like you've had a bit of fright.' A copper Leah didn't recognize leant forward over her desk. 'Have you got someone to stay with while your family is away?'

'Yes,' Leah said quietly, hoping her breath didn't smell of wine. She'd got a taxi to the station even though she'd never felt more sober.

'And, I need to ask you. How much have you drunk tonight?' The policewoman smiled, then went back into resting inquisitive face, and poised her pen.

'I couldn't give you the units. Maybe a bottle of wine,' Leah said flatly. She knew it didn't look good.

'Well. We've been in contact with your husband. He is very upset and concerned. He said you'd argued and that he will be staying away from the family home for a few days.'

'Yes. I told you that.'

'Right.' The policewoman, younger than Leah, of course, but not by much, looked up. 'He says he's been with a friend all evening.'

'He doesn't have any friends,' Leah said. She didn't mean it. He did. Just none he would admit his marriage was crumbling to. They were all university friends, the good ones. And they all lived at least two hours away. He wouldn't have gone that far, would he?

The policewoman shifted in her seat, and fixed her pale-blue, watery eyes on her file. 'We did speak to the, erm, friend, and she said he has been at her flat all evening.'

'Is her name Alice?' Leah said. She almost didn't want the policewoman to answer.

'No,' the policewoman said, riffling her papers. 'Elizabeth Walker.'

Leah let the words hang in the air, then felt every last bit of fight escape from her body like a punctured balloon.

Bunty? She felt like she'd been punched in the stomach. 'He's with her? He's with Bunty?'

The policewoman nodded.

'And there's no fingerprints? Nothing?'

'Nothing at the moment. We spoke to Tilly's family. But they said you'd visited them yourself?' The policewoman raised an eyebrow at Leah.

'Yes,' Leah said. 'I just, I just wanted to apologize. That's all.'

'Well, Mrs Bowers found the visit somewhat upsetting. Can I suggest you keep your distance from now on?'

'I upset her?'

'Not enough to hang a scarecrow from a tree in your back garden, but yes, I think it dredged up memories.'

'Listen.' Leah sat forward. 'I know you can't give me details of the case. But is there any reason to think that Tilly is alive? Could she be doing this?'

The policewoman coughed and Leah noticed the hairgrips in her ginger bun were coming loose. She had an overwhelming urge to push them back in.

'Your husband said you've been a little ... unwell recently.'

'You think I did this myself? You think I hung a scarecrow with a dead girl's hoody in a tree? Put candles round myself while I slept?'

'I'm not saying that.'

Leah stood up. 'I want to go.'

'Wait.' The policewoman stood up quickly. 'We just need to make sure you're not a danger to yourself or ...'

'Or to anyone else?' Leah finished.

'Leah, please. I'm here to help you. Now, who is the friend you're going to stay with? Let me call them.'

'Forget it,' Leah said. 'I want to go.'

'Leah, can you think of any reason why someone would want to hurt your dog? The RSPCA have reason to believe he was poisoned.'

'What? No, he's been sick for weeks ... They think someone did this to him? What did they say?' Leah's eyes filled with tears.

'I'm afraid I don't have any more information. We are still waiting for results. It's with the RSPCA now,' the police officer said gently.

'Would he have been in pain?' Leah's throat swelled and her eyes stung.

'It may not have been intentional; it could have been something he ate at home or while he was on a walk, even.' She took a deep breath. 'But I need to ask you about Sam, Leah.'

'I told you everything,' Leah said numbly. 'Like I said at the start. It was just a stupid kiss.'

'To you, maybe. Where was he tonight?'

'I don't know,' Leah shrugged. 'We haven't spoken since.'

'Well,' the police officer said briskly, 'we will be contacting him too.'

An hour or less later Leah left the station, the officer driving her home, and she felt her stomach rumble. Her phone was dead, finally killed by the constant messages from Bunty and Chris. She hadn't read a single one.

She knew the curtains would be twitching as the police car pulled up at the kerb.

'Are you sure you're going to be OK?' The officer looked at her in the rear-view mirror.

Leah nodded mutely.

'My colleagues have checked everything in the house. There's nothing there now. We've taken away the candles and the . . . the scarecrow. If anything else at all happens just call 999. Otherwise, we'll be in touch.'

'What kind of case is this?' Leah said finally. 'Is it . . . harassment?'

'Harassment, intimidation. Could be counted as a hate

crime. But my guess is it's over now. As soon as police start getting involved this kind of thing tends to dry up. These idiots are just cowards. All mouth and no trousers.' She smiled kindly. 'Have a shower. Things will look brighter after you've had some sleep.'

They didn't. Leah slept fitfully. It had been days since she had slept through the night. Her cheeks were hollow and her eyes were puffy. Even a hot shower and fresh clothes couldn't disguise the sallowness of her skin, the willow-tree hunch of her frame. She dried and straightened her coconut-scented hair and breathed in and out, finding solace in the ritual of the long, smooth strokes. She listened to the birds in the back garden, the rev of a car down the street. Smelt the singe of her slightly damp hair between the irons, the honey of her shower gel.

She grabbed her bag, her keys, her purse and went down to the kitchen. This time she didn't look outside. She gathered The Moog's water dish and food bowl and put them in a plastic bag, trying not to think about what she was doing as she dropped them in the bin. He didn't have a bed. He'd always slept on her bed or on a worn cushion at the side. That, she'd always keep. She wanted his thick little sausage body back. No way would she let the vets cremate him. He belonged with her, in her little back garden, overlooking the woods. She'd dig a grave when she found the strength. She spent the next couple of unsociable hours cleaning, wiping, scrubbing. She bleached out the bath, hoovered the stairs, put on the dishwasher. Even cleaned the inside of the microwave. Each stroke was soothing: the rhythm, the whir and the cycles of the white machines.

When the clock finally dragged itself round to 9 a.m., she chewed on an apple she didn't want and a slice of toast she couldn't taste, slicked on her best lipstick, and yanked the charging cable out of her phone. It was only half charged, but it would have to do. It rang almost immediately, and if she hadn't been so startled she wouldn't have answered.

'Leah? Leah, where the fuck are you? I've been going out of my mind.'

'I know Chris was with you last night,' Leah said stonily. 'The police told me. At least, that's what you said. So, either he was with you. Or you're covering for him. I don't know which one is worse right now.'

'What? Leah . . .'

'HOW COULD YOU DO THIS TO ME?'

Leah hung up the phone and wished she could slam it down like it was the Nineties. It just didn't have the same drama when she aggressively tapped the screen. She grabbed her keys and slammed the door. It almost seemed pointless to lock it, but she did it anyway.

'Leah?'

Leah opened her car door as Sam jogged across the street, still wearing those goddamn shorts.

'Are you OK? I saw the police car.'

'Well, someone hung a scarecrow behind my house and murdered my dog. But apart from that everything is just fucking great.' Leah tried to sit in the driver's seat, but Sam blocked her and banged the door shut with his hip.

'What? What's happened to The Moog?'

'They think someone poisoned him.'

'Jesus. Is that why he's been off? You said you thought he was sick. Did he eat something? You know, I heard something about slug pellets . . .'

'Someone did this deliberately.' Leah felt sure of it.

Sam's eyes darkened. 'Leah, you're not safe here.'

Leah sighed. Behind him she could see Hannah, her ghostly face at her bedroom window, with someone, Charlie by the looks of it, rummaging through an open wardrobe. 'Just go home, Sam. Just go home.'

Sam grabbed her by the top of the arm and tugged. Not enough to drag her exactly, but enough for her to lose her footing and stumble after him as he pulled her round the side of the house.

'What's going on?' Sam let go as soon as they were out of sight and crossed his arms.

Leah's back was up against the wall. For the first time she wished the back garden wasn't so enclosed. She looked out into the woods, but they were still.

'What do you mean?' She looked at Sam and found his eyes were cold.

'You know what I'm talking about. Why aren't you answering my texts? You said it yourself. We need to talk.'

'I . . . I haven't seen them,' Leah said honestly. 'I didn't realize . . . look . . . Chris saw them. They were on the iPad . . .'

Sam let out a low whistle. 'You didn't delete?'

'I didn't realize. Look, it doesn't matter now, does it?'

'So? What's happening? Are you . . . splitting?'

'Honestly, right now, I don't know. I think . . . I don't know what I think.' Leah's eyes filled with tears and Sam drew her close and put his finger under her chin, lifting her eyes to his.

'Stop pushing me away,' he said. 'Why won't you let me take care of you?'

Leah closed her eyes and felt him come closer, his lips touching hers so gently, his arms around her waist, pulling her towards him.

He kissed her and began to open his mouth over hers. For a second she let him. It felt so good to be wanted, to feel safe. Believed.

'You and me, Leah. You and me against the world,' he whispered and kissed her deeply, pressing his body up against hers.

Leah opened her eyes and looked at the woods. Luke's treehouse was just visible through the spindly trees.

It wasn't her and Sam against the world.

It would never be. It was her and Luke against the world.

She turned her head and put up her hands against his chest.

'Sam. No. I'm sorry. I can't do this.'

'Why not?' Sam's brow furrowed. 'What's stopping you now? He's gone, right? I saw him leave last night. I know he's not been back.'

'Look, it's not about Chris. I just . . . I can't deal with this now.'

'Deal with what?' Sam grabbed her hand.

'For fuck's sake, Sam!' Leah snatched her hand back. 'I don't want to.' She tried to push past him, but he pinned her back against the wall.

'You don't know what's good for you, that's all.' He kissed her again, hard, and shoved his knee between her legs so she couldn't move.

'Sam,' she spluttered, 'I said NO.' Fear started to rise inside her and she began to pummel at his arms, his back. But it felt futile. He even laughed.

'So this was just a bit of fun for you, was it? Bored house-wife? Needed an ego boost? You selfish fucking cow.'

He let go suddenly and stepped back. Leah's ribcage filled with air and she took a deep breath.

'No. Sam. It wasn't like that.'

'I told you stuff, God, I opened up to you. And you treat me like this?' Sam's face crumpled and for a second he looked like a little boy, told off for something he didn't think he'd done wrong.

'Sam . . . it's not that. I'm sorry. I'm scared.'

'I thought . . . I thought this was real.'

'I don't know what's real any more.' Leah felt a tear run down the curve of her cheek. 'I have to go.' She ran to the car, wiping at her face furiously. She got in and reversed away from Sam walking slowly down her drive. In her rear-view mirror she saw Hannah's face. Still at the window.

*

By the time she parked up at the run-down car park at the wrong side of the pier, she couldn't even remember how she'd got there.

'Excuse me. I'm looking for Dakota,' Leah said, standing in the doorway of Hollywood Nailz, a depressing-looking salon fronted with a broken fluorescent light-up sign that flashed only the red letters of Hollywood. The blue Nailz just buzzed and flickered.

A large lady with mermaid-style hair and a lip ring looked up from her customer – a young, emaciated-looking girl with slicked-back hair and bad skin who was having three-inch acrylic nails fused on. She reminded Leah a little of Hannah, the way her body was almost concave, and her eyes shadowed.

'She's not in yet. Got an appointment?'

'No, actually . . .'

'Hang on.' The woman squeezed herself out from between the small lamplit tables and shuffled over to the tiny desk at the front. 'She can do you at 10 a.m. You wanting gel?'

'Um . . .'

'Or summat else?' The woman looked up and raised her very skinny brows. 'Overlays? We've got some half-price offers on fillers.'

'Gel is fine. Thanks,' Leah said hurriedly.

'£20 up front.'

Leah handed over a note and sat on a plastic couch with yellow foam oozing out of the cracks.

She opened the messages on her phone. Two voicemails

from Bunty. One from Chris. Another from Sam. She deleted them all without listening. What was the point?

The Moog flashed into her mind. She took a deep breath and stalked Luke's Insta, then Dave's. More beach pics. A meal overlooking the sea. Louise looked good. The chemical smell of the salon was giving her a headache and the air felt too solid. She took a few breaths, five in and five out.

'You all right, love?'

Leah looked up and Mermaid Hair's doughy face began to swim.

'Sorry. Just a bit dizzy.' Leah rubbed her eyes.

'Hang on, I'll get you some water.'

A glass was placed next to Leah. It had obviously had some kind of decoration on it once, but it had been washed away to just a black smudge and half a heart. Leah sipped at the tepid water gratefully.

'Sorry. Thanks for that.'

Mermaid Hair sat back down with a loud *ouf*. 'Morning after?'

'Something like that.' Leah laid her head back on the sofa just as the door opened with a little jangle.

A curvy woman with complicated braids came in and dropped a brown paper bag on the desk. Her jeans were slung low and there was a thick roll of shiny brown skin that sat on display round her waist, underneath her Ivy Park crop top.

'She's for you.' Mermaid Hair nodded at Leah.

Dakota turned round and swept her eyes up and down Leah. If she recognized her, she didn't show it.

She looked down at a scruffy appointment book. 'Can you just give me five minutes to eat my butty?'

'Of course.' Leah smiled and took another gulp of water.

Dakota looked at her again, longer this time, then shook her head.

'You're wanting nails?'

'Yes please.'

Dakota brought her paper bag over to the towelled bench and motioned for Leah to follow.

'Oh please, eat your breakfast. I'll wait.'

'Nah. I can do both. And I've got another lady in at eleven. Sit.' Dakota nodded at the stool by the bench and held out her palms. 'Let's have a look, then.'

She put her hands out and watched as Dakota turned her hands over and stretched out Leah's palms.

She looked younger in the flesh than on her Facebook profile. The lines not so pronounced. Her mouth was wide and her cheekbones high. *If she smiled, she'd be stunning*, Leah thought. But her lips were mushed together and her eyes stony.

Then, oddly, she closed her eyes, breathing in deeply, the same way Leah did when she needed to root herself.

Dakota bunched her braids in her fist and let them hang over her shoulder. 'You carry guilt,' she said, opening her eyes.

'Sorry?' Leah tried to laugh but felt herself shiver.

She tossed Leah what looked like a giant ring of keys with a clack. 'Pick a colour.'

'Oh, erm . . .'

'How about a nice ombré? Match your top. Bit of sparkle? Like, gradual. On your thumb and ring fingers? Right classy.'

'Er . . . sure. What do you mean about . . . ?'

Dakota inspected her fingers. 'Christ, your nail beds are in a state.'

Dakota turned Leah's hands back over and traced the thick, deep line in her right palm with a sculptured fingernail.

'There's an . . . intrusion.' She looked up sharply. 'You need to start looking after these cuticles.'

She picked up a nail file and began to work it like a bow over a harp.

'Are you . . . you're psychic?' Leah asked quietly.

'Oh, bloody hell, don't get her started.' Mermaid Hair put a mug of coffee down on the counter a little too hard and it sloshed over the rim. *Keep Calm and Get Your Nails Done.* 'Stop freaking out the clientele, will you?'

'Nah. I just work with hands all day, don't I? I like the lines. They speak to me.'

'And . . . and what are mine saying?'

'There's a fork in your lifeline. A path. You've always wondered if you chose the right one.'

Leah took a deep breath. 'I think . . . well, yes. You're right. It's . . . well, to be honest, it's why I'm here. It's to do with a friend of yours. Tilly Bowers.'

Dakota looked at her without expression for a moment, then leant back and fished in her coat pocket, producing a

311

pack of cigarettes. She offered one to Leah, who started to shake her head, but then, on second thoughts, took one.

'Fag break,' Dakota said abruptly and stood up. 'Come on.' She marched out to the back, ignoring the scowl on Mermaid Hair's face. Leah followed her meekly through a beaded curtain and out of the back door onto a shaky metal staircase.

'Matilda Bowers. Fucking hell.' Dakota lit her cigarette then leant forward and lit Leah's.

'I used to work for the newspaper, and I know . . . I know I handled things badly back then.'

'Oh, it's you. Wouldn't pay out. You tight cow.' Dakota's face split into a sharklike smile. 'I remember you now. What, you want an interview now, do you? Now it's all back in the media? How much?'

'I'm not a journalist, well, I am . . . I mean, I don't work for the paper any more. I'm not trying to do a story. Someone is sending me threats. Clippings from the newspaper. I know it sounds mad, but I'm scared. I think someone is going to try and hurt me. For what I did.'

'What did you do?' Dakota exhaled a long plume of smoke and steadied her eyes on Leah's.

'You must remember? I didn't give Tilly enough coverage when she first vanished. We lost valuable time, witnesses who could have come forward, CCTV footage – anything that could have helped her be found.'

'Listen, girl. Some people. They don't *want* to be found.'

Leah felt something reach deep down into her chest.

312

'What do you mean? Tilly . . . ran away? Does that mean she is still alive?'

'I dunno. She *was* alive. I don't know if she is now. Police were right. She was doing one.'

'How come you didn't tell anyone? The police? Her family? They've gone through hell.'

'Her fucking family is the reason she left, and the more agony she's put them through, the better. You think they really gave a shit? They wanted money. Always have, always did. Money from the papers, the TV. The supermarket magazines. Anything. Then when the offers started drying up, they went on their little anti-media crusade. More offers. More appearances.'

'But I remember, you came into the office. You wanted to talk . . . to me. To the paper. You talked about it to the nationals. You said she had secrets . . .'

'I know I did. God, love, we all have secrets. I needed the money.'

'Where was she going?'

Dakota shrugged. 'London. See her half-sister. Just get away for a bit, I think.'

'But why? What was so bad?'

'Well, that's Tilly's story. Not mine.'

'Why are you telling me this now?'

'You paid me.'

'Fuck. I should have paid you back then. Can I ask you one more thing? The necklace? What does that mean? It was found on the beach.'

'Yeah. Well. Her family reckoned it was her most prized possession, and all that bollocks. But I'd never seen it before. She can't have had it long. I reckon she chucked it there. Faked her own death. She wasn't book-smart, but she was fucking clever, you know. Once, when we were kids, she dug up worms and sold them for 10p to the fishermen down at the docks. Then she had the bright idea of doubling her money. So she cut them in half. Doubled the price. Just sliced them up with a bread knife. I was screaming. But she just did it. Her eyes were, like, dead. You know. I mean, she probably robbed that locket. It wasn't exactly *her*. White gold. Locket? I mean, come on. That's a white girl's necklace.'

Leah paused. 'But there was a picture of her inside it?'

'Exactly. Who wears a locket with a picture of themselves in it?'

Leah had just left the salon when the rain came. It started with a couple of drips and then it was as if someone had turned on a tap, full blast. Leah watched the beach empty, the people scattering like insects bursting from an ant hill. Parents grabbed shrieking, gleeful toddlers, grandparents held deckchairs up above their heads for cover, all of them doing that peculiar high-kneed run through the yielding sand. Shop porches bulged with people, gazing dejectedly out at the grey skies and the rain that hammered on the canopies.

There was a small gang of teenagers on the beach still, down at the shore. A boy, fifteen or so, not much older than Luke, grabbed one of the girls and hoisted her over his shoulder, pretending to drop her into the crests. She squealed with fake outrage as her friend looked on and wished it was her, hugging her arms around her waist, hair matted and tendrilled.

Leah took off her sandals and headed down to the beach, pushing against the throng who were still elbowing their way up the concrete steps, thick with brown puddles of wet sand. Her top was clinging to her and the thighs of her jeans were soaked, but she didn't care. She walked down to the shoreline. The teenagers were beginning to disperse, their leader obviously bored now, and off in search of a pub that might serve them under age.

The waves beat at her feet and the sand bubbled between her toes. The air felt fresher now, and for the first time in weeks, Leah felt as if she could breathe.

Some people don't want to be found.

As she walked up in the direction of the pier, the rides were shutting down, the attendants zipping their anoraks and pulling up the carriages, battening down the admission windows. All but the funhouse, whose lights were fuzzy and warm against the rain, while tinny pop musak still vibrated on the wooden boards, playing chicken with the storm. The kids had run up their crab buckets from the end of the piers and Leah waded out, the bottom of her jeans now drenched, her ankles red and chafing, to the big rock under the pier. Underneath the flooring, there was some shelter from the rain. Leah climbed up onto the rock and stood, one hand against the metal scaffolding next to it. The rain was still coming strong and the ashen sea was bleak and merciless. She watched the water pound against the rock and thought of Tilly, here, under the pier, where her necklace was found. She closed her eyes and tried to hear her, feel her ghost on the crown on the waves.

'Where are you?' she whispered.

A white girl's necklace.

And then, as a wave cracked and smashed the rock, engulfing her thighs and soaking her with dark salt, Leah remembered. She'd seen it before.

24

December 2002

I was running. My legs were wobbly and my breath was raspy. There'd been a brief moment of hope when I saw the bus, still at the stop, its tail lights shining red. I'd picked up speed, forced myself to push with that last tiny bit of power I had left, the kind I would reach deep down for in the cross-country race a metre behind the girl in the lead. I wasn't the type of girl to come in second.

My knees banged on my Christmas shopping bags and the plastic twisted tightly around my fingers, so tight they were beginning to leave long, deep indentations. It was the last bus. If I missed this, I would have to get a taxi or walk the hour home. Taxis made me nervous and I'd already spent my monthly allowance on presents. I'd have to ask my dad for the money. I didn't want to have to ask him for anything.

I was sweating inside my duffle coat. It was freezing cold and the sea wind whipped across my face, but my double layers were keeping my body hot. Too hot. I reached the side of the road and willed the woman with the Asda bags to take her time getting on the bus. She was the last one in line. A car beeped at me as I took one step off the kerb, and it swerved. I blushed, but thought the driver was being a bit dramatic. I hesitated, though, and waited a moment too long to check both sides of the road were clear. The bus pulled out of the stop just as I had made it to the other side of the road. I stood dejectedly as it drove away, bags in both hands. A boy I didn't know laughingly gave me the finger from the back seat.

I hated teenagers.

My mum said I was a forty-year-old in a fourteen-year-old's body. I took this as a compliment. I had friends at school, other girls like me, who studied hard. Captains of sports teams. Most of us had reached a top grade in an instrument. Cello, for me. We had nice-girl names: Ruth, Rebecca, Faith – biblical. We had nice-girl hair: shoulder-length, shiny, blow-dried perfectly straight. We did nice-girl activities: cinema, bowling sometimes. I worked as a stable girl on Saturdays. We had clean, unpolished but shaped fingernails and waxed eyebrows. No foundation, but expensive mascara. We were late starters. I still wore pads rather than tampons. There was the occasional tooth-clashing French kiss at the birthday parties the whole year gets invited to, or ones in village halls. No seedy cider-fuelled basement hangouts for us.

Our parents were friends. They sometimes came round for dinner or went to restaurants together. Leave the girls at home. Absolutely no concerns about parties or boys. We were all babysitters. We came to cheer each other on in concerts, or sports meets. We swapped clothes. We could have swapped heads and no one would have noticed. We were completely and utterly interchangeable.

I hated every single one of them.

The past year I'd started stabbing myself with my compass during class. Just a little. In the fleshy bits. Through thick woolly tights. It excited me. No one knew what I was doing, under the table. I caught Steven Thompson looking at me once in Spanish when I was doing it. Maybe he'd caught something. The look in my eye, perhaps. The sweet relief on my face. It made me push down harder. I even answered a question while I did it. I was fluent.

I started looking at Steven Thompson a lot after that. Waiting for him to look at me again. I wanted to feel it. To see if his eyes fixed on mine would give me that electric feeling in my tummy again. I began to stare. Willing him. After a while I could see his friends noticing so I had to tone it down. It was too late then. It was all round school that I fancied Steven Thompson. It was easier just to go along with it. He was nice enough. Brown hair. Good at cricket. Really good at maths. Not, of course, as good as me. But that was a given.

Eventually we ended up sitting next to each other on a Geography field trip to Flamborough Head. There'd been much orchestration for it to happen. Rebecca, Ruth, Faith. They'd giggled at me in the hallways and spun me a confusing web of Chinese whispers involving various boys' names that meant nothing and conversations that just seemed banal, regarding who would sit with who on the bus to make sure he and I were together.

He smelt of Pears soap, which I liked, but he still wouldn't look me directly in the eye. He shared his Chewits with me, and by the time we'd arrived, we were 'going out'. I found the entire concept bewildering. We never actually went out anywhere. In fact, we'd studiously ignored each other until a week ago at the school Christmas party, when he'd taken my hand and kissed me up against the Biology life cycle of a frog poster after a couple of his friends had started teasing him about being chicken.

His mouth was wet and his lips didn't move the way other boys' had, like they were sucking on something. But he'd looked at me afterwards with some kind of triumph in his eyes. All I felt was a huge, crashing disappointment. I felt nothing. That night I moved the compass towards the inside of my thigh. The red, purply dots were getting more visible when I got changed for PE.

We broke up after that. Steven told everyone it was because I had as much sex appeal as a goldfish. My friends were outraged on my behalf. I thought it was probably good that someone was. I couldn't have cared less. In fact, I thought he was probably right. I tried to touch myself. In the bath. At bedtime. I'd had to Ask Jeeves for some direction as I couldn't quite work it out. It just felt numb. I just felt numb. I went back to the compass after that.

And here I stood, in the biting winter wind, having missed the last bus, the one that should have taken me back home to our four-bedroom, detached, beige box where my mother would be cooking dinner, and my dad would still be at work, and we'd pretend we felt sorry for him for having to stay so late, but we would both actually be relieved.

Those times, when it was just my mother and me, were peaceful. I'd help cook. We'd chat about the tennis, old movies, what we were reading. I liked the rhythm of it, even though she disgusted me. Sometimes I wasn't sure what I found more abhorrent. My father's arrogance, or my mother's compliance. It was fun, sometimes, trying to decide.

Just as I was about to turn and head to the taxi rank, a girl pushed past me. She smelt of strawberry nail polish. The kind you get when you're little, that peels off. She was shivering, in just a blue hoody zipped up to her chin and a pink and purple knitted hat that made her huge black curls sprout out either side of her head.

She looked at her watch then peered at the timetable board in the shelter, running her finger along the bottom row. She stopped, checked her watch again, then swore under her breath.

I couldn't move. There was just something about her, the pinkness in her cheeks, her dark, purplish lips. She swore again and then, I swear to God, stamped her foot, like a child. I bit back a smile as she looked up and caught my eye.

'Was that the last bus?' she asked, pointing her thumb behind her shoulder.

'Which one?' It didn't matter. I knew there were no buses after 6.30 p.m. This wasn't a city. There was no evening service.

'The 110?'

'Yeah. Sorry. I missed it too.'

'FUCKING HELL.' The girl turned and leant against the shelter. 'Shit.'

'Yeah. I know. Long walk home.'

The girl eyed me up and down, then spat out her chewing gum straight on the floor.

'Must be tough, having to carry all that shopping.'

I put the bags on the floor and held out my palms. 'I know, right. Look at what it's doing to my fingers.'

She looked back at me in disbelief, then let out a short bark of a laugh and looked away.

'Oh,' I said quietly, feeling stupid.

The girl reached into her pocket and pulled out a packet of ten cigarettes. Cheap, cut-price ones. My dad smoked, even though he was a GP. I knew my brands.

'Got a light?' she asked bitchily. 'Actually,' I beamed with pride, 'I do.' I went into my handbag and pulled out a box of matches, left over from Guides the night before. We were doing campfires with the Brownies. I didn't tell her that, though.

'Oh. Cheers.' She looked surprised but stepped towards me. I tried to light one but the wind blew it out straight away. 'Here.' She unzipped her hoody and pulled either side up towards me, so we were cocooned together in a little dark hole. I tried again and she cupped her hands around mine to protect the flame. I huddled in close.

'Got it.' She puffed hard on the cigarette, ensuring it was fully lit. 'So, how you getting home now, then?' She looked at me carefully.

'Walking.' I shrugged, trying to look rueful. 'I'd get a taxi but I've got no money.'

'Oh.' She looked like she was losing interest. 'Can't someone pick you up?'

'Mum doesn't drive. Dad's at work.'

'Looks like we're walking, then.' The girl zipped her hoody back up. 'Fuck, it's freezing.'

'Here.' I delved into my shopping bags and deftly ripped a tag off the gloves I'd bought for Rebecca. 'Wear these,' I said, handing them over.

'Aren't they new? I can't take those!'

'No, not new. They're old. I just brought two pairs. Don't know why,' I tried to joke. We both knew I was lying, but she went along with it.

'Where do you live?' the girl asked. 'Which way are you going?'

'Meadow Estate. What about you?'

'Berry Brow. Where's Meadow?'

'Just past Berry Brow,' I fudged.

'Come on, then.' The girl smiled and her whole face changed. Her teeth were bright and her lips redder on the inside. She pulled on the gloves. 'I'm Tilly. What's your name?'

'Hope.' I smiled back and it felt like the moment lightning cracks before the thunder.

25

Leah buckled her seat belt and the car began to steam up immediately. The rain was breaking now, and the air was warm. She yanked her phone out of her bag and pulled up the picture on Tilly's Myspace page. She was wearing the necklace. There it was, nestling over her collarbones. So this picture must have been taken just before she disappeared, if Dakota said she'd never seen it before. Or Tilly had hidden it from her best friend.

She magnified the picture and looked more closely at the necklace. The way it sat, in the hollow of her neck.

Suddenly her phone rang and buzzed in her hand, causing her to jump. Dave's name flashed up.

'Dave. Is everything OK?'

'Leah, is . . . is Luke with you?'

'Luke?' Fear ran down her spine. 'No. Why would he be with me? Why isn't he with you?'

'OK. Please keep calm, but when we got up this morning, his bag was gone.'

'What the fuck? Have you called the police?'

'No, not yet. We had a bit of a row last night; I think he's probably just gone and jumped on a train home.'

'A row? What about? The train? With what money?' Leah's words tumbled over each other.

'He's been attached to his phone for the last couple of days. I . . . well, I had a bit of a go about it and tried to take it off him. He went ballistic. Leah, something's not right there.'

'He's a teenage boy. They are all attached to their phones. Have you called him?'

'Of course I've called him,' Dave snapped. 'It's just going straight to voicemail.'

'Shit. *Shit*. Call the police. *Now*.'

'OK. OK. I will. Just let me know if you hear anything from him.'

'David, if anything has happened to him, I will *kill* you. Do you understand me? I will *kill* you.'

Leah hung up the phone and ran two red lights getting back to the house. She didn't even pause to shut the car door when she got there, running from room to room.

'Luke!' she called fruitlessly. 'LUKE!' She grabbed her phone and called him, but as Dave said, it went straight to voicemail.

'Luke, call me now. Please. I'm not mad. I just need to know that you're OK. Please, please. Don't do this to me.'

Leah hung up and glanced out of the living-room window. Sam's car was in the drive.

She ran over the road, not even pausing to shut her front

door, and hammered on Sam's door, before flinging it wide open.

'HANNAH?' she yelled. 'HANNAH! Are you home?'

A dishevelled-looking Sam appeared in the hallway, as if he had just woken up. Even from a few metres away, she could smell alcohol on him. Not fresh, not quite stale either. There was a stain on his T-shirt and his hair stood up in peaks and troughs that just a week ago she would have found cute. She was barely able to stop her lip from curling up in a sneer.

'She's not here,' Sam said quietly.

Something cold trickled down Leah's spine. Something in his eyes that made her take a step back.

'Where is she? My son is missing. I need to speak to her.'

Sam stared at her then slowly shrugged.

Leah felt for her phone in her pocket and glanced backwards to check that her door was still ajar.

'Sam, you're acting weird. Are you sure Hannah isn't here?'

'Why would I lie?' Sam took another couple of steps towards her. 'That's like me saying are you sure Luke isn't with you?'

'He's been in Devon with Dave. But he's disappeared. His phone is dead. I thought Hannah might have heard from him.' Leah stepped back. There was something unsteady about Sam's gait. 'Never mind.'

Leah began to turn away, but Sam came towards her suddenly and grabbed her arm.

'Maybe she has. Maybe she's with him. Or maybe he did something to her.' Leah felt his grasp tighten around her bicep. 'He's been sniffing around Hannah like a dog for weeks.'

Before she'd even had chance to think about it, Leah raised her other hand and slapped him as hard across the cheek as her twisted body would allow.

Sam stood firm. He barely even flinched. But his eyes grew darker and his mouth curled into a snarl.

Leah closed her eyes just for a second, and was about to open her mouth to apologize, when her body was yanked forward. She lost her footing on the step and stumbled, only half standing, into the hallway. Sam pushed her up against the magnolia wall with the oak-framed pictures of him and Hannah, and slammed the door. The smell of him was worse close up. Like men's toilets. Leah's stomach churned and she moved her face away from his mouth.

'Don't you dare hit me, you little cock-tease. I'll tell them you're violent. They'll take Luke away. All this paper dolls and candles crap . . .' He brought his lips so close to her ear she could felt the wetness of his mouth. 'It's all in your head.' Then, just as his tongue darted into her ear canal, she heard a strange sound, a clacking of heels, but moving very fast, like Morse code. The door burst open so fast it hit Sam's back. His head flew into the panel and he staggered back in surprise as Leah heard a familiar voice.

'Get off her, you piece of shit.'

'You crazy fucking bitch,' he whined, rubbing the back of his head.

'You come near Leah again and I'll cheese-grate your cock.'

Bunty tossed her hair over her shoulder. Then she looked over at Leah. 'Do come along, darling, you're really slumming it over here.'

'Lock the doors,' Bunty commanded as she strode into the house and went straight for the kettle. 'No wine. I'm making you a sweet cup of tea for the shock. Did he hurt you? I saw him push you against the wall before he slammed the door. Are you OK?'

Leah sat down gingerly on the bar stool at the counter and shook her head. 'No, he didn't hurt me.'

'Now. Listen. I am *not* shagging your husband. He's very unattractive to me and makes nowhere near enough money to make me think five minutes of him pumping away on top of me would be worth losing you over. No offence, but I should imagine sex with him would be like doing the washing-up. Only not quite as wet.'

Leah looked up at up at her and noticed that her eyeliner was uncharacteristically smudged under her eyes and that her hair had a slight kink in it. The Bunty equivalent of dishevelled. 'Chris came over. Yes. He was with me. I tried to call you, but you were probably asleep. You've been hitting the bottle a lot and I don't blame you. In fact, I'm your bloody enabler. Maybe I should watch that, actually. But he's devastated. And so he should be. He's just as much to blame for this as you are. And I told him that.'

'What . . . you know about Alice?'

'Who the fuck is Alice? Hang on, I've got déjà vu.'

'Oh God,' Leah sighed. 'I'll show you later. I'm sorry, Bunty. I shouldn't have thought, I don't know, I'm so mixed up. Right now, I just want to find my son.'

'What do you mean?'

Leah pulled out her phone and started tapping away at the screen.

'Dave called. He's gone. Somewhere. He's not answering his phone. There must be something that will tell me where he is. Somewhere. His Insta. A Snapchat story. When did he last check in?'

'Breathe, babe.' Bunty tried to calm Leah.

'I can't. I need to focus on finding Luke right now. Because what . . . what if the person who has been targeting me has something to do with Luke's disappearance? They killed The Moog, Bunty, the police said he was poisoned. What if they hurt Luke too?'

'OK. We'll find him.'

'Do you believe me, Bunty?'

'I always believed you, chick. You just didn't believe yourself.'

'OK.' Leah hung up her phone as Bunty reversed out of the drive. 'I've called all of his friends who I have numbers for. But no one's heard anything. They all thought he was still in Devon. If anyone knows anything, it'll be Hannah and Charlie Bates. I bet Charlie knows where Hannah is, at the very least.'

Bunty made a sharp right and flipped off an oncoming

driver who had the audacity to glare at her as his brakes squealed. 'Jesus, what is wrong with people? He was miles away. OK, direct me to Charlie's, then.'

'Head towards Berry Brow.'

'And what have the police said about Luke?'

'They said to call round his friends. Check his socials. I don't think they start looking at his phone records until it's been twenty-four hours. They are checking CCTV at the station, though.'

'But are they taking it seriously?'

'Of course,' Leah said grimly. 'He's a middle-class white kid.'

Bunty stared straight ahead and gave a pointed eyebrow raise.

Leah's leg was jigging up and down, faster and faster. 'I bet hundreds of kids go missing today. Hundreds of kids who don't live in the suburbs with vets for dads and failed journalists for mums. Kids who don't make good headlines. I bet you for every Luke out there right now, there's fifty other kids who haven't been seen since last night who aren't being looked for on CCTV. That's how they become ghosts.'

'Leah, we've been through this,' Bunty said gently. 'You weren't to know. The police said . . .'

'The police said she'd run away before. But why did that make such a difference? She was the girl who cried wolf. Surely, if she'd run off before she should have been even more important. It meant that she really needed help.'

They sat in silence until Bunty turned into the estate. The

car shook with a sudden force and jolted forward, before stalling and cutting out.

'JESUS,' Bunty shrieked. 'What the fuck was that?'

Leah whipped her head round and felt her neck twist in a way that she knew would cause pure misery for the next few days.

'Football,' she said shakily.

She watched as a small boy with tight black curls in a red hoody pegged it across the concourse, grabbed his ball and then ran off towards the bins.

'Shit. It scared me. My foot slipped off the pedal,' Bunty muttered, but Leah was watching the boy.

'I think that's Charlie's little brother,' she said, unbuckling her seat belt. Just then Charlie, dressed in overly baggy bright-pink tracksuit bottoms and a tight camouflage vest, threw open the cracked glass door at the bottom of her block and shouted something that sounded like 'Bailey'.

'Oh, that's her, isn't it?' Bunty said as she slammed the car door shut. 'Christ, she's got bigger tits than me.'

'HEY!' Leah shouted across the car park. The little boy looked up, startled, then ducked behind Charlie's legs, bleating something about driving into his ball.

Charlie straightened up and yelled back. 'He's just an effing kid! Let him kick his bastard ball around!'

'No, Charlie.' Leah picked up her pace to a stride, with Bunty just behind her. 'It's Leah, Luke's mum.'

'Bailey, go inside.' Charlie nodded at the boy. He scampered off to press the button for the lift, eyeing them suspiciously.

331

'Have you seen Luke? Or Hannah?' Leah asked urgently. As she got closer she noticed Charlie's eyes were puffy, as if she'd been crying. 'Charlie . . . what's wrong? Are you OK?'

'I'm going to see if I can crash a fag,' Bunty said tactfully, and took a few steps away. She never had been good with crying women. 'Surely there must be some old-fashioned smokers around here.'

Charlie rolled her eyes. 'Who's she?' She jerked her head in Bunty's direction.

'My friend. Immie Walker's mum. Seriously, though, Charlie. Luke is missing. Sam hasn't heard from Hannah. What's going on?' Leah said again.

Charlie jutted out her chin. 'I don't have to tell you anything.'

'Charlie,' Leah said and took a step forward. 'They're your friends. Are they in some kind of trouble?'

Bad thoughts, like big black insects, began to crawl up her throat. She could feel their thick hairy legs creeping higher and higher.

Charlie clenched her jaw and sucked in her cheeks but fixed her eyes in the distance. Her face began to crumble.

'Charlie . . .'

'I don't KNOW,' she suddenly shouted. 'I DON'T KNOW BECAUSE SHE WON'T TELL ME. SHE'S RUN OFF WITHOUT ME.'

'Charlie . . .' Leah reached out and tried to draw the girl towards her, but Charlie's body stiffened and Leah let her arms drop. She knew better than to try and comfort someone who couldn't bear to be touched.

'Don't,' Charlie said quietly, a tear escaping from one dark-brown eye. 'Just don't.'

26

21 March 2003

'If you could live anywhere in the whole world, where would it be?' Tilly asked me. The sun was ripe for May and the gardens were dewy. The shrubs had morning breath and the benches were still gleaming from the spring rain. Tilly rolled onto her front and kicked her legs back and forth in the air. She was childish in so many ways.

'Canada,' I said, picking a daisy with a thick stem and handing it to her. 'Vancouver.'

'How come?' Tilly wrinkled her nose and didn't wait for me to answer. 'I'd live in Magaluf.'

'That's so déclassé,' I said, poshing up my voice. It wound her up when I did that, but I liked getting a reaction.

'My sister went to Magaluf last year with this guy. They got jobs handing leaflets out, you know, outside bars. Trying to get people in. And then, they got like drinks and free entry to all the clubs, all night. I think that'd be sick.'

'It would be disgusting,' I said, but made sure I rewarded her with a smile, otherwise she'd give me a puppy-dog look.

I'd upset her once. About a band she liked, but really shouldn't. She didn't come to the caravan the next day and I panicked. I waited for her. All day. I didn't dare leave, in case she came looking for me.

When dusk fell and I knew I couldn't lie to my parents any longer I took my compass and carved our initials in the velvet bark of the boughs outside.

It was Tilly who'd found the caravan. We'd been walking Jasper, my springer, and she saw it and ran over, like a kid who had spotted an ice-cream van. Jasper had followed. He loved Tilly. He hated everyone else. Even me. And I was his favourite family member.

It became ours then. We dressed it up. Cleaned it. Even hid extra clothes there. We pretended it was ours. Our house together. Where it was just us. Tilly and Hope. No one else. Our hideaway in the Canada mountains, where it was just her sweet strawberry lip gloss smell and damp blankets. We padlocked it and laid our claim, like kids with a treehouse. But it was more than that. It was where I started to come, when it got too much. When I couldn't stand up straight and my thighs were sore from riding. When my head was too full of facts and my heart was too shallow. When I heard my father late at night, whispering vile things to his mistress with his thick, lying, rubbery lips, and my mother popped another pill. When I watched the back of their heads pretending to watch documentaries, the blue glare of the television and their revolting, waxy, unmoving faces. I played my part. I am the sweet, doting daughter who wins the gymkhanas and practises jumps until my thighs are rubbed raw and my lower back can no longer curve. I am a doll. A cut-out paper doll, strung up. But one day, I'll blow the house down.

When Tilly didn't turn up, I trashed it. I carved our names and then I kicked down the shelves. I pulled down my knickers and I pissed on her jumper. I smashed our cups, the ones we'd bought from the charity shop. Finally, I dragged my arm across the broken edges and howled.

Then I brushed my hair, straightened my jumper and went home and baked cookies with extra chocolate chips for my guide pack.

I called Beth and Rebecca and listened to their frivolous chatter and wanted to tear out their tongues because nothing they could say or do or be would ever compare to Tilly.

And she had gone.

That night I counted out all of my meds and laid them in concentric circles. They had reminded me of tombstones before I swept them back into the bottle.

'What are you thinking?' Now, Tilly rolled onto her side. 'You're doing that rabbit nose thing.' She strokes the top of my arm and brings me back. To her.

'Nothing.' I rolled over too so we were almost nose to nose. 'Tilly. I'd do anything for you. You know that, don't you?'

'Don't be gay,' Tilly laughed, but her eyes were bright.

I remembered the night in the caravan when I'd kissed down her body and heard her sigh, her head tipped back and her neck exposed. There was no moon that evening and the candles flickered with menace in the twilight. I felt the eyes of the woods on me.

'I mean it.'

336

'Good friends help you bury the body. Best friends bring their own shovel and don't ask questions.'

'That's cool. Who said that?'

'Saw it on a card.'

'Am I your best friend?'

'You're everything.'

The bruise on Tilly's arm was beginning to fade, the purplish tinge turning to blue. But she went back. She always went back. I let my finger tickle her bicep.

'I'm going to get you out of there, Tilly.'

'Do you promise?'

'I promise.'

27

'I mean, I'm only, like, meant to be her best friend.' Charlie looked sadly at Leah.

They were sat on the steps in the stairwell, so close their knees were touching. Charlie obviously was not the kind of girl who shed tears in public and had ushered Leah into the block as soon as she saw a group of lanky boys striding round the corner, skateboards over their shoulders like fishing rods.

'You really don't know where they are? Please, Charlie. This could be serious.'

'No. Hannah's not replying to my messages. But I know she's getting them. I can see the ticks. It's like, all fucking year I've . . . I've like, stayed at hers for two-week streaks. And I'm the one who, like, forced him to hang out with us. I saw the way she looked at him.'

'But you think she's with Luke now?'

Charlie nodded and Leah felt relief flood her body. He hadn't been taken, he was with Hannah.

'I think so. I mean, they are always texting. Like, all the time.'

'Charlie, do you have any idea where they could be? Or why Hannah wanted to run away?'

'We had an argument.'

'What? When?'

'Last night. I said something . . . maybe something I shouldn't have.'

Leah leant towards her. 'What did you say?'

Charlie looked over Leah's shoulder into the distance and chewed on her lip.

'She won't get undressed in front of me.'

'What? What do you mean?' Leah asked, confused.

'Hannah. She won't take her top off when I'm in the room. Even when we're getting changed for bed.'

'Well. Some girls are just like that. I hated to get changed in front of people when I was your age. I had no boobs until I was fifteen.'

'I don't think it's that.' Charlie shook her head. 'Sometimes, sometimes she winces. Like when we're messing about. Like she's in pain or something. I saw a bruise on her back a couple of weeks ago when she was reaching for something.'

'Are you saying . . . somebody is . . . hurting her?' Leah felt a coldness in her spine.

'I'm not saying anything. Just, I don't know . . . And then I fucked it all up. I shouldn't have said anything.'

'What exactly did you say, Charlie? Did you ask who hurt her?'

'I know who's hurting her. Why do you think I'm always there? I stayed at hers. All those nights. *For her.* I know you probably think it was for me. Because of where I live. But the truth is, my life here is great. My mum's my G. She works three jobs; we don't have a man around to boss her about or give us shit. We're a team.' Leah felt a stab in her gut, sharper than she'd ever felt before.

'Are you saying *Sam* is hurting her?'

'I asked her. Outright. She started screaming and crying and told me to get out.' Charlie's eyes started to fill up with tears. 'I didn't mean to upset her.'

Leah's mind flashed back to the scrunchie in Sam's bed. Hannah's baggy clothes. The weight loss, her gaunt face.

The knife in her stomach twisted and Leah felt vomit rising in the back of her throat.

Charlie's hands were shaking and, for the first time, Leah thought how young she looked.

'He's funny, right? He's a good dad. Or I thought he was. I thought he liked having me there. After that water fight, when we came to yours for tea. He said I could borrow his T-shirt, and then he didn't leave. He said he'd just close his eyes.' Charlie started to cry now. Really cry. 'And then Hannah started calling for me. Like she was scared or something.

'Then another time I was getting a drink and Hannah was in the living room. He came up behind me and put his hands on my waist. He told me I looked so pretty. And then . . . I didn't like being on my own with him. So we started hanging out more with Luke. Playing outside. Getting out of the house. But I couldn't say anything. I mean, he hadn't done anything. What if I was wrong? I could lose her. Maybe I already have. Maybe I've lost my best friend. I feel like I can't breathe.'

Leah drew Charlie to her chest and held her there, doing everything she could to keep from screaming. She waited until Charlie's sobs became whimpers, then she stroked her hair.

'I need to find Luke and Hannah, Charlie, and make sure they're safe. But then we need to speak to your mum and to the police.'

'What if I'm wrong?'

'What if you're right?'

Charlie smiled sadly and again, in that second, with the sun coming through the windows, she looked just like Tilly.

Bunty was waiting by the car when Leah emerged.

'So what did Charlie say?' Bunty asked as they climbed into the car.

'Jesus, Bunty, I don't know where to start,' Leah said.

'You OK? Come on. Let's go back to yours, pack your stuff and get to mine. You can tell me on the way.'

'I can't not be at the house, in case Luke comes back.'

'OK. Well, I'll stay at yours, then. We can check in with Dave and the cops – see if they have heard anything.'

Leah nodded.

Bunty took a hard right out of the estate, cursing as she narrowly avoided piling into the queue at the traffic lights.

Leah took a deep breath, trying to swallow back the bile

in her throat. They drove in silence until Leah managed to find the words.

'Sam has been abusing Hannah. That's why she ran away. Charlie thinks Luke is with her.'

'Fucking hell.' Bunty's mouth had literally fallen open.

'I just can't believe I missed it. How did I ever let that man touch me?'

Bunty didn't answer. She was staring at something straight ahead, her mouth slightly agape.

'Bunty?'

Leah followed her gaze.

Grey plumes were rising through the trees ahead.

'Fire,' Leah whispered. 'Oh my God,' her voice croaked. 'Is that coming from the cul-de-sac?'

'Call 999,' Bunty said and floored the accelerator.

Leah opened the car door before Bunty had even pulled over. 'It's not the house, it's the woods,' she said pushing past the small crowd of neighbours that had gathered in the street.

She could hear the snap and crackle of the trees burning. Running down the path by the side of the house, she threw open the back gate. But there was something horribly wrong and for a second she couldn't make sense of what she was seeing. The grass had turned to paving stones. No. A carpet. A carpet of black and white, stretching out before her. Her eyes took a second to focus. Every single inch of the garden was covered with newspaper. With Hope's face. Tilly's face. Candles, all lit, holding down the sheets.

'Fuck,' Bunty whispered behind her.

For a second Leah could feel Luke's small, fat hand in hers. The boughs were knitted over the skyline and the spikes and spears of the branches were like cramped, arthritic fingers, clawing at her as she started to run.

'LUKE!' she screamed. 'LUKE!' She ran towards the smoke, feeling the muscles in her legs and calves push forward, as if all that training, all the running, had been for something after all. The smell of the smoke became heady and the crack of branches rang out like shots.

She could see the flames now: ribbons and tentacles curling round the floor of the treehouse in the old oak ahead. She threw herself at the stout trunk, scrambling up onto the first bough.

There was a scrape and she was sure she could hear coughing, a splutter. 'LUKE!' Leah could see orange flames beginning to lick the planks of wood at the sides. Taking one deep breath, she yanked herself up and reached up through the black smoke. The heat was strong and the hairs on her arm singed and frazzled but she felt nothing but the need to get to Luke.

She saw him. In the hospital, how they had lain him on her breasts and how she'd smelt the blood on his head, felt the squirm of his stomach on hers.

The tree was filling with black clouds of ink. Leah's fingers were flying, searching for the rope, but they just trailed through the air, grappling against nothing. She could hear Bunty shouting just below her.

Her throat was scorched and her lungs were so tight they felt like they were about to burst, but her fingers finally found the cord. She pulled. To her horror there was a rattle but nothing budged. It was locked. Or swollen from the heat.

Leah couldn't help it. She opened her mouth and inhaled a huge drag of smoke. It filled her lungs and made her eyes bulge from their sockets. Bunty clambered up behind her and tugged violently on the back of her top. Leah turned round and Bunty pressed something into her hand. The smooth handle of her claw hammer.

Leah began to pound blindly at the wood until there was the sound of splintering and a huge crack. She began to pull and yank at the broken wood. It came off, plank by plank, the nails scraping Leah's arms. The smoke swirled inside the glowing hatch.

Leah pushed herself up through the opening and could just about make them out. Luke and Hannah; curled together like terrified children from a fairy tale.

'MUM!' Luke reached his hand towards hers just as there was an almighty crash from above, and the treehouse tilted slightly. Leah felt the edge of the hatch scrape into her chest.

Bunty screamed. 'The branches are going!'

'LUKE!' Leah reached for her son. 'Come on.' He looked at Hannah next to him. Her head lolled.

'Get Hannah out first! Please.'

The floor shook and the heat was blistering, Luke's comics whooshing up, perfect kindling. Leah hoisted herself into the flames, and reached out. There was a scorching pain on her shoulder and if there had been any air she would have howled. She crawled forward.

'MUM,' Luke cried, shuffling towards her, his arm around Hannah's chest, half dragging her.

'I'm OK,' Leah gasped, taking Hannah from Luke's arms.

The treehouse began to rock as their weight shifted. Bunty's arms appeared through the hatch and grabbed Hannah's feet and began to pull.

Luke was face down now, not moving. Leah couldn't feel any pain in her body any more, as she began to drag him towards the opening. Then there was a flash of light, a bang so loud it felt like the world had exploded, and they were falling.

Leah didn't feel her body hit the ground, exactly. Only the seconds of pure, clean oxygen, which filled her lungs before it was smacked out again by the impact of their landing.

Above her, the fire raged.

But she could only feel the body of her son, his stomach on hers. The smell of blood on his head.

28

3 July 2003

Tilly's beautiful face. That's what I see. When I wake up. When I go to sleep. Sometimes, when it's swollen, or she has purple shadows, I think she's even more beautiful. There's something ethereal about her. Which I always find interesting as she is the most real person I have ever known.

I saw her yesterday. In town. I was with Beth; we were going to the riding shop. I needed jodhpurs and Beth needed a new crop. Beth was droning on and on about exam revision and how she couldn't possibly stick to her timetable and do her stable-girl duties, and did I have any advice, because I'm the most organized person she knows. I was answering, but I felt like a ventriloquist's dummy. I know all the answers. I always have. I don't even have to think about it. It's like I'm possessed by the Other Hope. Sometimes I'm scared that Other Hope will take over. Other Hope will stamp me down in her cloud of CK One and blazers. Other Hope will ace her GCSEs. Her A levels. Other Hope will get her bachelor's at Cambridge and her master's

346

at Oxford. Other Hope will get married, perhaps to a nice boy with brown hair who rows. Other Hope will spawn his children and raise them properly while holding down a part-time job as a solicitor. Other Hope will smile in the playground and drive me down every time I try and surface, spluttering and crawling up her throat. Other Hope will kill me.

Without Tilly, I won't exist.

But she needs me now too.

I made her think it was her idea. To keep us secret. Better no one tries to convince us we're not good for each other. Tilly's so scared all the time. Always looking over her shoulder.

She is the queen of the castle she is locked into. I am going to set her free.

She was there, outside KFC. With the people who think they are her friends. That awfully common Dakota. She thinks she knows her. But she doesn't. No one knows Tilly like me. No one knows how she thinks. How the patterns in her brain are different to everyone else. She moves differently. They don't know how she tastes. She doesn't give them what she gives me.

Tilly's leaving school after her GCSEs. She won't do well. She's going to get a job. It's a bit embarrassing, really. But I can't sit them for her. I've tried to study with her. Her brain is incredible, but she can't focus. There's nothing for her here.

It's time for us to go.

29

'You need to go back to your bed.'

Leah glared at the nurse, a woman in her fifties with a no-nonsense bun and lipstick that had bled into the smoker's creases around her mouth. She bustled past Leah and checked the drip feeding into the back of Luke's hand. He looked so young, his head against the pillows, the oxygen mask still on his face.

'I mean it. You need to get back into your bed.'

'I feel fine,' Leah lied.

'We're not discharging you until your oxygen levels are where they should be. You're only making it harder on yourself. Don't you want to go home?' The nurse tutted and checked Luke's pulse.

'Looking much better here.' She dropped his wrist and put her pen away in her top pocket.

'How's Hannah doing?'

'Same as she was ten minutes ago.'

Leah sat down next to Luke.

Leah didn't say anything and stroked the hair away from Luke's face.

'Come on, Leah. Go back to bed. ' Chris came up behind her and put his hand on her shoulder. 'I'll stay with Luke.'

Leah looked down at her son. The pain was becoming unbearable; it was horrendous and she was still dry-retching into the grey cardboard bowl in her lap, her cracked rib making her yelp every time.

She did need to sleep.

'Have you heard from Dave?' she asked, standing up shakily and pulling her gown shut behind her.

'He'll be here very soon.'

'Are the police still here?'

'No, I think they've gone now.'

'And Sam?'

'I think they've taken him with them.'

'Good.'

Leah looked away and felt the sickness start to rise again. The thought of his hands on her made her want to claw at her skin. How could she have been so stupid? So blind? *Another girl I have failed.*

'Leah . . . Did he hurt you? . . . Force you?' Chris said, with quiet anger.

'No.' Leah shook her head. 'But I'm sorry. I'm so sorry.'

Chris stood up and looked out of the window. 'He used it, you know. The candles and the dolls. He used it to get close to you. That's why he pretended to believe you when no one . . . when I . . . didn't.'

'Chris, I found the pictures,' Leah said quietly.

'What pictures?'

'The pictures of Alice. You left your Facebook open on the laptop.'

'I don't know what you're talking about.'

'Pictures. Naked pictures of Alice. Chris, at this point, please don't try and pretend . . .'

'Leah.' Chris sat down at the end of the bed and reached for her hand. 'I really have no idea what you're talking about. What pictures?'

'Oh God.' Leah turned her head and felt the tears start. 'Do not tell me I'm making it all up.'

'I'm not.' Chris squeezed her hand. 'I'm not. I believe you. I'm so, so sorry I didn't before.' He put his head down. 'I can't believe I put you, and Luke, at risk like that. I will never do that again.'

Leah squeezed his hand back. 'Do you really mean it? You had no idea that Alice had sent you pictures?'

'No, I didn't have a clue. You know I'm never on Facebook. Show me when we get home. Did you really think . . . is that why you . . . kissed Sam?'

'I wish I could tell you it was. But no. That's all on me . . .'

'It's on me too. Fucking bastard. The more I didn't believe you, the more . . . fuck. I feel so stupid. Baby, please don't cry . . .'

'I'm not crying for me.' Leah shook her head. 'I'm crying for Hannah.'

*

When Leah woke the ward was quieter and the soft amber evening lights above the bed no longer stung her eyes. She rolled onto her side to face the window and saw someone curled in the green plastic visitor's chair, her eyes closed, a dressing on her temple.

As if she could feel the weight of Leah's stare, Bunty opened her eyes and smiled. 'Hey,' she said softly. 'How are you feeling?'

'Weird. How are *you* feeling?' Leah pointed to the plaster on Bunty's forehead.

'All good. Your doctor gave me proper fizzy knickers. Do you think there's a dating app just for people in the medical profession?'

'You're not in the medical profession.' Leah sat up experimentally. Her stomach let out a small growl.

'Yeah, but *they* don't know that.'

'What happened to your head?' Leah asked.

'Twatted it with a branch.'

Leah grimaced. 'Sorry.'

'Stop saying sorry to everyone . . . how's Luke? What's he said about Hannah?'

'Nothing yet. He's not been awake long enough. All I know is Hannah called him, hysterical, apparently. She was at the train station. But she had nothing. No bank card, no money. Not even a coat on. He just jumped on a train and used my Apple Pay.'

'Couldn't he have just let you know where he was? Selfish git.' Bunty shook her head.

'I think Hannah begged him not to say,' Leah said. 'I hope . . . well. We don't know anything for sure. I've told the police what I think. What Charlie thinks. I guess I can't do any more now.' Leah screwed her eyes tightly shut. 'Every time I think of how I let him get close to me . . . Bunty, I want to tear the skin off my bones.'

'What did the police say?' Bunty moved onto the end of Leah's bed.

'I think they listened. That fire was no accident. Bunty . . . he could have died. They could have died. All because of me.'

'OK, stop making it all about you. Get yourself down off the cross. This has nothing to do with you – the weirdo with the Tilly obsession is the one who is crazy. You are *not* responsible for Tilly's disappearance. They found a load of her stuff at the beach, right? If she killed herself, that is not on you. And who knows, if you hadn't put that white girl on the front page maybe they would both be dead. No one ever says that, do they? No one ever mentions you might have saved a life?'

Leah sat back, feeling her brain begin to whir.

A white girl's necklace.

Leah grabbed her phone and opened a new tab, then froze. And swiped back. *It was her. She was right.*

'Bunty, you're a fucking genius. Look!' Leah googled Hope's name and the picture from the front page popped up, over and over again.

'Hope is wearing the necklace – Tilly's necklace! The one they found on the beach, with her picture in it.'

'OK . . .' Bunty stared at the image on Leah's phone. 'But, you know, lockets are pretty popular. It could be an Argos job, you know?'

'No. Hope's family weren't the kind that shopped at Argos. It's expensive. You can tell. Look at the chain. That's a snake chain. I'd bet on that being white gold. And look . . .' Leah scrolled back to the last tab and pulled up Tilly's Myspace. She flicked through to the picture of Tilly laughing at the camera. 'Look. Look in her sunglasses. Look at that reflection. That's Hope!' She widened the picture with her thumb and forefinger.

'OK. I'm not saying it's not.' Bunty squinted over her shoulder. 'I mean, it kind of looks like her, but all blonde girls look the same at that age. But what does it prove? That Tilly knew Hope? Maybe they were just, I don't know, acquaintances.'

'Tilly's picture was inside the locket and you don't lend a necklace like that to an acquaintance.'

'You could be right. But why would . . . I don't get it, what are you trying to say?'

'Why would two girls who were friends go missing on the same day? And then Hope not even mention that they were friends when she came back? How did no one make the connection? There was nothing, *nothing*, from anyone to suggest they knew each other.'

'Where did Hope say she'd been? When she came back? I mean, why did she run away?'

'Oh, I don't know. Teenage drama shit. Police said it was a family matter and then we all went on our ways.'

353

'So, you think Hope was involved somehow?'

Leah's phone buzzed, making them both jump. Bunty grabbed the phone from the bedside table. 'Message. Unknown number.'

'Open it.' Leah's eyes were wide.

'The pier. Now. Alone,' Bunty read out. 'Oh my God. As if you are going to do that.'

Leah had already thrown back the bed sheets.

'Oh. Looks like you are . . . Don't be an idiot, Leah. This is the bit in the film where everyone screams at the TV.' Bunty jumped up. '*Do not go* to the dodgy pier alone. Call the police.'

'I'm not going alone.'

'I'm just going to say this, I'm not convinced I should be driving with a head injury.' Bunty grimaced as she reversed Chris's car out of the parking spot. 'I cannot believe this just cost me £20. Hospital parking is just fucking ludicrous. I mean, aren't people who come to hospital already having a bad enough day without being robbed? So do you think it's her? Hope?'

Leah nodded grimly.

'Should you be wearing a wire or something?'

'Jesus, Bunty, you watch far too much TV.'

Leah's phone started to ring. She looked down at the screen.

'Oh shit, it's Chris.'

'Answer it.'

'No, I daren't.'

'Answer it or he will call the police. You've just done a bloody runner from the hospital.' Bunty paused. 'Actually, don't answer it. I still think this is a ludicrous idea.'

Leah sighed and answered.

'Leah. Tell me where you are,' Chris barked.

'Chris, I can't. But please. *Please*. Trust me.'

There was a long silence.

'I do trust you,' Chris said quietly.

'Thank you,' Leah said. 'Stay with Luke. I will be back as soon as I can.'

'At least tell me you're safe.'

'I'm safe,' Leah said. 'I'm with Bunty.'

'Oh, for fuck's sake—'

Leah grinned and hung up the phone.

'Are you sure you don't want me to come with you?' Bunty asked, as she pulled over, half a mile away from the pier.

'No. She might not come out if she sees you. I need to know what's going on. I need to know if it's her. I need it to be over.'

Leah got out of the car and started to walk towards the pier.

Dusk was sinking over the sand and the beach looked smoky. The flickering lights of the funhouse were almost comforting. The clinking of the shutters from the cockles and mussels stand was almost rhythmic. The Blue Anchor was still bustling out the back. She could smell the Marlboros and hear the ping of glasses.

Leah wished she looked more conspicuous, somehow. But she felt like a ghost as she began the slow walk to the end of the pier. The last embers of the day had hit the line of the water and the sea stretched out into the void.

The old carousel was still turning at the bottom. The last ride on the pier. There was only one family. A laughing mum, an awkward and bemused-looking dad. Their toddler trying to clap with one pudgy hand holding a toffee apple. It was the last bit of charm left on the pier. The music box grinding. Round and round. Day in. Day out. The horses always dancing, whatever the weather.

Leah leant on the railing and looked out to sea. The water was beginning to get choppier now and the night was coming in thicker. She watched until the music died and the horses stopped dancing, the pier was still and the sea was black.

'Hello, Leah.'

Alice leant her forearms on the wall, matching Leah's pose exactly. Leah felt a jolt of shock. She didn't have time for this. Hope could be here any moment. She wouldn't come near if she saw someone with her.

Then Alice turned and faced her directly.

She still had the same look. The bright eyes. The glossy hair. She'd lost the puppy fat around her cheeks, making her bones sharper. How could Leah not have seen it before?

'Hope?' Leah whispered.

'Did you know that more people run away from seaside towns than any other type of location?' Alice said conversationally. 'It's partially to do with economics, of course. Places like this, well, people often want to escape. Seek their fortune. But it's equally about the horizon. Makes people want to just . . . sail away. It's a siren call. Oblivion.'

'What's happening? I don't understand,' Leah said.

'What do you think is happening, Leah? It's what you think that counts. Right?'

'It was you? All along? But how?'

'It really did take you longer than I thought it would to work it out. I mean, how much more obvious could I have been?'

'How . . . ?' Leah stuttered.

'Well. Once your husband hired me it was very simple. That man is far too trusting. Really, what is the point of changing your locks if you're just going to leave the new keys hanging on the hook at work? And then he gave me every password. Really. I could have been some kind of psychopath.' Her laugh was like a tinkling bell. 'Oh, the irony.'

'But why?'

'You know why. You put me on the front of that paper and . . .'

'I know I made the wrong call.' Leah jumped in. 'And I am very sorry that I didn't give Tilly the coverage she deserved, but . . .'

'Oh darling, no. Let me finish. You've got it so wrong. I'm not angry Tilly *wasn't* on the front of that rag you called a paper. I'm angry that *I was.*'

'What?' Leah's jaw dropped.

'You splashed me all over the front of all those papers. I

357

couldn't have escaped if I'd tried. I didn't have a prayer. I was getting coffee for us at the station and the man next to me was holding the paper. I was right there on the front page. I was so shocked I spilt my drink everywhere. I knew that second. I knew she was going to have to go and I was going to have to let myself be found. We wouldn't have made it further than York together.

'It was OK for Tilly. No one recognized her. You made sure of that. She still had a chance. She got to go. She would have thanked you for burying her story. But not me. Do you understand that? Because of you, I couldn't go with her. Either I had to let myself be found, or both of us were screwed. I couldn't make her stay. Not in that family. Not in that life. We were going to be together. Forever. You made sure that didn't happen. *You.* It was *your* call. I didn't know that until that godawful documentary. But I know it now.'

Hope turned and leant on the wall, resting her elbows behind her, staring down the empty pier.

'Have you ever thought that maybe missing people don't want to be found?'

'But . . .'

'Me and Tilly. It was perfect. I had the money. She had the reason. Her family, Jesus, the way they came out afterwards, it made my stomach turn. Their precious daughter. Funny how they forgot about that when her dad was beating the shit out of her every night and her mum just watched. Did nothing. We were going to be free. Together. I was going to save her.'

Hope's face was unmoving. Her features frozen, her skin waxy.

'So Tilly's alive? She just ran away? All this time, you've watched people grieve and search and you've known all along where she is?' Leah felt as if her heart was about to burst. Relief and anger were battling one another inside her.

'Not quite. At first it was like that. It was very entertaining. Like I said. Her parents deserved it.'

'And then?' Leah asked.

'There's something vulnerable about you, Leah. Almost the same quality that Tilly had, really. Perhaps that's why I'm drawn to you. I wasn't expecting to be. After all, you are just like her.'

'Hope. Where is Tilly?'

Leah stared at the young woman before her. The eyes that had looked out at her from that paper so many times.

'I put her on that train. Gave her all the money. I sacrificed myself for her. She said she'd come back for me. I waited every night. Every night in that fucking caravan. Waiting. Holding that cheap hoody of hers. But she didn't come.

'Then one day I just saw her. On the pier. It was like I'd seen a ghost.'

Leah watched as Hope's jaw tightened and she turned again to look out to sea. You couldn't see the edge of the water now. Just the deep blackness.

'She was just there. In that horrible, chavvy Adidas jumper. Hood pulled over her head. No one noticed her. Or cared, really. Just another girl from the estates. She was back. I don't know whether she had been back for an hour, a day, a week. But she was there. She had taken the money, but she hadn't started a new life. Not like we had planned. And she hadn't come back for me, either. She'd cheated me.'

Hope's face had stilled and her eyes were wide, frozen in some kind of remembered rage.

'I chased after her. Along the pier. I called her name. She heard me. I know she did. But she just carried on. I ran until we reached the steps. She was walking fast. Taking the shortcut under the pier. She hadn't come back for me. After everything I did for us.

'But I was always faster than her. OK, I admit, I got a little rough. She tried to scream. At first, I just tried to cover her mouth. But it felt nice, the way her body bucked and writhed under mine. So I put my other hand on her throat. Just to see what it felt like. I think that's when my locket, the one I gave her, came off her neck. She must not have had it fastened properly. I didn't notice. All I felt was her life running through me, running through my veins, and I couldn't stop. It was electric. When her body went limp, it was the sweetest kiss I've ever known.'

'I lay with her for a while, while the sea lapped and licked at our toes. Her head was on my chest. She always said it was her favourite place to be. She said it made her feel safe. I thought about burying her in the sand at the time, but really, how childish. I didn't like the thought of the crabs having at her either, although the thought of some child finding her while building a sandcastle, I have to admit, did make me laugh.

'I stroked her hair and murmured soft lullabies to her as she slept. Then when the skies darkened I floated her out into the water, filled her pockets with rocks and watched as the current swept her out with the tide.

'Sometimes I hear her still when the waves break. Her siren's melody . . . There's a Joni Mitchell song, *Carey*, where she accuses the bright red devil of keeping her in a seaside town. I thought perhaps she was my devil, that she would always keep me here, that I would never be able to leave this place. But I did leave. I went to study. And then, of course, I had a charming little spell in a psychiatric ward. But I came back. Didn't I, Tilly?'

Hope turned to Leah, who saw for the first time the scalpel up her sleeve. Hope let it drop now, between her fingers. The lights of the pier caught the blade. For a second it looked almost beautiful.

'It's your fault she's dead. It's your fault we're not together. If we could have just got on that train together . . . she would still have loved me. We would never have been apart.'

'Hope. You need help,' Leah said steadily. She could feel the bulge of her phone in her back pocket and slowly began to reach for it.

'You've not been well either. Have you, Leah? Poor Chris tells me everything. He has been ever so worried. We're not really having an affair, though. I planned on it, of course. Said the right things, made the right noises. He started staying late when he didn't need to. Looking at me that bit too long. But he never made a move. I wouldn't have even bothered with those pictures if I had known that you were busy destroying your marriage all by yourself. You took everything from me. I wanted to take everything from you.

'It wasn't Chris, though, was it? He wasn't the one that meant the most to you. I had the wrong guy. When I saw Luke and that girl sneak up into that treehouse, it was perfect. It went up like a giant tinderbox. I mean, I had to do something to get your attention. It was taking you far too long.'

'But what is it you want from me? I don't get it. You've tortured me. I'm sorry. What can I do now?'

Hope lunged for her so quickly that Leah barely had time to duck. A flash of light sliced down through the air and Leah twisted away. But her cracked rib made her cry out in pain as she bent double, holding her side. Metal slid into her shoulder like a knife into butter and scraped the bone. It was the kind of pain she never imagined she could take. Her vision flashed white as she fell to her knees.

Leah put her hand to her collarbone and felt the blood seep between her fingers. Beside her, the dead, black eyes of the carousel ponies looked on.

Hope's face came into view above her. So close to her own. Hope bent down and Leah felt the soft, warm hairs on her cheek caress hers.

Hope whispered in her ear, 'One day you'll understand.'

Leah looked at the blade and thought of Luke. Then,

ignoring the agony in her shoulder, she shot her arms up and grabbed Hope around her thin, pale throat.

She squeezed as hard as she could. Hope's eyes began to bulge and she tried again to bring the scalpel down, but Leah's arms locked firm.

In the distance she could hear sirens.

Leah felt a searing pain as the scalpel sliced across the back of her hands, again and again, but she didn't let go until she saw the sweep of the cold blue lights.

Hope looked up as the police cars squealed to a stop.

And started to laugh.

'Finally, boys. What took you so long?'

30

One year later

Leah picked up her coffee cup and rinsed it under the tap. The house across the road was silent. The new people hadn't moved in yet. The grass was brown and tinged with neglect. But the *Sold* sign was still hanging there jauntily.

'Guys!' she called up the stairs. 'Hurry up, if you want a lift to school. Otherwise you're on the bus.'

She opened the fridge and pulled out two Tupperware boxes of sandwiches and crisps. She had got into the routine of making them the night before, so she could run first thing in the morning. Every morning. Pickle, the one-eyed Staffie, sat at her feet. Chris had brought her home six months before.

'Coming,' Hannah shouted and appeared at the top of the stairs, hair pulled back from her face in a ponytail and her eyes framed by just a touch of mascara. Leah thought it was a good sign.

'Shout Luke again for me, sweetheart,' Leah said, putting her MacBook into her handbag. 'You've got your session with Mrs Harrow at 6 p.m. tonight instead of tomorrow, don't forget.'

'Yeah, it's on the planner.' Hannah smiled and took the Tupperware box. 'Thanks, Leah. Are you coming with me?'

'Of course I am.' Leah smiled and squeezed her hand. Hannah let her.

'Are you nervous? About today?' Hannah asked, zipping up her schoolbag.

'No. Not really,' Leah shrugged. 'Hopefully it will give me some kind of closure. And it's going to be such amazing material for the book.'

'You're brave.' Hannah shook her head.

Luke thundered down the stairs. 'What have we got?'

'Ham and cheese.'

'Oh, Mum. Fuck's sake.'

'Pack your own lunch, then.'

Chris came into the kitchen, already in his scrubs.

'I'm going now, but call me after, OK?' He leant forward and kissed Leah's cheek. He smelt of sandalwood. 'Guys, where is everyone tonight?'

'I'm at counselling,' Hannah said, pulling on her duffle coat.

'And I'm at Warhammer,' Luke said.

'Loser.' Hannah grinned.

Their romance hadn't lasted long. Hannah hadn't been

in any fit state for it. But the bond had lasted. Sometimes, when they watched TV together in the living room, Hannah would rest her head on Luke's shoulder.

The process of fostering had taken far too long. Six months. It had been Chris's suggestion. They'd sorted out the spare room and done all the checks, all the courses. She'd always wanted another child.

They'd celebrated at Pizza Express and Leah had given Hannah a locket with a picture of her mother that she'd found at the house when she had been helping Hannah to pack stuff before she'd been taken into emergency care.

She'd taken Hannah just once to see Sam. The girl had asked to go. Leah wasn't sure why, but the counsellors had suggested she go along with it. He was at Wakefield Prison. *Monsters' Mansion.* He had at least pleaded guilty, so there had been no need to put Hannah through a trial. He had sat there, those eyes all wide and pleading. He'd claimed he was sick. That it wasn't him. That he was getting better.

Hannah hadn't said a word in the car home. She'd never been back to see him again.

Leah dropped her kids as near to school as she could bear to get. Charlie Bates was there, perched on a street sign, e-cig in one hand, phone in the other. Leah smiled as she watched Charlie give Luke the finger as he walked towards her.

The drive took longer than she thought – it was almost lunchtime when she arrived at the facility. The building was low and squat. Almost like a country house. Nothing like the tall imposing one that housed Sam.

Leah sat for a minute, reapplying her lipstick for no good reason. She just needed a moment to gather herself.

The book had been commissioned almost immediately. She still had friends in the tabloids, people she'd trained with. They'd suggested a publisher. She even had the title ready: *Paper Dolls*. She'd interviewed up and down the country. Families with children who had gone missing and had been given media attention. Families whose children hadn't. Children who had returned. Children who didn't want to be found.

Inside the building it was austere and clinical. Nothing like the outside, with the grounds, the willow tree, the bedding plants. This was all metal stairs and white walls. Leah signed the visitors' book, handed over her driving licence and was given a pass.

She was walked to the visitors' room. Hope was sitting there already. She looked immaculate. Hair glossy. Skin clear. A flicker passed across her face when Leah sat down opposite her.

'Oh, it's you.'

'Who did you think it'd be?'

'Doesn't matter.' Hope drummed her nails on the tabletop. They were ragged and bitten to the quick, skin puffed and swollen, bulging over the beds. She noticed Leah's glance.

'I know. Can't even give myself a mani-pedi in here. No one trusts anyone with a nail file.'

'How are they treating you?'

'Oh, it's all very tedious. You'd hate it. Such routine. No creativity.' She smiled almost conspiratorially.

'I'm writing a book,' Leah said. 'About Tilly. And the hundreds of other girls like her.'

'There's no one like Tilly.' Hope smiled. 'Is that why you're here? Am I being interviewed?'

Leah shook her head.

'How disappointing.' Hope's face clouded over and her eyes dimmed.

'It wouldn't be ethical of me to interview you while you're in here. You're vulnerable,' Leah explained.

'So why are you here?' Hope sat back in her chair.

'To tell you. About the book. Everything that happened. It will be in there.'

'But I don't get a say?'

Leah shook her head.

'Well, I think we're done here, in that case.' Hope frowned. 'Did you really have to come here to tell me this?'

'I wanted to see you,' Leah said quietly.

Hope gazed back for a while, before her face broke out in a huge, teeth-baring grin.

'I made this. Consider it a present,' she said, and pulled out two paper dolls, their hands holding, joined together in one shape.

'Is that you and Tilly?' Leah asked, taking the dolls and turning them over in her fingers.

'Of course,' Hope said. 'But my doctor said she thinks that really they're both me. Hope. And Other Hope. They want me to be Other Hope. You know. The nice one, the good one. I can feel her sometimes. When I take the meds. She's getting closer.'

Leah stroked the dolls, seeing that they had been clipped from a sheet of newspaper. It had today's date at the top.

'Who's Other Hope?'

'She's *awful*,' Hope hissed. 'She'll be the death of me.'

'Which Hope was it, that sent me the dolls? That tried to hurt my son?'

'Silly goose.' A playful smile flickered on Hope's lips. 'That was me, of course.'

Leah put the dolls back on the table and pushed them towards Hope. Hope picked them up and held them to her chest, like a child cradling a teddy.

Then she widened her eyes. 'You'd better go,' she whispered. 'She'll be here soon.'

The weather outside had darkened and the sky was roiling.

'Goodbye, Hope,' Leah said. And walked away.

Epilogue

Poor Leah. She doesn't understand the paths of the brain. The ebbs. The flows. Not like me. I do hope she's sleeping better. She deserves it. After all, she's played her part nicely, even if she is a little egotistical to think this was all in the spirit of revenge. That would be like a pulp fiction novel.

Please.

She's coming to see me today.

When I think of Tilly now, I don't think of her smile. Or her face. Her body. Instead, I think of the way she couldn't pronounce her aitches properly. The way she used to like to tumble down grassy banks and thought Hollyoaks was a real place. She made beautiful daisy chains. I admired how precise she was with them. Each slit in the stalk an exact length. She had so much potential.

It's been sixteen years. I wonder how she will look now. In my mind, I imagine that she will be a little plump.

It's true what I told Leah, about the waiting. I did wait. And wait. I waited sixteen years. The rest of the story I told her on the pier was somewhat fantastical.

Of course I dreamt about it. My hands around Tilly's throat in the shallows under the pier. How I could watch the life drain out of her eyes, how her face would slacken, her body grow limp. All mine.

But she didn't come back.

She never came back.

But I know she will now. I know she will. God, I thought the police I called were never going to show up at the pier. At one point I thought that dreadful woman was going to strangle the life out of me. Luckily the cuts were enough to get me in handcuffs.

I did need to get charged for your murder, though. How else could I have made you show up? You might have abandoned me before, but I know you would never let me get a life sentence for a crime that you know full well I didn't commit.

We've been all over the front of every paper. Our faces together. The schoolgirl killer. Oh, Tilly. It's been so beautiful. I've cut them all out with my ridiculous safety scissors. Our faces, the headlines. I made them into bunting, rows and rows of paper dolls hung all over my room.

You never came back.

But you will now.

You won't leave me here, taking the blame.

I need you. Like I said, I don't exist without you.

Without you, there is no Hope.

Acknowledgements

To my husband Mark, and my sons, Tommy and Oscar, for being my inspiration and cheerleaders every single day. Mark, you probably know the characters in this book better than me. Endless dog walks, bottles of red wine and drives where I have talked of nothing else. You have always, always listened and been next to me on this journey every step of the way. I love you so much.

Being published is a childhood dream come true, and one that wouldn't have been possible without some pretty incredible women. So this bit is for the girls. My wonderful agent, Jo Williamson, thank you for always believing in me, and my amazing editor at Quercus, Rachel Neely, for loving, living and breathing *Paper Dolls*.

Which brings me to all my Buntys. You know who you are. I am honoured and humbled to have such an incredible, supportive group of women around me. Karen Cockerham, Lucy Mizen, Becky Mills, Ruth Lockwood, Carolynn Williams, Cat Ross, Arlene Lawler, Sarah Goodwill, Becca Milner and the Sheff Chicks. Without your never-ending support and love this book would not exist.

A huge thanks to the entire Quercus team, Rachel Wright, whose copy editing skills are almost biblical, and to everyone who championed this book, especially the Scribblers, my online writing friends, who have cheered me on through the darkest hours. I can never thank you enough.

Thanks to my blended family: my dad who still thinks I'm the best girl in the whole world despite being in my 40s, my in laws, particularly my father-in-law Steve, who died just before this book was published. He sent me a message when he heard the news *Paper Dolls* was going to be a paperback. 'Well done, kid.' I'm forever grateful you left this world proud of me.

And finally, this is for the two kick-ass women in my life. My sister, Suzanne, and my mum, Joy, who first put a pencil in my hand and taught me how to love words. Us three. Always.